A Pig's View
Of Heaven

Stephen McQuiggan

A
Grinning Skull Press
Publication

ISBN: 0996223223 (paperback)
ISBN-13: 978-0-9962232-2-5 (paperback)
ISBN: 978-0-9962232-3-2 (ebook)

DEDICATION

For Mum and Dad (for being there)
And for Dawn (for being her)

CONTENTS

ABOUT THE AUTHOR

ACKNOWLEDGMENTS

Big thanks to Anton, Nick, and Lou, and especially to Brackagh and the Forestals. Thanks also to Mike and Harrison at Grinning Skull Press.

Part One

Eileen sits with her back to him, like a cat waiting for rain. Even from this distance he can see her skin peeling, the dry glue of sunburn on her shoulders. The park is full so he can watch her safely. He does not stand out from the dog walkers and the families playing catch, their kids screeching like gulls until he has to bite down the impulse to scream. Just another sun worshipper lounging on the grass nodding hello to passers-by, smiling at a nun, waving at a small Down syndrome boy. A sensitive soul. He is free to relax, to watch, and to listen to the voice.

The voice is always with him now.

He pictures it as a Brainworm, burrowing into his synapses, eating away all rational thought, yet he loves its soothing tones, adores the things it whispers. It is a quiet voice, but the world slows down to listen. He is unsure if others have a Brainworm of their own, or if he is somehow special, so he never mentions it, not even to Samuel. He is no fool; the Brainworm sees to that.

It was the angel over his father's grave that first spoke to him, scared him so badly he blamed the drink he had taken to. Now the voice comes from everywhere, from cats and flowers, from cars and lampposts. It seems that everything has something to say, something urgent to relate.

He isn't naïve; he knows they are only manifestations of the voice in his head, knows it is only the Brainworm playing games.

He likes games.

He plucks a few tufts of dead grass and watches her chat to her little friends. Whenever the carrier bag beside him speaks, he cannot help but smile.

"No more rehearsals, Paul; this is it."

In the distance, getting ever closer, the cacophony of an ice cream van forces him to clench his teeth. As if on cue her friends get up and fix their hair, pat down their school skirts. He grits his teeth harder against the jangling muzak as he tries to place the tune; Mozart? He would ask his brother; Samuel would know.

He holds his breath until the rage passes, and the Brainworm whispers relax, relax.

He watches the girls, their laughter full of corners and angles, watches Eileen take her goodbye and stride away on coltish legs, clutching a schoolbag to her burgeoning chest. He places a yellowed stalk of grass between the gap in his front teeth and waits until she is almost out of sight by the duck pond, then he follows her.

He passes her friends, bowing his head at their inane chatter. Tomorrow one of them will try to describe him to the police, but all she will remember are his eyes. His cold shark eyes. The detective will put this down to the romantic fantasies of a grief-stricken teenager, but the Brainworm concurs; "Don't look at them, Paul," it whispers. "They will remember your eyes."

It is hard not to sneak a peek. He dreams of fucking a schoolgirl in a hearse. It is his way of showing that he does not fear the grave he also dreams of; dreams so real that when he awakes he can still smell the cloying perfume of attar and feel the crumbling earth in his throat. But they are only dreams.

He stays far behind her on the bike path. She is wearing her too blue skirt, the one so dark it looks like it is made of cardboard and still contains the pins. He hates that skirt; it is more of a veil than an enhancement, yet it cannot hide her glory.

Some girls pretend to be happy, burying their bodies under chocolate, little more than waddling advent calendars, but her body is a ferocious joy, hungry and lean. He hides in her shapely shadow, cooled by the waft of her invisible wings.

She flicks a glance over her shoulder; so cold, yet it warms him, bringing the blood to his face. She wears the expression of a hood ornament, aggression coupled with triumph. He sees her perfect skin as a pasture, as something to feed on.

She floats, yes, floats, this creature of air and light, close to the shortcut through an overgrown copse, the same one she has taken every day for the last fortnight. He begins to pray the way his brother has taught him to.

A swish of a hip and she disappears into the bushes and he begins to run, crunching twigs, cursing, stealthy no longer, reaching into his carrier bag for the hammer just as she is about to turn, and he strikes her as hard as he can between the shoulder blades, sending her sprawling, shedding library books instead of tears, her ponytail spinning, her face buried in foul-smelling weeds.

She moans and he strikes her again, cracking her skull, then rolls her over and closes her vacant eyes. They are staring straight into hell, and they unnerve him. He has an erection, but the voice urges patience. She may be still alive and he cannot touch her until she is dead. He doesn't have the right; Eileen is too far

2

above him, but Death is a great leveller whispers the voice.

Her angelic face is ruined, and he shudders at the thought that she might suffer. Is it too late, can he fix her still? He begins to cry. There is no room in this world for such beauty, for such … freaks of nature.

"Yes, freaks," whispers the Brainworm. "Abominations, cold-hearted teases. Only the Devil could bleed so sweetly."

He puts his hands around the tidemarks of cheap jewellery on her throat, squeezing until he feels all the little bird bones snap. Her eyes open again but he closes them. It is time for his reward.

Though his pounding heart seems to accelerate the moment, he takes his time undressing her, wiping the sweat from his face as he gazes on her nakedness, his breath broken by her small perfect breasts, the wispy V of her sex. He forces himself deep inside her with a dry rip.

"IloveyouIloveyouIloveyou."

He doesn't know if this is the Brainworm or his own voice. He is told not to bury her, not even to cover her, to leave her as a sign.

The Brainworm is silent all that next day. He is left alone with the papers and the gossip and his own rising panic. The headlines shame him. Headlines, head lice; they itch just the same. On the television they shuffle their papers at the end of each broadcast and he realises it is all just a dance, all just steps in a timeless ritual.

He had worn gloves, conspicuous on such a hot day, but necessary. There had been so many people in the park, it would be impossible to pick him out over such a small detail. But then he had taken his reward so eagerly, so thoughtlessly, shooting his code into her, his filthy code, his filthy issue seeping out of her.

They can crack that code, no doubt about it. You read about it all the time; DNA may as well read RIP. His code was probably still drip, drip, dripping out of her, running down her cold thighs, pooling on some slab, ready for some nosey lab coat to poke and analyse.

He doesn't need the Brainworm to tell him his next course of action. It is fitting that he will join her. All he wants is to be with her now, to die in her dead arms. Samuel has told him there are no bodies in the next life, and his brother is learned in such things. He needs to hold her again because he will not be able to hold her in Paradise.

He hides. He waits.

Under the oblivion of night he goes to her. The wind is so angry, screaming at him, trying to roar the world awake, but as he reaches the cemetery gates it turns its back on him, refusing to speak. The wind is unpredictable, the wind is a woman. He removes a binful of wreaths with his spade.

It is harder than he expects, the soft ground giving way to shoulder sapping clods of clay. The spade bites deep but does not yield easily. He fears he will have to abandon his labour, that soon the sun will uncover his dark toil, but the thought of her keeps him going. He can almost see her, glowing by the slender light of a toenail moon, standing by the edge of her grave, urging him to ignore the blisters that burst wetly on his palm, cajoling him in her tinkling voice.

He digs. He digs until his fingers bleed, and each stone jars his bones and shakes his teeth; each stone another hard memory of her.

He strikes wood, a hollow dent in the graveyard hush, and he digs more frantically now, suppressing a cry, using his hands, breaking his nails, his clothes and skin so begrimed he looks a living part of the grave itself.

The little plaque on the coffin is too encrusted to read, but he knows what it will say—Thank You, Paul. He leans over this receptacle of so many things—of kisses and dances, of homework and tears—and places his lips on the broken pine.

He levers himself between the earth and the casket to get a handhold on the lid, jamming a chisel under it, cranking it until there is a crack and it rises on a sickly sweet miasma that makes him gag.

She is lying with her eyes open, waiting for him, her face porcelain perfect.

A movement catches his eye, a cry freezes him. Something crawls by her feet.

A rat? He cannot bear to think of her being so defiled. No, not a rat. It looks up at him, lurching feebly into the light of the jaundiced moon, its eyes knowing, sparkling.

A baby.

Impossible, impossible—the mantra loops like a Tilt-a-Whirl through his mind—impossible, impossible.

The child raises a hand toward him, and he reciprocates the gesture as if in a trance, touching the tiny fingers, feeling their oily texture. The child is soaked in blood he realises, as he clasps it to his chest. He can see the bloody chevrons of her dress where the child has chewed its way through.

"Dada," whispers the child into his ear, and the Brainworm tells him this is true.

Chapter 1

Carrie Anne Bradfield lay in her coffin, thin as a whisper in a hospice. They spoke in hushed tones as they waited patiently for their turn to shuffle forward and stare at the lifeless doll, their tongues slapping louder than the words they formed; in the overcrowded sitting room their murmurings sounded like the beginnings of a forest fire.

Malcolm tried to catch the words, the smallest of talk in the biggest of situations, but the voices were lost in a haze of whiskey and cheap aftershave. Through the bay window the late December sky fell in to pay its respects, and it too was dressed in black.

"Hard to believe she's gone," said Dobson. "I guess girls like Carrie Anne don't have to try too hard to make people hate them."

Malcolm grunted, glancing at the photograph of Carrie Anne above the fireplace, wearing the smile that had burned him all through high school. In a town the size of Ellsford, where a stolen bike was news, her murder was already as legendary as the previous one twenty years before. It was impossible to think that she would never curl her lip at him again or slight him with those dark eyes.

It was harder to believe he was even here at all.

Not one of the dough-faced mourners would give him the glad eye, and not just because he had brought Dobson Heather, though that would be their excuse. They could smell failure on him. It was a pack thing: he bore a mark that only they could see, and they shunned him for it.

5

Malcolm could see it in their eyes as they acknowledged him with sharp little flicks of the chin, and how they avoided Dobson's gaze altogether.

"Whoever killed her must've had a reason," said Malcolm. "Maybe one of the girls in Shoe Express finally had enough."

He coughed, almost hearing the swivel of eyeballs as they turned to glare. Funerals always gave him the sweats. Malcolm had a fear that he would end up with something cynicism couldn't make light of. Like Carrie Anne. Staring at her coffin he realised there were no novelty key rings for the likes of this. He imagined her dad at work, his mobile jangling with a comedy ringtone, only to be told his daughter was dead.

From where he stood he could just make out the waxy tip of her nose, a shock of nylon blonde curls, before his view was blocked by a large man with a silver streak in his oily midnight hair pushing his way to the front. The man leaned over the casket as if surveying a buffet, mumbling quietly to himself.

"What the fuck is Silver Cunningham doing here?" whispered Malcolm.

"Who knows," said Dobson. "Maybe he's gonna try and resurrect her."

Malcolm snorted, feeling his face burn as he tried to hold back the taboo laughter, but the high squeaks he emitted caused him to convulse even more. Out of the corner of his eye he could see Dobson's shoulders heaving, his small head drowning in the plaid expanse of his long-dead father's Sunday best.

The man with the monochrome hair turned to face them, and their laughter choked, spluttered, then stalled abruptly. He regarded them a moment before making his way toward them.

"There's a new face in Jerusalem this very day," said the big man with a smile, "though her sins must have been very great indeed to call down such a judgement. Mr. Heather, I trust your mother will be attending Group tomorrow night?"

"Dunno, Mr. Cunningham. I expect so."

"Tell her seven thirty sharp. We're making progress, boy, with the Lord's help of course. Perhaps you'll join her?"

"I'm not ill, Mr. Cunningham."

"We are all *ill*, son," he said, glancing over his shoulder at the coffin. "We are all dying. You do know God is watching you, Dobson? Always."

Then he was gone, leaving only a minty aura. Malcolm felt the anger rise in him, breathing deep to still his tom-tom heart. Fuck Samuel Cunningham and his happy clappy routine. What good was a faith healer at a funeral? And to come to *this* funeral, after what *his* brother did. Talk about bad taste.

"I'd like to lay my healing hands on him," he said to Dobson, "Right round his bloody bull neck." He reddened again as he realised what he had said.

Malcolm looked guiltily at the picture of Carrie Anne on the mantelpiece, wearing the pink dress she had worn all last summer. Were there still marks on her tender neck, faded now to accessories; if he pulled her blouse down would he be able to see the killer's prints still embedded in her throat?

The rotund figure of the Reverend Craig, grown fat on funeral fare over the years, bobbed among the mourners shelling out platitudes, Hell never far from his grey lips. He seemed less substantial than those he bleated to, diluted like a cup of milky tea, flittering amid a pervasive odour of self-denial.

"Such a tragedy, such a waste," he said, spotting Malcolm and Dobson, his sheep face breaking into a smile as it always did when chatting with the "young folk".

"Sometimes the Lord leaves us looking to the heavens askance, searching for His designs, but of course we can never hope to comprehend. It is our duty to accept, not to question."

"He raised Lazarus from the dead, how come—" began Dobson, but the Reverend was an old hand at deflection.

"He did indeed! You've been reading your bible I see. I was just saying to poor Mrs. Bradfield that all the answers can be found in that blessed tome. Aren't the sandwiches a credit to her? I mean, under the circumstances she has managed a wonderful spread. Carrie Anne's memory has not been tainted, I assured her."

Then he was gone, latching onto another, then another, like a dog in a butcher's shop that could not settle, his voice mingling with others, becoming so much white noise. Funerals were always full of such gossiping teeth-melters.

"It's just like when we were kids," said Dobson, as their turn came to shuffle forward and peer into the box. "When Skinner's dog got mangled under the tractor, and he charged us all to see it."

Suddenly this didn't seem like a good idea. What if her body was as mangled as Mutley's? What if her eyes were torn out, swirled in the bloody stew of her face, and what if one of those eyes flicked open just as her buckled hand reached out and—

Even in death she wore too much makeup. It was a shock to see her like this for Malcolm had always believed the adverts, believed that beauty was somehow immune to such degradation, but without a sparkle in her eyes her waxy face looked bony, hungry.

Twenty was too young to die. As a kid you couldn't wait to grow up, to reach the top of the hill, but nobody ever told you about the crap view from the summit. Malcolm backed away. Reverend Craig would have his work cut out explaining God's mysterious plan with this one.

He looked over to where the minister sat with Mrs. Bradfield on the enormous beige settee beneath the window, a twang of eucalyptus emanating from him as if he had a perpetual cold. "The undertaker's spade covers many a mistake," he was saying to her, in his professional role of Job's Comforter. "She's only sleeping," he soothed.

I've a hundred says she's dead, thought Malcolm, turning away. Brian Craig preached recruitment, not redemption. Malcolm had no patience for his voodoo.

He could hear Dobson's laboured breathing, feel it slide warmly against his neck. "You okay, Dobs?" he asked.

Dobson didn't answer. He was fighting an urge to touch her, to run a finger down her shiny cheek, to feel her coldness for himself. She looked aloof as always, unaware that she was news, that her death had rendered her more popular than ever. She just looked bored and perhaps that was all that death actually was, the ultimate boredom.

Dobson tore his eyes away from the silver cross that lay against her chest and let out a ragged sigh. "Looking good, girl," he said, his voice tender. "Doesn't she look great, Mal?"

The words brought Malcolm back to school, staring at Carrie Anne instead of the blackboard. She had her hair cut short, a severe amalgamation of angles that seemed to squash her face; squash it so hard that tears fell from her eyes, as if the end of the world had been shorn onto her head. Her hair bore the distressed look of something that had been tortured and teased, scrunched and gelled, an entire sleepless night. She slumped at her desk, a female Samson, her head unable to rise on a neck broken by shame. She had dismissed her court of admirers and hangers-on, intent on grieving in public solitude.

His first awful thought was that she had cancer or something unpronounceable. He did not realise the source of her misery was the little blonde helmet that sat so awkwardly atop her head. He could hear her chanting quietly, "I'll sue", over and over with such conviction that he expected lawyers in the hallways, and TV cameras in the playground interviewing eyewitnesses of the tragedy.

You'll get your TV cameras today Carrie Anne, he thought.

"Someone must know something!"

Mrs. Bradfield had broken from the Reverend's consoling shackles, knocking a plate of egg and onion sandwiches from her lap, shouting in the high-pitched tones of grief that knew nothing of embarrassment.

"One of you must know who did this!"

Her plea was so visceral, so bereft, that Malcolm felt like running, convinced that she would point her trembling finger at him and the mourners would fall on him and tear him apart.

"Come on, Dobs," he whispered. "Let's blow town before they wheel out the burning staves and pitchforks."

But Dobson wasn't listening.

He was peering over the coffin, his face paler than the corpse beneath, his mouth open as if to kiss it, vomiting a freight train of brackish water and offal, a steaming deluge of sour glory that gushed over Carrie Anne's immobile face. The needle smell of bile assaulted the room, mingling with the sickly sweet smell of roses, as if Hell's gate had been cracked ajar.

"Jesus Christ," said Malcolm, his voice sharp enough to burst the silence.

A fist flew through the swell of gasps, landing squarely on Dobson's nose. Malcolm could see the mucus bubbles fatten and explode in his nostrils as Dobson slumped to the floor. A hand grabbed him in the confusion, spun him round.

"Get that little shit outta here, or I swear there will be two fucking funerals this day!" Spittle hit his face, burning like chip fat. Mr. Bradfield's eyes were raw, the lines beneath dug like trenches, a long vein pulsing the length of his bald head. Unable to meet those eyes, to be sucked into that terrible abyss, Malcolm fixed his gaze on the wiry black hair that snaked over Bradfield's shirt collar, each one bejewelled with a tiny bead of sweat.

"I'm sorry, Mr. Bradfield, he—"

"Get the fuck out of my house, now!"

The collective eyes kaleidoscoped from shock to rage as arms reached out to restrain the father. Malcolm helped Dobson up, steering him through the press of bodies, navigating their way by the faded diamonds on the carpet, unwilling to look at those who backed away.

Typical that *he* should get the blame.

Every time Dobson messed up Malcolm always had to pay the piper, as if he were somehow operating him by foot. The worst of it was that he *felt* guilty; guilt gripped him like the bloody flu. He felt obscene.

Yet wasn't the very idea of lining up to ogle a girl who had the life squeezed out of her obscene? Wasn't that enough to turn your stomach as they handed out the strong tea and biscuits? They were all guilty of obscene curiosity. Maybe Dobson's reaction was the only truthful one you could possibly have.

A cardboard reindeer stood guard by the front door, a forgotten remnant of a Christmas now cancelled; it looked capable of eating them both. They stepped out into a coal black street that was trying to swallow the snow, the door slamming righteously on their hunched backs.

"Mal, I thought I saw—"

"Just shut it, Dobson. We're lucky they didn't lynch us in there. What the fuck is wrong with you!"

"Sorry," mumbled Dobson, wiping a bloodstained piece of carrot from his tie. "I guess we'll miss the burial."

"You think?"

Despite the heavy sarcasm the thought actually cheered Malcolm. He would not have to sit through the interminable service, the Celine Dion song they would undoubtedly play as they hoisted her out of the church, would not have to bear witness to the incongruous menagerie of stuffed toys littering the grave as if they buried a child and not a woman. He would not have to listen to Reverend Craig bleat, "Blessed are the dead who die in the Lord", or read the pathetic euphemisms for the horror of the void.

Dobson was pressing a small wad of dirty snow against his busted nose. "Sorry, Malcolm. I never saw a dead girl before."

It was easy to forget what age Dobson was sometimes. The small frame, the large bullock eyes, the hair that looked like it had been cut with a knife and fork, conspiring to make him look a little boy. That, and the fact that he never stopped smiling, made him seem younger than his twenty years. Even now he was grinning round the ruins of his nose. People tended to mistake his natural optimism for backwardness.

"Come on," said Malcolm turning his collar up, "before my ears start bleeding."

The biting wind cut through the greasy air of The Frying Saucer on the corner, as they plodded through slate grey lumps of slush, turning onto the long road of shoe shops and discount stores that Ellsford called a High Street.

At the bus stop Malcolm lit a cigarette, its fiery tip changing colour with the passing traffic in the Plexiglas until he smoked a carnival. Behind him the distorted image of Dobson blew smoke rings, his fingers barely reaching beyond the sleeve of his dead man's coat. A bus lurched to the kerb, splattering them with icy water, turning their cigarettes to mulch; it coughed, spluttered, the hiss of its opening doors its final breath.

Sitting in its dirty tube of light they didn't speak, letting their words dry out with their clothes. Rubbing condensation from the window Malcolm watched the parade of storefronts give way to washed out streets, then fields of mud and virgin snow that slipped by like sunken wedding cakes.

The bus shuddered as they reached the churchyard, moaned, and then gave up the ghost once more.

"Approaching Shit Central," said Dobson, using his hand as a radio mike, "please prepare to disembark."

Home again thought Malcolm, feeling the familiar depression seep into him along with the chill air. Romannon Street was a small concrete tapeworm secreted in the bowels of Ellsford where the birds never sang, just gossiped and cleared their throats. He had lived here his entire life; sometimes he told strangers he lived on Knox Avenue just to escape for a while.

Clouds hung like smoker's lungs over the grey rooftops above as they skirted deepening puddles, heading toward the squat rows of houses at the street's twisting conclusion. The moon was up early, but its batteries were weak and it looked sick and jaundiced. Two mongrels screwed enthusiastically in the middle of the road, holding up a few cars that blared their horns as they rusted impatiently. A thin blade of light broke through the clouds, stabbing the pavement as they reached Dobson's house, illuminating a pale bare leg that emerged from his front door, the veins scribbled up it in felt tip scrawls.

Joyce Heather popped out before them wearing only an outsize t-shirt, Monroe's face twisted into a freak show by her expansive breasts.

"Did you bring me back some vol-au-vents?" she cooed in a little girl voice.

"Get inside, mum, before someone sees!" She was the only one who could embarrass her son.

"Was there many at it?" she asked Malcolm, ignoring Dobson completely.

"There wasn't room to turn a sweet in your mouth," he said, feeling uncomfortable. There was something dirty about her that made him itch.

Her laugh echoed over her broken teeth, and Malcolm waited for her lips to crumble as if her face was made of sponge; he knew if he dug his nails into those painted cheeks he would expose thick rivulets of jam.

"Mr. Cunningham wants to know if you're going to Group tomorrow night," said Dobson. "I told him I didn't know."

"Course I am! I *never* miss. I never give up hope." She turned her attention back to Malcolm. "I'm dying y'know, but I'm determined to live life to the full."

Malcolm forced a smile. Bloody hypochondriac would outlive them all.

"Would you grant a dying woman one final wish?" She began hiking up the bottom of her t-shirt to reveal a pair of lace panties. Dobson succeeded in ushering her inside as Malcolm felt the snow melt on the blaze of his cheeks.

"See you tomorrow, Dobs," he managed.

"Bright and early, Mal."

The door slammed shut, the way it always did in the Heather house, as Malcolm crossed the road to his own front door. Twenty-six paces; once, when life was simpler, it had been twice that.

After he had closed the door, Dobson's habitual smile slipped from his face like a slug from a dog bowl. He needed to talk to some-one, tell them he thought he had seen Carrie Anne's eyes open, but who would believe him? Certainly not Malcolm; Malcolm had no time nowadays for anything he said. Dobson put his hand into his pocket and took out the cross he had stolen from Carrie Anne's corpse, still congealed by the lining of his gut.

"I'm sorry I was so squeamish," he said to the empty room, then gave the cross a perfunctory rub on the sleeve of his father's coat.

He pulled a box out from under his bed and, kissing the cross, placed it beside the other necklace he had found in the sewers all those years ago.

Chapter 2

The rain started to fall, a cascade of tiny pins washing way the slush and the mud that choked the gutters, but the world still looked filthy. Samuel Cunningham strode briskly, trying not to dampen the shine on his heavy black boots, whistling softly to himself in a bid to ease the mad pounding of his heart.

It was beginning, he thought, *the girl's death was a sign.* Her killer had made the days bright once more, brought purpose to this shabby little town.

He soldiered on, his steps punctuated by the tinny drone of carols. Santa and Elves, their girth and their mirth at odds with the thin, miserable street, appalled him; Christmas was a time for suffering and penance. The cold gnawed at him with kitten teeth to reassure him this was true.

The tinsel had run amok, took root and prospered like a gaudy weed. He could not decide if the forced good humour that surrounded him was cynical or merely insane. He wanted, above all else, to absorb some goodness. He needed to find something pure to hang onto, to get him through the coming darkness, but that was the one thing not on sale.

And yet he knew of a vessel. The Heather boy; he had sensed it in him before he had been told.

Staring at the pavement as he walked, at the countless sparkles of frost on mica, he imagined them as forgotten souls begging from the depths of a black Hell. All around him was a fool's idea of heaven, a cartoon neon soup as shallow as it was loud. He would rather be with the sparkles.

Cutting down Hollywell Road on his way to Romannon Street, he couldn't help but smile at the sudden row of gardens that popped up beside him; oasis allotments in the relentless grey. So many signs today, and he was privy to them all! He frowned at the pampas grass though; too showy, too pretentious. Pompous grass would be more apropos. People should stick to roses, for God loved the basics.

An old woman watched his progress from behind a net curtain, chattering away soundlessly on her telephone. He waved cheerily at her, but she let the gauze drop and carried on watching him from behind its milky shadow. He refused to let this spoil his day; perhaps God was not omnipresent after all, perhaps he just hired fat nosey women. The snub heightened his anxiety. He hurried on, eager to reach his destination.

It was imperative that he persuade Joyce to bring her son to Group tonight. His presence was vital, that much had been revealed to him. In all the visions that plagued his sleep, the chaotic voices that frazzled his waking hours since the Bradfield girl's death, one thing alone was clear—Dobson Heather was the key Paul had spoken of. He felt the truth of it in his bones, in the flutter of moth wings in his belly even now.

The boy was an idiot of course, but he had been chosen nonetheless and Samuel would have to abide by the Lord's decision.

A scream broke the silence, startling him, sending the sparrows flapping into the air like filthy rain.

"They are not cows, they're dogs!"

On the other side of a matchstick fence Bob Turk was beating his four-year-old son with the flat of his hand as two Dalmatian pups yapped at his feet.

"Are you stupid? Have I raised another fucking moron!"

The little boy cried lumps of broken glass. Turk looked over at Samuel, guilt on vacation, and mumbled something that could have been "Hi" or "Die"; he was a clever man that way. Despite the chill in the air, Turk was wearing a luminous muscle shirt and a pair of shorts, the better to show off his tan. This depressed Samuel more than the beating of the child. He hated those tanned enthusiastic types who openly pitied you when you revealed you weren't holidaying abroad this year.

He could never explain to them how he preferred possessions to memories, solids to shadows.

He ran his fingers through his hair, conscious of gaining power just by touching that streak of silver, the mark of God, that shot through it, and hurried on, confident that misery would find Bob Turk before the suntan faded. It was a shame that so many girls would suffer, that the killer would pass over men like Turk, men who did not deserve a lungful of His blessed air, yet who could question the divine plan?

He felt out of place here. He had few followers here, for money took away real belief. It was only in the council houses, in the cramped confines of places like Romannon Street, that the truth really blossomed; faith came to those houses as readily as brown windowed envelopes. He would receive no salutes here, no recognition of his gift. Their doors would remain closed to him, even if he could save their slutty little daughters.

After tonight that would all change. Faith would be bestowed on them, slowly but surely, like a dripping tap, and they would all come to wisdom.

His shiny boots beat out the glory of Christ as he marched on, contemplating the destiny so devoutly assigned to him, and to him alone.

The houses began to huddle closer together, whispering of his approach. He slowed as he reached the church, its spire scraping the grey underbelly of cloud that smothered it, its walls thick with damp green moss, its dull stained glass lifeless. He had never liked churches, could never understand why the house of God should look so foreboding.

Surely only a wicked thing could abide in such a nightmare.

Nor could he understand the pious sheep who flocked there in their brand new clothes, a fashion parade, to indulge in an exercise in tedium they laughingly called worship. He sighed; *I guess we must all throw our pebble at the wall regardless.*

He was about to move on when he spotted the Reverend, a gnome amid the gravestones. He walked through the gates as the church bells rang out, the difference between notes as hazy as the gradations between sins. Reverend Craig was hunkered on the steps to the vestry, scrubbing furiously. Samuel knew it would hold him back, but he could not resist the chance to point out the Reverend's flaws.

"Beautiful day, Mr. Craig," he said, strolling briskly toward him. The Reverend looked up at the pregnant sky about to miscarriage and smiled back doubtfully.

"I suppose so, Samuel, but we must remember it is a sad day too for one poor family in this town. And how are you?"

"Well, I'm above the soil, can't ask for more than that." Samuel was upon him now, gazing over his shoulder at the bucket of soapy pink water, at the brush in the Reverend's hands, its bristles stained with the blood he was trying to scrub from the steps.

"I'll have to have a word again with the police, about the young ones drinking here," said the Reverend standing up. "I don't mind the bottles so much, or the butts, but when they start fighting … Here of all places. So little respect."

"What makes you think it was kids?"

"Well, who else, Samuel?" The Reverend's tone was testy, resigned to the unwanted argument he saw coming. "Is there something I can do for you? As you can see, I'm rather busy."

"I was wondering what you think Isaac might have said to Abraham after he tried to sacrifice him. 'You never even paused, dad, you were really going to do it!' 'I had to. He would've killed us both. Never a word to your mother mind, you know what she's like.' Long journey home don't you think?"

"Ah, Samuel, Samuel," sighed the Reverend. "Must you keep coming round here and blaspheming? Have you no decency left, son?"

Samuel knelt down and dipped a finger in the clotted mess on the steps, then held the dripping digit under the Reverend's nose.

"'And Moses took the blood, and put it on the horns of the altar round about with his finger, and purified the altar.' Leviticus eight, fifteen."

"Don't you quote the scriptures at me, Sammy boy! I baptised you in that font in there, and your brother too. I'm too old a cat to be lectured by a kitten like you, heathen that you are."

"Have you read your bible lately, Mr. Craig? This is the blood of the lamb, shed as a sign."

"Why do you go on with this, son? Can't you see you're not well? You drove your poor mother into an early grave with this nonsense, and not content with that you have to take the vulnerable away from the bosom of the church, people who need it most, with your yarns of healing hands. You pour your unctions into peoples' eyes, but you pour something more dangerous into their hearts—hope. False hope. Can't you see the harm you're doing?"

Samuel wiped his bloodstained finger carefully on a small tissue he pulled from his pocket, taking his time, recovering his composure before answering.

"So you think the miracles have stopped. Do you think God has fallen asleep?"

"I'd think it a miracle if you came to your senses. You're a rare breed, Cunningham, a circus barker, not a miracle worker. In all these years you've not cured so much as a wart. You couldn't cure bacon, and yet you carry on oblivious."

"And what of you, Reverend? You're … expletive deleted. My soul is green tea and cucumber fresh, can you say the same of yours? Maybe if you came to Group tonight you would change your mind, but I doubt if even the good Lord could work such a feat."

The Reverend threw the brush into the bucket, splashing Samuel's boots with bloody suds. "Just go, Sammy, go home and rest yourself."

"You're blind, Brian Craig, blind to the plans of the God you pay lip service to, and I fear you are a long way from Damascus."

"You're sinning your soul, Samuel. I'll pray for you, son, I surely will. Doesn't it ever bother you what comes out of your mouth?"

"Does it ever worry you the amount of graves you rob to line your own? Save your dusty prayers, you talk only to yourself."

Reverend Craig reddened, using the voice he normally hurled from the pulpit, "Is it any wonder the world's in such a mess with false prophets like you roaming through it! Any wonder the devil stalks these very streets! I saw you at that young girl's house yesterday, wallowing in her death. God forgive you, Samuel Cunningham, God forgive you for even being there."

"I had every right to be there," said Samuel, regarding the swirls in the pungent pool of Domestos.

"After what your brother did? Do you think people have forgotten?"

"Her parents are my people—"

"Listen to yourself, 'My people'."

"—my blood-bought people!" He kicked the bucket over as his hemlock rage, his nettle anger, boiled over. "Those girls were sin offerings, mere sacrifices. My brother burns in Hell for what he did. I am not accountable for his wickedness."

"No, Samuel," said the Reverend quietly, sadly. "But you are accountable for your own." He turned his back on Samuel and walked away.

It was a low trick to bring up his brother like that, and one that he should have been ready for. The day grew darker as if God were frowning on his weakness.

"Angels are among us!" he shouted at the retreating figure. "Your favour is slipping, Craig, you no longer have the power!"

Samuel trudged down the avenue of brown windblown flowers, the puddles beneath his feet sparkling with the pleas of countless lost souls, his brother among them.

"You don't have the power," he whispered to himself.

Paul's memory was forever etched on the small mind of the town, and, of course, when the Bradfield girl was found naked and battered in the park the talk immediately returned to him.

Even some of his own people had turned from him, finding an abundance of chores to keep them from Group. He had went to the Bradfield house to show that he was spotless, free from the perceived sin that stained his brother, but he would always be marked by it; like the silver streak on his temple, his brother's act would always define him in the eyes of others.

If only he could heal himself.

He thought of Eileen, turning her image over in his mind like a magician toying with a coin. She was barely sixteen when Paul raped her, when he crushed her skull, and though he could feel nothing but sorrow for a life snipped so brutally short a surge of joy overwhelmed him.

Paul had known one thing—you have to take a life to get a life.

My brother knew the secrets, the truth behind what was taught. He knew it all and shared it with me; before he had a hair on his chin he knew the workings of this world.

Samuel wandered round the corner of Hollywell, cutting across the patch of wasteland that separated it from Romannon Street, thinking now of another teacher; his father.

Father's knowledge was more frightening, lent gravitas by his booming voice, and he spoke only of earthly things, things more terrible than the demons that plagued his brother's every waking thought. He remembered how his father had come to their room late one night to tell them the facts of life. He told them it was called "pussy" because once it had its fill it grew arrogant and snooty and wanted nothing more to do with you until it was hungry once more; just like a real cat, he said. He taught them to fear this independence. Samuel had learnt the lesson well and never married.

As he stopped outside the Heather's front door his mind returned to Eileen, how he used to write her name with a heart above the "i", her long sleek legs, her smile. Yes, she had made him the man he was, and Carrie Anne would take him to the next level. The ones yet to come would take him all the way.

Smiling, he pushed the doorbell.

She must not have been expecting him for she was soberly dressed.

"Silver!" squeaked Joyce, then with a crinkle of her stonewashed eyes she corrected herself. "Samuel, do come in."

"Mrs. Heather," he said, bracing himself as he pushed passed her into the manky darkness of the hall, holding his breath in case she touched him. She was so wanton, like the girls under his bed made skin and sweat. The way she decorated her meat drove him to distraction; *she is my Magdalene*, he thought.

She waved him on through, her eyes on full beam raking over his skin. "Shit before the shovel," she said, and even her vulgar laugh aroused him. Her crudeness often vexed him, but he never checked her; he knew her profane bluster hid a pleasing vulnerability.

"I didn't know you were coming," she said, her voice perpetually breathless around him, "or I would've cleaned."

It would take a strategic air strike to clean this house, he thought. How she managed to live under the burden of such squalor was another of her charms. Her home resembled a neglected zoo, the hallway filled with the constant shadow play of cats, feral little brutes that stalked the menagerie of caged birds that trilled incessantly of their danger. "My ornaments," Joyce called them.

He wrinkled his nose at the sharp twang of urine that seeped up through the carpet, dismissing her apologies with a wave of his hand. "You know I love how close you are to nature, Joyce. I've come to talk to you about Group tonight. There is a favour I need to ask of you."

"Cup of tea, Vicar?" she giggled, taking him by the arm and steering him into the kitchen, managing to squash her breasts against him even though it was the most spacious room in the house. He would have to be careful; she would run up the back of your neck to get to your head.

"No sugar, that's right, isn't it? You really should develop a sweet tooth, Samuel, it makes you seem so stern without one."

Rolling up her sleeve she extracted a soiled mug from the sink. Two terrapins lay encased in a strange green fuzz beside what appeared to be a bowl of dysentery. He waited as she boiled the kettle, stranded on the lino in a minefield of cat shit, unsure whether to head for the detritus of the table or stand his ground.

"Joyce, it is imperative that—"

"Sherman got another one, mum." Dobson stood in the doorway cradling a tiny kitten, its head dangling in a precarious position. "Oh, hello, Mr. Cunningham. I didn't know you were here."

The boy looked pale, a stranger to sleep, but his smile was extraordinary and those huge eyes, the shaving mirrors of the soul. He held up the fluffy corpse. "He didn't eat it this time though."

A low rumble seemed to shake the peeling walls. Sherman, the enormous fang-ridden beast they called a dog, padded in with a baby doll clamped in its dripping teeth. Its eyes locked on Samuel's as it growled; you could hear the bite in that wicked hum. It dropped the doll, unleashing a howl that sent a shiver up Samuel's back, then sat quietly, Japanese in its silence. They said that when a dog howled like that it meant someone in the house would die; if that were true, the whole street should be a ghost town by now.

"Take it outside and bury it with the others. And take Shermy with you, he hasn't emptied himself today." Joyce handed Samuel a mug of tea, her breasts an exhalation from his chest.

"Actually, it's about Dobson that I called."

"What about him?" she asked, regarding him with a raven's eye, always so protective of her only child.

"The voices have started again."

"Oh Silver, after all this time!"

"I have had a message. Dobson must be at Group tonight. I don't pretend to know why, only that the Lord promises great progress if we carry out His will."

She turned to her son, her slippered feet squashing a pungent little turd. "Do you hear that, son?" she said, pride glowing in her voice, "Mr. Cunningham has invited you."

Dobson started to fidget, unconsciously stroking the dead kitten. "I'm going out with Pruner tonight, there's a band on, BullSkull, and—"

"You're no such thing, you are coming to Group."

"But mum, I—"

"Do as you're bid! Go upstairs and get your good shirt and I'll iron it for you." Dobson flinched and Samuel sympathised; her tongue was a ripcord for a panic alarm when her temper was up.

"Sorry, Mr. Cunningham, I already made plans." Dobson's eyes pleaded with Samuel's but Samuel turned away. He knew what was coming next.

"They were here again, Dobson, this very morning, first thing. They asked me if you were being good and I told them yes, I said you were ever so good. Don't make mummy out to be a liar."

There was no need to ask who "they" were. They were the ones who called to make sure he went to work, ate all his dinner, obeyed her every whim.

"Mum, I'm not a baby."

"Then stop getting on like one and do as you're told. Your dad would be spinning in his box if he heard you giving me back cheek."

Phase two, thought Samuel. Any mention of the boy's father hit home hard he noted, filing away the boy's pain for future reference.

"I'm dying, pet," she said, rubbing her hands over her face, smearing a rainbow of makeup around the knife wounds of her eyes. She held her hands out for his inspection, a cosmetic stigmata. "Do it for me while you still can. Do it for me and you dear dead daddy."

She was in disgusting, filthy health. It radiated from her, but her ridiculous claims always had the desired effect so Samuel bit his tongue. The doctor was always prescribing her potions for her notions when all she really needed was faith.

"Okay, okay, just don't cry. I'll bury this first, then I'll go tell Malcolm—"

"You'll get your shirt first," said Joyce, snatching the kitten from him and flinging it in the sink. "I don't have all day to run after you."

"Sherman would probably have dug him up again anyway," said Dobson to Samuel, shrugging his shoulders as he left the kitchen, Sherman taking point.

"See," she beamed when they were alone. "Simple as dimples. Anything for my Silver."

He reddened, setting down his tea untouched, feeling the mug stick to the table. "I'll see you both tonight then."

Joyce laughed, jiggling her ample bosom. "I never go anywhere without them."

He muttered a prayer to ward off temptation as he hurried into the hallway. He could feel her breath hot on his neck, sweet as attar, as he yanked open the front door, letting the cold air purge his body.

"Mrs. Heather. Joyce. I realise this might seem an indecorous question," he said, as she laid a firm hand on his arm.

"Yes, my Silver?" she asked, her eyes illuminating the dank hall.

"Do you still have my brother's finger?"

Chapter 3

The Cove Bar always reminded Dobson of an old hooker, one who had outlived the bad reputation of her youth to reinvent herself as a venerable old lady; a lady with too many facelifts and a wicked glint in her eye perhaps, but a lady nonetheless. For Dobson, the whole town was a monochrome stage set, save for the small splash of joy that was The Cove.

Her dour red façade was embellished by a few hanging baskets and a stunted conifer in a pot by the door. An Olde Worlde sign in bald white lettering implied simple but prolonged pleasures. The other bars in Ellsford, notably Benson's across the street, had succumbed to the awful trend of becoming quasi restaurants, divorcing themselves from their natural audience by seeking the kind of clientele that simply did not exist in the town. They had become a haven for college kids too young to hold their ambitions let alone their liquor. The Cove watched them all come and go, and if she didn't shed a tear at their passing, she never raised a smile either.

His spirits dipped as he saw Drew Proctor's Yamaha parked outside. If that slabber was here he would never get a chance to talk to Pruner about Carrie Anne (but perhaps that was a good thing for in the cold light of day he didn't believe it himself); Drew's mouth craved feet, hungered for them, and after a few pints he always got the munchies. Dobson had no idea how to hold a conversation with him; he was a completely different species. For one delicious moment he considered kicking the bike over, then shivered at the thought of the revenge Drew would exact.

No sooner had he stepped through the pub doors than a cheer rose to meet him and the beer mats came flying in his direction.

"Duh-obson!"

He saw all the pretty girls sitting in little pockets of perfumed air, ready and willing to be plucked from the herd, shunning the raucous laughter, turning away their snooty little noses when they saw its cause.

His eyes darted behind the bar to see Tommy's reaction, but Tommy merely carried on pulling a pint and chatting away to some old wheeze bag. He wasn't barred then. He had no memory of the last time he'd been in, of what he had said or done, but Tommy hadn't pulled him aside for one of his frequent private chats so he must be okay.

With that monkey off his back, Dobson started to relax. He felt like a cowboy, the local gunslinger coming in to take his lumps and shoot down his detractors. He'd need a lot of bullets. Everyone here knew his name but nothing else. It was only jokes and jags they wanted with him, they didn't give a damn how he really ticked.

The bar swallowed him whole as he pushed his way through the crowd, through the artificial birdsong of the poker machines, through the blare of the racing commentary, through the fog of aftershave that smelt like it was sold by the gallon, past the phallic beer pumps that shone like alien candles in the gloom; the tweed and the designer labels fusing into one around him as the young merged with the old.

Nothing changes, thought Dobson.

People die, pints are downed, and the whiskey drained. The Cove was God's waiting room; when a man fell, a new one took up his stool and carried on supping. Even now a generation of characters and bores were being spawned so that one day they too could make their stand here, in this their Stalingrad, their field of Megiddo.

Nothing ever changes, thought Dobson, *amen to that.*

Except maybe it did. There was a killer in their midst, after all, sitting by those pretty girls for all they knew, admiring their trashy hairdos and leering at their frozen chests. Dobson knew in his gut the killer wasn't finished yet, and when he was done could things ever be the same again?

He manoeuvred his way out to the beer garden, spotting Mal and

Pruner sitting at the table underneath the huge cartwheel that hung on the back wall, only their bravado protecting them from the elements. He tensed as he saw Drew; even seated his every movement threatened violence. Sucking up his breath, he walked over, glad when Pruner broke into a smile at the sight of him.

"Dobson, you mad wee fucker! What's all this I hear about you taking a dump on Carrie Anne Whorefield's stiff?" said Drew, far louder than was necessary.

"That's not exactly what happened."

"I heard you spread your bony arse cheeks and squished a hot log on the bitch's face."

"I'll get a round in will I?"

As he headed back into the bar, grateful for the brief respite, he heard Drew laughing ("Did you clock his shirt?"), then Pruner's voice, soft but forceful, "Cut it out, Drewcifer". Dobson pushed his way through the crowd feeling ten feet tall. At least he had one real friend in this world.

"Hey, Moses!" he called to Tommy's back, "Four pints of Guinness and a couple of bags of cheese and onion!"

Tommy folded his paper and made a face and Dobson laughed. He always laughed no matter what Tommy did; laughed too hard, too long. He hated himself for being so hand rubbingly obsequious but he had an almost pathological need to be liked. The fact that he himself only truly liked a handful of people didn't matter; he needed the people he despised to like him too.

"Why do you always call me Moses?" asked Tommy, setting the drinks before him.

"Well, every time I see you I just think *profit*."

"No-one likes a smart arse, Heather."

Don't I know it. People shunned him because they thought he wasn't the full deck, worried that his stupidity might be catching, but perhaps they feared him too, suspected deep down he was too clever by half.

"What can I say, Thomas, I'm an enigma."

He carried the tray of drink back out to the beer garden where Drew was gesticulating wildly, no doubt livening up another dull anecdote with a thuggish mime.

Drew Proctor was a hard man, at least to listen to. Hunched over the damp table, head shaved down to the wood and glowing under the three bar heater, his bulging arms a mess of Indian ink tattoos that resembled doodles on a school jotter, Drew rode the conversational merry go round; dipping, falling, rising, the hostility so thinly veiled. His face was a tiny afterthought in the squat centre of his meaty head.

Even from this distance it wasn't hard to work out what he was pontificating about; from school his head had been filled with nothing more than tits and tanks. The son of a former local hell raiser, Drew Proctor cared for nothing outside his own heartbeat.

He glued a smile to his face and walked over, unable to take his eyes off Proctor, off a mouth so slack it was capable of forming only crass clichés. Drew's arm shot out in a wide arc before zooming back to pluck the cigarette from his lips, blowing the smoke from a pinhole in the corner of his mouth.

"So, tell us about the dead whore then," he laughed, and even his laugh was hard; it could beat up your laugh, and your dad's laugh too. "Your little bud must've stood seeing her up that close, eh?"

"Enough, big man," said Pruner. Drew smiled coldly, then quickly changed the conversation back to himself.

"I was just telling the boys about the ride I got last night. Popped both the balls in. She bent over so far, if she'd opened her mouth I coulda used her as a fuckin telescope!"

"Still living the Fleming novel then, Drew?" said Dobson, pleased to see Pruner grin; he owed him, he usually only told him jokes he'd heard off the telly.

"You think you know everything, Heather."

"No, I don't," said Dobson dealing out the pints. "I just know a lot, and come tomorrow, I'll know even more."

"I'm talking about that Deirdre Wright bit, total cockaholic, not that you'd know anything about that. The only thing you ever shagged was that Brady tart, and you had to lace her with voddy first. Christ! What an ugly bitch. You would've been better off drinking the Smirnoff yourself and having a wank."

"Whatever you say, Studley," said Dobson, feeling awkward because Drew was closer to the truth than he knew.

"Fuckin A, virgin hole! I'm ball bag dynamite." He rubbed his denim crotch in Dobson's face and cackled. He had developed a comedy laugh over the holidays to make himself more interesting, and Dobson suspected he never found anything funny after the decision to adopt it; when he was laughing, he was really just practicing.

Dobson laughed too, hating himself for feeding the myth.

Drew lifted a leg and farted, a long, drawn-out, creaking B-movie door of a fart that made everyone at the nearby table look over. "Excuse me, ladies," he said, patting his ass, "I've a Womble to dispose of," before marching off in the direction of the toilets.

Malcolm was laughing too hard, the strain showing in his eyes. *Is that what I look like?* wondered Dobson, *because if I do I'll open a vein.*

It was clear Malcolm was desperate for Drew's approval, had been from their school days, hoping that some of that bad boy swagger might rub off by mere proximity to his idol, but the sad truth was that if it wasn't for Pruner, Drew wouldn't give him the time of day.

"Listen, lads," said Dobson, "I can't make it tonight. I've been roped into going to Silver's shindig by my mum." There was a silence that stretched across the frozen beer garden, punctuated by a few grave-yard coughs.

"Fucksake, Dobson, what age *are* you?" said Malcolm loudly; it wasn't enough to let Dobson know he thought he was a big kid, he had to make sure everyone else knew too.

"What time's it at?" asked Pruner. "I wouldn't mind seeing the old badger work his hoodoo."

"Round seven." Dobson didn't know what was sweeter—Pruner's support or the look on Malcolm's face.

"What about you, Mal, fancy some old time religion?"

Malcolm sniffed. "You serious? Is there air getting in?"

"That'll be a no then," said Dobson, relieved that Malcolm wouldn't be dragging his dark cloud along with them.

"You two idiots enjoy yourself, I'll just go to the gig with Drew."

Good luck with that, thought Dobson, trying not to smile; the day was turning out a lot better than expected.

Drew returned, his hand hovering over the numerous pint glasses that clogged the table. "Where am I parked?" he asked, and Malcolm pointed out his pint, nearly knocking it over in his haste.

"Ah," sighed Drew after a long swallow, his breath blooming like a jellyfish in the freezing air. "That was some shit, six on the Richter scale at least. Do you think queers get turned on when they have a crap? What do you think?" he said, slapping Malcolm on the back. "I hear you're a bit of a double adaptor, Weir, take it both ways."

"You wish," said Malcolm reddening.

"What the fuck do you mean by that? You saying a man of my

28

calibre would give you one, you baldy wee prick!" The fact that that he pronounced calibre "kal-eye-bree", and that his own head resembled a dinosaur egg was lost on Drew in his fury.

"No," Malcolm panicked, "no, I didn't mean … I'm not bald!"

"Who you trying to kid, Weir. Your hair's combed round in so many circles it looks like an ice cream."

They all laughed, but Dobson knew that Malcolm would soon be in the toilets checking himself out in the grimy old mirror in order to reassure himself that Drew was only messing. It was Pruner who excused himself first though, and Dobson followed soon after.

The urinals were blocked again, brimming over with an orangey fluid that looked like melted lollies but smelt like laughing death. He added to it self-consciously, watching its skin ripple with the flow. Among the floating cubes a cigarette butt was riding high on the brine and he focused awhile on pissing it over the drain.

"Don't let Mal get you down, Dobs." Pruner pulled up his zip and let out a cough. "Head's up his ass as usual."

"It's not him that's worrying me, Billy," said Dobson, pushing open the crapper door to make sure they were alone.

Pruner's face knuckled up; Dobson rarely used his real name. "Is someone giving you grief, wee man?"

"Nothing like that," said Dobson, glowing at his mate's obvious concern. "It's Carrie Anne. I think—"

"Ah, Dobs," sighed Pruner, putting his arm around Dobson's shoulder, "I know you liked her, and I'm sorry she's gone, but trust me, she was no lady. She'd been cocked more times than John Wayne's rifle. What existed up here," he tapped Dobson on the forehead with a damp finger, "bore no relation to reality. She was a bitch, Dobs. No point in being a hypocrite about it."

"That's not what I mean."

"Well, what then?"

"Christ, this is going to sound so fucking nuts."

"When did that ever annoy you? Listen, mate, ding dong the witch is dead, rest in peace, yeah?"

"That's just it. I don't think she is, I mean … I don't think she's resting at all." Silence enveloped them; the trickle of water down the urinal, the muted voices from the bar—all seemed to fade away. "I just feel that if I don't explain this properly then something bad's gonna happen."

At the sound of his ragged voice the spell broke and the door opened, the urinals flushing like applause. Suddenly the toilets filled with drunks, their words buzzing in the stale air. The chance of conversation went up the wall along with their frothy pish.

As he slipped back outside he felt the old familiar sadness sink into his bones; *don't ever make the mistake of thinking that you are popular*, he reminded himself, *your face does not show its depths and people are blind to nuance*. It was time to go home. He arranged to meet Pruner, took the inevitable insults from Drew, the aloof silence from Malcolm, and left The Cove on a wave of catcalls and jeers.

He began the walk home feeling sorry for himself, without enough courage to tell Pruner that Carrie Anne's eyes had opened in her coffin, without enough alcohol in his system to dull his fear. Even the wind bullied him. He hunched his shoulders as he passed beneath power lines slumped under the weight of electricity. At the road works the turn boards flipped and for a moment he fully expected them to read—*Doom*.

The streets were filling up with early evening drunks; he acknowledged them all by name as they lurched by like buckled frogs. As bees dance to tell their kind of pollen, so drunks stagger to inform each other of bargain wines.

Was this his destiny?

To hallucinate over corpses, to end up a member of the Brew Crew, joining the infamous ranks of Catman, Firedancer, Sniper Hanlon, and Sneezy John? The thought turned his mood a shade blacker; he would spend his life alone for sure then.

The grinding of a gearbox broke his reverie.

A yellow car, thin and sharp as a dart, growled alongside him before stopping and purring idly. A smoky window rolled down and he saw a pale figure beckon to him. He looked around, scanning the street, but he was the only one there.

"Me?" he mouthed, feeling stupid as he pointed to himself. The pale figure nodded its head. He ambled over, noticing how the car's interior seemed to suck the last of the day's feeble light into itself. He didn't want to touch that shiny metallic carapace; it looked like it might take his hand off.

As he stepped closer he felt his head reel. Not from the stench of decay that seeped unbidden from the open window, nor the sight of the stick thin figure behind the wheel, grinning through a starving death mask. It was the noise.

It made him sway with a nauseous vertigo, tried to pull his fluttering gut up through his throat; a discordant cacophony ebbing and flowing in tactile waves from the car stereo, sucking on his skin, crackling in his hair. The windscreen was spattered with something, as if it had rained inside. When the door opened the air that rushed out was so fetid it was visible. The man behind the wheel smiled at him.

He had a pronounced underbite and a half-cooked egg of an eye. His hands were blotchy, the skin a purplish blue and veined like corduroy. His hair was sparse, clinging damply to his skull, a skull so white it seemed to push through the skin that draped it. His nostrils flared like camera shutters snapping another desperate slice of life. Dobson realised that what he could smell was the accumulation of the man's breath.

The noise stopped as the keys shut off the engine. The sudden silence was as disorienting as the aural chaos that had preceded it.

"You're the one they speak of," said the stick man. Dobson stared into the Noh mask of his face, hypnotised by his voice even as he recoiled from the storm drain of his mouth.

"Who are you?"

"I'm here to make good on the promises of the past, and to make sure all the little ladies find their way home safe." He stroked Dobson's cheek with a gnarled fingernail that cracked and broke.

Then the noise began again in Dobson's head and the day turned hopelessly black and a forgetfulness enveloped him like a swaddling smog.

Chapter 4

William "Pruner" Rose had only come along for a laugh.

A room full of coffin dodgers, that old badger Cunningham laying on hands and talking in tongues, it seemed too good to miss, but the fun was seeping out of the occasion with indecent haste.

Dobson had been uncharacteristically quiet the whole way there, unresponsive to Pruner's boisterous attempts to shake him back to his goofy self. All he wanted to do was talk crazy shit about Carrie Anne, about ghosts, or apparitions, or whatever they called the ones that didn't speak or move things; figments of the imagination.

"They're all in your head, Dobs," he'd tried to reassure him, though in truth he had only been half listening.

"Isn't that the worse place they could be?" replied Dobson.

The poster pinned to the front door of the community centre proclaimed—*A Healing Explosion! Samuel Cunningham Presents An Invasion By God!* The hall smelt of almonds and urine. Pruner heard the false laughter of women taper off as he shook out his coat; their sing-song voices, their bland formalities, set his teeth on edge.

They settled in near the back, on contoured plastic seats designed for stacking not for sitting on, fidgeting like kids in church until the hall gradually grew quiet, became a room of autumn looks and winter sighs. The aura of hushed reverence made Pruner squirm. Beside him Dobson was sweating profusely, his wan face glowing under the dim lights.

He bit back an insult.

Dobson was always too vulnerable, there was no need to hurt his feelings even more. Pruner could remember how, even at primary school, the bruises smudged his skin like dirt where his bastard of a dad had beat on him. No-one ever mentioned it, not even the teachers, even though when Dobson changed for PE he was the dirtiest boy alive, covered head to toe. Now his head was full of ghosts, though his father was buried beneath the bruises. Yet he could still hoist heaven with a smile, and that was the real reason Pruner was there.

And it was why he would stick it out to the end, even though he felt so awkward amid the pastel hues and the reek of Parma Violets that barely covered the miasma of pensioner gas. Across the aisle sat Joyce, and Pruner was glad for small mercies; he was out of reach of her wandering hands.

Society admires the stupid and labels them brave. Maybe he should've gone to see BullSkull with Drew after all; he had a feeling this was going to turn into a bloody cult rally. To his right Dobson began to shake like a palsied dog.

"You okay, Dobs?"

He muttered something that was drowned out in a burst of spontaneous applause; when Silver took the stage they would be resolutely sitting on their hands, disappointment on their faces, for no-one is more disappointed than those cheated of their health. Oh, and how he would laugh at the big phoney. It would start with a snort, sicken to a grin, then convulse into hysterics as Silver died up there on his big cold ass. His momentary doubt left him; he was looking forward to it again.

Another round of imbecilic clapping and Cunningham appeared, a beard of shadows flitting across his face.

"Good folk of Ellsford," boomed Samuel, flanked by posters for Mother and Toddler groups, cake sales and diabetes. "We are gathered here to ask God to touch us with His compassion. I am His conduit, His wand and His staff. Work through me this night, Lord, or call me home right now!"

The crowd applauded appreciatively as he revved up the Messiah dynamic. *He's strutting round up there like he's at an audition*, mused Pruner, *like they're casting Jesus.*

"Pray for me and I'll be cured!" shouted a woman at the front when the forest fire of clapping died down. There was a manic glee on Cunningham's face at the sound of her desperate voice. Pruner was sure that the only spirit Silver had direct access to was in a hip flask, and judging by the old biddies huddled together with their Rudolph noses and roadmap veins, he wasn't alone.

"It's a hands-on job but one I love," Samuel was saying, drawing a spattering of polite laughter for a line he probably used at every meeting.

Pruner scanned the herd of heavy coats around him, the nodding heads and the tea cosy hats, wondering which ones might have a bottle of gin tucked away between their bus pass and their stuttering hearts, which ones might be tempted to part with it for a few flattering words. Then he caught sight of the ones in the wheelchairs, the mangled ones with arthritic claws, silent hell in their rheumy eyes, windblown by the storm of passing years, and he felt a sudden rage at Cunningham for exploiting them with his promises of healing. There are some people only a razor can cure.

Not that Cunningham ever asked his flock for money or conned them out of their savings; no, Silver was too crazy for that—he actually *believed* he could help them. He was a vampire, feeding ravenously on their fading hopes, their wilting dignity. Like the God he claimed to speak for, he felt hard done by because no-one understood him.

"There is power in this room tonight. Can you feel the ever-loving power this very night?"

And the strange thing was Pruner could. The hackles had risen on the back of his neck, sweat beading his skin even though the chunky old radiators creaked and clunked with the cold. A collective moan ran through the hall and Dobson's was loudest of all. *Christ*, thought Pruner, *this is Jonestown for the blue rinse brigade.*

"Lord, I ask you! I demand you! Work through me this night! Here is Your flock, bleating at Your gate, but unless You give them signs and wonders they will never believe. Work through me now, show these sinners that disease is the Devil's lie, a manmade illusion they cling to. I summon an intervention here tonight, Lord!"

A truckle of pleas—pick me, pick me—begun to trundle around the hall. Cunningham was sweating now too, the streak above his temple now luminous, a crow wing that had brushed the hem of Jesus.

"Bring Molly Stone to me!"

There was a gasp, and even Pruner held his breath. Everyone knew Molly Stone.

She had taught Maths, and a vicious old bitch she was too. She had been crippled for as long as anyone could remember, had probably been born with wheels. They had called her Wooden Tit at school, and Dobson had taken one hell of a beating when she caught him in the Super Ser, acting her at the back of the class. Before the first blow of the skinny cane he managed to ask her if her maiden name was Davros. The memory made Pruner smile.

He was excited now, genuinely glad he had come.

This was no insomnia, no indigestion, no stress rash or vague complaint. Cunningham was going for it; there could be no turning back. Already the squeaking of unoiled wheels echoed off the floorboards and across the murmuring hall.

Molly Stone appeared more interested in timing spit bubbles on her chin than the faces gaping at her; only her hair, sitting upright on her shrunken head, seemed surprised. The wheelchair was attempting to eat her whole and, judging by the way she was slumped, had managed to digest most of her backbone already. She was drowning in the quicksand of her own flesh, clinging to a Thermos like it was a hoary old branch. She was a half-finished magic trick, a rolling advert for euthanasia. In her eyes nothing but confusion, a wonder that fate had dealt her such cards when she truly loved the Almighty.

"Me? You want me?"

She was barely audible over her grumbling wheels, her voice vinegar on paper cuts, her teeth blowing strange whistling chimes, the act of speaking grinding her brittle old jaws to powder, sending little puffs of dust from her bacon rind ears.

"Me?"

She sank further into the chair, deflating the closer she got to the stage. Pruner fought the urge to run to her and tear away her tartan blanket. In his mind he heard the sticky sound it would make as he peeled it off; there would be no legs under there, only a car battery and a set of crocodile clips attached to her saggy grey nipples, or maybe a dwarf with a starting handle.

"Me?" She shed a tear that cracked her dry skin.

People were jabbering, chanting words that jangled the insect brain, turning his skin to bubble wrap, as an old man pushed Molly further up the aisle, a wizened Sisyphus struggling with his burden. Cunningham made no attempt to help. He beamed down on them, a wild light in his eyes.

"Come to me, Molly. Let me take away your pain."

With the aid of a few more robust members of the audience, Molly was hoisted up onto the stage. Cunningham stood behind her, wheeling her around to face the assembled believers. It was quiet now, quiet enough to hear her breath scrape across the room.

"People of Ellsford!" bellowed Cunningham, "I know, though it hasn't been said to my face, I know that there has been much talk of me lately in this town. Spite and malice spat at my back, accusations of evil. Tell me, isn't that brush big enough to tar us all? Yes, I know, I have heard. God abhors black talk as much as he abhors the coward. I stand before you now, brazen with the power of the risen Christ because I fear no slander!"

Silence. Even the ragged gasp of Molly's breath had ceased.

"I do not hide my brother. Judah said, 'What will we gain if we kill our brother and cover up his blood?' I seek only to redress the balance, to atone for his perceived crimes, as God so wills it."

He laid his hands on Molly's head, her hair as hard and unyielding as a toffee apple. "I kiss the cross and pray," he said, almost to himself, "memorise and say every day." He glared up at the ceiling, holding his arms out to crucify his silhouette. "My brother was shadow but I am sun, and light destroys all darkness!"

Cunningham began to babble, a strange, nonsensical chatter, but to Pruner's chagrin no-one was laughing. Were they really buying this? Surely the old badger's spells would stutter in this clogged cauldron. He turned to Dobson to make some withering comment but found him uttering the same strange invocation word for word.

On stage, Cunningham clapped his hands together like thunder.

"Behold the touch of the Almighty!"

There was a scream, though Pruner couldn't tell from where; it was as if the very atmosphere had cracked and cried out. Molly was tottering up from her wheelchair with all the grace of a newborn foal.

"He is among you and you do not know him!"

In a vacuum of sound Molly stumbled to the front of the stage, each step stronger, more determined than the last. The crowd gaped, question marks like fish hooks in their mouths.

But it was her eyes that reeled in Pruner, her eyes were all wrong. The confusion there was gone, replaced by a terrible clarity. Her piercing blue eyes, obscene in an old woman, sparkled down on them all; Pruner could not bear to look into those seascape eyes.

He felt numb, unable to move, and for one horrible moment he was convinced that Silver had transferred Molly's paralysis unto him; cursed his unbelief, smote the unbeliever. His sphincter felt like a molten rivet.

The crash beside him broke his trance.

Dobson fell to the floor, arms and legs jerking frantically, a thin string of white gruel dangling from his mouth.

The people around him ignored him.

They were all standing now, concentrating solely on Molly as she walked serenely down the aisle; even those whose chairs were kicked and toppled barely gave Dobson more than a cursory glance before returning back to the approaching vision.

"Somebody help him!"

Pruner tried to put his weight on his friend, to still him by force, but Dobson flung him off with one vicious jolt.

"Somebody fucking help him!"

Dobson went limp, his fingers drumming, clawing at the floor, his face suddenly calm. Pruner looked up to see Cunningham above them, a vast shadow that stole the light from his eyes.

"'And a great crowd of people followed him because they saw the miraculous signs he had performed on the sick,' John six two."

From somewhere in the pressing crowd, Molly started laughing.

Chapter 5

They can probably see me from the moon, she thought, as she hurried through the snow in her shiny red coat. The man in the moon had his cold eye on her alright; he was put there for chopping sticks on a Sunday, that's what granddad used to say. She missed granddad so much, the way he used to take off his spectacles to thread a needle always tickled her; furnace burn he would explain, from stoking the ships, though dad said he had never been on so much as a canoe.

She missed the way he called her Princess.

Now everyone called her mousy Nadine. Even dad called her Squeak, though he did so with a twinkle in his eye. She had no interest in music or boys (kiss a boy and a germ might run up your leg!) like all the other girls in school. The time between classes was interminable, the corridors stretching out like wormholes between dimensions. Why was she seen as an outcast just because she wanted to learn?

Thank Christ for the Christmas holidays, she thought, then blushed at her blasphemy; doubly sinful in a Reverend's daughter.

That was another stick to beat her with, but she was proud to be her father's child, proud of his convictions, his faith. Without faith there would be no miracles, and you only had to listen to what everyone was saying about Mrs. Stone to know that miracles were real and God was among them.

Daddy said it was a trick of some kind, that Mr. Cunningham was a charlatan, but that was because he was old school; he didn't realise

38

that God needed to adapt to fit into the modern world. Dad was fond of saying He moved in mysterious ways, and didn't that explain why He would cure old Molly Turnip Toes whilst He let young girls be murdered? *Oh that's a sin Nadine Craig*, she chastised herself, *you're sinning your soul, my girl.*

They would laugh at her no matter who her parents were, laugh because she didn't have a boyfriend, or her navel pierced, or a tattoo above her butt, or some other trivial thing.

They thought these fads made them rebels, *that* was the truly laughable thing because *everyone* had them done. She was the *real* rebel, the one who dared to be different, to stand out from the herd.

Not like Adele Roberts, who often pretended she didn't know where Nadine lived; it was indicative of her vanity that the only estate in Ellsford she claimed to be aware of was Adele Heights. Little immature kids, that's all they were, spoilt little brats. Not like her. Only the other day she had heard Mrs. Turk remark to her dad, "Your daughter is older than you are."

She smiled, wiping the snow from her glasses with the damp finger of her glove.

Two weeks off.

Two weeks to be herself, two weeks to breathe, free from petty criticism. It was Christmas Eve, her favourite night of the year. "Only one more sleep til Santa," she said with a giggle. I bet Adele and the others think I still believe in Santa, even though I'm nearly fifteen. *Who cares*, she thought; she wouldn't let them ruin this most special of nights.

Christmas Eve was Games Night, just her and mum and dad and the traditional Craig family tournament—a round of Ludo, a round of Ker-Plunk, a round of Buckaroo—that went on and on until the Christmas Champion was declared. She had won the last two years on the trot. The crystal jelly bowl that dad bestowed upon the winner took pride of place on her bookshelf, right beside the weird shaped bottle she had found in the park when she was little and kept because she was convinced it was worth a fortune.

She laughed as she hurried through the snow, remembering the last time dad had won, hoisting the bowl high above his head, referring to her and mum as his loyal subjects right through to the New Year.

All the games were *ancient*, salvaged from the attic, not a plug nor a console between them. How all her classmates would sneer if they knew—no X-box or PSP or internet. They would label her a freak, as if she had a monopoly on that; she smiled at the unintended pun. It was a day for smiling.

She had never had any real toys for her parents thought them frivolous. When she was younger she had spent so much time visiting with her mum, especially the Bradfield house. She had been so small then, and the house had seemed to grow around her and it was bursting with toys, but because they weren't hers she found it impossible to play with them. They could never *feel* like hers. She could never take them home and tell them how much she loved them, give them their secret names, allot their roles in the never-ending, always expanding epics she was constantly creating.

She imagined that one day she would have toys of her very own, but she never did. She would outgrow their need before they would be condoned.

Ah Nadine, don't you wish you'd stayed a child and kept the ghosts of those little summer friends with you forever?

She still had Harry though, the one concession, the mouldy old Polar Bear that mum had bought her (because she had been a wee winter baby), and whom she had named after granddad and loved beyond reason. Harry wasn't stuffed with rags or wool but secrets and dreams, for she whispered them to him every night. Her wonderful pink bed that looked like a great big sweet, so cosy and warm, was his haven. She would say her prayers then climb in beside him, making sure her hands did not stray to that awful place between her legs that seemed to grow itchier every year, and then she would talk to her beloved bear.

Poor old thing was as yellow as auntie Joan's fingers (forty a day she smoked, no matter how many times dad warned her) and mum was forever telling her to throw him out. *As if.* She would take him to the grave.

The thought made her stop.

She thought of Carrie Anne, the strange young man vomiting over her. Carrie Anne so cold in her coffin, so lonely in her grave. Maybe that was karma.

Nadine!

She reached the church and opened the gate.

In a way this was her favourite part, walking home with dad, anticipating all the fun that lay ahead. Better even than Christmas dinner, though maybe not dessert—rhubarb crumble; rhubarb—nature's dynamite! Or the tiny biscuits mum would be baking even now, little animal shaped cookies. All the animals you could not, or would not, eat; crocodiles and frogs, giraffes and monkeys, all covered in chocolate with a jammy little heart. Dragons too, for even mythical beasts could slide down a young girl's throat.

And there would be sweets too, a special treat only slightly ruined by the fact that dad always paired them up after he emptied them out—two Milky Ways, two Snickers, two Bountys; a part of her hated him for this, it took all the mystery out of things.

She felt the staggered crunch of snow beneath her feet as she made her way through the tilting headstones. She wasn't scared of graveyards, not one bit; she had grown up around them after all, played in them her whole life. Daddy called them marble orchards. She scorned the soppy girls who would wet themselves if they were here, yet tonight she felt a chill that had nothing to do with the weather.

A scream made her jump, her heart settling slowly as she realised it was only the banshee wail of fornicating cats. Evil little heathens. *Nadine*, she chided herself, *you truly are the yellowest cornflake!*

Her feet echoed on the cleared path and the world sounded hollow, her breath streaming out before her in great horsey gusts. A sliver of moon hung in the sky sharp as a blade, and the air tasted almost too fresh to breathe.

She halted before a thick bank of gnarled trees, now just a hole in the gloom. The crows lived here, squawking their dire warnings all the live long day, driving dad to distraction. He said at least there would be no hoof marks in Heaven, for he couldn't abide animals and believed they were soulless. She would bite her lip when he ranted; this was her secret doubt, one only Harry knew.

She blushed, thinking of all the times she had walked with him here, her stream of nonsensical questions that must have drove him crazy. Did daddy think kids were soulless too?

"What would crow taste like, daddy?"

"I don't know, dear."

"Would they taste like blackcurrant?"

"Well, I doubt that. I think they would taste burnt, least they would if your mother cooked them." A wink. "I think they'd be greasy, don't you?"

"I think they'd taste sweet, because of all the apples I leave out for them."

"Well, I tell you what, why don't we have a crow supper tonight and find out for ourselves."

And they had, or at least they had eaten chicken and pretended it was crow. That was a metaphor for faith. Now looking at the trees she wondered what lurked in their depths. Perhaps a giant web spanned their black trunks, a horse caught in it, its blood all drained out and—

She was being watched.

Her stomach turned to curds and whey. Her red coat began to glow. Suddenly she felt way too visible amidst the white. A twig snapped somewhere to her right, somewhere over by the graves.

"You're a little loud for stalking!"

She hoped she sounded braver than she felt. She scanned the plots for any sign of movement but her glasses were all fogged up. She knew sometimes couples came here to *do it*. She had heard dad telling mum (though he'd go through her for a shortcut if he knew she'd been listening), and once she had found a condom draped over a grave, its nebulous head filled with goo. How could people be so low, so pathetic, as to sin against the dead? And as for sex, she didn't understand *that* at all, give her a good singsong or a good book any day of the—

Another snapping behind her.

Louder. Closer.

Just the wind baring its teeth she told herself, but she ran all the same toward the dark shadow of the church, its spire puncturing the moon.

No such things as ghosts, Nadine, except the Holy Ghost of course. The dear departed don't come back, they don't miss us at all. Death is a one-way street, no turning back. Ghosts are just the screech of brakes, the honking of horns, distant traffic on a busier road, don't tell dad that, he'll just say—

She heard a clomping noise behind her, then the world kaleido-scoped away from her and she fell headlong into a dream.

She came to amid the headstones, the sharp light of a torch playing over her face. She tried to move but she was bound tightly, her thrusting causing the marble chips beneath her to grind loudly in the damp silence. Her head throbbed malevolently. A shadow moved behind the light and she made butter in her bowels.

"Please don't hurt me," she squeaked; oh yes, *now* she was a mouse,

42

a tiny little mouse under the paw of a tiger cat.

"Hey there, Little Red Riding Hood, do you know me? Do you know who I am? The wolf is scared of me, and Granny had better watch out."

"I want to go home, please let me—"

A hand shot out from behind the light, striking hard enough to rattle her teeth, the explosive flash of its connection blinding her.

"I only crossed your path by accident, little girl, you should be grateful. Now, once more, do you know who I am?"

She shook her head, snot and tears mixing with the blood rolling down her lips. He had broken her glasses. She was lost, no breadcrumbs, no way home.

"I am a monster, and I cannot be trusted."

He's going to rape me, she thought, *he's going to tear off all my clothes and*—

There was a click as the shadow fumbled with some machine.

"You can make your noises now, I'm ready."

Her mind fled her. She was at home, one round away from claiming the bowl once more. She saw a Cluedo envelope and a card that said Nadine Craig, another that said Graveyard, one more saying— what? She could not make it out. She began to pray.

"Enough. Save your voice, little girl. God's good, but Satan's quicker."

She heard a guttural laugh. Something glinted above her and she realised what the third card had read.

"Hatchet," she whispered, and before she could scream it fell, and then all the games were over.

Chapter 6

Christmas day.

Turkey, warm beer, unwanted jumpers and flatulent uncles.

Malcolm's mother gave him a coat which his other coats jealously rejected. He knew that when he opened his wardrobe on Boxing Day they would all be wrapped around the interloper, creasing and choking it. He would have to hide it under his bed or its plaintive cries would keep him awake.

His father gave him a lecture and a bottle of something he didn't know whether to drink or rub on.

Over dinner he aged a year with every brussel sprout, with every jaded cliché his family trotted out. By the time he lumbered from the kitchen to the living room, his insides bloated bicycle tubes, he had outlived most of the biblical patriarchs. Pruner had his own flat; surely it was time now for him to fly the nest and escape this random collection of idiots that posed as his family. Malcolm sat a lifetime away, watching them from the window seat, feeling like an actor, feeling the camera zoom in, feeling alone in extreme close up.

His aunts yammered tirelessly, straining their plum lips. His Uncle Tommy scribbling furiously on a pad, the power of speech having left him years ago; Malcolm's mother crumpling the notes up after a cursory glance, the power of handwriting having left him after two bottles of table red.

Malcolm hated them.

Hated their tweed breath, the leather patches on their brains, the pointless conversations, saying the same things over and over as if repetition could somehow make them relevant, hated the very blood that clogged their veins, hated their 'And let me tell you another thing, my boy,' hated their endless reminiscing.

"I have no concept of what size that actually is. I can't picture it," Uncle John was saying, apropos of what, Malcolm had no idea. Uncle John always looked on the verge of anaesthesia, the pockets of his trousers hanging out so that he resembled a panting dog from the waist down.

His father feigned sleep, John's creepy twins bouncing on his lap in a manner that would make a social worker blush.

"Look at them, they love it, that's who Christmas is for. It's not the same anymore, not like when we were kids, eh, Tom?" sighed John, as Tommy scribbled another note, his pencil blunter than his senses. "An apple, an orange, and then off to church. It's all about money nowadays."

"You're not joking there, Johnny," piped in his mother. Johnny? She was never usually so informal; were they having an affair? Could crumbly old John possibly squeeze any more festive pleasure into his life twixt citrus and clergy? Any free time he had would surely be better spent at an ear barber.

Malcolm smiled to himself. The thought of his mother cheating on his dad was just too ridiculous. No, Sheila was incapable of such a thing. Besides, dad would kill them both.

Malcolm yawned. He wasn't tired; it was just a habit. Tommy carried on writing away, his polished brogues fast disappearing under a mound of paper, aunt Emily smiling at him the way you would smile at an imbecilic child. Uncle Eric had joined Malcolm's dad in a pseudo Neverland as the twins turned their attention to his bony milk crate of a lap.

Eric was the only one of the clan he had any time for; his father's brother in name only. On the fireplace was a photo of Eric standing by some ruins, Cyprus or Greece or somewhere, and Eric was laughing, irreverent as always, his moustache like a Rorschach inkblot beneath his nose. *If Eric had been at the crucifixion he would've pissed himself*, thought Malcolm, *he'll be laughing at the gates of Hell.*

The rest of them were a humourless embarrassment. John had nipped into the kitchen to fart, unaware he had returned bringing the host of the undead with him. His aunts were burping like a swamp of frogs.

"Anyone have any New Year revolutions?" asked his mother in her cuckoo clock voice; no-one could accuse her of not knowing how to keep a party swinging. Malcolm bit his tongue, longing to correct her, to yell "Re*so*lution!" but he knew his dad would slap him down if he dared.

She could pronounce the names of tablets—huge, unwieldy word snakes that could break your teeth with one swish of their Latinate tails—but words like "menthol" or "detective" were apparently beyond her.

Uncle John cleared his throat in preparation for some long-winded speech, but Malcolm's dad beat him to it with a sheepish, "Not to make any resolutions."

Nice one, Cyril Weir! Do you have an agent? Even the twins laughed, a bloated duet that proved they hadn't an ounce of wit between them.

"Isn't that right, Malcolm?" Aunt Bet was talking to him, her needle voice jabbing at his ear.

"I don't know, Bet. Maybe if I'd been listening I might have agreed with you, but as it is I'll have to remain neutral."

His dad shot him the rooster look.

"I was telling you about my side," twittered his aunt. "I've awful shooting pains all along it. Cheese would do that, wouldn't it? I was telling Sheila the cheese would do that." His relatives invariably viewed him as a locum as he had a Biology GCSE. "Thing is, the pain never sits, it's always changing sides."

"That'll be your apostate gland, Auntie Bet."

Bet puffed out her spindly chest as if a medal were forthcoming. "I'll have to go and see that Silver Cunningham. He's a friend of mine you know. Maybe he'll do something for me; those doctors don't have a clue. You'd be dead before they give a damn."

"That's so true," said Uncle John. "Many's an undertaker's spade has covered up their mistakes."

"I saw Mrs. Stone up town the other day," said Sheila, her eyes flicking up to the ceiling to seek verification from on high, her hand clutched to her heart to contain her disbelief; this was performed routinely for miracles and mundanity alike. "Walking she was! Large as life and *walking*! That Mr. Cunningham must be touched by angels, it's a gift from—"

"Ah, catch yourselves on! It's a trick is all it is." Malcolm couldn't listen to this nonsense again, even Pruner was at it. They stared at him, waiting for him to elaborate. It was so quiet he could hear the fizzle and fart of woodchips in the charnel tube of tobacco between his fingers.

"What? Molly will probably be dead by New Year and you'll find out there was nothing wrong with her legs in the first place. He's slipped her a mickey or something."

His father opened one eye. A dragon. There were things that Cyril Weir did not like, things that *just weren't funny*. Death and blasphemy were high on that list, as was doubting the wisdom of your elders. Malcolm went upstairs before he was forced to go through that list once more.

He hurried up to his room, stopping outside the nursery to listen to the cries that seeped under its door. Santa's early little present was obviously upset. He hesitated before entering, his damp palm slipping on the handle.

The baby lay in apparent agony; pink and sticky, a half-chewed sweet in a shit-stained nappy. The baby monitor had been switched off.

"Is oo hungwy?" asked Malcolm, his baby talk shaming the infant into silence. "Is the ickle man hungwy wungy?"

The child was evil. It had been here before, this was merely its latest guise. It watched Malcolm with old, knowing eyes. "Is oo gonna fuck up or does oo wanna smacky wacky?" A river of snot and tears in answer. The baby's skin raw and new, the mother's price tag still attached, stained grey where the tears festered.

Graham. Little Graham Weir. Wee Gramgrams. A gift to his mum, and at her time of life too, a trick that even Silver couldn't pull off. He was crying because he wanted to be fed. Malcolm would feed him alright, feed him his fist, bury it in the tiny fudge gums, then etch his name with a dirty fingernail in that putty soft skull. Hug him, squeeze him, kiss him better, his very own little brother, inheritor of bad breath and worse luck.

He was a hideous little thing though, but then all babies were. There were so many ugly words connected to the birth process—cervix, placenta, child support—it was only fitting that the end result should be so vile.

He pinched the baby as hard as he could, sending it into paroxysms of wet screams. He closed the door behind him, leaving the cries to fumble blindly downstairs in search of their maternal slave.

He lay on his unmade bed and lit a cigarette he didn't want, pondered having a wank then decided against it. He could think of nothing more depressing than masturbating on Christmas Day. He felt his rage start to flare.

Closing his eyes he fell into an uneasy slumber, floating on the surface for a time before giving up and drowning. When he awoke shadows had spilled into the room, squatting in the corners, watching him intently. Over the canned hilarity of the television downstairs he heard a heavy knock on the front door.

Dobson.

He hadn't seen him since the night of Silver's shindig. Pruner told him that Dobson had taken some kind of fit. He was going to have to do something about Heather, his Siamese disaster. Perhaps he would make a New Year's resolution after all; New Year, new start.

He pulled on his new sweater, (replete with the pattern of a digital Christmas tree, courtesy of his senile Aunt Gloria who could not attend Sheila's soiree due to the fact she was lying in a care home marinating in her own urine) feeling the static prickle his ears.

He didn't bother with the landing light even though the stairway was gloomy. Dobson's face would illuminate the entire street anyway, especially if Joyce had bought him something halfway decent this year.

He opened the front door, letting in an icy blast that momentarily stole his breath. A girl stood on the other side wearing the cold like a winding sheet, her eyes enormous behind her glasses, a crumpled polar bear clutched tightly against her bright red coat. A bundle of ethics draped in sensible clothes.

Malcolm braced himself, preparing the line he always used on such occasions, "No thanks, I'm a Satanist," as he waited for her to produce a copy of The Watchtower or some such rubbish. *Is there anyone left to save?* he wondered. Surely there were only Japanese schoolgirls and the unemployed left to judge, and he didn't fancy their chances. Jehovah's Witnesses were the worst; witnesses of an evil God, hiding behind watchtowers when they should be using them as vantage points.

"I didn't think your lot believed in Christmas."

She grinned. Maybe she was a Mormon, though she lacked the fascistic dress code and Beach Boy smile.

"Yes?" he snapped.

She carried on grinning. She looked vaguely familiar, but he couldn't place her. Not surprising really; she was a bit of a dog. Why should he waste his time filing away images of all the mingers he ran into. She looked a bit retarded too, her face a blank canvas waiting for a personality to be drawn there.

"Look, I'm not interested okay? I believe in the Prince of Darkness—"

"Don't be silly, Malcolm," said the girl, "you've never believed in anything. But we're going to change all of that."

"How the fuck do you know my name?"

"Dark clouds told me, black clouds of billowing sin."

The snow was falling again in thick jaundiced clumps that began to erase the street, but the girl was dry, the snow passing her by as if she were encased in a glass dome.

"Listen, you freaky little bitch, if you don't—"

Malcolm's voice caught, slid back down his throat, as she let out a brain-blistering shriek. Her head caved in by some unseen force, shards of her skull spraying over Malcolm, over the door, tinkling on the brass knocker in the sudden silence, little shavings of bone showering into his eyes as he watched the stain of blood spread blackly over the ruin of her head. Snow was landing on her now, her wound soaking it up, turning it into a scarlet Slush Puppie, her brain a pulsing grey.

Malcolm could only stammer, waiting for something to throw his mind a rubber ring.

"Remember what you did," said the girl, her teeth broken, her mouth torn. "All of you."

Then she was gone, the snow where she had stood only a moment before pure and unbroken, free of blood. Malcolm emptied his guts into the street, steam rising from the bile like a camp fire. The chatter behind him grew louder as the living room door opened and closed, then the shadow of his father fell across him, chilling him, putting out the flames.

"What the hell are you playing at? Can you not hold your liquor yet! What's wrong with the toilet you've to puke in the street like a fucking tramp. Get in quick before the bloody neighbours see you."

Malcolm felt the neck of his sweater tear as he was hauled back into the broody darkness of the hall, his dad shaking him as he flicked on the light. "What have you done to your face boy?"

Malcolm saw no concern, only disgust in his father's eyes. He put a hand to his cheek and took it away to find it covered in blood.

The door banged violently again.

"Don't open it, dad!"

Too late. Snow ushered Bob Turk into the hall. Old Moonface Turk squeezing sideways past Cyril who frowned, checking his visitor's shoes for vomit.

"Sorry to bother you, Cyril, it being Christmas, but the Reverend's daughter is missing. Hasn't been seen since last night. They found her coat over by the Bradfield girl's grave, and what with what's been going on lately … You know the Craig girl, hardly the type to go on the lash and run off. We're getting a few people together to go looking for her. We could use your help, big man. You had your tea yet?"

"I have, and a good walk will help it down." This was Cyril's comfort zone, the civic leader, the moral heartbeat of a tight-knit community. *It's why I hate him,* realised Malcolm, *because I'll never be him.*

"I'll meet you by the church, Bob, we'll fan out from there. Give me twenty minutes or so to round up a bit of a posse." Cyril smiled, indicating the living room with a curt nod. This was the best present he could have wished for.

Malcolm could see him formulating stratagems, already breaking the bad news to Elsa Craig, her broken daughter limp in his manly arms. Turk, the dutiful corporal, echoed his solemn nod and stepped back out into the evening's cold maw.

"Get your coat, boy," said Cyril. "And for fucksake smarten yourself up a bit."

Cyril was already in the living room marshalling the troops before he could reply. Malcolm heard his aunts tutting and sighing over the "poor wee lassie," already anticipating a month of gossip.

His father herded his uncles out on a wave of *you be carefuls* and *watch yourselves,* as if they were heading into a war zone and not Ellsford's grey, abandoned streets.

"Hurry, boy, the hare's running."

"I'm not going," said Malcolm quietly.

"What did you say!" Cyril's voice rattled the portrait of Churchill on the wall.

"I'll only get in the way. Too many cooks and all that."

"There's a wee girl out there, you waste of skin."

"I'm not well. I think I saw ..." He turned away from his father's contempt.

"Keep dodging me, boy. I'm nowhere but right behind you."

The door slammed and they were gone, the echoes of their leaving still humming on the painted wood. Malcolm climbed the stairs slowly, listening intently to the soothing voice that was worming its way into his brain, a voice he had only heard before in dreams of the sewers.

Chapter 7

Christmas morning, and Jason Turk wandered the streets alone.

It was too cold for the other kids to be out. They would all be nice and snug indoors playing with their presents. He burned with the injustice of it all. It was Sunday, so dad wouldn't let him have his presents until Boxing Day, like he was some big Christian or something; big hypocrite more like, for when Jason had left the house he had been sitting with a bottle of whiskey and mum hadn't even put the sprouts on yet.

All morning he had pleaded and bargained for just five minutes with his toys, but dad had told him quietly, "Shut your trap or I'll knock your head off." That's what he always said, *I'll knock your head off.* He would as well.

So Jason had taken the dog out, wandering the empty streets, the wind mocking him as the Dalmatian yapped and crapped with surprising frequency in the most awkward and public of places; he was a dad now, too, and like all dads, he was full of shit.

Aimless steps took him past the women's refuge, and he smiled as he recalled how he and Tony Webb had rang them up and ordered battered wives and chips. His smile soon died though when he realised that was where his mum might end up if he told his secret. His secret weighed so heavy sometimes he thought it would cripple him, but he must never tell.

Think of something else.

Think of the presents that would still be fresh tomorrow morning, think of the bliss of ripping off all that wrapping paper! Dad didn't believe in bliss, the hateful old Scrooge.

Passing rows of silent houses he imagined all the families inside, proper families with no secrets, where kids were working up an appetite by making lazy movies with their new action figures, or averting the apocalypse on their X-box.

But Sunday was Sunday, Christmas or not, and because it was Sunday his father had stuck his finger up Jason's ass. *You have to be clean, son, I have to check.*

Santa came calling early. As Jason listened to the heavy footfalls on the stairs, his stomach plunged down a manhole. His little brother sleeping sound, or at least pretending to, his snoring a little *too* loud.

Not that that would help. Dad liked you wide awake to receive your gifts.

Was it worth a remote control car or a new football kit, or whatever else his mum had bought him in the long gone sun of August?

Bite your lip. Bear it.

And if it turned out to be some awful jumper or outdated game, well too bad, he would never tell. Dad would kill him. Kill mum. Kill them all.

Of this he was certain. It was in his dad's eyes, in the way he made them say "please" before and "thank you" after, in the way he'd once made them beg. It always started with the finger. He could black out everything else save the finger; rigid and hurtful and accusing.

Once he had thought of telling Aunt Lydia, convinced that she of all people would know what to do, but then he had caught Aunt Lydia with her head buried in dad's lap, eating at him like a pig in a trough, and his secrets had doubled. Lydia could not be trusted. Lydia probably *liked* the finger.

What did dad need her for anyway, when he had him and Jake?

Maybe he would tell. They could all die for all he cared. He felt a sudden urge to kick the dog as it snuffled through the frozen remains of a Chinese takeaway. Samson had gotten his present this morning; a big chewy pigskin bone by the fire, and he was promised a leg of turkey.

Dad always got a leg too, and unless they had started breeding turkeys differently that meant none for him. He would be stuck with horrible old dry white meat and it would be the worst Christmas ever.

He felt the tears come but he fought them back. If dad knew he had been crying he'd be done for. "You have to be brave, son," he would say as he crept into their room. "And clean too. I have to check".

He circled the grey streets for hours until he found himself at the back of Ellsford primary school. He climbed through a hole in the hedge, intent on letting Samson run amok on the playing fields. Sitting down by the goalposts, he hoped the dog still had enough left in his bowels to give Poker Hanlon, the bald caretaker, a dinger of a headache come the new term.

He hated this place, so why come here?

It seemed as if he were determined to make this day thoroughly miserable. On his first day here his mum had walked him across this very field, and he had gripped her hand *so* tightly, as all the other kids (he had never seen so many!) scuttled by, laughing, bumping him in their eagerness.

"He's very nervous," mum explained to the stern woman who came out to meet them, as he sought invisibility in the folds of her skirt.

"Don't worry," said the stern woman attempting a smile. Her name was Mrs. Duggan, and he would never see her attempt one again. "He'll be just fine, won't you, Jason dear?"

His mother put his hand in the teacher's and kissed him on the forehead. "You have to be brave, son." *Brave and clean.* Then Mrs. Duggan led him through the heavy doors and he jumped when they snapped closed; later that week they would snap the end off a girl's fingers and be replaced by glass ones.

They had bitten off Mrs. Duggan's approximation of a smile as well. As soon as they banged closed she leant over him, too close, her breath reeking of Juicy Fruit. "What's wrong? Have you wet your pants? We don't tolerate dirty little boys here."

The tears came now and he didn't try to stop them. They blurred his vision, the Dalmatian becoming nothing more than a blur of black dots, a swarm of flies against the snow.

Everyone lied to him, and here was the birthplace of all those lies.

He *was* a dirty boy. His nose was running and he rubbed the snot all over his sleeve with a vicious glee. Maybe he *would* wet himself just for the hell of it; it would warm him up if nothing else.

Someone had built a snowman over by the fir trees that lined the far side of the football pitch. Jason frowned. He had passed this way yesterday, and it hadn't been there, he was sure of it. Perhaps some of the big kids had built it last night. The snowman wore a grimace instead of a smile—the same his dad habitually wore—and as the snot hardened on his glistening lip a thought crystallized in his mind.

He scanned the darkening school grounds, making sure he was alone. Not even a crow tore the blank page of sky. He grinned, running full pelt toward the snowman, a wicked laugh spewing from his throat.

"I'm gonna knock *your* fucking head off!"

He launched himself at it, burying his fist into its face, letting out a yelp of pain as he connected with something unexpectedly hard.

There was something underneath. He brushed away the snow. A girl, encased like a nut in a shell, her face grey and blue, her eyes open and full of ice. Her lip was curled, and Jason knew that, if he dared, if he reached out and touched that lip it would snap off with a crunch.

Her mouth was full of broken teeth. He had little crescent moons of blood riding along his knuckles where he had punched her. He screamed until it hurt, but the nearby houses had their backs to him and no-one answered his calls.

He backed away, tripping over himself, scrambling to get up, making frantic snow angels in his efforts to right himself, his screams spent, only little moans escaping him now, little fragile notes of despair that cracked and shattered in the brittle air.

He could not take his eyes off the dead girl.

She was dead, *really* dead, not dead like in the movies dead, or trying to scare your brother by holding your breath dead, but really, awfully, reach out and drag you down to Hell with her dead.

Samson came bounding over, his tail wagging excitedly at his master's discovery, planting his paws on the snowman's chest, sniffing, chewing on the frozen meat, a large red lump falling from his messy jaws, the crack of tooth on bone like gunshots in the empty playground.

He found his legs and ran, ran from the dead girl and the skeletal trees that tried to grab him. In his terror he could hear her heavy corpse footfalls pursuing him relentlessly, could hear the snap of her remaining teeth, feel her chill breath on his neck; running so hard his side was pierced with daggers.

He fell by the hole in the hedge, scrambled onto his back to face the nightmare but there was no-one there. The snap of teeth had been nothing more than the bounce of the buckle on his hood. Samson licked his face, filling his nose with the stench of cold dead meat.

He gagged, glad now that he had missed his dinner. He pushed the dog away and clambered back out onto the street, running again, speeding round the corner onto Hollywell road and into a crowd of people.

"Whoa there! Steady on, lad!"

It was Mr. Weir. He was safe now; Mr. Weir would know what to do. He chanced a glance over his shoulder. There was no sign of the girl.

"She … She … She only has half a head. I knocked her teeth out but it was an accident, swear to God, I didn't …"

He saw his dad pushing up front, a stick in his hand, a stick he knew well, a stick for dirty boys that dad called *The Settler*. He felt content now. This was a fear he could handle, a fear he understood.

His last thought as he felt himself slide away was that maybe now he would be allowed to open his presents.

Chapter 8

Malcolm closed his eyes, feeling the water slip over him like an army of marching ants, then slide down over his back with a soft caress, tracing intricate ticklish patterns over his skin.

Indoor rain, washing away the sludge of thought.

If only it were possible to open a flap in your skull and wash away your thoughts completely, the whole grimy past that clung stubbornly in the creases of the brain. The scrubbing brush tore at his skin; reborn pink and sweet and insubstantial.

He held onto the shower door as if he might follow the water down the drain. Twenty-two years old and already over the hill and far away, galloping from admiration. There were no niche websites for this body.

A whisper in his ear.

Someone saying his name.

He shivered though the shower grew hotter, his skin now lobstered red. Unseen hands slid under his arms, circling his nipples. He felt a teasing bite on his shoulder, then the hands moved down to his groin. He closed his eyes, groaning, as they slithered over his shaft, so hard now it hurt. He bit down on his lip as something enclosed him, a water-tight shield that made him explode.

Jesus Johnson!

He turned the water off, panting furiously, semen dangling from the hair on his legs. Christ, that had felt so real. Had Uncle Eric spiked his drink? Either that or he was developing schizophrenia. They said that ran in families, and his were an entire fucking relay team. They would stick him on tablets and he would end up like Sandy Newell; big as a house, standing in the middle of the road haranguing the clouds.

Most likely he was just tired, and what with all the booze he had been downing lately he'd got the horrors or something. The soothing voice returned, running calm fingers over the jangling creases of his brain, and told him it would all be okay.

He stepped out into the cold of the bathroom feeling that something essential had deserted him, evaporated in the cooling mist. He felt dirtier than he did before he showered.

He heard the front door slam and the excited chatter of his parents. Stepping onto a sodden towel, he tried to make out their conversation but his ears were clogged with steam.

He was about to cover himself when the bathroom door swung open; old Ma Weir was quicker than she looked. She stared at his xylophone ribs, beads of sweat trapped between them like musical notes, at his wrinkled member curled up like an evicted snail, and felt a momentous instance of shame for the thing she had raised.

She turned away quickly in case he saw it in her eyes.

"Sorry," she said, embarrassed even though she had seen his pizzle countless times. Once, when he was only a nipper, she had been drying him, and he had taken an erection, all the age of him too.

"Did you find her?" asked Malcolm, having no real interest; it was intended to fill the awkward silence.

"Yes, son, that's what I came up to tell you. Poor wee thing's dead. Murdered. God help her poor family. World's gone mad, son. God help us all." Then she was gone, descending the stairs, treading the day's forgotten laughter into the carpet.

Later, when she was sure he had vacated the bathroom, Sheila returned. Tutting at the mess he had left, scooping up towels (how could one person use so many towels?), she found herself grateful for something to take her mind off the horror of the evening.

She could not remember a worse Christmas, not since—

No matter, the day had been totally ruined for her. How could Ellsford harbour a monster in its midst? The idea was nonsensical.

Yet Cyril said the wee girl had been nailed up on a pole like a scarecrow, like the blessed Lord, and covered up with snow. It didn't bear thinking of. To leave her like that for people to find (that poor Jason Turk, scarred for life), a sick joke, it was the end of days, it really—

There was something lying by the shower drain.

Sheila stooped, tutting once more. A pair of pants; lazy hallion never would pick up after himself. She reached down and wrung them out over the drain, frowning as she unfolded them.

A pair of cotton panties.

Girl's cotton panties.

On the label, in felt tip now blurred and smudged, a name still legible.

Nadine Craig.

Sheila felt her breath escape her in a single sharp blast: *My son,* she thought, *oh please God, not my son!*

But he's not your son, is he? This thought came so clearly it was almost as if it had been planted in her ear and set burrowing calmly into her mind: *You raised him as your own but he was never really yours now, was he?* Sheila listened to all the voice had to say as she carried on cleaning, her fear curdling to anger. Anger was good, according to the voice.

Chapter 9

It was colder in here than it was outside, thought Samuel.

It was too bright, lit like a morgue, which in a way it was. He surveyed the tins of ravioli and sweet corn on the shelves, the birds hanging upside down and naked in the window, their skin still puckered where the feathers had been ripped out, their dead eyes curiously accepting of their fate.

Butcher's shops always gave him the shuddering creeps.

Cully, the family butcher.

Samuel smiled as an image of a long flat knife hacking through some anonymous wife and kids sprung to mind; you just couldn't trust a man whose profession was slaughter.

Not all here were shopping for the last supper though; a rose had bloomed amid the craggy thorns. She was by the counter gazing at the pies, a lump of meat herself, the tastiest on display. A decrepit old man was staring at her tight powder blue denim buttocks and licking his lips; he kept winking at Cully, who thought this genuinely hilarious.

She was pretty, even with her wicked curves, but not in a showy way, not like most of the other sluts. Samuel had seen her before. She worked in the library.

Her dark hair was shoulder length, neat and clean and tidy. She had no visible tattoos or piercing, although her shirt was emblazoned with the logo of some satanic rock band. It was a pity about the jeans. A woman shouldn't dress like a man, or vice versa, *for all that do so are an abomination unto the Lord.*

"Deuteronomy, twenty-two, five," he muttered to himself.

Still, Samuel liked her, a helpful girl when he ordered religious tomes, and not flashy at all. She didn't have to try too hard to affect the air of one who didn't care. She was probably a hellcat in bed.

Samuel caught the thought and strangled it quickly.

The thought of her naked body was appealing so long as she remained upright. The very thought of her bent over, splayed for easy access, appalled him. Female genitalia were so ugly, so *violent*. God had forgone a lot of his usual aesthetic impulse when He had sculpted the rib.

He watched her pay, watched her small clean hands. Better. She left with a wiggle, the old man still ogling her. She walked so straight and upright. Better still. If she remained upright, hiding her hairy sin, he could take her from behind—

Cully was talking, cutting into his reverie. He sighed, turning back to the counter. It might be weeks before he could conjure up such images again.

"We'll be doing well if we get to his age and we're still thinking about women," Cully was saying, indicating the dirty old lech. "Did you see his face? Happy as a goat a hanging."

Samuel smiled, said nothing. *If I were to live that long*, he thought, *I would be stooped and glassy eyed from the accumulation of sorrows, the unbearable weight of sin upon my shoulders, not revelling in carnality.*

Perhaps the old man's soul was clean, that would explain his vigour, or perhaps he was just an empty husk devoid of conscience. Maybe he was full of vinegar. His mind certainly was active, if it was *his* mind; perhaps there was a new tenant in that old house.

If I were to lay a cross on that scalloped forehead, would those lively eyes roll back as it seared the wrinkled flesh? Would a torrent of voices spew forth in a cascade of obscenity?

He watched the old man hobbling past the window, putting his stewing steak in his pocket, wondering if he had discovered yet another agent of the Devil.

"We'll be doing well if we get to his age at all," said Samuel.

"Still, it would be nice to go out with a hard on, eh?" Cully grinned.

Death. Death and sex.

That was all he ever yammered about. Hadn't he heard of life, sweet life? Had he not heard of the wonders performed in this very town by the quiet man standing right in front of him?

Samuel bent his head at the vulgarity, rummaging in his oversized Tote bag, looking for the purse he used for small change. "Half a pound of sausages, please."

"Size of that bag, I thought you'd be buying half the shop," said the butcher; a joke with a jag, the disappointment evident on his face. "I've some lovely venison, perfect for New Year—"

"Oh no, no. Deer is a spiritual creature, a symbol of life. Herne and all that."

Cully looked at him blankly.

"In Christian terms it would be like eating Jesus." Samuel was disheartened by the vacancy in the butcher's eyes. "I'm happy as Lawrence with just the sausages, really."

"I've some lovely Cumberland's," said Cully, brightening at the prospect of unloading some of his most expensive. He lifted one slimy sausage and wobbled it between his legs. "Now that's what you call a widow's memory!" His laugh was a drum solo played with hammers.

Samuel blushed, trying to hide his discomfort by mirroring the coarse humour. "I'd dare say that would be no good to that wee girl that was just in. She'd have the likes of that for breakfast."

Cully wheezed and snorted more than the comment merited, no doubt due to the unlikelihood of its source. Feeling more uncomfortable than ever Samuel waited for his sausages to be bagged, paid with a trembling hand, turned to leave, and bumped into Bob Turk, who had slipped in on cat's paws. Turk was hovering too close, bursting Samuel's personal, sacred bubble.

Turk was looking a blend of serious and smug, and had been since he had found Nadine Craig. Or rather since his son had, though that hadn't stopped him and Cyril Weir taking all the credit. Staunchly refusing to discuss it, batting away all enquiries with a weary shake of the head, and a terse "I'll be having nightmares 'til I'm sixty", they both acted as if they had just returned from the front line instead of a primary school playground.

For people who could not bear to discuss it they had appeared on every newscast, been interviewed by every gore hound hack that snooped and swooped on vulture wings around the town. Whores, the pair of them.

I have healed!

I have performed a miracle!

Not stumbled on a corpse like a dog on a fresh turd.

He dropped the sausages into his bag and brushed by Turk, Cully's crass laughter pushing at his back. He heard the butcher sneer in a mock whisper, "They're all the same, those Holy Joes: cock in one hand, bible in the other."

The rain-washed streets, wet as a baby's eye, were filled with drunken harpies even though it was barely after midday. Tomorrow they would all be rushing like the Gadarene swine to the New Year sales, seeking trinkets to ornament their grey sinful flesh.

He fought back the urge to yell "I have healed!" in their ungrateful faces. He had given back life, but people were only interested in death. He should be the focus of all eyes.

It was only pride that wished it so, a desire to outshine the lily in the field. The town was filled with television cameras and death junkie reporters. They had no time for silent miracles. God was testing him, teasing him, dangling dreams of mammon before him. It had been that way since pussy was a cat.

Not for him the glory; his job was to prepare the way.

He must be patient. There would be other miracles. He must keep his brains in his boots so he could think on his feet. For now, he must concentrate on the sick; they were everywhere if they only knew it.

I shine, oh how I shine, I shine already!

Between Cully's shop and Minnie Finlay's hairdressing salon was a lane just wide enough to drive a car down. It ended in a cul-de-sac with the Ellsford pigeon club blocking off a postage stamp of a car park. The backs of several houses overlooked the car park, and there was a fence crowned with barbed wire that segregated the rest of the lane from the railway tracks. Cully's house lay at the rear of his shop, a small gate opening onto a narrow path and the butcher's Spartan garden.

Samuel looked left, then right, opened the gate and slipped quickly through it.

"Here, Bony," he called quietly.

A scuffle of nails on the path, followed by a whiney growl. Bones. That was its name. Samuel supposed that was supposed to be ironic or something, for Bones was one fat tub of a dog; the body of an overinflated water bottle and the sad, gentle eyes of obese things species over. Or sarcastic. Probably sarcastic. Cully was a very sarcastic man.

STEPHEN McQUIGGAN

"Here, Bony boy," clucked Samuel, pulling a sausage from the depths of his bag and waving it aloft. "I've got a present for you, straight from daddy's shop."

The little dog sniffed the air, trundling forward with all the grace of a landed walrus, eyeing the meat with the hunger that only true gluttony knows. *If he eats this he'll explode*, thought Samuel as the terrier shuffled closer, its belly grazing the ground. To come back as a butcher's dog, now that was good karma; Bones must have been Gandhi in a previous life to have been so blessed.

The dog never tasted the sausage, just swallowed it whole. Samuel glanced over his shoulder. The lane beyond the gate was empty, the curtains still pulled on Cully's kitchen windows.

He produced another lank sausage and dangled it above the dog's dry nose, leading him toward the waist-high back fence, climbing over onto the short steep bank that descended down to the railway tracks.

"Here, Bony boy," he urged, the slap of chubby paws stopping as the dog halted by the fence and issued a tiny cough of a bark.

"Come on, boy, don't you want a lovely sausage?"

The dog regarded the tracks, then the house, then the sausage, its brain reeling from years of conditioning never to leave the boundaries of this canine nirvana.

"Lovely boy, lovely saussy."

Greed won the short skirmish. With a grunt and a squeeze Bones slid through the slats and almost tumbled down the bank. Overhead the smoky clouds broke to let through an overdiluted light, as Samuel popped the remaining sausages into Bones' greying muzzle one by one, wincing at every shark bite snap.

"You really shouldn't bolt your food like that, Bones."

He lifted one of the large rocks strewn by the sleepers, turning it slowly in his hand, hefting its pleasing weight, all the while scratching the mutt behind the ear, gratified by the pleasant whine it emitted.

"Good pup, good boy," he soothed, and Bones rolled over, exposing his swollen belly taut as a drum skin. This act of submission touched him deeply and he felt the sting of tears.

"That's right, boy, I'm the alpha male."

He rubbed the dog's bloated gut, causing its stubby legs to cycle, its penis emerging wet and sticky and shockingly pink.

"Oh Bones, that's so ... inappropriate." He felt the familiar hug of disappointment.

64

He brought the rock down, down, down, in his head the litany *one, two, skip a few, ninety-nine, a hundred*; his hands soaked in warm blood, crunching in his ears. Bones was still, somehow already less.

He put the dog inside his bag and began to walk.

He had only a mile to go to Troughton's Moss but the railway lines seemed to stretch on forever, the illusion of eternity comforting him. The weight of the dog bounced against his back as he kept to the stones by the side of the tracks in case the sleepers hypnotised him with their constant repetition, the way they had when he was a boy and his brother forced him to—

He stopped to shake the memory away. He was alone, hidden from view by the trees and scraggy bushes; the banks steeper now, flanking him. The raucous crows were his only company, calling out his progress. The cold seeped into his bones and made them brittle. How he wished it was summer. His faith was never this weak in summer.

He left the tracks, circling by the crossing gate, and headed up a country lane. A barn of steaming cows lay to the right, their pungent, earthy aroma wafting over him; frozen hay and manure crackling beneath his boots as he climbed over a stile, taking the age-old shortcut to the Moss.

He had buried his own dog here once, and Paul had dug it up again when the floods came to bury it on higher ground.

"Where did you put her?" he had asked his brother.

"I buried her deep inside me," said Paul.

The cows watched him pass with their stupid doll eyes, chewing moronically like the silly little girls in the mall. If only he could get a cow, but the logistics of actually killing one, of moving it … He shook off the idea as the cows shook off flies. Bones would do for now.

The tarmac ended, giving way to frozen muck and dead grass. Civilisation only stretched so far. Hidden beneath his feet were seeds, seeds filled with ineffable power, waiting for the sun to light their fuse. Here even his breath bloomed in botanical glory. This was where the magic was. This was the birthplace of wonders.

He could hear its song underneath the wind, haunting and deceptively sweet; the melody of venom. To be this close to wonders! No, better than that, to be a collaborator of wonders! To be a lackey of the infinite meant more than anything the material world could offer. This power was all around him and knew his name. It had summoned him here. His whole life he had been sleeping; he was a seed too.

The Moss always made him think of Paul.

When they were young they had been close as wind and rain, and where one stalked the other was not far behind. Together they were a storm. They foretold each other.

Every stone, every bush held its ghost. That old tree over there—the Umbrella tree Paul had called it—that was where his brother had first been called and where Samuel had first seen him cry.

"Look at my hands," he had said. "They're like an old man's."

In the bleary light Paul had reached up the elephant bark of the Umbrella tree and his skin had seemed to fall away from the bone.

I cried too.

He looked away and the ghost faded. Deep down trees, especially old ones, wanted to eat you. Paul had told him that. He wouldn't listen to the Umbrella tree's lies anymore, though its memories lingered.

Paul was wild at school, a big fish in a small pond, but bright as the dog star itself. Boys much bigger are scared of him, some of the teachers too. They sense something in him. His intelligence bothers them; if only he were stupid they wouldn't feel so guilty wishing him on the scrap heap. One day Jenny Hare stands up in class and makes some sweeping statement about how Paul will come to a bad end. It hurts *so* much.

Because he thought she liked him.

It hurts because the teacher does not slap her down, because the whole class agrees, hurts because I feel Paul's power slipping, hurts because she is right. Paul smashed her teeth in on the way home.

For you, Sam, these are for you. Little tusks of ivory pooled in blood in his outstretched hand.

As he trudged into the Moss, the dead dog beating on his back, the bag strap garrotting his shoulder, the thought occurred to them that they were finally running out of time.

Time had done a Dooley.

When was the last time he had thought of Dooley? Just being here in his childhood stomping ground brought so much back.

They had been halfway down Horseshoe Lane, on the other side of the Moss, when Paul grabbed Dooley and demanded to know where his coat was. Samuel didn't intervene, for one thing it was too damn hot and his throat was full of flies, and besides, Dooley shouldn't have ditched Paul's jacket in the first place.

Sure, it was a heavy leather, too bulky to cart about on such a scorcher, and yes the tarmac was bubbling and sticking to their Doc's as they stood and argued, but Dooley was the youngest and so it was only fair that he should carry Paul's coat from the quarry like he'd been told to.

Paul looked at Samuel and Samuel looked away. It was the only permission his brother needed. Paul grabbed Dooley by the scruff and marched him up the lane. Samuel slumped on the verge to wait, sipping the last of the warm Fanta, and dozed. When Paul returned, coat under his arm and face badly scratched, there was no sign of Dooley.

"He ran off," said Paul without being asked.

He must have ran a long way for he was never seen again.

Had Samuel known? He thought he probably had, though he pretended not to when the procession of police and parents flashed their desperate questions in his eyes. Did Paul dig up Dooley too, bury him on higher ground when the floods came and the Moss turned into a swamp?

The trees thinned out, the path tapering, as he entered Troughton's Moss proper. A blasted landscape, the scene of some long-forgotten war. Hard to believe that in a few short months it would be transformed into a fecund jungle of frogs and ferns, and gunship dragonflies scratching like pen scrapes across the sky.

Eyes were upon him, not the watchful wary eyes of the carrion shredders and starving foxes, but patient eyes, eyes whose hunger ran to silent depths.

"Preacher man."

A whisper in the wind.

He could see nothing save for the bushes decked out in the spectral bridal lace of cobwebs. He knew where to go, his feet taking him to the overgrown path he had found only a few weeks before.

"Preacher man."

He stopped at the cross he had made, seven feet tall, the wood plain and stained, a marker for the church he would build here, black like his dream. He had been told to put it on this very spot, a link to God in this most special of places.

There were wounds on the face of the earth—the planet was bruised and raw—and sometimes when you put your foot on such places they bled. This wound where he stood was open and festering.

The crows knew it; that was why they gathered here, their eyes filled with a dark semblance of life, eager for pain, the thin trees bowing under their weight.

He shivered as the sweat cooled on his skin. The wind had stopped. The grey day paused. The Moss took on the feel of a stage set. He felt he could rip down the slate sky backdrop and see the celestial engineers at work.

He dropped the bag, his arms fizzing with relief, and shook out the dog's body, the rest of the sausages stuck to its matted fur. He kicked Bones, rolling him over and over with his foot, until the corpse rested beneath the cross.

"I bring you …" *A sin offering? A sacrifice? A bribe?* "… What you asked for."

Silence.

He wanted to run but he did not dare. Down the long kaleidoscope of time he heard his brother's voice, "You smell like rats." Paul always said that, and now for the first time Samuel believed him, could smell them on himself. He had been stained, marked by something awful.

He bowed his head, fighting back sudden nausea. Sometimes you have to make yourself sick to get better he thought, sometimes we all smell of rats, sometimes—

The silence was shattered by a tooth-rattling roar, a howl from the draining depths of Hell.

He did not raise his eyes. Even when he heard the icy undergrowth snap underfoot, even when hot breath misted his forehead, even when he heard the guttural gargle, even when he heard his name mangled by a mouthful of dead meat.

"What *is* this, Samuel?"

No, he did not look, but turned and walked slowly away, only running when the scream tore the sky asunder, showering the crows to heaven in a coal storm. He did not stop, not when his breath knifed his throat, not when the remains of the butcher's dog struck his back, soaking his hair with entrails.

"What *is* this!"

He ran on, tripping over broken promises.

Chapter 10

Why did he have to meet them in the park of all places?, wondered Malcolm.

Not only would half the town see him pushing a pram but he was bound to run into Dobson and be forced into some kind of conversation with him. It was New Year's Eve, a boring goalless draw of a day. He should still be in bed conserving his energy for tonight, not dodging embarrassing parasites like Heather.

Being seen with a baby was bad enough, being seen with Dobson *and* a baby was too much to contemplate. People would see it as confirmation that they were paedophiles or a gay couple or something. At the very least they would assume Dobson stole it. Why the hell did he get lumbered with the brat anyway, and why here, in the very public place of Dobson's employment?

It wasn't like it was his mother's idea. She hadn't so much as spoken to him all week. She had been avoiding him since Boxing Day.

He could remember the chill in the kitchen that morning, though the heating had been up full for once, and how he had prodded listlessly at his eggs, mentally processing the awful dream he'd had of the girl at the door, and trying to think of something to say to drag his dad away from the paper and his mum from the sink.

"So, what happened to the Reverend's daughter?"

His dad was about to answer, eyes squinting in anticipation of reflected glory, when there was an almighty crash. He turned to see his mother stooping to the floor, surrounded by a million glistening shards.

"For fucksake, Sheila!" Cyril was pumping himself up to deliver a lecture on the price of crockery but she shot Malcolm such an accusatory glance that even Cyril seemed to cower. It was only a brief glance but it turned the eggs to crud in his mouth.

Cyril coughed and returned to his paper. "I don't want to talk about it. It's not a fit subject for breakfast time. For any time. Drink your tea."

Malcolm stuffed some toast in his mouth to bind a reply, then left the table, halfway upstairs when he heard the argument roll in like a thunderhead, an argument about what he could not tell, though he was sure it had little to do with broken plates.

He spent the next few days trying to puncture her silence, but the more chores he'd done, the nicer he was to her, the colder and more impregnable her defences became.

On Tuesday he had even brought out the rubbish—the last of the turkey bones, the Christmas telly listings sodden in vino and swollen to the size of phonebooks, all squashed into one thin-skinned bin liner. On top of the bin was the little figurine he had bought her, Marie Antoinette scrawled on the base in spidery gold lettering, lying on a bed of leftovers and tattered wrapping paper.

His mum had always loved such tat, every nook and cranny of the house filled with porcelain statuettes of society ladies, each one the quintessence of virginity. Like its namesake, his present had been beheaded. He fished it out determined to confront her with it, to demand an explanation, but she refused to even look at him, seemed to be listening to something else as she cocked her head to one side.

"I dropped it," she said.

He reached out to touch her, to tell her it was alright he would buy her another one whenever he went back to work, but she flinched from his fingers as if they had been rat tails.

Dropped it.

No excuse, no apology, just the dry fact. Oh, she had grown clumsy of late, hadn't she? Clumsy and full of lies.

Then only this morning she had decided to get her hair done. He was about to offer to walk her as far as Minnie Finlay's when his dad decided he too would go to town, thus leaving him stuck with Graham for the day. Only then was her silence finally breached.

"You can't leave the baby with him!" she said, as if Malcolm were some pervy uncle, as if he hadn't babysat countless times before. As if he wasn't there. "I'll mind him myself, or maybe our Bet could—"

"I'm not running after people when I've got a perfectly good babysitter built in," said Cyril, one foot already in The Cove. "One who's not going to cost me a packet and eat all my bloody biscuits. Now there's an end to it. Get your coat on and give those bastarding jaws of yours a rest."

Dad had won. She was more wary of him than Malcolm's childminding skills.

"And you, boy, meet us in the park at one and we'll walk home like a proper family. You hear me, boy?"

Malcolm nodded; the whole damn street probably had.

There was a group of girls further on down, walking past the redundant sundial, chewing and gabbling as they came; a giggle of fannies, to use Drew's collective noun. All school age, all huddled together because that's what you did when a psychopath was thinning the herd. Now everywhere you went you had to wade through hordes of stroppy little bitches who were impossible to intimidate in a group.

The last thing he needed was some sniggering little cow making some smart crack about him being a granddad when his nerves were as raw as ropes to begin with. He pushed the pram into a nearby bush, partly concealing it, then crossed to the far side of the path by the dog mess bin where he could still keep an eye on it. He lit a cigarette. If mum turned up early he could always claim he didn't want to smoke round the baby.

Now, standing all by himself, he felt like a bloody flasher.

He tried to look nonchalant as the girls approached; five of them, jailbait every one. Their voices stopped tinkling as they drew near. He could hear their heels clipping on the frozen gravel, little lust pony steps quickening as they eyed him warily. He flung them a yellow smile that hit them like a hand grenade, sparking dark muttering as they hurried by, craning their heads over their bony shoulders to make sure he was not following, accusations in their heavily made-up eyes.

His face grew hot, turned a new colour on the Dulux chart. It didn't take a killer on the loose to draw glances like that, like so much pus from an open wound. He had been a magnet for such looks since the day his bollocks dropped. Now even his mother was adding to his collection.

He flipped his cigarette onto the path and obliterated it with his boot, pretending it was the face of the prettiest girl who had walked by. Then he fired up another, striking his last match, dropping it to the ground with the burnt remains of the others in the box. It looked like a tornado had blown through a small homogenous forest.

He hawked up some phlegm from the back of his throat and spat it on top of them. He got most of it out but there was a bone at the end of it and it swung from his mouth, an X-File, a mucus pendulum, and he had to snap it off with his fingers. As he rubbed his hands on his trousers he looked up to see a girl watching him, her lip curled in disgust.

Not any girl. Kate, from the library. Kate, who looked like a vampire and smiled like an angel. He was planning on asking her out, to go down to the library without Dobson for once and just ask her out.

"Hi," he said, but she hurried on.

If he had a horned helmet she'd love him. Bad boys could get away with spitting. Bad boys and Vikings. He could sail into the library and throw her over his shoulder, her screaming face buried in his musty furs, carry her back to his longboat and pillage her loins. Then burn her on a pyre.

He waited until she was out of earshot then yelled, "Bitch!"

He went to get his brother, thinking it might have been smarter to have kept him by his side in the first place; sensitive boys got away with spitting too. He pulled the pram from the bushes and felt his heart grind to a sudden halt.

A short laugh escaped him when he saw only a few leaves where Graham should be, the blankets pulled back to reveal a few damp twigs.

A short laugh before his heart lurched back into gear, hurtling into rally mode, a short laugh because it was the worst thing that could possibly ever happen, a short laugh rapidly turning into high-pitched keening as the empty pram blurred into a watercolour.

His dad would kill him, rip him limb from limb, and his mum would chew on whatever fragments he left behind.

He had only been gone a minute!

He tore his way through the brambles, scratching his face and tearing his clothes, feeling the pain as somehow noble, evidence of his sincerity, his worry. He just prayed his dad would see it like that. With suicidal thoughts plunging silk thorns in his brain, he broke through to the other side.

It was impossible that Graham could have crawled away all by himself. Someone took him. That blatant fact drove him on.

The park opened out in a wide vista of pale green and ice. Straight ahead lay the duck pond, cold and uninviting even to the grumpy mallards and scrawny moorhens that shared it with the litter. To his right was the playground, its garish skeleton frames empty, the rusty squeak of the swings audible in the breeze. To his left the path disappeared around a bend of evergreens leading to the front gates.

Malcolm ran toward them. Whoever had snatched Graham must have come this way, if he was quick he could—

Something caught his eye by the pond. A dark stick figure, a shadow dancing against the grey water, with a bundle in its arms. He heard a cry he had heard countless times before; had his brother's hateful squeal ever sounded so beautiful?

Powered by fear and righteous rage, he ran to the water. He would kick the living shit out of this guy, save Graham and be a hero, make the front page. There were enough journos in town, he might go national. He might even get a handshake and a manly chat from Cyril.

The figure turned at the sound of his approach and all heroic thoughts left him.

Standing knee-deep in the pond, cradling his baby brother, was a man so thin that for a moment Malcolm mistook him for the silhouette of some monstrous heron. The water pooled around his trousers like an oil slick; he smiled at Malcolm, his lips parting to reveal desiccated gums.

"Give me him back or I'll—"

"Or what?" His voice, black as his suit, shook Malcolm; he could almost *taste* it, like a live battery when you put your tongue on the end of it.

"I'll …"

The stick man's smile grew wider. The breeze ribbed the pond, carrying his scent. He smelt like he'd recently spent the night in a butcher's skip.

"You'll what? Kill me?" He laughed, thin wisps of hair dancing on his skull.

Malcolm waded out toward him, the icy water stealing his breath. He thought he heard music, distant and sickening. "Just give me back my brother."

"Your brother? You mean this?" The stick man held aloft the child in one long, thin claw as if considering it for the first time. "I have no interest in this … yet. I wanted to meet you is all."

"Give me him now, or I swear I'll fuck you up, you anorexic freak."

"Dogs only bark when they're frightened, so stop your growling, boy." He dangled the baby between them but Malcolm hesitated, struck by the irrational thought that if one of those pale spidery hands so much as brushed against him he would wizen up and crumble to dust.

"Little Moses saved from the bulrushes," laughed the stick man. "Who saved the Saviour in the sewers?"

Malcolm was in over his knees now, the cold water shrivelling his testicles and erasing his breath. He reached for his brother as the stick man ran a long black fingernail down the child's forehead drawing a long dark worm of blood. Graham howled, his face turning an apoplectic scarlet.

"Ah skin," hissed the stick man, pulling out the sibilant. "I love its feel, its texture, so rough, so smooth. They say that, don't they? You have to take the rough with the smooth. Easy to cut, easy to pierce, hell, you can even sew it! It's what sex is really all about. You know of sex yet? Of girls? They are God's ejaculate made flesh. I'm going to eat yours soon. Catch!"

He flung the baby in the air, and as Malcolm caught him he heard far off a woman's scream, turning to see his mother running down the bank with lunatic velocity, jettisoning her shopping bags, soup cans rolling round her feet, her heavy cardigan billowing, her new hairdo barely moving. Behind her, dad, running like a pensioner's tap, face set in habitual anger.

"What are you doing!"

The stick man was gone, leaving not a ripple; the pond deserted save for a few miserable ducks, the far bank lined with the frozen smudge smoke of denuded trees. He was alone.

"What the hell are you playing at! Give him to me!"

There were tears in her voice; boiling, scalding tears. She was in the water before he could climb out, grabbing at the child, and when she saw the blood on Graham's forehead she shot Malcolm the same look as she had on Boxing Day, only this time cubed, and Malcolm realised with a jolt what lay beneath it.

Hate. Pure hate.

"I told you!" She was a spitting cobra, yelling to his father as he huffed up to the water's edge, the Daily Mirror clamped under one arm. "I told you he couldn't be trusted. He was trying to kill our only son, our baby boy!"

"What the fuck have you been at?" Cyril's voice was dangerously civil, though his frown lines were set in granite. It was clear he intended to take all the discomfort of this very public humiliation out on Malcolm. Yet there was something else there too—Fear? Was Cyril afraid?

"There was a man ... I saved ..." He lost the answer somewhere in the telling. Something his mother said was jarring his grasp of the situation. "What do you mean, 'Only son'?"

Cyril blanched, tried to coax his wife out of the pond, but Sheila ignored him and lunged deeper into the water, splashing her brown stockings black, a triumphant look on her face.

"You're not mine!" she said, snapping the whips of her lips. "That's right, you're nothing but a *bastard!*"

Malcolm laughed nervously, but her face was rigid; *the truth doesn't have a sense of humour*, he thought as he looked into her eyes.

"Sheila!" Cyril was using his parade ground voice, but he looked cowed, beaten. "This is neither the time nor the place."

She waded out to Malcolm, hugging Graham like a talisman, close enough to press her face into his. Up close Malcolm could see the welts the shopping bags had left on her wrists.

"I couldn't have children, doctor told me so years and years ago." She was vomiting the words out now. "Your *father*," she laughed bitterly, "that man behind me, thought it was his fault, thought himself less a man. I always believed it was down to me, but we were both wrong. Look, look at this little boy. God gave us this miracle when we'd stopped even dreaming. *You're* not our son, you were a parcel on the church step. A foundling that we adopted. We thought we couldn't have our own, and you were the price we had to pay."

She was whispering now, her grey batwing voice oozing over him. "I know what you did. I found her pants." She looked shocked, afraid she had said too much, went too far. She looked frightened of him. She turned quickly and clambered from the pond.

"Where's the pram?" Cyril was unable to meet his eye, unable to soften his voice.

"Dad ..." The word embarrassed them both.

"We'll talk when we get home. Where's the damn pram?"

Malcolm pointed in the vague direction of the bushes, his hand shaking. A crowd of dog walkers and joggers had stopped to rubberneck but moved on quickly when Cyril stormed toward them, head held high, clutching his newspaper like a sword.

It all made sense now. How could he not have known? He felt green as snot; hadn't he always felt different? *Didn't I tell you so?* cooed the voice inside him.

When he got back his mother, or rather the woman he would always think of as his mother, was in bed. Hiding. Cyril was waiting for him on the offensive, his chosen form of defence.

"What happened in the park with the baby? Don't lie to me, boy, or I'll knock your melt in."

Malcolm found he was no longer scared of him, his power had diminished with his paternity. He mumbled some halfhearted rubbish about jaggy brambles, about trying to clean the child's cut in the water. He didn't mention the stick man; in truth had almost forgotten him. That snaking voice had told him to crush his thin memory, to concentrate on what was important.

"Is it true? What mum said?"

For a second he thought Cyril would deny it, put it down to post-natal depression, wrinkle his nose and say "periods", and a sudden savage joy whelmed up in him.

"I raised you. You always be mine, no matter what."

Malcolm left as the final nail was hammered. He went to bed, hiding too. Later he heard the phone ring, heard his dad (so hard not to think of him as that) actually *knock* on his bedroom door.

"Call for you, son."

He feigned sleep until he heard the soft click of the door and his father's retreat. He lay staring at the ceiling, eventually falling into a fitful slumber, his body struggling, writhing in the grabbing dark. And in his dreams the voice returned, louder, stronger—he tried to ignore it, to stew in silence, but in that silence the wormy voice jabbered on, impossible to ignore.

Outside the New Year was born with a drunken scream.

Part Two

It's Dobson's idea. The bad ones usually are.

Although it is barely midday the heat is already heavy and their shirts are glued to their backs. As they cut behind the Esso station a couple of guys shout abuse at them from the forecourt and this too is Dobson's fault; Malcolm knows they would have been ignored if Heather wasn't with them.

"Don't worry," says Pruner. "Thick as mince, the pair of them."

Dobson is a bully magnet—everything he does attracts their attention. Like the name he has chosen for their gang: Flea Force. It is so childish it makes Malcolm squirm, but Pruner likes it so he has to go along with it. Pruner always lets Dobson have dibs on things like that because he's so small, and because he's so small he chose bloody Flea Force. Not The Grifters like he had suggested. As usual Pruner had lapped it up, shouting it out during the quiet bits in assembly and inventing a daft one-fist salute.

You can see Dobson's pride at this, his big eyes bulging with secret signs, codewords kicking at his teeth to get out. He thinks Pruner can pick a rainbow from his nose but Pruner isn't all that. Pruner is always on about starting up a band, but the name—Polio Assmeat—is just fucking stupid. Now he's telling them it should be Natas because that's Satan backwards and what could be more evil than that? If anything that's even dumber.

He'll probably let Dobson come up with the name and if he does Malcolm will leave the band before they've bought any instruments.

The Hawks would be a cooler name, anything but Flea Force.

One break time last week they had met by the Monkey Tree outside Miss Wilson's room. They had to be very quiet because Miss Wilson's class were "special" and had different playtimes, and smiles so wide the slobber just dripped out of them. They had given the salute, preparing to swoop down on the playground with their coats tied around their necks like capes and scatter the hopscotch girls, when Drew Proctor and Skinner Morris showed up and asked them who the fuck they were supposed to be.

"We're Flea Force," said Dobson smugly and Skinner had almost pissed himself, and Drew had punched him so hard on the snout he had to take the next day off. His freaky mum Joyce had turned up later on, shouting so loud you could hear her all the way down in the woodwork room.

As they crawl through the fence that separates the Esso from the fields and the Moss beyond he has his school tie wrapped around his head, bellowing "Red sky, shepherd's pie!" No wonder those two goons on the forecourt are laughing at them.

They cross the scorched lion's back of the close cropped fields, the stubble razor like and flyblown, until they come to the entrance of the sewers; a large open pipe that smells obscenely damp in the drought of the day. They are silent awhile, passing a cigarette amongst themselves, coughing occasionally when they accidentally inhale.

"Will we have to crouch the whole way?" asks Malcolm. "I mean, if I come home covered in shit my mum'll go through me like a dose of salts."

"If it wasn't for your right hand you'd be a virgin, Weir, you know that?" says Pruner. "I already told you, Skinner says you can walk upright for miles, right under the whole town."

"Maybe we should just go a little bit. I'm supposed to go straight home after school. What if we get lost and—"

"Look at you, you're bricking it, the gravy's running out of you! You truly are yellow, Weir. Why do you think we brought spray paint?" says Pruner patting his school bag. "Now let's go, we have a kingdom to conquer. Dark adventure awaits us in the shitpipes of Ellsford!"

Dobson laughs and Malcolm forces a smile. Although their friendship hasn't crossed the finishing line yet he's sure if Pruner says it's okay then it surely must be okay. Still, he wishes they were hunting ghosts in the graveyard like last week. The graveyard wasn't scary at all during the day.

It will be dark in the sewers, miles and miles of bible dark if Skinner is right and, flashlights or not, in the dark make believe can become real.

"Flea Force!"

Dobson runs into the pipe, bouncing on the wire grille they had ripped off the day before, and disappears into the black. Mad little bastard, thinks Malcolm, he knows he'll never be popular so he's decided to be dangerous. At least if there is anything down there it will get him first. Pruner takes a torch from his schoolbag and dances it over the opening.

"Ready? Course not."

He takes a deep breath and follows, leaving the sucking demon heat behind, stopping to look back at the circular shot of early summer at the end of the tunnel; an ingenious painting hung in hell to torment the damned.

Wrinkling his nose, he jogs to catch up with Pruner's light, a Will-o-the-wisp that always seems to be one turn ahead of him.

"Holy shit! Hurry up guys, you gotta see this!" Dobson's voice echoes back to him, raising the hackles on his neck.

He hurries on, feeling as he does so that he is running deep into the town's colon, spraying a ragged asterisk at every corner. This is gonna all go egg shaped, he thinks, this is a proper maze, Dungeons and Dragons for real.

Anything could live down here, rats grown huge on human shit, feral dogs … the Devil himself. It's so easy to believe in the Devil down here, easier than believing in the Big Beardy in the sky at any rate; he could use his pitchfork to shovel away the turds.

Pruner and Dobson have stopped up ahead, their beams lapping and interlacing over something he can't quite see. The dark is cold on his skin, his eyes feel as slimy as the sweating walls. Now the stink really kicks in; it smells worse than Dobson's house down here. He adds his own torchlight to that of his friends, confusing the scene rather than enlightening.

Then he sees.

Cats.

Lots of cats. Mangled. All heaped together in a broken, bloody nest. Dobson's torch flickers across their decaying faces, staining their fur a sickly luminous yellow. The blood seeping from their twisted carcasses looks fresh. Malcolm doesn't want to look, scared he'll puke, but he can't tear his eyes away.

So many, their tails knotted together, their bodies contorted and full of holes, holes that look like teeth marks, like—

"Something's been eating at them," says Dobson. "Probably rats."

But rats can't tie knots, and rats don't have teeth that big, and where were they? Weren't sewer rats supposed to be cocky, unafraid?

Pruner stretches out a leg, presses a distended gut with a shoe, and a high pitched whine of escaping gas fills the tunnel as the cat slithers off the pile with a wet, gloopy slop.

Dobson reaches for something underneath its chewed corpse. Malcolm feels his gorge rise as he watches him pull up a string of veins, but as Dobson wipes away the gunk he realises it is a necklace.

"Eileen," reads Pruner, training his light on the pendant as Dobson wipes

away a viscous clod with his thumb. "Dumb name for a cat."

"Here, Mal," Pruner says, flinging a wad of gore and bone and Malcolm ducks; in the movies that would have went right down my throat and—

A howl punctures the silence, bouncing off the corrugated walls, clutching their hearts in its needle grasp.

"What the fuck!" Malcolm knows now he is going no further, no matter what Dobson says, no matter what Pruner calls him.

"Probably a rabbit," says Dobson. "I heard one Skinner caught in a snare one time and it—"

"What would a rabbit be doing in a fucking sewer!"

"Might have fallen down a storm drain or something."

The howl bursts again before logic can batter Dobson's argument; higher this time, glacial, a freezing death cry that hurts to hear.

"I'm outta here," says Malcolm.

"Surprise, surprise. Keep your hair on cunty balls and don't be such a weenie," says Pruner. "That's one hell of a riff, we could use that on the first album." He turned to Dobson. "Shall Flea Force investigate?"

"Aye aye, Commander."

"What about me?" asks Malcolm.

"Why don't you go and see if you can rustle up some carrots," says Pruner over his shoulder as he leads Dobson further up the tunnel. "Our Bugs sounds very hungry."

Oh, how he wishes he had the nerve to tell Billy Rose to take a fuck off tablet. He hangs back until their glow and their laughter are swallowed by the dark, twitching to follow, acutely aware of the feline charnel mound beside him.

Can he remember the way out, has he marked every turn? What if he gets lost and—

A guttural roar fills the pipes, so loud it sounds like industrial machinery. Malcolm flees on leaden legs, schoolbag beating out a frantic tattoo on his hip, running like he is enveloped in some death dream.

"Fuck off, Dobson!"

He doesn't really believe it's Dobson messing, no he really doesn't believe that at all.

He reaches the final turn, skidding, one hand flapping against the sticky wall, as a figure emerges from an adjoining pipe ahead casting a thin silhouette on the disc of sunlight at the tunnel's end.

Malcolm splashes to a halt though his heart gallops on ahead, letting out a low moan he is convinced is his final breath. As the figure stands upright he sees it is a child his own age, naked and covered in shit and blood, with jutting ribs sharp as blades.

In its hands the child is clutching something tightly.

For a moment he is sure it is a head, a severed human head; he can almost see the slack jawed moronic glare of death on its face, but a sudden slash of sunlight reveals it to be a raggedy old teddy bear, one arm missing, its original colour lost in a glaze of dung.

The roar sounds again behind him and the child answers with an unholy whine. Malcolm uses the only weapon he has. Swinging his schoolbag, adding his own terrified yell to the din, he charges at the child.

Chapter 11

Morris Skinner swerved, avoiding the kerb by the skin of his yellow country teeth, and sucked in a deep breath. Jesus, that was close.

He forced himself to concentrate on the road ahead but his eyes were continually drawn to the mirror, to the reflection of Molly Stone in the backseat, pruned and wrinkled, her hearing aid squatting like a space station on the surface of some arid planet. Her face was custard yellow flecked with rhubarb veins. She reminded him of school desserts. The knuckles of her hands gripping her knees, sending fleeting stegosaurus shadows across the dash.

"You okay back there, Mrs. Stone?"

He would never dare call her Molly. People like her didn't have Christian names, they lived on some higher plane that prohibited familiarity. Her husband had probably called her Mrs. Stone too, or Mother, as he wasted away under that unforgiving gaze. On her headstone it would say "Mrs. Stone" and—

"Of course, I'm not an invalid," she snapped.

Oh but you were, Mother dear, and not so long ago at that.

He had picked her up so many times before, literally so, carrying her small bird frame, her useless legs dangling like straws as he put her in the taxi, feeling guilty as he strapped her in, guilty at the thought it would be a mercy if she just plummeted through the windscreen; cursing as he folded down her tank of a wheelchair, all pity leaving him, as he humped it into the boot.

84

But today she walked from her front door, sans Panzer, climbing into the car reeking of health as much as lavender.

Had that Looney Tune Cunningham really fixed her? He had heard the rumours, of course, but dismissed them as nonsense, one more tall tale in a town hysterical with murder. And yet here she was, vital *and* vertical.

"I must say, Mrs. Stone, you're looking well."

She glared back at him in the mirror, scratching herself like a mongrel by a fire. Her handbag seemed to be moving under its own steam.

"What are you wittering on about, boy? And don't drawl so; enunciate, boy, enunciate!"

Hot blood rushed to his face, the way it used to in class when she would single him out for one of her barbs, feeding like a vulture on his dialect and ignorance.

"You were always the same, your brother too, and your father before you. Country mumblers all."

"I was just saying you looked well. It's a miracle isn't it?"

"Do you know what a real miracle is, young man? Travelling from A to B without some ignoramus prattling away ninety to the dozen."

Morris sighed. Normally she was a gasbag. She reminded him of a news bulletin—she started with death and ended with the weather. He should be used to such rudeness by now. Old things, people as much as books, tended to be difficult. He had picked up so many belligerent drunks, and even more cranky pensioners, he really should learn to keep his trap shut.

He liked to talk though.

It was a lonely job driving these same old roads hour after hour, day after day, with only his wife's metallic voice barking out fares for company. Maybe he would catch a decent run to the city or the airport, or better still, maybe he would get a call from Christa Finchley.

He had run her home one night before Christmas and she claimed to have no money. Grinning drunkenly, she had spread her legs, her short skirt squealing up her thighs, "But I did bring my hairy chequebook."

He had come like the kingdom.

If Beth ever found out about that little caper the next car he'd be in would be a hearse. Was it any wonder he strayed occasionally when all he ever got at home was grief? He needed to sort himself out, give his brain a spring clean, what Les would call "a good dung out".

Beth didn't want him out driving—he was a partner in the business, he shouldn't be out slumming it—but they only had two drivers, so he had to go out to make the money she so readily spent. He couldn't ask the old man to bail him out, not since the farm had gone belly up. He had debts like boa constrictors. She didn't seem to realise they weren't just broke, they were beyond fixing.

Beth didn't like his brother either—he was rude over the radio and smoked in his cab—but he was the *senior* partner. That's why it was called Les Cabs; she didn't like the name, said it sounded like a French skin disease. Lately she had taken to pointing out that he was as bad as his brother.

At school people had tended to mix them up, even though Les was a year older and a lot heavier. Old Ma Stone had referred to them as Skinner Lesley and Skinner Morris and it had stuck. He supposed he should be grateful, before that his nickname had been Pigman.

Beth didn't like people calling him Skinner Morris. Beth didn't like much of anything at all.

Morris got a daily run down of the things she didn't like, both old and new, over the breakfast table, over the airwaves, and over the top. Trapped in the cab he had no escape. He loved her, he really did, but lately he found himself daydreaming that the killer would take her next. He was genuinely shocked each time at the thrill this shot through him.

The sympathy he would garner, the pity that would be lavished upon him. He could take Christa—

"Where do you think you're going!" Molly was prodding his shoulder with the warped root of her finger.

"Where I always take you. Evanston Home."

"Did I ask you to take me to Evanston Home?"

He couldn't remember, he had just assumed. He always brought her there to see her sister; he hadn't expected to bring her anywhere else. Then again, he hadn't expected to pick up a biped. He pulled the car over at the end of Hollywell. All the shoppers looked the same, as if they had all bought the same expression, as if there were a sale on boredom.

"So, where do you want to go?" He turned to face her but she was glued to the window, transfixed by the sight of a young girl pushing a pram. "Mrs. Stone?"

"I suppose you have bred."

"Pardon?" It would only lead to more pedantry not to be polite.

"Have you any children?" Her voice was distant, her one good eye fixed firmly on the child in the buggy whilst its neighbour circumnavigated its socket with a manic glee. "A horde of double glottals and slurred vowels no doubt, all dreaming of following in your illustrious footsteps."

"No, not yet. Plenty of time for all that."

"Who says so? Are you a fortune teller on the side?" Her eye was on him now, its harsh intensity freezing its companion in its tracks.

Christ, she's worse than Beth, he thought, *baby this and baby that. One minute she's talking about budgets and belt tightening, the next baby-grows and bibs—who could understand the mind of a woman?* He was only twenty-one. He would rather choose voluntary brain death than have a kid right now. Maybe when he had saved enough, bought Les out of the business, but that was years down the line. He quickly smothered the thought that a baby would only trap him.

"Where to, Mrs. Stone?"

"Bring me to Troughton's Moss. I have to see a man about a dog." She laughed as he pulled back out into traffic, the dry click of her throat louder than the indicator.

"You sure? I mean ..."

What exactly *did* he mean? Would the old pishmare be able to traverse the Moss with its overgrown ruts and sudden swamps, or was it merely superstition that nagged him?

He had played there as a boy, spent as much time out there as he had on the farm, it had been the setting of his dreams. A fecund canvas; sometimes Middle Earth, sometimes the wilds of Borneo, sometimes the Spanish Main. But those dreams had clotted and soured.

In his head he told himself it was because he had discovered that they had found Paul Cunningham there, after he had raped and murdered and then dug up that girl. Once he knew that he had avoided the place. It had been tainted. But his heart knew different, his heart whispered it was because of that time he had gone to find the buzzard nest and met that guy who called himself Dooley and—

"I mean it's dangerous down there."

"What are you yammering on about now? You always were a yammering fool. Time has done nothing to alleviate your idiocy."

Another thing Beth would agree on.

"I need to stop for fuel." He needed to get out of the car, away from her pious stench.

He drove out of town, the small outcrop of houses giving way to frosted fields and skeletal trees. He slowed as the road snake tongued, turning onto the gravel track that was Horseshoe Lane, the heater on full, the smell of cow shit pervading the cab, mixing odiously with the stench of Magic Trees and old woman.

He wondered briefly if she had soiled herself. It had always been a concern of his that someday the old witch who couldn't move her legs would nonetheless have no difficulty in moving her bowels.

A private concern now, for he had once mentioned it to his wife and she had got up on her soapbox pointing out he never worried about picking up the Brew Crew (and for nothing! Imagine!) who were far more likely to dirty the upholstery than a lady like Mrs. Stone.

The reason she was so quick to defend the old crone was because she had been a swot at school; one of the only students to ever receive a muted compliment from Molly. Finishing top of Wooden Tit's maths class three years in a row had earned her the glowing accolade, "At least Miss Watson can count on more than her fingers and thumbs", but it had also nurtured her otherwise inexplicable belief that she was somehow superior than everyone else, especially her dimwit husband.

That was why she handled the accounts; her nose plunged into them, an unerring rudder guiding them to untold, and so far unseen, riches.

It was all besides the point anyhow. Ma Stone could walk again. Silver Sam had no doubt tightened up her hoary old sphincter into the bargain.

He rolled down the window and let in some icy air. Mrs. Stone was loosening her seatbelt in preparation for a quick getaway. He grinned as he imagined her trying to make a run for it to dodge the fare.

The winter sun was strong. As Skinner searched for his sunglasses by the gear stick he felt a rough-skinned hand round his throat; the stench of lavender and stale urine suddenly overpowering.

He had almost time to issue a nervous laugh before another hand clamped his windpipe, squeezing until stars burst across his windshield. He tried desperately to unhook the wizened claws as brambles scraped the side of the cab, the car veering ever closer to the drainage ditch running parallel to the lane. Her breath was fetid, rotting, the breath of the Moss itself, mocking the lack of his own as it smeared his face in a liquid sheen.

There was a bone-rattling jolt as the cab smashed into a tree and he slammed into the steering wheel, blood spattering from his forehead. The airbag popped out belatedly in bloated surrender.

"I'll walk from here," he heard her say.

The door banged shut as he passed out, slumping down into the airbag that shone like Heaven's gate.

Chapter 12

With Bob Turk on holiday, Dobson had the storeroom all to himself. He could have taken the day off too, Turk would never have known, but Dobson couldn't wait to get into work; he loved the park at this time of year.

The store loomed around him, clung to him like a rumour, as he rocked on the little complaining stool staring deep into the shadows cast by long-dead lawnmowers and the teeth of rusted bucksaws. The old shed hissed and crackled to itself, senile old wood babbling to dribbling old felt. A soothing sound broken only by the pistol crack of the clock that Bob dusted everyday as if to placate its anger. If Dobson closed his eyes he could pretend he was on a steam train.

But he didn't dare.

Lately, when he closed his eyes, all he could see was the skinny man; the skinny man and the fish-eyed dead girls from his dreams.

He pulled his monkey hat down over his ears, protecting himself from those who would burgle his thoughts. He stepped out into the mint-crisp morning, looking like an inkblot on virgin paper, the wind a thousand rodent claws racing on his skin.

You're alright son, leastways you'll do. That's what the doctor told him after he had collapsed at Silver's meeting.

Dobson never mentioned the dreams of dead girls, nor of the thin man who revved his car outside his house in the wee small hours. If he had, then Doctor Dear would have told him he wouldn't do; no, he wouldn't do at all.

Exhaustion. Been burning the candle both ends have we?

Chip bags danced a tango in the breeze. He walked, hunching his back, uphill toward the pavilion, relishing the empty crunch of his boots, the unashamed nakedness of the horizon. He felt like he was walking on the surface of an enormous egg. At last the world was ready to hatch, and he was to be the only witness. By the time he reached the pavilion he was sweating, his breath a tracker dog before him.

The squat building always depressed him for he could remember carrying sandwiches up here to his dad when he worked here. It was one of the only memories he had left of him now and the main reason he had applied for the job in the first place; and if Turk was to be believed, the only reason he got it.

Have you had other episodes like this?

All that week after his dad died, when he had been fed nothing but chocolate and sad eyes, and the house so quiet he thought it had died too, Dobson had stayed in his room. He didn't trust the world anymore. If he ventured outside then whatever had taken his dad might just snap him up too.

Reverend Craig had practically moved in, smelling of talc and boiled sweets, smelling of school toilets, his breath foul with lies. "Don't be sad, Dobson," he said, the hairs in his nose glowing like fibre optics. "Your daddy is in a wonderful place now."

That only made him feel worse—why hadn't dad brought him with him then?

"We should be celebrating! It's a glorious thing to be with Christ Jesus! We should have a party, not sit around moping. It's a sin to mourn so, the same as not believing. You do believe, don't you, Dobson?"

He wondered if old Baa Craig believed now, wondered if the crushed head of his daughter had also crushed his faith. He fought the sudden uncharitable urge to go round to the manse, slap the Reverend on the back and say, "I heard about Nadine. Congratulations, you must be over the moon!"

His coat billowed as he fumbled for the keys. The pavilion's glass doors were vain, begrudging his reflection. His hand stuck on the steel handle, stealing skin instead of fingerprints. He went inside flicking on the lights; they flashed teasingly before settling, humming an insect dirge.

Any olfactory signals? Did you smell anything beforehand?

He blew into his hands, rubbing life back into them, watching them redden and curl; bargain bin Lazarus, five a pound. It was colder in here than it was outside, the air cruel enough to sharpen pencils.

He entered the toilets where the rats and spiders lived. He placed a boot on one of the rims and hoisted himself up, checking for any sign of malevolent eyes in the yellow water below, seeing only cracked porcelain stained by excrement fingers. He opened up the window above the toilet halfway. From here he could see right down to the park gates. He watched people enter the park, pause briefly, then leave as if its emptiness recalled something within them they would rather keep hidden.

Any fever or casual vomiting?

With a belch that turned the air violet, Catman, the town drunk (known to the law as Brendan Harper), staggered through the park gates on his biro refill legs, a bottle of wine in his hand; or was it *part* of his hand, the next logical step, along with a shorter neck and hollow legs, in the evolution of the chronic alcoholic.

His two children, tied to his waist by a length of clothesline, falling from their rollerskates and scraping their knees on laughing tarmac with every unpredictable lurch of their sodden father.

Do you drink to excess? Do you smoke?

"Take me, God! Take me now, you bastard!" Catman raised his arms to the sky, sending his kids flailing once more on their plastic umbilical cord. "Beam me up, Scotty!" He waited a few moments, for effect or orientation, then moved on, dragging his family behind him like the unwelcome past.

A flash of colour by the gates caught Dobson's eye, a burning sun seen through its black iron ribs. She was here at last.

Michelle Mason, dressed in red head to toe, oozed into the park pushing a baby buggy, the child swaddled in a plague of anorak. Her short mousy hair had retracted to hide from the wind that had set up fruit stalls in her cheeks. She pushed her daughter along at a dangerous pace, her knuckles swollen and angry from the cold or lack of a wedding ring. Her pug nose seeped watery snot onto her top lip, where it encrusted, reflecting the dishwater sun like a second-hand bauble.

Dobson watched her breath hang in the air as he held his own. She was a contradiction, beautiful yet not. She was Christa Finchley's best friend.

Michelle used to sit beside him in English and Maths, her days as barren of affection as his. A plump lonely girl, her eyes vacuuming up every detail, her body built for comfort not for speed.

They said the kid was Drew's.

She always smiled when Dobson played the fool, handing out laughs like loaves and fishes, but her smile was more of a question. She could see through the act; she always listened to him, maybe she would listen to him now.

Do you ever have strange dreams?

Listen when he told her that Christa was in danger. He had been dreaming about Christa, dreaming about her all week, only they didn't feel like dreams, they felt more like memories. Memories of things to come. Michelle would want to help if he could explain it properly; if he didn't use words like "murder" or "mutilation" and end up convincing her in the process that *he* was the threat.

A spider bungeed down, thought better of it, scuttled away. Closing the toilet window, he jumped onto the puddled floor and hurried back out into the blank wasteland. He tried whistling in the biting air, his breath bellowing out like his lungs were on fire. He sounded like an ice cream van. His boots lost traction on the ice and he almost went head over breakfast down the pavilion steps.

He could see Michelle trundling her way to the bandstand where she would stop for a crafty cigarette as usual. Dobson marched after her with careful strides, faltering only when he saw the figure sitting on the bench watching him. He put his head down automatically and picked up his pace, sneaking a glance as he drew near.

Have you ever suffered from hallucinations?

It was that girl, Kate, from the library, the end of her nose a bright shade of red, her hair tucked under an unflattering cap, her hands hidden in little girl mittens.

"Dobson?"

It pulled him up short. He felt a sudden blast of heat envelop him. She knew his name! Maybe she thought it was his surname and was trying to be rude—a lot of people got caught out like that—but he didn't think so.

"Where are you off to in such a hurry?"

I'm off to tell that fat girl that I've been dreaming her best mate is going to be chopped up into little pieces. "Hi Kate, I was … I work here. You work in the library."

She laughed. "I know. You bang your head on those steps or something?"

He tried his best to assume a carapace of indifference. "No, I'm fine. I just meant I've seen you in the library. Working." *This is where her smile dies and she tells me to jog on*, he thought, but instead her smile widened.

"And I've saw you in the library," she said. "Reading."

She was wearing faded denim jeans and an army jacket. Her hair hung wet from the edges of her cap, sticking to her forehead like some drunken take on the Cyrillic alphabet. The scar on her temple glowed a sickly pink. He wanted to reach out and touch it, to brush her hair back into place, to hold that small perfect face, studded with such green eyes, in his hand. He wanted to run.

Harpooned by her looks he could not run far. Her smile, the glint in her eye, was the secret behind every love song ever written. He didn't want to come over all Mills and Boon but, Christ, she *melted* him.

How could she even speak to him?

Not a cursory conversation either, she seemed interested—now even laughing at his clumsy jokes, and in the right places too. Within a few seconds of her company he was her biological slave, within a few minutes he contemplated tattooing her name across his chest, and all that time the word "love" sang deep inside him.

Stupid, girly, adorable, wonderful love.

He had wasted his life on sorrow and self-pity. Sure, he felt sick and time was speeding up and slowing down alarmingly, but that was okay; love was Alzheimer's, love was cancer, love was inevitable.

All he could do was grin back. She had never spoken to him before, not really, barely ever looked at him. He grinned so much it hurt, grinned so much he forgot her name.

"Kate," he said aloud.

"Yeah?" For a long awkward moment he stood gawping, unaware of where he was and fumbling for something to say.

She giggled, derailing his runaway train of thought. "You okay, Dobson? You zoned out there for a moment."

"Yeah, yeah, fine … Do you know what time it is?"

The old fallback, as dependable and as exhausted as the weather. She pointed to the large clock face that hung above the pavilion he had just left, and he felt all hope deflate. She was new to town, did not hang with anyone he knew, had not witnessed the worst of his excesses, know the worst of his upbringing—he was *clawed* up people said—and yet here he was, convincing her all by himself, sinking fast into the old routine of slack-jawed stupidity.

thing. It was like he was trying to keep him alive."

"Praise his soul," said Molly, and the air seemed to darken and the room fell away and Samuel found himself a boy again, at the dinner table, his ears echoing with all manner of praises.

"Praise God for the carrots, praise Him for the potatoes, and praise His ever-loving heart for the lamb that gambols no more, and for the gravy that covers the flesh."

"Praise Father God!"

Sometimes the meal was cold before they could eat, his father praising the condiments and cutlery, once the very tablecloth. You had to put your knife and fork down between each mouthful and chew twelve times, once for each apostle, even sly Judas. Once Paul had chewed thirteen times not knowing father was keeping count, and he had been slapped upside the head and made to spit it out.

"You have the devil in your mouth, boy! What would you do if he got into your workings!"

Mother would sit quietly, pushing the pin deeper into her palm as she chewed to take away any pleasure she might receive from the food. By the end of the meal her plate would be spotted with blood but she never winced, not once, and father would smile at her show of strength then praise the custard and bless the jammy cake.

And all the while stern Jesus frowned down upon them from the beauty board. His dark eyes said *He* had no time for desserts; it was only blood that piqued his appetite.

Was it not fitting that his father should sing hallelujah to God's fare? Though not the turnip, his father viewed the turnip as the heretic of the vegetable world, an "unclean root." So often had he railed against it that even now Samuel held an aversion.

Father had so many prejudices—coloured sheets, scented soap, peat briquettes, any ice cream save vanilla, and the television presenter Dickie Davies; all were base.

Their neighbour Mrs. Robinson, a kindly woman with a crab-apple tree in her garden, suffered from diabetes—a fact which, when revealed, caused father to issue an injunction, delivered in the *strictest* manner, that on no account was any member of the family to so much as look at her.

"It is sin that courses through that harlot's body, sickly sweet sin, and that is the most contagious of all. Shun her, spit at her feet, run if you have to, but never look her in the eye. Heed me well."

"So you work here? I see you here all the time. I thought maybe you were just a really blatant paedophile." Her tone was playful rather than cruel.

"Yeah. I mean I work here. I'm not a perv."

"Relax, Dobson, I don't bite."

"Do you think you should be sitting there?"

Kate surveyed the park then brought her big greens back to rest on him. "I didn't realise I was breaking any laws. I don't see any signs."

"No, it's just what with everything that's been going on, maybe you shouldn't be out all alone. It isn't safe is what I'm saying."

"Well, why don't you sit down beside me and protect me."

Do you ever experience euphoria for no apparent reason?

He laughed, absurdly pleased by the notion. "I wouldn't be much use I'm afraid. If we were attacked we'd both wind up dead."

Her eyes sparkled, mimicking the frost. "You find this approach usually works?"

Approach? Did she think he was chatting her up? Was he? It was *her* who had spoken to him first. Was she teasing? Girls did that a lot; cats playing with their prey.

"And there's me thinking I'd found someone brave enough to walk me home. Guess I'll have to stay here and take my chances. But please, if I make the front pages tomorrow, don't feel guilty. You were honest about your shortcomings upfront."

He was about to answer when a scream rent the park.

Catman's kids, torn free from their bonds, running down the path toward them, hand in hand, fat tears rolling down their skinny cheeks.

The scream, louder now, desperate.

"Jesus! What's—"

Dobson was already gone, loping past the crying children holding out their malnourished arms to him, skidding by them, windmilling for balance, running toward the increasing howls, all the time wondering what the fuck he was going to do when he got there and remembered he was a coward.

And still the screams.

Do you have any problems shifting your bowels?

He came upon them in the playground. Michelle pressed up against the jungle gym clutching her baby to her chest, its tiny legs waggling each time she vented her lungs. Catman, drool cascading from his lips, clumsily trying to negotiate his way past a carved wooden rabbit, a knife in one hand and a cheap bottle of wine in the other.

"Help me, Dobson, he's trying to take my Lizzie!"

"The Devil's in the Moss!" said Catman, as if in agreement.

With the severed clothesline still clinging to his waist, he resembled some primeval beast that had burst its bonds. He seemed quite lucid today; he usually spoke (shitfuckfuckfuckshitfuck) like he had just stubbed a toe. He ignored Dobson completely. His wet doll eyes, sunk in the scarlet swamp of his face, were fixed firmly on the terrified girl and her bawling babe.

"Call the police, Dobson!"

"I invented the fucking police! I invented everything!" cried Catman cheerily.

Dobson heard footsteps behind him, turned to see Kate panting, her pale face flushed. Catman turned too, his eyes as unsteady as his feet. "Why do you want a little baby in the first place?" he asked, addressing the trees, then winced as if he was being yelled at. "Okay, okay, I'm doing it, stop your bloody nagging!"

Up close Catman appeared to have fallen asleep by a raging fire, melted, then cooled to his present shape in the sharp morning air. His eyebrow ridge, banged on so many kerbstones and walls, was a swollen crown of lumps protruding in Neanderthal glory. His ears were hellish flowers, mazes of flesh to trap unwary voices. The few teeth that still remained to him, browned to wooden pegs, clung on resolutely, lighthouses in his stormy mouth. His nose pancaked across his face in a brutal swipe.

"I'll rip your heart out!" he bellowed good naturedly. It had become his catchphrase over the years, losing all meaning and threat in the process. Kate circled him, but he was oblivious to all now save the squealing baby with the face like burst fruit. "I am your smokescreen," he slurred. "I'll do whatever you want, just get out of my fuckin' head!"

"Brendy, calm down, mate, put down the knife, okay?" He knew his words had no chance of penetrating Catman's frazzled brain, but what else could he say?

"Why does he want such a little thing?!" asked Catman, still regarding the child from beneath the mountains pushing through his forehead.

Kate was lifting a wooden squirrel, bringing it down with a hollow thunk on Catman's walnut of a head. Brendan went down in instalments, as if even unconsciousness struggled to gain a hold on his skewed reality.

Dobson stared at the worm of blood emerging from Catman's ear, transfixed by its shocking brightness, by the purity of its colour, that it was, in fact, red rather than the urine shade of wine. One of Catman's teeth jutted from his mouth like a tusk; the great beast had been defeated.

Do you ever feel shortness of breath?

Michelle broke the spell, standing over Catman she sank a small Ug boot into his head. Dobson turned away. He could hear the frost settling, cracking comfortably into place. He looked at Kate, the squirrel still hanging loosely in her grasp, her mittens stained a pestilent green. Over her shoulder he caught a glimpse of movement.

The sun stung his eyes, giving everything a starry aura, so that at first it seemed like one of the young saplings had uprooted and was walking off. He squinted away the blurring tears.

"Dobson? We should call the police. Dobson, you okay?"

Kate's voice was as thin as the figure he saw clearly now. He sucked in a ragged breath as Kate turned to see what spooked him so, and he wanted to tell her not to bother, the thin spectre was for his eyes only, a personal haunting, a private delirium, but as she covered her eyes and stared into the copse by the playground she spoke in a quiet, quizzical voice.

"Dooley?" she said.

Chapter 13

Even the air was different here.

Samuel breathed in deeply; oh, to be free of the council estates and the filth, if only for a few hours. Pepper's Trees lay before him, regimented, its bricks shining with a golden haze, not a milk bottle unwashed or out of place, the avenue of oaks lining the road like gentlemanly behemoths. As a boy in church, listening raptly to stories of Heaven, this is what he had envisaged lying behind the pearly gates.

The people here had full cream in their fridge, free-range eggs and briotta cheese. They had BMWs and Mercs in their double garages. They had respect in the community. Pepper's Trees was a quiz show of wealth and aspiration—*What's behind Door Four?* Why, the palatial living room of Doctor Dear. *Who's behind Door Six?* Only Stanley Simmons the bank manager, so upright he can't tie his own shoelaces. *Who would live in a house like this?* Why you, Samuel, and very soon, when the murders stop and the Moss yields up its secrets and the town turns to you for guidance. Then you'll be free of the rat-run estates forever.

So soon, Samuel, you can almost taste the crustless cucumber sandwiches, and smell the wood smoke as you lounge by the tennis court of Rodney Forsythe, MP, at his annual barbecue and fundraiser for the great and the good.

Mr. Forsythe probably paid someone to pull his zip up. Money was all about banishing embarrassment. That was what wealth meant.

As he walked the path to Molly's bungalow (like a man invited, not a skulking salesman) he caught a whiff of baking from her open windows. Baking! He was used to the ding of microwaves but now his talent had brought him here, to manicured lawns and wholesome air and the smell of baking.

Molly's garden was a patchwork delight, free from snow and ice, of litter and weeds. He climbed the ramp to her door, stroking the long handle that adorned the wall; no need for that anymore. She could buy herself a house with stairs again if she so wished. She had the momentum now, and she certainly had the money.

Samuel's heart fluttered. Perhaps some of that money could be earmarked for his church; a small sum, a trifle, a widow's mite. Was that too much to ask when he had restored her legs?

But he would not ask. No, he would wait until it was offered as it surely must. The good Lord would loosen her purse strings and then things would move on apace.

He pushed the doorbell expecting to hear Strauss, but instead it issued the clunky strains of a demented ice cream van; taste and wealth were ever uneasy bedfellows. There was a shuffling behind the door, as if his arrival had roused a nest of cloth serpents. *Probably the rustling of Molly's dewlaps*, he mused.

The door opened on her eager smile. He had barely time to say "Mrs. Stone" before he was ushered in, squeezed into an armchair and fussed over, his health checked and double-checked and his appetite fretted over.

"I'm dandy, Mrs. Stone," he assured her, feeling masterful and huge in her spotless dollhouse. He loved it all; the glass bowl with the porcelain cat and mouse, the radiogram, the mothball odour. It was all so homely. "What news?"

"He was asking after you, Samuel, and he sounded *so* angry. Why would he say such things? You of all people." Molly leaned forward in her chair. "He said you had strayed from the Lord."

"We must forgive him. He always had such energy for misunderstanding. You delivered my message of course."

"Of course." She slunk back into her seat, offended by the implication.

"Of course you did; you *are* my rock after all."

She beamed back at him, eyes as bright as hunter's lamps. A trapped breeze rattled at the door, as if something were trying to get in but lacked the strength.

"I'll need you to return to the Moss. I have something for you to place at the shrine."

"A thing of wonder?"

"An offering," said Samuel. "A completion if you will. A nod to past mistakes."

"And our church …"

"We'll build our church, Mrs. Stone, on that very spot. It has been foretold."

"The true church is in our hearts, that's what you taught me."

"Not I. The Lord Himself declared it. What we build is a focal point for our hearts, a place for them to beat together."

"Until the reckoning," she said, scratching contentedly at her lizard throat.

"Yes. One more visit to leave the offering. Bury it exactly where I tell you. I won't return there until I receive a sign. My intentions have been misunderstood."

"Isn't that always the way? Christ Himself—"

"Now, Mrs. Stone, I can hardly be compared with the Divine."

"But you are, Samuel. You are His messenger as surely as Christ was. Pure as the risen, bane to the followers of the dark, to the sneering wicked running from the path."

"I think you need to spend a little more time on your bible, then you will understand."

"I've no time now for musty old books. Why should I bother with dry words when I have them in the flesh to instruct me? Would you have me waste my few remaining years on ink when I can learn at your feet? Your modesty becomes you, Samuel, but it would be a sin to let it hamper your deeds. Tea or coffee?"

"Tea." Samuel's heart beat ever faster. To be appreciated in Pepper's Trees! As Molly hobbled off to the kitchen he picked up a newspaper then threw it away, the headline sticking in his craw.

The television had been full of the same nonsense all morning.

Although they were careful not to say as much, you could tell by their smug smiles and frantic scribbles, the use of so many well-informed yet anonymous insiders, they thought they had their man.

And what a man.

Brendan Harper, town derelict. A brine-pickled weasel incapable of rational thought. Preposterous. They would seek alibis for the dates in question but Brendan would have no notion of his whereabouts of the previous hour let alone the previous month.

Another murder would soon strangle their relief.

So why did he feel so angry; was there a gnawing doubt that this lumpen drunk was actually the killer? Absurd.

Molly returned with the tea tray and he concentrated on her instead, on his glory (*now, Samuel, don't be vain, you were merely the conduit*) personified. It did his heart good to see the result of his faith tottering before him. And they thought it could end so soon, and all because of a man who drank meths with aftershave chasers. Nonsense!

"You look very serious, Samuel. Have I done something wrong?" Molly set the tray down on a dainty little table, the tea still arcing, spilling over the rim like stray tears.

Samuel picked at the antimacassar, stirring a maelstrom in his cup. "It's all this rubbish in the papers. Brendan Harper. Are they so desperate they put their senses on hold? They'll be arresting you next."

"Me? What for? Do you want me to kill someone, Samuel? If it is for the good of the Lord—"

"No, no, Mrs. Stone. You have a role to play, as we all do, but our hands will not be sullied by blood. Our work is to bring forth light from this darkness. It's all part of His plan, and I can assure you His plan does not include a sodden wretch like Harper."

"He's not the killer?"

"Ridiculous. He once threatened me with a screwdriver for some spare change. I shook him like a bag of crisps. The sequence isn't finished yet. He wouldn't jeopardise it by entrusting it to an addict of the Devil's urine."

"I didn't think so, not really. There'll be more murders then?"

"Unless the police get lucky, I'm certain of it."

"God's good," soothed Molly reaching for a biscuit. "Why, they didn't catch that Sutcliffe for *years.*"

She offered him up the plate and he sat munching awhile in thought.

"You wouldn't believe how such a little thing can take you so far back; a song, a smell, a snatch of laughter. Take this chocolate lime, this … time machine. My father used to eat them every Sunday. He would let me and Paul have one, and one only, and while we gorbed ours he would nibble his. He was a big man, but so delicate, mannered as an old maid. You could still smell them on his breath when he kissed us goodnight. They were his sole decadence. Paul copied him in that of course, he mimicked him in all things; the tie, the hat, every-

His uncle always said father was odd as two's even, but he had raised them right—scared and moral.

"Penny for them?"

"Nothing, Mrs. Stone," said Samuel with a smile. "Silly really. You know Paul was eating one of these the night he ... I remember I was so angry with him. He was quoting scripture at me, accusing me of not reading my daily bread. I jabbed a finger in his face. Shouted at him. 'I would never do that to my brother,' he said. I think my hair streaked white that very night."

"The Lord touched you."

The room was drifting again. As Samuel took another bite of the biscuit it floated away completely.

"'Was it you, Paul?' I asked him. I didn't mention Eileen, but straight away he got defensive and that cemented his guilt for me. 'It's not what you think,' he said. 'Not what I think? You killed her!' I yelled. God forgive me, I didn't know."

"How could you have? The Lord had not lifted the scales from your eyes."

"I was hoping he would admit it, claim it was an accident. Paul laughed at me. For the first time in my life I hated him. All I could think of was the shame he had brought down on the family, of my father in Paradise, and how his laughter mocked us.

"'You've damned your soul,' I said, and that stopped his cackling. 'No, Samuel, I've joined the ranks of the marching saints! I set her free on His command and He welcomed me into His loving arms—I go to be with Him this very night!' Then he told me he would return, lead me to the light. Told me of the Moss and its secrets ... How could I have ever doubted him, my holy brother?"

Samuel brushed the crumbs from his trousers, watching the static pull at the hairs on his knuckles.

"'Samuel, thy name is Cain,' he said. He could see my doubt. He pulled a knife from the drawer, a cleaver that Joyce used to chop up bones for the mongrels she collected. Looking back, Paul had just been another stray; she was good to him though, good *for* him. For a moment I thought he meant to attack me. Yes, even I believed him capable. The veins were pulsing in his forehead, his face paper white, the rage sucking all the life out of him to stoke his hellish heartfire.

"'I give you this as a reminder, rather than thrust it in your face.' Before I knew what he was doing, before Joyce could stop him, he brought the blade down. I remember the glint more than the noise. The spray of blood, his gasp, like a man dunked in an icy pool. I remember his finger in a lake of crimson, for all the world like a squidge of pasta. But in dreams I hear the thwack. It sounds like the gates of Heaven slamming shut on me forever."

The doorbell went, the tinny muzak breaking Samuel's reverie.

"That'll be your special guest," Molly said. "The whore."

"Now, Mrs. Stone, we've discussed this. You must be nice to her, she's very important to our ministry."

"She's a Jezebel, Samuel, but I'll try for you. My Ernest would turn in his urn if he knew her batter-dripping cunt set foot in this house."

He was shocked by her language, still found it hard to believe she had such a primitive core. "Joyce suffers from a surfeit of love is all. It takes all sorts to spread the Word. Look in your heart for some charity and ignore the whispering Devil. She was Paul's choice after all."

"I understand. She is your Magdalene."

"I'm not Christ, Mrs. Stone."

She placed a hand barnacled with arthritis on his knee. "Aren't you?"

He was about to chastise her for her blasphemy but found he couldn't. He *was* a saviour of sorts, an amateur in the face of the Divine, but a saviour nonetheless. It would be more of a sin to deny it.

"Let her in, and wheel out some of your carrot cake. She'll like that."

The smell of gin seeped into the room before her. His heart sank when he saw her face. It seemed to have plummeted south, her grin like a child's finger tracing a crescent in dough, her dull eyes full of lascivious mischief. Please, Lord, don't let her flirt with me in front of Mrs. Stone.

"Hi Ho Silver!" She licked her lips as she rubbed at her crotch, her large breasts squeezed into a top that a ten year old would find constricting, her nipples jutting out blatantly. *You could hang a wet duffel coat on one of those*, he thought before he could stop himself.

"Hello, Mrs. Heather."

"Oooh, Mrs. Heather! We are very la-di-dah when we're out and about." Truly, she could make an onion weep.

"You've met Mrs. Stone?" He knew she had, knew Molly had taught her, her mother too no doubt, but it was something to say.

"We go way back. I was a *bad* girl then wasn't I, Wooden Tits? Not that I'm entirely good now, I've just got better at not getting caught." She giggled; a dirty, trouser-tightening giggle.

Samuel began to sweat. She was vice insatiate. He could tell what she'd had for lunch by looking at the stains on her top. He gave a tentative sniff; chicken korma. Yet evidently she was still hungry.

"I could eat the beard off Moses," she said, flopping herself down and helping herself to biscuits. The capacity of her mouth mesmerised him. She started sucking on a chocolate finger, her dimples flexing, and he had to utter a silent prayer for strength as her slurping filled the room.

Mrs. Stone was right. She was a Jezebel, a beautiful devil.

"Did you bring it?" he asked, not daring to look away from his Fig Roll; he was very aware she was sitting with her legs akimbo. He could swear he could feel the heat emanating from *there*.

"Of course, my Silver," she said, draining the last of her tea from her saucer. She had absolutely no manners, was thoroughly wanton. A hussy.

She was the antithesis of his mother, the kind of woman his father warned him of, right down to her coloured bra. *God lend me fortitude in this, the hour of my temptation*, he thought, as Joyce placed a small jewellery box on the coffee table.

"It's a bit smelly I'm afraid."

He could feel Joyce's breath on his neck as he leaned over, smell her cheap perfume mingled with sweat, and his hand trembled slightly as he removed the lid. Inside, on a bed of velvet, lay what looked to be a moldy twig. It smelt bad, eclipsing even Molly's scones.

His brother's index finger.

A peace offering. A completion. A way of saying he believed him now.

"I've tried everything to keep it good. Kept it in the back of the freezer for years, until Dobson came home drunk one night and bunged it in the pan with some bacon."

"A relic. A holy relic," said Molly, almost to herself. "Dare I touch it? Dare I lick it?"

Before she could reach out to snatch it, Samuel had it in his palm. As soon as he touched it the rain began. A rain of blood. Inside the house.

"Spiders and slugs and goats and monkeys!"

A pool formed on the carpet, the curtains stained with vital red death, and the walls shook with a wicked guttural malice. Teeth fell from the ceiling, and as Samuel stared up at the sudden deluge several fell into his open mouth.

They said Nadine Craig's teeth had been beaten out, he thought as he gagged. Samuel put his hands over his head as they rattled down upon him like rotting popcorn, covering his lap in yellow shale. Some of them still had strands of bleeding gum attached, as if they had been torn from the jaw. He hunkered under the onslaught, hearing Molly's frightened yelps, feeling Joyce's long nails pierce his skin.

"Don't worry," he said as the brief shower began to peter out. "It's not real, it's just a show. He is putting on a show just for us."

Chapter 14

He had never really paid much attention to her scar before—her hair usually covered it—but today she wore her hair scraped back and the scar was a livid red snake curling round her temple. Dobson liked it. If anything it enhanced her beauty.

He had her cornered, pressed against a clunky carousel of bulky holiday novels, their fat spines barely legible. He was feeling bloated too. He had just had two plates of what his mum called "spaghetti hogdown", and he could feel the sharp press of gas blocking his tubes. He was acutely aware now was not a good time to break wind, especially in the echoing sepulchral confines of the library.

"Hello hero, hero hello," Kate said. He wasn't sure if she was mocking him; he had been pretty useless after all, though her eyes were kind. "What's the name of that aftershave you're wearing—Overcompensate?"

"It was the last of the bottle. You're the hero," he said sheepishly. "You didn't half clobber him."

"I just got in before you did. Thanks for taking the credit though. I told you Michelle would be too stressed to remember much. Last thing I need is the press round my house. My dad … he'd go ballistic."

"Thing is," said Dobson, "I don't think either of us are heroes. I mean Catman? Brendy Fuckfuck? I've known him all my life, he's just a pisshead. The only thing he's murdered is his brain cells. You haven't lived here that long, but surely it's obvious he's no criminal mastermind."

"We did a *good* thing, Dobson. He scared the crap out of that poor girl, who knows what he's capable of. If he's innocent they'll let him go soon enough and, from what I hear, he's not exactly new to Her Majesties' hospitality. It'll give him time to dry out if nothing else. It's all good, Dobson."

"I guess."

The library was empty save for a few elderly blow-ins who had wandered by to flick through the papers, scanning the obituaries to see who they had outlived, and a fat woman who was a regular, devouring equally fat romances on the spot as if she couldn't wait to take them home.

He was safe here. For Dobson the library held all the awe and sanctuary of a church. Now Kate was here and it seemed complete. It felt like she had been born in the stacks, a product of classical imagination and daydreaming.

"So, where's your friend?"

A simple question but Dobson was sure the crack of his heart was audible over the muted coughs and spluttering. How could he have been so foolish to think that a girl like Kate would be interested in him? Of course she was using him as an in with one of his mates. Pruner most likely. Dumbass Dobson—taken for a mug once more.

"Which one?"

"You've more than one?" Her eyes were playful but her words stung nonetheless. "That guy used to come in here with you sometimes. The grumpy one. Looks like he irons his hair."

"Malcolm?"

It was worse than he thought. Pruner he could handle, it had the law of inevitability to it, but Malcolm—that was a kick in the balls by laughing Satan, that was just—

"That his name? He's a bit of a geek. He comes in a lot now, not that he ever takes anything out, just hangs round by the CDs."

"I haven't seen him much recently; he's got a bit strange. I don't know what I've done on him."

"You're better off without guys like that, trust me. He's a bit creepy, don't you think?"

Her bluntness cheered him; she was what mum would call an "earthy type with no back doors." He felt no guilt, only relief, putting the boot into a lifelong friend. Part of him revelled in it.

"He is a cold fish, I suppose."

"I'll say. He stands over there for hours, staring at me. I'm beginning to think I've a stalker."

"He probably fancies you."

"You think? Well, he's definitely pissing up the wrong lamppost. I'm *so* not interested. I've got my eye on someone else."

She blushed slightly, lowered her gaze, then looked back at him full on; a challenge, a declaration. Dobson, victim of low self-esteem and crippling insecurity, felt his head bump the ceiling as his heart kickstarted and raced headlong into pastures new.

He could only stare back at her, aware he should say something but totally devoid of any notion of what those words could possibly be. She dropped her eyes, disappointment etched on her face, and before he could rectify the situation she said, "You're staring at my scar. I'm not deformed, y'know. Don't treat me like a freak."

"No, Kate, I wasn't … I didn't even …"

"Notice it? Come on, Dobson."

"Of course I noticed it, not that it's … Ah Christ, Kate, I was looking at *you*. I'm useless at this." He looked around, expecting a shepherd's crook to appear stage left at any moment. "I thought you were coming onto me and no-one ever does that and … You're so beautiful. I could stare at you all day."

She blushed fully now, the blood dancing under her skin, and Dobson had to bite his tongue as a playground taunt entered his mind—*Tomato Head, round and red!*—his mouth had got him into enough trouble.

"I *was* coming onto you, dummy! Do you always make things complicated or where you just born clumsy?"

"Tripped over the umbilical and went ass over tit into the bucket."

Everything apart from her face began to dissolve, to fade away in a murky bleached fog, whilst her features took on a clarity that almost blinded him. The snake-like scar became more prominent, racing across her skin like molten lava, cracking at his eyes like a whip. He felt irretrievably lost.

"So, the scar. What happened?"

"Quit while you're ahead, boy. Let's just say I was a tomboy as a kid, a bit wild. Will I see you tonight?"

"Yeah, sure, I mean, if you want to. I'll pick you up. Where do you live?"

"No, that won't work. I'll call for you. My dad's a bit funny about me dating. Only child, y'know the kind of thing."

Dating. A date. He was going on a date with a girl. Malcolm would have a fit!

"You don't know where I live."

She pointed over to the computer squatting on the counter. "See that big magic box over there? It's got all your details in it, even your phone number."

"See you later then."

"About eight."

"Where would you like to go?"

"How about we be spontaneous. You can be spontaneous I take it?"

"Yeah, given enough notice. Eight then."

"Bye, Dobs."

"Oh, Kate, I almost forgot to ask you. In fact, it was why I came in. That guy in the park, Dooley you called him. Do you know him?"

"Dooley? He comes in sometimes, reads the papers over there in God's waiting room. Why?"

"You know where he lives?"

"No. I figured he was homeless by the look of him."

"I don't think so. He has a car."

"He does? Maybe he stole it, or maybe he is an eccentric millionaire. Listen, Dobson, I really better get back to work."

She gave him a peck on the cheek, whispered, "Eight o'clock." The proximity of her mouth was enough to buckle his spine. Then she wandered off through History into Fantasy, her ponytail swinging hypnotically.

"What a girl," he thought, Dooley forgotten, as he floated through the library doors and out into the street, where even the icy raindrops were an echo of her kiss.

Chapter 15

Pruner stood by the door of the church hall collecting the money. Scene of such recent miracles, it would be a wonder if he broke even tonight he thought sourly. Where was everybody?

The band was on in ten minutes and the place was barely half full. It was typical of Skinner not to show for his getting out of hospital bash, but where the fuck was Dobson? He hadn't seen him in weeks. Had he gotten too big for his boots since he crigged Brendy Fuckfuck?

He wasn't expecting Malcolm to show; in truth, he hoped he wouldn't. Malcolm had barely spoken to him since he had asked to move in with him, and Pruner had laughed in his face. Malcolm had looked haunted, diluted somehow, but Pruner had problems of his own, and unlike the popular theory, *his* misery was definitely a soloist. Besides, the thought of sharing the flat with Malcolm Darkcloud was too ridiculous for words.

Yet would it have killed Skinner to pop his face in for five minutes after all the effort he had put in?

Skinner had crashed on the back roads. He hadn't been travelling fast so, apart from a rather hefty blow to the nut, he was fine. But Pruner couldn't help wondering if he was back on the soup— God knows he could put it away when he started. As a kid his capacity was legendary; he could drink grown men into oblivion, and not just piss beer either. Skinner was a whiskey head.

Drew had once, in a fit of bravado, drank plum poteen with him.

Skinner had put him to bed within an hour, informing them the next day that Proctor was "merely a kitten." All farm boys had such bottomless appetites. Skinner had left the farm now, and the boozing too. They hardly ever saw him down The Cove now unless he was picking up a fare. He was like a tortoise; he never left home.

He was stand-offish now, though he would relate his money worries at the drop of a hat. No, "Hey Pruner, how's you these days?". Just mortgages and the price of diesel. The cops had been hounding him lately, too, questioning him about the murders; what with him being a cabbie, they figured he had easy access to the girls and, lacking a natural suspect, they'd been leaning on him hard.

Now he had wrecked the motor, or rather his brother's motor, and his income was lying in a heap in Hunniford's breaker's yard. If he had been drinking—and claiming you had been attacked by Ma Stone seemed to back that up—his license would be down the drain with his livelihood.

His brother Les wasn't talking to him, nor his wife Beth. Pruner had tried to do something nice for him to cheer him up and he had shunned the gesture offhand. Fuck him; let him stew in his Bush and his Bells. *To be fair*, he thought, *if I had a wife like her I'd be on the sauce every fucking night.*

According to Drew, who always seemed to know such things as if he were tabloid made flesh, Beth had left all his gear round the hospital and told him not to come home. She always was a vicious, money-grabbing little bitch. Could be the accident was a blessing in disguise.

Not that Morris would see it that way, soft touch that he was. He was probably broken hearted as well as just plain broke. A time to turn to your friends, or to wallow in self-pity? Looks like Mo had made up his mind on that score.

Pruner warned him years ago not to saddle himself with that mare and he had gone ahead and did it anyway. That had been the start of the divide.

Drew had told him of the break up with a manic glee in his eye. Drew had always had a thing for Beth and, though his neck would always be thicker than his wallet, she returned the interest. Pruner had noticed; they all had, apart from Skinner, the dozy cunt.

All he could see were his debts, the ones his bitch of a wife dangled constantly in his face. He probably dreamt of invoices and final notices.

He was better off without that succubus. The thought cheered him. Maybe now Skinner would return to the fold, would join them once more on long drunken weekends (*And what bar shall we frequent now, Mr. Skinner? Why my favourite, Mr. Rose—The Open Door*) and things would stop slipping away and getting so goddamn … grown up.

Let Beth hound herself out some other mug, like a pig snuffling out a truffle, all the while moistening herself at the thought of a brain-dead bad boy like Drew. Then things could be the way they used to be. The way they were *supposed* to be.

They could all head down to the Moss like old times, a perfect reunion, and camp out when the summer came. His sudden enthusiasm cooled. In his mind his heartbeat sounded like a solemn gong. The Moss … it scared him a little to think of there. He'd been dreaming of it lately, dreams he'd rather forget.

He heard the first twang of a bass string, the first thwack of a snare, and a few half-hearted insults. Bullskull were on. "Take over for a while, Drew, okay?"

Drew turned from the underage girl he had been hypnotising with his wit. "No probs, *mein kommandant.*"

He would likely pocket any cash that happened to drip in at this late hour, or exact revenge in one of his many ongoing feuds with the clientele, but Pruner had had enough; he was determined to enjoy the fruits of his labour even if no-one else did.

He entered the hall as the first song started and was bored by the first strangled chorus. To think he once thought these guys were the dog's balls. Now they sounded so prosaic it was untrue. All music bored him now; soon a car alarm would be released as a single and make number one. *This technological advancement,* he thought, *had the ability to make you despise what you once loved.*

It wasn't the band's fault to be fair. Lately he had been developing at such a rate he couldn't even listen to his own albums, he was so busy making his own sound. He was so far ahead of the game, so *beyond* the concept of music, that he burst out laughing at the half-assed applause that greeted the end of the song.

Not that he expected anyone to appreciate his opus, not for years at any rate, but that was a burden he was willing to carry, something all innovators had to shoulder. Dobson might though; Dobson was *smart*, Dobson had an ear. He was tempted to let him hear it; even though it wasn't finished, he was so sure he would get it. Where the fuck was he?

He scanned the meagre crowd again, his eyes sticking on a pair of legs straight out of a fantasy poster; Amazonian legs, tanned and muscular, topped by a belt of a skirt that hugged impossibly round globes. A long mane of honey hair halfway down her back, not an inhibition in sight. He felt his chest tighten, grow cold. Who the—

She spun round, gyrating in anticipation of the first chord that duly struck as her breasts' orbit swung into view.

Christa Finchley.

He felt a sudden lash of hatred. He despised being fooled like that, but then again who else could it have been, who else was built like that in Ellsford. She might have the personality of a dung beetle but she had been sculpted by a horny adolescent God. As Drew was wont to point out, "She could make you spill your milk at the gate."

He watched her dance, his eyes glued to her perfect skin just like every other hairy eyeball in the place; and man, didn't she know it. He felt a stiffening in his jeans despite himself. Disgusted, he drained the last of his can and, thinking "Death's a girl," headed out through the fire exit into the sharp, wit-clearing night.

When exactly would his opus be finished? That was something to concentrate on. Every time he thought he was nearing completion it seemed to grow, to expand in ever new directions. Already it was a truly monstrous length. It had taken on a life of its own, but he would know when it reached fulfilment; he would *sense* it. It was part of him now, as integral to his existence as his heart, his lungs.

He fired up a cigarette, watching the stars wink back at him from the black shroud above. They looked sharp enough to shave with. His ears needed popping on one side. At night in bed he could hear his heartbeat in his skull, the sound of someone pounding on a distant tin gate, and it kept him awake. He must have water in it or something; it had been driving him crazy the last few days. That and the serpentine voice that sang to him. Now he wondered if he might not just have discovered the perfect intro to his masterpiece.

He took out a half bottle of vodka from his coat pocket and raised it to his lips. "To the death of matrimony, nuclear families, work in the morning and responsibility." He took a long tear-inducing swallow. He wasn't a little kid anymore; he was a fucking artist.

"My, my, Billy Rose. Don't you know there are no chemical solutions to spiritual problems?"

He looked up to see Christa closing the fire door behind her. Although made for sunlight, for total exposure, she looked spectrally beautiful in the moonlight.

"Looks like even you can't stand the band, and you booked them." She staggered toward him, giggling as she nearly fell, and he realised she was more than a little loaded. He couldn't remember if that dulled her awfulness or merely enhanced it.

"You seemed to be enjoying them," he said. "Quite the show you put on. All was missing was the pole."

He turned away, unwilling to give her the enjoyment of his gaze; she was an attention junkie, she fed on eyes. She had once won The Flower Of Ellsford, but she was no rose; she was a penis flytrap.

"I like dancing," she pouted.

She stood toe to toe with him, forcing him to look into the vast natural valley of her décolletage, or her piercing green eyes that glowed with a catlike luminosity. They implied a deep intelligence, one she never revealed in conversation.

She grinned as his eyes gorged themselves on her, shaking out her smooth doll hair that reeked of coconut and God knows what other unpronounceable extracts. Her teeth were blindingly white; shark teeth. He shivered, though the night was mild, the season on the turn.

"Bullskull are a fucking great band, but I guess an airhead like you can't appreciate anything more complex than a nursery rhyme."

She moved ever closer. He could smell the Juicy Fruit on her breath. "On the contrary," she said, her voice little more than hot breath on his neck. "I love to bump and grind. I love rock."

She touched him, and he flinched, as if a tarantula had crawled up his skin instead of her perfect little hand. Her lips were so close now. Pruner felt his body tense like catgut. Then those lips were on his ear, her hands unbuckling his belt.

"And I *love* cock."

She was on her knees, those bright red lips encasing him, the scrape of those ivory fangs sending him back against the wall gasping. "If you don't exercise the pig," she said, "the bacon will be all rind."

He watched the top of her head awhile, bobbing professionally, her slurping louder than the drums clattering under the door, and felt nothing save mild loathing. The smell of urine caught his nostrils as a breeze picked up, and for a moment he saw himself as from above, as if he had soared from his body in contempt; a young man in a piss-streaked alley, a cheap tart chomping on him like a piglet at a trough.

A shaft of light fell on him like an epiphany as the fire door opened. Christa stared up at him with vacuous eyes, eyes that looked painted on, eyes too big for her face. He looked up to see Dobson silhouetted in the doorway. Before he could explain himself, before he could extract himself from the empty skull devouring him, the shadow departed.

Ah Christ, thought Pruner.

He grabbed Christa by a clump of her supernaturally soft hair and pounded his frustration into her mouth, working his hips into a frenzy. Apologies could wait until after gratification, however fleeting or meaningless either might be.

Christa moaned in pleasure; pain was second nature to her kind.

Chapter 16

Drew gave the cloth a final swoosh across the leather seat and stood back with a satisfied grin. Perfect. The bike gleamed as if it had just popped out of a genie's lamp. Man and machine faced each other in total disparity, for Drew was caked in grease and sweat. Still, at least he had got the rest of the badger off his wheels.

"I nearly hit a badger," he said aloud. No-one was ever interested in his bike stories so he told them to himself. "But I just give the wrist a twist and lightened the front wheel, didn't want barbecued badger on my pipes now did I? Remember, just give the wrist a twist."

He ran a finger along the bike's sleek, gleaming surface. "You're so beautiful," he said softly. "So damn sexy." Lately he had taken to sniffing the petrol in her fuel tank to get a cheap high, but sometimes his mouth lingered there in an almost kiss.

Talking of sexy, what about Beth soon to be no longer Skinner.

How horny was she.

She had always given him the glad eye, but a couple of nights ago he had bumped into her over at the Cedar Inn in Blackmore, where she'd been dancing with some skinny bit with no jugs and a wonky eye (hot girls always knocked around with total skanks he found). Rolling drunk, the pair of them.

As soon as he realised her prick of a husband wasn't there he made his presence known, and it was Bacardi Breezers all round.

I'm a predator at the watering hole, he thought, giving the tank a lingering rub. *I'll drill that little slut given half a chance; I'll make her cat bark.* She had told him that she and farmer boy were over in no uncertain terms; something about not being a provider, or some other chick rubbish, he was barely listening. He went stone deaf when she grabbed him by the crotch.

"Why don't you drop by some night," she whispered, "make sure I don't get lonely."

Tonight's your lucky night. He climbed onto the bike. He wouldn't bother washing, all that sweat and oil would be a real turn on for her. Girls like her, all stuck up and frustrated, loved that mucky shit. Tarts like her were so damn dirty; they just liked to hide it.

Part of him wished it was Christa but, as he started up the Yamaha, letting it sing, he knew he was invisible to that bitch no matter how loud he revved his bike. The noise of the exhaust soothed him. *That's the sound of my ballbag,* he thought, *I'm a fucking Tyrannosaur.*

His mother appeared in front of the handlebars and he killed the engine.

"I've told you before, wheel that deathtrap to the bottom of the street before you start it. You know your dad's on shifts. Where are you off to anyways? Where's your helmet? Are you going near the shops?"

"I'm just popping round to a mate's."

"Not Elsie Rose's boy I hope. I've warned you about him before. They say he's on them drugs, and God knows what else."

"Pruner's alright, mum. Anyway, I'm heading round to Skinner's."

"Morris Skinner? The taxi boy? That's worse! You've heard what they're saying about him? Those poor wee girls. If you think Brendan Harper, God help his poor wife, had anything to do with those murders you must've been born in a bean tin. Did you say you were going to the shops or not? I need eggs—"

"No, I'm not. Skinner lives the other side of town."

"You be careful, you hear? Police are never away from that house lately. Now mind you wheel that thing clear before you crank it. Clear mind, hear me?"

There was more chance of her klaxon of a voice waking his old man, but he bit his lip.

"Will you be back for your tea?"

"Not if I get lucky?"

"What?"

"I'll get a Kentucky."

Drew trundled the bike down the path and out through the gate, pointing it toward Mill Street at the bottom of the road. He jumped on the Yamaha, stoking it up to a vengeful howl, speeding out of Mill Street like the coming apocalypse, heading out to God's country, to Troughton's quarry and Skinner's house and the Moss beyond.

The Moss.

It had been years since he had been down there, though he had practically grown up there. So many good times, so many *great* times— he'd popped his cherry down there when he was only thirteen—but he had not been back since the day, what, five or six years ago?, when he and Pruner and Mad Dobson and Dutch Holland had gone down to build a hut.

The bike hit a patch of ice and wobbled alarmingly before he got it back under control. *Fucking amateur*, he berated himself, his heart pounding, but it wasn't the wobble that caused it to race; no, it was thinking of that day down the Moss, that day with the bloody crows.

He hadn't thought about that in so long, hadn't so much as mentioned it. None of them had, like it would be bad luck to bring it up, or they had made some unspoken, collective effort to forget.

He wondered if the others had the nightmares too.

He pushed it to the back of his mind, convinced it was an ill omen that it should crop up again now for no reason, but as he sped down Horseshoe Lane and the turn off to the Moss the image of all those birds, and Dutch's screaming face, refused to go away.

He hared round a bend, giving the machine far too much juice, taking it far too wide, almost smearing himself against the grille of an oncoming truck, pulling by it on in instinct only, its blaring horn chasing him on to ever greater speed. The breath inside his helmet grew stale, the sound of his heart heavy in his ears, but he could not outrun the memories that came clawing back.

It had been a glorious day that summer; his whole childhood seemed to be made up of such sunny days, each one melting into the other. They had trekked down to the Moss just as they had on countless other days, armed with a frying pan and bacon and eggs and whatever else they could scrounge off their mothers.

The rain started, splashing on his visor, blurring the horizon, but he didn't slow down nor dare look in his mirrors. He could feel the Moss crouching at his back no matter how fast he went.

They went swimming in the pool by the quarry first, and he remembered his pride amongst all those skinny runts; dressed only in a pair of footy shorts, his burgeoning muscles oak hard, his chest a barrel and his back an upside down triangle.

Pruner never took his top off, he'd wear an anorak in a sauna, and Dutch was built like a pull through for a rifle. And Dobson, fucking hell, how many times had he threatened him that summer that he was going to ring the Welfare? His spine was so thin it had a joke wrote on it. He had never seen anyone so skinny. He could've got a job on a ghost train. The heaviest thing about him were those big bullock eyes.

They had dried themselves on the bank after dinner—did anything ever taste as good as bacon and eggs cooked on a campfire on a summer's day?—and after rehashing the long-running debate of whether Spiderman should have eight legs, the talk got round to the serious business of building a clubhouse.

They built one every year, spent months renovating them and building extensions before abandoning them when school kicked back in, starting from scratch again the following year. The Moss was strewn with such deserted derelicts. In a thousand years archaeologists would uncover them and ponder over this previously unknown civilisation.

Because of problems last summer when some older kids had found their clubhouse and burnt it they had much to discuss. One of them had even taken a dump on his seat, and used the best porn mag he had to wipe his manky arse. The big question then was where to relocate. Most of the supplies grew naturally, and the construction site by the quarry was always a goldmine for gear. They just needed somewhere off the beaten track, somewhere *nobody* would find.

Enter the Dobson, as Pruner was wont to say.

No-one knew the Moss like he did.

"I was conceived here," he used to brag. "So my mum says." And as much as Drew hated to dwell on that he figured it must be true, for that little ferret could sniff his way round there like a bushman. No matter how many times they went down there, Dobson always managed to find a new turning, an unexpected path to an unforeseen clearing.

So naturally it was Dobson who said he had found a new spot, one that was perfect. After a smoke and a gallon of water, after the sun had dried the last of the murky pool from their skin, they followed him into the heart of the Moss until every tree looked the same, and all but

Happy Heather were hopelessly lost.

It was so alive, you could almost hear it growing, the air filled with smudge clouds of midges and gridlocked with birdsong.

Drew felt sick. He remembered that vividly, could taste the metallic backwash in his mouth. Then Dutch threw up. If it hadn't been for Pruner he probably would have decked Dobson.

"You and those fucking eggs!" Pruner had laughed, and so had he, but it was a thin laugh full of nerves. Looking back they had all felt it.

Felt the *wrongness* of the place; it kind of started in your feet and oozed all the way up into your guts and into your brain. But Dobson was whistling, and there was no way a two-stone gerbil was going to show Drew Proctor up, so he followed on, shouting a battle cry to show he wasn't scared, even as his balls shrivelled up into a walnut.

The cry died in his throat when he entered the clearing.

He slowed the bike down; the turn off to Skinner's was close. His breath was galloping away from him, steaming up his lid, fogging his senses.

There was a large tree at the back of the clearing that dominated the saplings around it. It was quiet here, far too quiet, and the sun hid behind a cloud as if ashamed to watch.

Hanging from the tree by their feet were hundreds of crows, blood dripping, falling in huge wet splashes from their ugly stony beaks.

No-one moved, no-one spoke.

Dutch broke the spell, walking forward, looking back at them as if *he* couldn't believe he was doing this either, reaching up to touch the nearest bird, sending it spinning like some hideous berry.

"It's still warm," he said, his voice full of awe. "It's still fucking warm."

Then Dutch froze, staring at something behind the trunk, something they couldn't see. Then Dutch screamed; screamed like all the hordes of hell were trying to crawl up his butt. Drew had never heard anyone scream like that, *never.*

They turned and ran. They didn't need to see what made Dutch Holland, who could fight like a fucking Trojan, lose it like that.

They would never know, not now, even if they wanted to.

Dutch died two years ago in a car wreck on the Old Park Road. Maybe Dutch had screamed like that once more, just before the car left the road and smashed into a telegraph pole. Maybe, but Drew doubted it.

Drew had run. He was faster than the matchsticks in front of him, but he was big and clumsy too, and the path that Dobson led them down was thin and full of brambles. He tripped on a root, and before he could get up something rolled him over, something with sharp claws that sank into his sunburnt flesh, something with hot stinking breath that made him screw his eyes up tight (yes, that was why he closed his eyes) as it sniffed him over, its drool falling on his skin, scalding him.

In his head a madman rattled the bars of his cage. He lost control and soiled himself. He cried. And he never mentioned it to anyone again ever.

With a roar the thing leapt from him, bounding up the straggly path after the others. He lay there a long time before finding the courage to drag himself up and run the whole way home. Next day, though no-one brought it up, they unanimously decided to build a tyre swing over the river by Hollywell, and the summer carried on, as long and glorious as it had ever been.

He never set foot in the Moss again.

It had been a dog of course. A big mangy farmer's dog out scaring up rabbits, or digging up badger holes. Yet before he had scrunched up his eyes he had caught a glimpse; dogs did not have such cruel, such human eyes.

He turned the corner, decreasing speed until he reached the lane leading to Skinner's bungalow. The cab wasn't there. It was wrecked after all. There was no sign of the hapless hick as he eased the bike down the loose gravel toward the house.

"It was a dog," he said into the padded confines of his helmet. "Just a mutt." He began to imagine Beth bent over the kitchen table to chase away those summer ghosts.

It was a cream bungalow with a bright green fence, its front garden perfect as pins; what his mum would have called a Babby House. There was no sign anyone was home. He hadn't even heard Max bark at his approach. The blinds were pulled on the kitchen window and there was no way to see in. Had he rode the whole cut out here for nothing? The door was open. Someone was home alright. He walked straight in, closing the door behind him, she had invited him after all. He would surprise her, take her there and then, she'd love that; dirty bitch.

The kitchen was a stew of shadows and half-light. It was a while since he had been here—Skinner wasn't much for the ol' hospitality lately, content to stay in and squirrel away his money as he pissed and moaned about his lot. No wonder his missus was gagging for it.

He remembered the little room they used as an office further down the hall, the one where they kept the radio, and that was where Beth was bound to be, directing her brother-in-law around the mean streets of Ellsford, Avondale, Blackmore and beyond.

The hall was long and narrow; no windows, no natural light. He hesitated with his hand on the switch. He didn't want to give himself away just yet. He could see the office door ajar, hear a blast of static, and he proceeded down the hall grinning, his heavy boots muffled by deep carpet.

The closer he got the worse he began to feel, his throat constricting, his erection withering.

Fucking Moss, he thought, *why did I have to go thinking about all that shit again?* He could not shake the feeling that once again he was walking into a *bad place*, and that this *bad place* might be even worse.

He heard the crunch of the radio, a muffled chirrup of a voice, but if Beth was in there she wasn't answering.

He couldn't go back now. He was no pisspants little runt like Weir. He burst into the office, his boots pounding on the wooden floor. No-one here. So why was he so scared?

A crunch of static once more. Something, some dim shape, slumped behind the desk. He flicked the light on by the door, temporarily blinded by the fluorescents, and moved to the other side of the room. He froze, at first unable to comprehend what he was seeing, then scrunching his eyes up to make it go away.

She was naked. Her head was gone. In its place was a rough-hewn spike, and sitting precariously atop that spike, dripping blood down onto her heavy breasts, was the head of Max, Skinner's docile old Rottweiler.

Another blast of static, more muffled voices. The radio mike was shoved in her pussy. Its crack and blur broke his trance and, stomach hurtling to the top floor emergency exit, he turned to run, slipping, crashing down into a pool of blood that covered his hands, his face; *it's so* red, he thought.

He heard Dutch say, "It's still warm", and a cry escaped him as he skidded to his feet, fleeing the Babby House, pinballing down the hallway.

Outside he ran on into the pouring rain, waiting for a roar that never came.

Chapter 17

The Wednesday Club was in session.

The bar was filled with betting slips and newspapers folded to the racing section, the television tuned to the meet at Haydock. The Cove would be virtually empty if not for the few hardy souls that made up the Wednesday Club—a squad of heavy drinkers and heavier gamblers, a cocktail of the retired and the unemployable.

The mood was quieter than usual, the drone of the commentators lulling the patrons into deep contemplation. It was raining needles outside. The beer garden was flooded so Dobson, Malcolm, and Pruner, choking for a cigarette but unwilling to brave the elements, huddled at a table inside, nursing a few unwanted pints.

The barman flicked the telly over to the news.

The newsreader, or presenter, or whatever these jugglers called themselves now, was standing imperiously amidst huge screens; a hall of mirrors reflecting only tragedy. On one was the Prime Minister, on another an Arab mouth open in mid-rant (it made it easier for you to realise he was the bad guy), on another the President of the Goddamn Yew Nigh Ted States. And there, in the middle, towering over the news seller in company too surreal to accept, was Beth Skinner.

"Another murder in Ellsford," said the hawker, making it real.

"It's hard to get your head round," said Dobson. "Do you really think Drew could have done it?"

They had all taken the day off when news of Skinner's wife had broken. They all agreed to meet up when they heard Drew was arrested. But only now, when it was on television, did it start to sink in.

"'Course he fucking did it!" spat Malcolm. He was, if possible, in a sourer mood than usual. His skin was tinted grey around his panda eyes. He looked awful. "Proctor's a fucking psycho, always was."

"Drew's a bighead with a big mouth," said Pruner, "but that doesn't make him Jack the Ripper."

"Maybe not, but his prints were smeared all over the house, his clothes covered in her blood, he damn near hit a truck flying from the scene—what more do you want? Cops didn't lift him for nothing Pruner."

There was silence, broken only by the three thirty at Newmarket, as they sat pondering these indisputable facts.

The rumour mill was in overdrive, spewing out wave after wave of gory detail; her head had been lopped off and replaced by a balloon, a football, a turnip; her legs had been fed to the dog; the killer had daubed a satanic message in blood, semen, stating there would be another three, four, five murders and soon.

For all the gossip, the bare facts laid out by Malcolm were set in stone. Frank McDowell said Drew had nearly squashed himself like a bug on his bumper, and someone on the police force had leaked the info about Drew's prints to the plague of journos descending on the town once more.

"I knew it," said Malcolm. "I knew that big he-bitch was bad news. Knocking round with us all this time, making jokes about this shit, the sick fuck."

"We don't know for sure though," said Dobson. He didn't really like Drew, never had, but he still felt the need to defend him, from Malcolm if nobody else. It was wrong to turn on your own.

"Yeah, well who else could it be, smart guy? Catman Harper? Maybe you're not as big a hero as you pretend to be, eh?"

Malcolm's anger only fuelled Dobson's; the dig at his brief fling with stardom was typical of him lately. Finding out the guy you thought was your dad was actually a stranger was a bound to be a kick in the clackers, but the truth was Mal had been a toxic pain in the hole for years. Chip on the shoulder? Try a hundred weight of spuds.

Dobson took a deep breath. "I'm just saying, why? What was his reason?"

"Hello! He's a psycho." Malcolm slammed his hand down on the table, sending a beermat gyroscoping off its edge.

"Dobs is right," said Pruner. "Think about it a minute, Mal. Who's been acting out of character lately, been a virtual recluse, who's personality has changed? Who's always moaning about money problems, problems at home, problems, problems, problems? Who had good reason to kill Beth and the opportunity to kill the others? Who's went AWOL since his wife was sliced and diced?"

"Skinner Mo?" Dobson's voice was small with shock. It seemed so obvious, but he hadn't thought of it before. "Jesus, Pruner, you don't really—"

"Just saying. Mal asked for an alternative. Drew might've turned up to console the lovely wife, we all know what he's like, and—"

"Bollocks! Skinner would never do that. It was Drew. End of." Malcolm got up and stormed off to the toilets.

"What's eating him?"

Pruner shrugged. "He asked to move in with me and I turned him down. He's taking it out on Drew because he's not here. He'll get over it. He's crashing with his uncle, or Cyril's brother I should say."

"Poor bastard."

"Poor bastard your arse. Karma."

"You really think it might be Skinner?"

"Dunno, Dobs. I really can't see Drew … He's full of shit, y'know? Remember the time we were at Avondale that weekend, and the kid got run over?"

"Yeah. Drew bawled his lamps out."

"Then he threw up and blamed the wine. He'd do more damage if he shit on you. He doesn't have the stones let alone the guts."

"And Skinner does?"

"He grew up on a farm. All that slaughter must desensitise you."

"I guess."

Pruner shot a glance at the toilet door. No sign of Malcolm.

"Listen, Dobs, I meant to say but I never got the chance to see you. Last week at Skinner's do, out the back, me and Christa—"

"You don't have to explain, Billy, it's fine."

"Yeah, I do. I know you like her."

"Why do you always say that? I had a stupid crush on her at school, who didn't? I always knew I'd no chance."

"You're always putting yourself down. She's a slag. *You're* out of *her* league, not the other way round. She came out when I was having a smoke and damn near raped me."

"Spare us the details. It's okay, seriously. You think I don't know what she's like? I'm not as stupid as I walk easy. I don't care, mate, honestly, fill your boots."

Pruner looked at him, gauging the truth of his words. "You sure?"

Dobson grinned, his mouth a hammock for his teeth. "I've met someone, Billy. I've been seeing her the last couple of weeks. I meant to tell you—"

"So that's where you've been, you dark gelding! I thought I'd done something on you. Who is she?"

"Who's who?" Malcolm had slunk back unnoticed, hovering behind them, lowering the temperature. Dobson's joy was suddenly doused.

"Our Dobson's only went and found himself a woman."

Malcolm expelled a blast of dismissive air as he sat down. "Yeah, right. When were you in Thailand, Heather, or is she of the inflatable variety."

Dobson stayed silent and wished Pruner would too, but he could tell Pruner was keen to big him up to get on Malcolm's nerves.

"No, true blue, he's been on the job hot and heavy this last fortnight. Haven't you, you little stallion?"

"So who is it?" sneered Malcolm. "Is it that blind mare that goes to Silver's voodoo club?" His curled lip was trembling; why couldn't he just be happy for him like Pruner was?

"Fess up," urged Pruner, "who is she?"

"She's nice. Her name's Kate. She works down the library." He couldn't bear to look at Malcolm, but he heard the intake of breath.

Pruner frowned. "Don't know her."

"Course not Bill. When's the last time *you* cracked a book?"

"True. I'm a watcher not a reader, though I always fancied those bookworm types. Hair up, glasses. Supposed to be hellcats."

Dobson laughed, grateful for the chance to relieve some of the tension.

"Do you know her?" Pruner asked Malcolm who, if possible, looked paler than usual.

"I think so. I mean, I've seen her around."

"What's she like?"

"Okay, I suppose, if you're into that kind of thing."

"What kind of music she into, Dobs?" asked Pruner. "Maybe she would appreciate my epic."

"Catch your fucking self on," said Malcolm quietly.

"How so, Dark cloud?"

"Seriously, Pruner, you've been banging on about being in a band since P7 and you still haven't learnt how to play anything. Come on, have you even so much as written some lyrics? You must, in your heart, know you cannot sing, know you are full of mad dog's shit."

"It's a collage."

"Convenient. Stop fucking waffling and actually do something. Then you can fucking talk about it, okay?"

"For your information, I've very nearly completed something that'll knock your little virgin socks off."

"Yet you can't play a note."

"Instruments are dinosaurs, Weir, the computer saw to that. What I'm doing is avant garde—"

"Avant what?"

"It's French for bullshit," said Dobson trying to lighten the tone. He couldn't believe Malcolm had the balls to attack Pruner about his music. The hurt look Pruner shot him made him feel like such a Judas he wanted to curl up and die on the spot.

"When my opus is complete, when Judy Holocaust is finally finished—"

"Judy Holocaust!"

"—you will be fucking awestruck, doubled over in penitent shame. And no apologies will be accepted, Weir."

"Whatever, William, keep taking the tablets, mate."

"One day, Mal, your kindness will come between us. I suggest you exercise your hand for the marathon ahead."

"I have to go," said Malcolm. "My dad ... Cyril needs me to give him a hand with something." He left without a goodbye.

"Man, I tell you," said Pruner thoughtfully, "one of these days I'm gonna stick it to that humpy bastard."

"He's a lot on his mind."

"Yeah, him and the rest of us. Fuck him. You like this girl or what?"

"Yeah, Bill, I really do. She has everything a guy could want."

"What? A big cock and a hairy chest? You okay with me having a little fun with Christa for a while then?"

"Well, if you don't mind hanging out at the clap clinic for the next few weeks, why should I?"

"Seriously, Dobs, I'm happy for you. Just don't forget your mates, okay? Don't do a Skinner. Now you've got a new arsehole don't forget your old one, capiche? When do I get to meet her? I take it they let her out of the Crunchy house at the weekends."

For the first time in his life Dobson felt like a grown up, talking to Pruner about women on equal terms, trading playful insults. "We'll have to organise something," he said finishing his pint.

"Another? My shout," said Pruner.

As much as he would have given his left nut to stay and talk he had things to do. "Sorry, mate, I can't."

"Fuck me, under the thumb already?"

Dobson grinned sheepishly as he stood up. *My life has been ruined for the better*, he thought. "I've got to get a Valentine's card before I meet Kate," he said in a voice that suggested he could hardly believe it himself.

Chapter 18

Christa Finchley lay under the protection of a butterfly duvet, sweating a vile syrup that blurred her thoughts, her father's head floating in the mire above her. He wanted to tell his wife to go, to leave her alone; couldn't she see daddy's little girl was dying?

Her mother was pouring yet another Lucozade into the orange caked glass on her bedside table. "Still feeling rotten, Honey?"

Of course she did! Even though the larder of her soul had emptied itself of every last carrot, every last grisly rind, even though the bile bottle was down to the toenails, she was still sick.

Trevor Finchley turned to his wife, angry as usual with her in their daughter's presence. "Are you blind, woman, she's burning up!" Babs merely answered with her trademark stare.

As he gazed down on his little puked-out princess, Trevor wondered for the umpteenth time how he had been blessed with such a beautiful child. Golden hair, glamour girl body, killer eyes and—as if God had said, "Sod it, I'm in a good mood, have the lot"—dimples.

She didn't favour his side of the family, that was for sure; he had a face like a welder's bench, and could peel an orange in his socks standing upright. Babs had been a looker in her day though, if not in her daughter's league. There was a French connection somewhere along the line, maybe that was it, maybe that would explain the exotic good looks that excited him so.

He found himself looking at her a lot lately, and with more than just pride. Instead of kicking up a racket those times when she would appear in a skimpy top, her nipples riding on the top deck, he found himself looking forward to them instead. Only last week during a rare clinch with Babs (who had finally run out of headaches) he had found himself fantasising about her. He had felt guilty, but wonderfully *free* too. He couldn't stop because he didn't want to; each thrust brought her pouting lips, her enthusiastic breasts, to his fevered mind.

It was natural; she reminded him of Babs when she was a girl, that's all.

"Let her sleep, Barbara, the rest will do her good." He guided his wife by the elbow, hanging back slightly for one last look. What was it Bob Turk had said down the Legion? Something about how your kids are only extensions of your own body. *Nothing dirty about it, nothing at all*, a voice piped up inside him.

Christa turned her head, buried it deep in her pillow, closing her Bambi eyes, and exhaled a munchkin breath through her pixie nose as she slid effortlessly into the land of Nod, to dream of soft drugs and hard sex and other things that pleased her.

When she awoke she felt healthier than ever, though something still sweated at the back of her mind. A shower and a phone call later she was in Ellsford High Street strutting her stuff. She knew she was taking a bit of a risk being seen with Simeon but it was Monday, and Mondays and Wednesdays Pruner spent religiously working on his "music".

Still, there was no point in pushing her luck. "Must you follow me everywhere, Simeon? I only wanted a lift, not a bloody chaperone. What do you think I'm gonna do? Can't you see how unattractive this jealousy of yours is?"

He was wearing that lumberjack shirt again. If she'd known he was going to dress like that she would have walked into town. All she wanted to do was go to the chemist, not the moon, not the stars.

She watched him chew on his girlish lips and wondered if he might be gay. He might only be going out with her to prove something, or as a decoy. Come to think of it, he was a bit quick on the job, like he couldn't wait to get it over with. God, what had she seen in him?

Deep down she knew; it was parked right across the street.

An Audi. A bright red, look-at-me Audi with leather seats that smelt like sin, and a kickass stereo system. Pruner didn't even have a bicycle. Simeon Mortimer was loaded, daddy's money all well and true, but he still clinked when he walked and if she had to put up with a two-minute grunt occasionally that was a small price to pay. As long as she had one immaculately manicured hand on his balls she would have one tight little claw in his wallet.

"You ashamed to be seen with me or something?" He looked genuinely hurt, which made it easier for her to put the stiletto in.

"What do *you* think, you little runt? Now, lend me a tenner, I'm in a hurry."

"I've only a fiver on me."

"Give me it, you can owe me the rest." She snatched the note from his hand. "Now, fuck off." That should do it. He wouldn't follow her after that, he was a sensitive brat.

She turned her back on him, hitching up her belt that held up her skirt, which held up the traffic. Hopefully she hadn't gone too far. She didn't fancy walking home, and she wanted him to be waiting here for her, begging for forgiveness. She would slide silently into the Audi, torturing him with icy looks and long drawn-out legs, then when he dropped her home she would finish with him. Better still, she'd get Michelle to do it for her, if she could get her to stop going on about that disgusting old drunk Harper for five minutes. Pruner was her one and only now. Perhaps she could talk him into buying some wheels.

She cut down Hollywell Street, known to all as HollyHoly due to the presence of the church and chapel that flanked either end like celestial bodyguards, thinking of a coat she had seen in *Baby Janes* as she opened the chemist door, smiling a "wouldn't you like to" smile at the decrepit old man over by the cough drops and pile creams.

Ordinarily she was more than happy to parade her boyfriends around the chemist, picking out the biggest condoms and enquiring about studs and strength to embarrass that dowdy little Jenny Bell on the counter. She loved to make that bitch blush because she was getting with a capital YES, whilst Miss Spot Cream on the till was still on two fingers and thumb.

But today was different, today she had to buy something personal and so help her if that drab little cow laughed. It was ironic, she supposed, especially after buying myriad rubbers she now wanted to buy a pregnancy testing kit, but there were times when it had been too much hassle to fumble about with those greasy little sachets. She would *never* go on the pill, she knew far too many girls whose arses had *ballooned* on it. Now she was late, waiting for the proverbial red bus.

Oh fuck, she was pregnant!

No, hang on, babe, she told herself, *you can't be a hundred per cent. Focus on the glitter, babe.*

But she was late and that was a fact. Usually she was the menstrual express, bang on time, but somewhere down the line there was a hold up. How could she tell Pruner she was pregnant? *Might* be pregnant—say your hard words easy, girl.

But what if Pruner was delighted at the thought. He *was* unpredictable. What if he burst into tears and proposed? A family, a husband, wasn't that better than a career?

Christa lifted a small cardboard box that couldn't even be bothered to rattle, indifferent of its ability to ruin lives, shatter hourglass figures, stain meticulous eye shadow with pointless tears.

She strolled to the counter, sticking out her chest to torment the Plain Jane pill counter whose name tag read: Emily. Christa had a granny or something called Emily. She gave her a cursory glance, curling her lip at the shop girl's shit-flavoured life. Emily drained of hormones as if Christa were sucking up her femininity by proximity, and immediately looked defensive as if she guarded something important, pearls instead of aspirin.

"I'll get this, Em," said Jenny appearing from behind a stand of lozenges.

Christa knew that Jenny was frowning at her hooker clothes, her siren-red lips, and thinking slut, whore, tramp; but they were her mother's words. She wished she had the nerve, the *body*, to carry off that look. She knew that just looking at her made Jenny want to give up; she was the goddamn Eyeful Tower, and didn't she just know it. And what was she? A little grey nothing.

"Anything else?" Jenny asked pleasantly.

"I'll give you the entire show in one mime," said Christa shooting her the finger. She scattered a handful of change on the counter like brazen rain, strutting out before it was counted because she knew she was short.

A rush of panic hit her by the doorway—what would daddy say if …

Where was Simeon? Did he really have the balls not to wait for her? Didn't he know she would claw his fucking heart out? She ran, her heels clicking like a gossiping tongue, her breath coming out in short cute gasps. Where was—

She heard the blare of a horn. He was parked on the other side of the street. She felt herself burn; he had seen her running, getting herself all worked up, and was probably laughing at her and feeling all masterful.

She slipped the tester into her handbag, the sun catching her nails, and walked on convinced steam was rising from her in thin knives. She heard the Audi purr sexily into life and sidle up alongside.

"Get in, baby." How could he call her that! Why use that word? Did he know, had he followed her after all?

"Fuck off, Lizard Scrote." She walked on faster, feeling uneasy, the first time in her life she didn't want a scene.

"C'mon, climb in, we can argue later. Then make up." He did something with his mouth he probably thought erotic.

She spun on him quickly. "Listen—"

The quiet milk and biscuit hum of the Audi was shattered by the blood-and-turd roar of a motorcycle that skidded dangerously onto the footpath, fire sparking from its exhaust. The rider was clad in padded leathers and exam-length boots, a dented, matt black helmet obscuring everything but his hungry eyes.

"Hop on," said the rider, indicating the back seat with a nod. "Live wild."

Could she get on a bike in this skirt?

"Listen, asshole," began Simeon, but the biker shot him a glance that drained him white and he drove off, crunching through the gears, in daddy's little runaround.

"Find 'em, don't grind 'em, wimp!" Christa shouted after him. She was shocked. Was she not worth fighting for? He was *so* getting a phone call from Michelle.

"Come on, Rapunzel," the biker's voice had a sing-song lilt, "let down your hair."

The evocation of fairytales swayed her. She was a princess after all, daddy always said so, and here was her knight on his Isopon stallion come to save her from the weedy villain who had abandoned her so cruelly. She swung her leg up over the bike and showed the world her breakfast.

"Hit it," she said, just like in the movies, her hair trailing out behind her like an advert for a hard on. She would definitely have to talk Pruner into getting a bike, it would *so* go with his image.

Street after street after street.

She was home before she could catch her breath. She snuggled in closer to him, digging her thighs in, relishing the throb. They pulled up outside her house with a black rose storm cloud spewing from the tailpipe.

Christa dismounted. She felt like lighting a cigarette she buzzed so keen. She ran a finger seductively round his visor, looking deep into those startling eyes. The rest of the world, finding itself ignored, halted momentarily.

"Who are you?" She pouted as if medals were at stake.

The biker removed his helmet and Christa experienced a dread that had haunted her all her life—she felt the butt of a joke. She looked around to see if anyone was watching, but the street was empty as if ashamed of the punch line. The rider smiled, his yellow teeth hanging like stalactites from his withered gums.

Simeon must have known, that was why he'd cleared off. He was sitting in that poxy car of his right now, pissing himself at the thought of it and wondering who to tell first. Then they'd all be laughing. Laughing at her.

"My name's Dooley," said the grinning skeleton.

With a viciousness born of beauty, she swung her handbag in wide, testicle-threatening arcs, then brought it down on his skull; a crunch of eye shadow and lip gloss as the bag rained down in a mushroom cloud of foundation. The bag's contents made a secondary charge, falling short, dancing like dying fish by the kerb.

A hairbrush, chewing gum, a CD (Christa The Hits Vol 1), a clean pair of panties just in case. A home pregnancy testing kit.

Dooley bent to retrieve them.

"Don't touch them!" She screamed loud enough to raise nearby blinds. She filled her bag with a deft sweep of her hand then composed herself with a flick of her hair. *I am a lioness*, she told herself.

"You're so fucking dead, fucker, you're so fucking fucked ..."

For the first time in her life Christa Finchley ran out of fucks. She stormed off, wiggling like a car with a blowout. "We'll see who's fucked, my dear," said Dooley, spinning away in a cloud of acrid smoke.

Christa ignored her father's red-faced enquiries, mistaking the remnants of Satsuma on his chin for angry bile. She locked herself away in her bedroom. *Oh Pruner*, she thought, *save me, save me from myself.* She put the pregnancy test under her pillow. She would use it in the morning. Things would be better in the morning.

Eventually sleep came, stronger for her rage.

Inside her belly something stirred; a child, a baby. Oh, the sheer amount of excrement it would smear on those expensive nails, the shame it would heap on the family name, the clubs it would bar her from, the potential dates who would yell rejection as the child yelled, "I want, I want, I want!"

Christa murmured happily in her sleep.

The child took this as a good sign.

It grew.

Chapter 19

It was so dark when he awoke that for a moment he wasn't sure he had. The room was filled with a thick shadow broth and, as his eyes struggled to adjust, it was impossible to tell if it was day or night. *If it is morning and I have to go to work*, thought Malcolm, *I will open a vein*. Death could be no darker than this.

The voice was his constant companion now and the voice knew so much. The "Brainworm" it called itself, laughing at the name as if at a private joke; a fitting name for he could feel it writhe restlessly in his mind, coiling and uncoiling with visions and threats. He didn't even try to untangle them now, just gave in to their suffocating reason.

He got out of bed. If luck was a contagion he was immune. He couldn't go out. Going out was fraught with the danger of meeting people. He was immersed in cabin fever, the house closing in around him until he felt trapped in the belly of a badly furnished whale.

He was alone in a silent house, the phone dead or dying, only the tick of the clock for company; a maddening metallic pulse that quickened or slowed with his mood. He whipped open the curtains and let in the diluted daylight. It was raining. Raining so hard he couldn't go out. It didn't matter, he had nowhere to go.

In the hallway mirror his reflection grinned back at him. Surely his own smile wasn't as wicked as that, his eyes as cold and mocking? The longer he stared the more his skin seemed to redden, until he gazed upon a picture book Satan. The world behind the mirror was more authentic than this one, that's why his image laughed.

I am losing my mind!

He wrote some poems; stupid, deformed, pleading things that shamed him. He tried to burn them but the fire kept spitting them out. He put them in a pedal bin which left baked beans on his fingers. He rubbed his fingers on his trousers because he could afford a new pair if he didn't go out, and he couldn't go out because it was raining so hard.

He could try...

What if he...

No. the rain was on for the day.

He decided to shave. He went to the bathroom to get a razor. His stomach smiled up at him from the U-bend and he smiled back, his face reflected in a pool of urine in the sink. Yesterday's beard still clung to the soap, floating in the piss like a strange speckled egg.

He couldn't breathe. He was going insane, he was going to die, they would find him here and say—

He didn't care what they said.

The umbrella, where was the umbrella? No, he couldn't go out. He went back downstairs to answer the phone, but there was no-one there because it hadn't rang.

He found the umbrella. It was ripped. It was the skeleton of a pre-historic bird. He had discovered it. He would be famous.

He had to get away but he couldn't go out.

He realised he was screaming, and hoped the neighbours would hear and call the police. He would answer the door, mild surprise on his face, "No, officer, nothing wrong here." He felt guilt; guilt, shame, the whole bloody lot. He remembered the razor and felt at peace for a short time.

Though his heart was trembling like a pup, Malcolm held the blade steady against his skin. He sliced deep, enchanted by the thick welt of blood that appeared on his arm in a devil smile, so mesmerizing against his pale flesh. The relief was momentary.

He sliced again.

Relief once more; fleeting, spectral.

He imagined he could hear the susurration of blood as it fled his body. How many cuts would it take to let all this pain out? His arms were laced with old scars, hardened like boiled sweets under the skin. Tears came, snot tripping from his nose, and he ran his arm across his face, smearing it with blood and snot, and hated himself a little more.

He should cut into an artery, a vein, but even in his miserable state he knew he was a coward. Why was he so alone when he had so much to give?

He could handle it all if he had only someone to share it with, but who wanted an equal slice of nothing, of fuck all squared? To make it worse, the one girl on earth he felt a connection to was going out with Dobson.

That ugly, ridiculous, trampy little toad.

He had prayed it was a lie, a bad dream, but the Brainworm confirmed it was true. He had hung around the health shop across from the library and watched them coming out together hand in hand like it was normal, like this was the way the world was meant to turn. He was forced into buying a bag of pecans and a box of green tea because the girl in the shop was getting creeped out by his loitering, his muttering. Seeing the two of them together was heartbreaking, and the tea turned out to be just as bitter.

The guilt at what he had done made him hate the little bastard more. He was about to slice again when he realised the best way to hurt yourself is to hurt others.

To top it all off, the cherry atop the shit pie, he was going crazy; slowly but surely going seven kinds of pure fucking nuts; seeing things, people, that could not be there. If only he could put yesterday down to a hallucination.

He had slunk into the library—yes, slunk—for that's what God-forsaken unfortunates like himself did, they slunk, and hung around the DVDs until he made sure Kate was alone and he could talk to her in private. He had come in with the vague plan of getting some books or leaflets that could help him trace his *real* family; he never meant to cross the line, at least that's what he told himself.

He had a nebulous vision of himself typing away at one of the consoles late into the morning before arriving at a eureka moment, his real parents appearing on his screen—then giving Ellsford two fingers as he jetted off to Monaco to join them and their celebrity-filled lives. He had no idea where to start though; this was no movie where everything could be sorted in a slick sixty-second montage.

That was the ostensible plan, but when he saw her, looking even more beautiful now that she was soiled and unattainable, a new plan formulated in his head and he dived in, accosting her as she headed down the stacks under an anvil load of Art books.

"Hi."

He didn't know whether to tap her on the shoulder or not. She turned at the sound of his voice, freezing his hand in midair. Despite the amount of time he had wasted in here lately her face showed no recognition of him at all.

"I'm Malcolm." Nothing. "Dobson's friend?"

"He never mentioned a Malcolm." Was that a smile on her lips, a thin mocking smile?

"I'm not surprised really," he said. His anger was on the boil, but he was still calm enough to realise that this denial played right into his hands. "We haven't spoken in a while. We had a bit of a fallout."

"Really." There was not the slightest interest on her face. She looked at him like he was a chair, a table.

"Yeah, that's what I wanted to talk to you about. See, I know him and you are … well, the reason for the big fallout was he came onto me. I'm not like that and—"

She burst out laughing in his face, hot contemptuous laughter that shrivelled all but his rage.

"Oh, I can assure you, *Malcolm*, Dobson's not gay."

"You don't know him as well as you might think."

She slammed the heavy books down with a thunderclap, narrowly missing his feet; several of the old folks over by Local History clutched at their chests and muttered disgustedly.

"Let me tell you something, Mr. Weir, you're even more pathetic than I thought. Just go, before you take all the fun out of it for me."

She was right. He was pathetic, whiny and childish and pathetic. He thought he had God by the toe but really he had the Devil by the tail. Bitch. Before he knew what he was doing he punched her, spinning her head round, knocking her into a carousel. She stared up at him, blood snailing down her nose. He ran.

She would tell Dobson of course, Dobson would tell Pruner, and there would be a showdown and he had no defence. He hadn't crossed the line, he had jumped it.

He dug the razor into his arm once more, gaining a momentary respite from thought. *Oh, I can assure you he's not*—did she mean they had … Christ, and he was still a virgin. He feared he would wank himself into an early grave.

"I hate you, Heather."

He was going bald on top of everything else. Just let me die without the bother of living.

Outside his window he heard the roar of a motorcycle at the end of the street, the satisfied purr as it stopped outside the house. He recognised that engine, knew who it was before he even looked out. Proctor, freshly released, come to get him because fucking lugnut Dobson had told him what he said in The Cove. Dobson couldn't hold his water.

Or had Dobson told him about Kate …

Malcolm felt sick. The tears were starting again. Another layer of shit to wade through. He lit a cigarette and pulled open the curtains, watching Drew dismount below. His swaggering persona was disconcerting. He seemed blissfully unaware of his misshapen head, his eminently punchable face screwed up like the knuckles it invited.

Drew looked, saw him framed in the window. "Hey, Malcolm Queer, I need a word!" His thick clotted voice betrayed by its very laziness the apathetic, narcissistic soul it vocalised.

Malcolm shot him the finger, held it up in plain view whilst he took a long slow drag, then his head was mashed up against the glass, his cigarette exploding in his face. His uncle had him by the throat, shaking him like a sauce bottle, beating his head against the window (which surely must break) in a raucous tattoo.

"You piss in my sink!" He had never seen him so angry before. "I go away for a few days and you destroy my house and piss in my fucking sink!"

Malcolm could see the joy etched on Drew's meaty upturned face before he was dragged back from the window and out onto the landing.

"I'm not well, John, I—"

"You dirty wee bastard!" His uncle punched him on the ear, and with a hard shove he introduced him to the stairs. Malcolm half fell, half floated, jarring his chin on the banister before landing in a heap in the hall. Through the blood curtains of his eyes he could see his uncle at the top of the staircase, descending, and for a brief instant he felt a certain romance; he was a fallen angel cast down by an unjust god. Then the pain kicked in as he felt the eight pints of his soul try to seep from his body. He was a glowing ball of agony.

"I want you out of this house by the time I get back!"

The door slammed. His tears returned like an inner faucet had been cranked and he thought he would not stop crying until he was dead, that his very heart would pour from his eyes. *I deserve this*, he thought. In his mind's eye he could see himself clearly, a shameful blubbering mess lying broken on the floor.

Now I have nowhere to live and nothing to live for.

A hand touched his shoulder and his heart tried to flip from his mouth.

Had his uncle come back, full of pity, his aunt—

He raised a bleary eyelid and made out a pair of biker boots studded with expensive-looking straps. His eyes climbed them slowly, traversing shapely legs, reaching the summit of the concerned face of Beth Skinner. He let out a helpless moan.

"Shh," she consoled him, and he found a whole new reservoir of pain to draw on. He was insane, the going part was done and dusted, he was already there, signed, sealed, and delivered.

"Don't fret, pet," she said, rubbing his thinning hair. "Settle petal."

"You're not real!" he screamed. "Not real! You're dead and in Hell!"

"Death doesn't make me any less real, Malcolm," she cooed. "And as for Hell, I'm in a much better place than that. Why don't you come see, you look ever so lonely."

Malcolm let out a long drawn-out sob. "Mother," he bleated.

"Your Mother hates you," said Beth, and her voice was that of the Brainworm's. "She knows all your little secrets. She thinks you're a killer and she hates you. They all do, except me. I'm the only one who cares about you now." Then she kissed him and the world turned black.

He felt that he was not emerging from darkness but from the earth itself, up into the light, a green, brackish light. He could feel rain on his face. A large burnt cross stood before him, a charred midwife at his birthing. In a circle around him stood Carrie Anne, Nadine, Beth and the stickman licking his bloodless lips. Another man, naggingly familiar, stood by the cross.

The stranger reached out his hand but as Malcolm went to grasp it something stirred in the bushes and stepped out into the clearing. A flood of images deluged his mind, a torrent of childhood memories drenched in the stench of the sewers, and he fell back into the earth, awaking at the bottom of the stairs, his bruised body feeling like he had fallen a thousand miles or more. At least one of his problems had been solved now.

He knew where he had to go.

The Moss was calling him.

Chapter 20

Sometimes his brain felt like it had swollen up and was pressing against his skull, threatening to burst through; sometimes as if a waspish voice was trapped in there; sometimes as if a vice were being cranked and his eyeballs were about to pop, or hot knives had been inserted into his frontal lobe. This morning it was just a nauseating dull ache that bleached the vibrancy out of everything.

By the time Pruner left the pharmacy, his Solpadeine forgotten, it felt like his head was about to explode in a mushroom cloud of burning dogmeat. Despite his pain he had managed a smile when he saw Jenny Bell behind the counter. Like all his exes she still held a candle for him. He was proud that not only was he still on amicable terms with his conquests (and he had *rang* that Bell, clanged it off the bloody wall) but that they still openly flirted with him; once you had been in the Rosebed you always wanted back, no matter how many thorns you encountered.

He queued behind a few oldies, his eyes burning under the ridiculously bright fluorescents, as they waited patiently for their prescriptions.

"Hi, Pruner," said Jenny, reddening slightly.

"Hi, Dinger," he said.

"Stop that!" she said, absurdly pleased and totally scarlet; God bless her little tomato head. *Ah Jenny*, he thought, *I bought that smile and still have change enough for your ass.*

"I need some headache tabs, strongest you've got."

She turned to survey the brightly coloured boxes behind her, handing him one with a big shit-eating grin plastered on her face. "I should think so," she said, ringing it up on the till.

"What do you mean by that?"

She took his money, gave him back the odds. "You're dating Christa, aren't you?"

He sucked on his teeth. Normally he liked to dangle his new beaus before his old flames, but for some reason he felt mildly ashamed.

"Must be serious," she said when he didn't answer. "Nearly two months. Must be some kind of record for you."

"Yeah, well," he said, uncomfortable now, his headache drumming at the back of his eyes. "Such is life."

She put the tablets into one of the fussy over-creased, over-folded little bags. "I guess you'll be buying a lot more of these in future, at least for the first few months." Her smile was gone. "I never pegged you for the type, Billy."

"What *are* you wittering on about, Jen?"

"Christa." She searched his eyes. "Oh God, you don't know, do you? Me and my big trap." She didn't look sorry, not at all. "She was in the other day, bought a pregnancy test. I thought you knew. Maybe she isn't and that's why she—"

The rest was lost, swallowed up by the hungry maw of his headache, his vision swimming, coming to rest on a display case of Durex, the rainbows and happy couples mocking him. He placed a hand on the counter to steady himself.

"Pruner? I'm sorry, I didn't mean to …"

But he was gone, out the door and sucking in breath far too quickly, his headache possessing him from toenails to quiff.

Now, sitting on his sofa with the curtains drawn and a glass of milk curdling in his hand, he felt much better; the belt had loosened, his brain shrunk back to its normal functioning size. His headache had disappeared like dandelion fluff on the wind.

He was calm.

Christa was gone and she would not be back. He had made damn sure of that. It left a sour taste in his mouth but it was over and for that he was thankful. He scratched at his bare chest, at the cold spot in its centre where no hair grew, where he sometimes struggled to find even a heartbeat, and frowned. Every time he touched his

146

eggshell chest his thoughts got all jumbled up and he drowned in an overwhelming surge of melancholy. It had always been so. Yet, he had so much to be thankful for.

No more would he have to listen to that awful droning voice (how could such an ugly sound issue from such a pretty source, such poison spray from such an exquisite fountain?), or sit through endless dreary monologues on Reiki and Hopi ear candling, gagging in the stench of incense and ginger and fucking patchouli. No more seething while she talked all over his albums, or slagged them off.

Why had he stayed with her so long anyway?

Her mate Michelle, a virtual heifer, was ten times the lay (fat girls were always more grateful), but then he couldn't be seen with her. Christa, on the other hand, was a great accessory—a breathing Harley, a long-legged Porsche. The idea of a child with her, the idea that she had trapped him, that she believed he would spend the rest of his life shackled to an inane robot, picking out bedspreads and rearranging furniture to maximise energy flow, had burst the numbing balloon of boredom that had encased him. And still the small things rankled most.

For someone who never ate anything, food was all she ever talked about, constantly harping on about calories and carbs and cooking preparations. She had ransacked his cupboards, lecturing him on their contents—"Do you have *any* idea what's in a Pot Noodle?"—and filled them up with bland cardboard dishes with zero taste and zero sustenance. Even a bag of crisps became a matter of hot debate.

He couldn't even fart. He would hold it in, his stomach cramping, until he left the room and let it go. He had the feeling she would not approve of such a function as he had never heard her make so much as a squeak, probably due to the oxygen diet she was currently on. Sometimes though she would go a slight shade of pink and the room would momentarily smell like cat food.

And she smoked!

What a fucking hypocrite.

Smoking was the real key to her diet, that and the fact that she could chug back vodka like any of the derelicts that hung out behind the Fire Station, claiming the mixers were part of her five a day. He could have put up with the self-delusion if only she hadn't dragged her joyless regime into every other aspect of her existence.

That was the main thing. She was boring. For someone so beautiful to reach the stage where you yawned at the sight of her in lingerie was one hell of a feat. She was boring in the kind of damp Sunday in church, howl at the fucking moon, tear strips of living flesh from your face way that could push you over the edge.

He waited for her, stewing in his own acidic juices. He had hardly let her sit her shapely rump down before he lit on her; her *Baby Girl* t-shirt had enflamed him; there was something too hard about her for pink.

"So, when you gonna tell me, eh? Planning a romantic candlelight dinner, hold my hand over the table and tell me I'm a daddy?"

"What are you talking about, William?"

William! The last few weeks he had become William, and he should have realised then, realised that Pruner was not an acceptable name for a father, husband, he should have twigged on there and then.

"I'm talking about you being up the duff! Tell me, did I offer to go halfers on a bastard? I don't recall."

"What!"

"Up the stick, my dear, bunged, ready to drop a litter. When were you going to tell me, or were you working out who the daddy was, narrowing down the list?"

"William—"

"Don't fucking call me that!"

"—I'm not pregnant!"

The relief was instant, liberating, though his chest grew colder. He was surprised by how calm she was; he had expected her to go down bitching, fighting, hissing.

"You sure?" He was aware she might be painting the truth with a shiny new coat. "You take the test?"

"How did ... I'd appreciate it if you didn't yell at me."

His anger came back, adding its own percussive accompaniment to the pounding in his skull. "You wanted to be though, didn't you? I got lucky this time, but you would've got me sooner or later. Jesus, you must think I'm an easy touch."

"Listen to yourself, you must think you're God's gift!"

"For someone like you I am, you desperate bitch. You can't wait to get your claws into the first guy who can stick you longer than five minutes, you dull whore."

She burst into tears. Pruner was struck by how unbelievably rancid pretty girls were when they cried. "Cue the waterworks! I should record this. Look on the bright side, love, what chance would a kid have with a mum like you."

"Billy!"

"You'd probably swap it for a pair of Jimmy Choo's on eBay."

"You bastard! I had a miscarriage once and it nearly killed me, inside, in here." She held a hand over her mammary-clad heart. For the first time in her life she genuinely felt in touch with something outside herself. "I'd be a great mum, and you'd be a great dad. Think about it, Billy, don't be scared. If you just give us a chance—"

He slapped her hard, snapping her head back against the wall, and was on her before she could react, his hands on her throat. *Yes, rearrange that face*, buzzed a voice in a dark tunnel of his mind, *see what that will do to her precious energy fields, see—*

"I love you," she spluttered.

He stopped squeezing, the waspish voice inside his brain stopped buzzing. His headache dissipated, his anger absorbed by the lightning rod of those three small words. He laughed at her, and his laughter hurt her more than his hands ever could.

"You bastard!" She spat on him as he lay on the floor clutching his ribs. "I fucking hate you! I never want to see you again!"

He laughed so hard he felt vomit surge up his throat in an oily backwash as she stormed out; then the slamming door, then the blessed silence. Then he had a Mars Bar and a cup of sugary tea because, "Sugar is worse than heroin," and he felt like a fix.

He sat quietly, the laughter gone, the pain hibernating, the skin above his heart ice cold, feeling calm if strangely hollow. His cigarette was burning on only one side, hooded like a cobra; someone was talking about him, but better that than someone talking *to* him. When the doorbell rang he jumped, spilling milk over his stomach.

The police again with the same old questions? They were as boring as Christa. God knows what yarn Drew had spun them. Or maybe it was Trevor Finchley, all pistols at dawn over his daughter's beleaguered honour.

But when he opened the door it was Dobson, or rather Dobson's grin hanging in the air like Alice's cat. He couldn't help but grin back. The sun was shining, he was a free man, and his best mate was here. Life wasn't so bad. Somewhere an ice cream van blared; the first ice cream van of spring. Pruner gave Dobson a mock salute and stood aside.

"Come in, Comrade Heather. Be careful when you enter, my house is full of wonders."

And to Dobson's eyes it was. Hundreds of albums, vinyl at that, were stacked neatly against the walls; boxes of CDs formed surreal forts in the corners. The stereo, mounted on a pristine mahogany table like a shrine, was flanked by two of the biggest speakers Dobson had ever seen; he had helped Pruner haul them back here and nearly had a hernia in the process.

"I think I know where Skinner is."

"You seen him?"

"No, but I know where he is. It's obvious."

"Well? Spit it out."

"The Moss."

Pruner sighed. "I doubt it, mate."

"Think about it, where else would he be? Apart from me, who else knows the place as well."

"It's been two months or more, Dobs. He's not Raoul Moat, how the fuck would he survive? Plus his card was used at an ATM in Scotland, it said so on the news. Face it, he's long gone."

"You know who's been to Scotland recently? Gus Hamill."

Pruner stared, his mental cogs not yet spinning. "Gus the mechanic who used to work on Skinner's farm?"

"Yep. Gus who lives on the edge of the Moss, Gus who is Skinner's mate, Gus who's probably feeding him and helping throw the law off the scent."

"I dunno, it's a bit of a longshot."

"Maybe, maybe not, but it *feels* right, Pruner."

"So what do you suggest we do?"

"Get a tent, camp out, sniff him out. It'll be like old times. The weather's on the turn—"

"What if he doesn't want to be found? As hard as it is to say, the guy might be a killer."

"He's also a mate."

Pruner felt the cold patch on his chest begin to thaw; *we should all have such mates as you*, he thought. "You're right. When do we go?"

With his usual economical thrift Dobson had a plan that would gather together all the essentials for less than the price of a pack of smokes. His excitement was contagious, and Pruner found himself looking forward to what Dobson kept referring to as "the mission." It was glaringly obvious that neither of them had the least idea of what to do or say if they found Skinner, if he was even hiding out there at all.

"So how's things with you? You look like a dog with two dicks, can't be all down to a camping trip."

Dobson blushed, then beamed. "Kate's pregnant."

Pruner hugged him like he had just announced he was terminally ill, more to hide the despair on his face than anything else. He was losing them all, one by one. He couldn't let his best mate see his worry. Beneath his embrace he could feel him shudder with pride. Damn. Damn it all to hell. Herod had the right idea.

"So you've ginger in the old loins after all! Ah fuck, Dobs, I'm chuffed for you mate."

He got rid of him as soon as he could, his face sore from smiling, the numb patch on his chest back and spreading.

Outside in the warm spring air, Dobson strode down the street like an invulnerable colossus, every step treading his old timid self deeper into the past. He had been right to tell Pruner first; his mum hadn't even met Kate yet. He felt fortified now for her inevitable rejections and threats. The sun shone *in* him, illuminating the day, banishing forever the chills of his childhood.

All his life he had been a toad in a world of poodles; how could he not believe that when every put down, every look confirmed it. If he had only been as stupid as they thought him he might have been happy, but he had always known what life *could* be, and the thought that he could never have it, that he was doomed to be a spectator on the sidelines to others joy made his torment harder to bear.

Like a pig with a view of Heaven, the knowledge of bliss denied was worse than it could be for the rest of his kind.

But now he had a girl, one that bore his child, and he could make his own family and put right all that had been wrong. Now Heaven was attainable even for the likes of him. Whistling tunelessly he floated home, thinking that surely if there were a Heaven it would be the Moss.

Part Three

At first he thinks Dutch has been shot; he has blood on his hands and the veins in his neck are standing out like corduroy. His screams are claws in his ears, dragging him off to some fearful dark place. Pruner is watching it all from outside of himself, thinking, "I am witnessing my own death."

Dutch's screams are no longer audible. All he can hear is the torrent of his own blood. Everything inside him is racing at a million miles per hour whilst the outside world has slowed to a stroboscopic crawl.

This is death, this is the end of everything, just like you thought it would be, here it is banging on the door, so soon, so soon, a huff and a puff and your straw lives are blown apart. And no-one will ever know, of that he is sure; we will be forever lost in death.

Suddenly the vomit he has been trying to hold down since entering the clearing escapes his mouth, his nose. As Dutch turns to run the normal thread of time reasserts itself and the natural soundtrack kicks in once more.

Drew is pushing past him, Dutch and Dobson running headlong toward him, the dead birds quivering on the tree. Pruner turns to flee as much from the look in Dutch's eyes as the horror that has caused it.

The air is too dense to breathe as he chases Drew's broad back up the narrow path, a swarm of crows falling around him into the sky until he feels he is trapped in some airless globe filled with ashes or black snow. He hears a roar behind him and part of his mind flickers on a memory of the sewers the summer before, a memory that is smothered by a cry from Dutch or from himself, he cannot be sure.

Drew is blocking his way, he will die if he cannot get past, so he sticks a toe between his heels, tripping him, almost stumbling himself. He feels no guilt, only the dried pull of brackish water on his skin, shining like a target.

Dobson and Dutch fly by, and only then does he find his rhythm, running after them, prepared to mow them down if he has to but their skinny bodies hare on ahead, Dobson's spine jutting luminously, a Will-o-the-wisp guiding him from this dank jungle.

Over his own desperate breath he hears Drew let out a magpie rattle—It's eating him, he thinks, it's eating him alive! He feels no compunction to go back and help his friend, only the hope that Drew's death will buy him the time to escape the Moss, to escape and never, never, never come back.

Knees pistoning, ignoring the fire in his lungs and the knives in his throat, he gains on the others. The Moss blurs by in a haze of greens and behind him something is coming, he can sense it, his skin prickling; he can smell it.

The path widens, forks in two. He knows where he is now, and with familiarity comes a sliver of hope. Dutch and Dobson run straight ahead, but Pruner takes the other path, the one that leads to Horseshoe Lane, to Gus Hamill's house. Gus is a big man, a big man with a shotgun, and if he can get there he will be safe. If whatever is chasing them goes after the other two (it's them it wants! It picked out Dutch first!) then he has nothing to worry about and—

And his legs, already numb and running on empty, bend like straws as he tumbles over a stone, his ankle twisting with a lick of white fire as he plunges down the sun-beaten bank, landing in a mass of clawing brambles and sweet smelling vetch by the edge of a greasy black pool that mirrors his startled face and the blue sky above.

His fingers clutch the crumbling earth as he waits for the killer blow but nothing happens save for a massive heron taking flight, flapping its ragged wings and almost bursting his heart with fright. Bastard bird, he thinks, I'll come back and burn your nest and ... In the pool he sees his eyes are exactly like Dutch's; no, no, I'm never coming back.

In his terror the world takes on a crystal clarity. He turns to look at the rock that tripped him: veined with red and blue, it shines with an inner light. A weathered tag is screwed to it—DUSTY: A True Friend. The Moss is littered with pets and their monuments, their bones sinking further down into the peat each year to merge with the prehistoric lizards beneath.

The broken snail shells littering the base radiate an ever-changing umbra. The splash of a frog in the pool is differentiated into a million individual notes, each one cast with a pearlish hue.

At least he is out of sight. If he stays quiet he can make it out of here; he will not be joining the oozing fossils below.

A heavy tread squashes his heartbeat. A sigh; or is it just a breeze tickling his imagination? He closes his eyes but the red blistered darkness only amplifies the half-heard noises. An obituary montage runs through his mind. A twig breaking, the slurp of a boggy sod. Something is looking down on him as he concocts half-legible prayers to a God he suddenly believes in very much.

He opens his eyes. The shadow that falls across him is a tangible, groping thing.

In the water is a reflection of a man, a young man perhaps, but one caught in the maw of a terminal disease intent on sucking the very life out of him, draining even the colour from his hair. His large eyes are brighter than the sun and when he smiles, revealing a mouth full of tilted headstones, the water starts to bubble and steam.

Pruner rolls over, his eyes squinting at the panting thing by the man's thin legs, the panting thing crawling toward him. The smell is unbearable.

Now its face blocks out the bleaching sun, its narrow mouth open to display rows of thorns, its eyes deeper than any devil lake; a thin line across its face where no fur grows; its tongue a bloated grey maggot of a thing, flicking, flicking, flicking.

"It's not him," says the skinny man, and the thing that has crawled on top of Pruner lets out a wail, a buzzsaw lullaby that shakes the leaves from the branches.

"Hush, child," chides the man. "He can still be of use. Remember what your father taught you. Think ahead."

Its panting becomes agitated, excited. Its savage black orbs rest on Pruner once more as it growls.

"That's right," coos the thin man.

One bark-like nail cuts deep into Pruner's chest, slicing away his t-shirt, then the snuffle of a snout against his bare skin. He feels the bite of the thorns, the delving of the maggot tongue, then the cold nothingness.

The sun moves far to the west before he rises. Shaking, disoriented, mind blind, he gathers pace though he can't remember what it is he's running from or where he is running to. The trees crowd him, trying to snag him. There are eyes everywhere in the verdant shadows, reflecting back from the stagnant pools, rustling behind the dog roses, watching quietly from barren nests.

By the time he gets home his chest has healed. Where the wound throbbed there is now only a Judas stain, and a pulsing coldness that will never leave him.

Chapter 21

"Bless you," said Samuel as a cat crossed his path. "Bless you," to a sparrow on a wall. "Bless you all," as it was joined by more of its dusty comrades.

He was feeling stressed, and when he was wound up (*Bless you*—a mongrel sniffing at a bollard) so tight he found himself handing out (*Bless you*—a pigeon strutting by the kerb) benedictions to all and sundry. He had to pull himself together before (*Bless you*—an insect of unknown origin sluggishly attempting to scale a window pane) this got out of hand. It was a form of OCD and would anger the Lord.

"Bless you," he said and stopped short; a plastic bag blowing across the pavement. It was a sin to praise the inanimate, God would unleash his wrath. He had to get a grip on this (*Bless you*—the thought of his damned self).

Self-praise was the worst of all. God despised vanity. When he got home he would pray, hurt himself if he had to.

"Bless you, Lord."

He would be forgiven. It was only a ritual and a holy life was nothing without ritual. Every night Samuel removed one of his pillows and put it safely under his bed. He had done that every night since childhood, when his father used to settle himself on the edge of the eiderdown and tell them Bible stories in his gruff tones.

Paul lapped them up, but they had always scared Samuel a little. He was too young to understand, but his brother explained they were *meant* to frighten you, that being scared was good because God fed on fear. When papa warned them to be good Samuel always prepared himself to be eaten.

In his fear he often misheard his father, so that for years when daddy left the room he did so with the bizarre injunction to "Say your pears." But it was the story of Samson that disturbed him most; the superman lion slayer brought low by a hussy (*you can tell a hussy by the colour of her underwear, boys*), the cutting of the hair (*such a sin, boys, such a sin*), the putting out of eyes.

The terrible vengeance when he pushed the pillows apart.

Even now that he knew better Samuel still maintained the habit of placing one safely under the bed lest he bring down the temple un-knowingly in the middle of the night. "Bless the pillows and the pillars." Oh, such blasphemy! You will pay for such weakness of lip.

He steeled himself against such thoughts for he had to preach this day. How could he deliver divine truth when damnation festered in his mind? Why think of death at all when Paul had shown that veil to be paper thin at best.

Maybe today he would do more than just preach—maybe today he would heal. How often had he visited with the drunks behind the Fire station and imagined driving out their drink lust like the Gadarene swine! Perhaps today he would do it, and without Dobson. Dobson was a mere battery to feed off until he was fully charged, until he learned to harness the power himself. He *felt* ready.

When the derelicts were gutted of their base temptations he would renovate them with faith; they would become his acolytes and what use he could make of such streetwise disciples. They would be the manpower to build his church. Oh he glowed this day, he glowed, bless the—

And if he failed that would be his funeral.

Now, Samuel, he chided himself, *don't be squeamish. It is the will of the great and terrible Yahweh not to be questioned. Did Paul fret over the girls' mangled and defiled corpses? Of course not, he only cared about the child getting stronger. Ours is not to reason why. If he had to spend a season in the fiery abyss, then what of it? Jesus Himself had descended from the cross to the charnel pits of Hell with a beatific smile on His face—and how many millions have died since to make strong the Word?*

On the Day of Judgement their sacrifice would no doubt be noted. "Bless you, brave sweet girls." Up ahead was the bank of fragrant pines that screened the grey block sheds behind the Firehouse. In his heavy coat Samuel began to sweat as he made his way toward them.

This was their lair.

Banished from bars and bookies, prohibited from public spaces, ousted from off licenses, they congregated here; a captive audience. He liked to proselytise to these lost souls. Soon he would be moving up and on, soon his ministry would be taken to the great and the good, but that was no reason to forget his calling. Jesus spent time among the lepers and whores, the sinners and the taxmen; it would be remiss of him, nay arrogant, to pass them by.

And when he cured them, what glory then?

It would be like Pentecost, for people would see his new recruits and say, "Those men are drunk," and he would reply, "No, they are filled with the Holy Spirit."

His visions of glory dissipated when he came across the scrofulous herd; the only thing they were filled with was meths or turps. He recognised most of them, but their numbers seemed to swell each year, attracting young wastrels like iron filings to a magnet; so young, so apathetic, pickling their brains in the fresh outdoors. Samuel ignored them as he made his way to the high table, to Catman, the king of this No-Man's land.

Sniper's skin was cut and bruised, a palimpsest of pain old and new. Doc seemed to be shedding his like an old bony snake, and Wheezel was suffering another bout of ringworm; strange crop circles on his cheeks gave him the air of a decomposing Aunt Sally as they undulated.

Samuel was loathe to proceed. Healing the sick was one thing, exposing yourself to contagion another. Who knew what parasites lurked here; they could all be riddled with the bloody plague.

Brendan was removed from the others, sitting by himself on a breezeblock, his head bowed over his bottle as if in prayer, but his eyes were focused and his mouth free of the manic Tourette's that was his trademark. Was he sober? It was almost noon, could it really be? A sober drunk. Oh, the signs he was receiving each and every day!

Brendan was the key, where he staggered the others would follow. First he must pass himself off with the lieutenants or he would never get any peace; five minutes of banter should suffice. Let them insult him, throw their jokes at his polished armour until they tired and returned to whatever occupied their garbled minds; the past no doubt. Those without a future were big on the past he found.

Brendan was eyeing him warily. There was something furtive in his feline eyes. Samuel had no doubt now; that gaze was a frightened one, but a sober one too. He approached the ragged scarecrows before him with a spring in his step.

"Morning, my good men. I didn't see you at Group this week."

He would call them by their given names, their *Christian* names. Not Sniper, Doc, Sneezy John, Wheezel, and Catman. No, he would not fall into that trap. Those debauched Disney names were the names of the demons sucking on them. They would swear and sneer but somewhere deep inside that vat of liquor they would listen, of that he was confident.

"If it isn't the Silver Surfer hisself!" Yes, the Silver Surfer, surfing on the ocean of God's love, praying to drown. "Sit yer arse down, brother, an' give us a bit a yer lip. None a that Jesus malarkey now, makes the vintage go down the wrong tubes."

Samuel took the proffered bottle. "This is my blood. Take. Drink."

"Monkey's blood is what it is," said Sniper.

Samuel winced, more from the harsh taste of the vinegar than Arthur's casual blasphemy. They had renamed this brand, the cheapest on the supermarket shelves—Wreck The House. Damn The Soul would have been more apt.

Samuel wiped his mouth on a pristine handkerchief feeling uncomfortably tidy in their flyblown presence. They had a uniform of sorts, one that may even have been stylish once before it was rescued from charity shop hangers. Sports jackets and baseball boots. Jeans or trousers optional, so long as they were baggy; not a problem, as to a man they were emaciated. *If they pooled their flesh instead of their Giros they would collectively make a smaller man than me*, thought Samuel.

"Who can afford to eat, price of drink these days?" Sniper observed as he caught Samuel's eyes, sticky with pity, alight on his pigeon chest.

"A loaf and a small haddock, I would feed you all."

"Will you stay and take communion with us, Sammy?" asked Sniper. "More than welcome, if you chip in."

"Another time, Arthur, I've people to see. A lot of frightened people in town just now who need the Word." Sniper looked ill. Samuel hoped he wasn't sick; watching people regurgitate was an emetic in itself.

"Your brother needed the Word, didn't he, Silver, eh? A bad egg to be sure," piped in Wheezel.

Lord, lend me your strength against this monodont, thought Samuel. Wheezel was an irritant, a mote in his eye. It was a wonder the others could stand him, though the bruises on his face were testament to the depths of their patience.

"My brother has served his time in Hell, I can assure you of that, Norman."

"Aye," said Sniper, "we all have at that."

Silence fell amongst the haunted wretches as they processed this truth. Samuel scanned the rubble where they perched, the broken furniture, the empty cans; *vermin*, he thought, *human rats eking out a parody of existence, the flotsam and jetsam of society. What am I doing amongst such detritus?*

I'm in a hellish wasteland this day, Paul, lend me your strength.

"If you'll excuse me, gentlemen, I need a word with Brendan."

"You'll be lucky," said Sniper. "Fucker hasn't spoke since they let him out."

Ye are of your father the devil, thought Samuel as he picked his way across to the solitary figure, *and the lusts of your father ye will do. He was a murderer from the beginning, John, eight, forty-four.*

"Brendan?" Catman lifted his head as if the name rang a distant, muffled bell. "You look unhappy, old friend. I can change all that you know. I can cure you. Throw away that alcoholic prop that sucks you dry."

"I believes you, Sammy, I do. I sees Molly Stone charging round town, how can I not? I sees many a thing, Sambo, that's why I'll carry on drinkin, ta very much. Your health, preacher," he said, tipping a bottle to his crusty mouth.

"Brendan, let me take that demon off your back——"

"Demon you say? Angel is what it is! Keeps me sane or I'd rip your heart out. I hears things. I *sees* things. I don't wanna be sober! I'm scared, Sammy, scared to know more than I already do."

"What do you know, Brendan? Do you know Jesus?"

Catman laughed. "Not so well, though I bet he's heard of me. I know if my missus hadn't left me I'd have kilt her stone dead. Kiddies too. Killed them and ate them or some fuckin thing. Bet the good Lord knows that too. The drink's keeping me from sin, Sammy, don't take it away from me or you'll be sending me to Hell, sure as God."

"That's the demon talking, Brendan."

"That's just it, can't you get it through them cloth ears of yours?

Fucking demon whispers to me all the time. It's only when I'm drunk I can block the bastard out." He rubbed a shaky hand over the mountainous bones of his forehead. "Always whispering, telling me stuff I already know, then showing me to rub it in."

Catman's voice reminded him of the old scratchy fountain pens they used in school. "Delirium tremens, my friend, a typical reaction."

"Yer arse, Sammy, no offence. I know more about coming down than your holy rollin bollocks knows about the Good Book. Don't try to teach Astaire how to dance or I'll rip your heart out! I'm telling ya, I seen him."

"Who, Brendan? The devil?" Samuel was aware he was leaning too close. He could see the dandruff on Catman's skull, like icing on a matted coconut; smell the stale urine emanating from the hardened tweed.

"Aye." Catman's eyes lost their focus. "Aye, maybe it was him right enough, though he wore a different face. See, Sammy, I knows you and your brother a long time, eh? School days an' all that. Knew your auld fella too, crazy as a shithouse rat. No offence."

"Expletive deleted, forgiveness granted."

"You was always the quiet one, auld sober sides, Sam. Wild as a whore Paul was. Hard to believe the two of you came out the same hole. Nobody was surprised he turned out the way he did, though I liked the cunt, don't get me wrong. I wasn't surprised y'see, cos I knew he'd been at it before."

He took a long glug of dark wine and bowed his head.

"Been at what, Brendan?"

"The ripping and the killing." Glug. "Leastways I suspected and the Devil confirmed it."

"Perhaps I'll come back when your mind isn't so polluted, then we'll talk." Samuel's faith suddenly felt very thin.

"You'll find no better time than now, Monsignor," laughed Catman ruefully. "No matter how much I slam down my fucking neck I can't get so much as a buzz. Believe me, I've tried. He said you wouldn't believe me anyways."

"Who said?"

"The Devil. Can't you keep up, or is the smell of my breath mangling your nut? I was down the Moss one day, years ago, back when dog turds were white and crumbly. I sees Paul and Dooley traipsing down the path and Paul has him by the scruff. I was lying down by

Gus Hamill's still—you remember that? Christ, that was some rocket fuel he used to brew! I hears a scream, and then I sees Paul coming back all on his lonesome. Just him and all that blood on his mitts. No-one saw Dooley again, not after that."

"Careful now, Brendan. You said yourself you were intoxicated, praising the might of Hamill's poteen—"

"Aye, that's why I never went to the law. That and I liked your Paul. I got to thinking I'd imagined it all. The auld nut's not as good at storing things," he rapped his head with a peeling knuckle, "as it used to be, and even back then it was full a shite."

He took another drink, kissed the bottle and hugged it to his chest. His smoke-stained fingers were like alien pincers daubed in luminous yellow paint. Those fingers would glow in the dark as they came to grab you but that's not what would wake you though, Samuel, no, it would be their smell, a smell of Sugar Puffs soaked in blood.

"Then a few weeks ago I met him. I met him and he talked to me and ever since I've been drinking more and more to no effect." Tears formed in his deep basilisk eyes. "I took a knife to that poor wee lassie so's they'd lock me up, told them I'd killed all them wee girls, but they knew I was shitting them, and they chucked us out. Now the drink's not working anymore, fuckfuckshitfuck!" For a moment the old Catman returned, raging just beneath the skin.

"Maybe another bottle would do the trick. Spare us the money for a bottle of Wreck The House, Pastor, you'll be saving my immortal."

Samuel absentmindedly held out a crumpled note. "You saw Paul then. I told him not to come to town, not yet. He never listened to me. Never." Still, no harm done. Paul wasn't foolish; no-one would believe a terminal sot like Harper.

"Not Paul, ya heathen! You think I'd be scared of the big fella that's been rotting these years? No, I seen the Devil, Sammy, the same one you've been threatening us all with for years. That's the boyo got to me."

"And what did he look like?"

"The spit of wee Marty Dooley, the picture a him, 'cept I had to look twice cos there wasn't a pick on him. Looked like he'd just crawled outta the grave hisself. You couldn't lend us a few shillings for some smokes? I'm fucking choking here."

Samuel rattled in his pocket. *It can't be. Paul would have told me.*

The girls were meant to strengthen the child, to bring about the rebirth of God on earth, not to flesh out Dooley's bones. No, Paul would never let that be, never throw lives away on a worthless one he had taken in the first place. Catman was mistaken, he was—

"He says the child's doing well, grown so big. Says it's high time you came back to see it."

The world shifted beneath Samuel's feet. He had been used, beguiled.

"They have gulled me," he said in a weak voice.

Paul would never do that to him, there had to be a reason why he never told him of Dooley; hadn't Paul told him many secrets were yet to be revealed? He snatched the bottle from Catman's adhesive lips and drained its bitter dregs.

"Steady on there!" cried Catman. "What do you think you're doing?"

Samuel had no idea. He would have to go back to the Moss to find out. He stumbled away, ignoring the sneers of Sniper and his cohorts, picking his way over a jumble of half-burnt tyres (*Bless you*), used condoms (*Bless you*), and dried-up glue bags (*Bless you all*).

In his mind the pillows had been united, and God would not go hungry this day.

Chapter 22

Joyce sat at the kitchen table, microphone in hand, reading aloud from a corrugated Mills and Boon that looked as though the plot had been sucked out of it. Beside her elbow a tape spooled contentedly, recording her shaky voice for the long dark days that must surely come.

She was convinced, and had been from an early age, that one day she would be struck blind. She accepted this as a basic truth, a badly stitched hem in the fabric of her being, one that even Samuel would be unable to fix as it was a judgement from on high, a judgement she deserved. Hadn't this morning's events verified that and brought her penance ever closer?

She wasn't scared; she was prepared.

She had already recorded the most vengeful verses from the Old Testament and the dirty bits from her stash of Jackie Collins, but the saccharine fare she held in her hand seemed empty, a hollow lie, and her voice broke before the heroine's first perfect kiss. She pressed the stop button with her thumb and hit rewind.

If only life could be turned back so easily, mistakes erased at the touch of a button. She would never have met Eddie Heather and Dobson would never have been born. She would have her tubes tied, she would be born a boy, she would—

She would still be in this position, for this was God's will.

There was no point in prayer. Christ had prayed on the cross and been ignored—what were the chances of hers getting through. Samuel had never spoken of Satan's role in all of this, but surely if they were involved in such a Holy endeavour, to bring back Christ, the Devil would not lie idle. Surely he would stick a hairy paw into the spokes, attack them at every opportunity with obstacles and doubts.

She would never have guessed the attack would come from such a quarter, or in the guise of her gormless son. Samuel had told her once that Satan was God's eldest son, and now she wondered if Dobson, on whom all their hopes were pinned, were not the child of the Evil One.

Eddie, the boy's mortal father, had been gormless too, but clever with it. Sometimes, though she knew it was wrong, she missed him, but it was wrong too, to wake in the night with the image of her husband being fed to Paul's ravenous child. Paul had explained it all, with the light of a toenail moon shining through the thin mist of his body in the rustling Moss.

"Not terrors," she heard Samuel say, "wonders, Joyce! Dust is good enough for man, but only blood will satiate God. You have been chosen, you will sit with the Holy family in the new world to come. Ignore the screams, the guilt, and think only of Paradise."

But here in her working kitchen, with a spider crawling across the savannah of the tablecloth, the ashtray full, and the bananas turning black in the fruit bowl, Paradise seemed a distant joke, a fairytale to placate a wayward child. A wayward child like Dobson.

If only she could have told him like she wanted to!

She had begged and begged, but Samuel refused. This was as much his fault as hers, and she would point that out to him whenever that vein in his forehead pulsed and he began quoting his beloved Leviticus.

No-one was to blame, not really. Who could have foreseen the events of this morning, when Dobson turned up with that dark little thing, holding her hand and beaming. Kate. The name was phlegm in her throat. They thought it was love at first sight, you could tell; it happened all the time in the movies. But in real life hearts were made of something less durable than celluloid.

Sherman didn't like her, and that was proof enough she was bad news. He damn near went for her (he could've swallowed the skinny bitch in one snap) and they ended up having to put him out. He had howled the whole way through, punctuating the long uncomfortable silences as Lady Muck sat sipping her tea and looking at Dobson with those proprietary eyes, flashing her mocking little smile.

She was a hungry-looking little mare with bony hands (no rings, no jewellery at all), and baggy boyish clothes—her big army coat from some surplus store, you couldn't even tell if she'd a chest on her—and her little talon hooked on her son's knee. She was pretty though, even with that scar on her face.

Something was obviously wrong with her; why else would she take up with Dobson? He was no catch. She could have dealt with that—a few threats and this unforeseen problem would soon iron itself out—until the bombshell, the bloody A-bomb that ruined everything.

"I'm pregnant," he said, blushing. "I mean Kate's ... We're having a baby." A big goofy grin like it's the best news ever, and all the while that little bitch's rodent eyes on her, gleeful.

Impossible that Dobson could do this, Dobson who had wet the bed until he was twelve, Dobson who still had a teddy, Dobson who cried at love stories and war films alike because he was soft. Or so she had thought.

She had thought his father soft too, soft and sweet as the ice cream he used to sell from his rickety old van. He had been drunk when he bought it, and the gears never worked properly. She hated the gaudy old thing but he had stood up to her over it. She got a wake-up call there too.

Oh what would the Cunningham boys say now? How had she not seen the warning signs? How could she when her boy was so ugly?

Joyce lit a cigarette, rubbing the ash spill from the tape deck. She felt old, sexless. How could her own flesh and blood betray her like this? He was so awkward and shy, so small and funny looking, she never believed this would happen—who would have him?—yet he had been here only this morning, talking of marriage and smelling of fucking.

The girl would have to go of course, and go quickly, completely. Would God send down His hand once more and have her killed? Surely he must, for without Dobson His child could not return. Born in the Moss, he was to be the groom of Paul's Child of the Moss, the father of the Second Coming. Such an honour, such ...

Her assumptions and her laxity brought this to pass. God would leave it to her to sort out.

She stared her blushing son down: "You're what!"

"We're getting married."

The budgies stopped chirping, the terrapins hid in their shells. The cats still pranced around Miss Callaghan but she ignored them. Never trust anyone who has no interest in animals, had she not drummed that into him his whole damn life?

"You were a beautiful child," said Joyce in a lilting rhythm that was almost hypnotic. "Eight pounds six ounces. A real bruiser. He used to eat soap y'know," she said, turning her eyes on Kate. "Toothpaste too. Always mucking into something, real little devil he was. Never thought he'd turn out the way he did."

"And what way is that, Mrs. Heather?" Oh, the cockiness of the little tart.

"Well, if you don't know by now, dear. He's a clever one, more smarts than a hedgehog's arse, though he likes to let on he's slow. He could buy and sell you, that one could. When I think of burping him over my shoulder, and him to grow up and take a blade to my heart. Should've kept the gas in and let him explode."

"Don't be like this, mum; can't you just be happy for us?"

"At the shops, at the school, at the effing front door. Always someone with a tale to tattle about that 'crazy son of yours'. Happy for you? I would've been happy for you if I'd squirted you out blue and put you in a wee white box instead of a wee white cot."

"Mum—"

"I defended you, always did. What mother would stand such things said about her own flesh and blood. They didn't *know* him, yet they queued down the street to crucify him. What good did it do me? They just turned on me instead—Loopy Ma Heather, someone to scare the kids with, accuse the hubbys of Whorebag Heather, Jumpleads Joyce— do you think I don't know what they say about me behind my back?"

"Mrs. Heather. Joyce. I realise you're upset. You think I'm taking your boy away from you but you've got me all wrong." The little bitch had the nerve to grin. "I'm not what you think I am."

"You're exactly what I think you are!" Joyce leaned forward, her nails digging into the cheap vinyl armrests. "A greedy little snatch intent on making him do your every whim while you service half the town. I know you alright, Missy, I *was* you. You're lucky I don't rip your tiny little titties off."

"I think we should go, Dobson," said Kate, taking his hand as if she were declaring ownership. "Best let mummy fume in private."

And when the door closed on the idiotic pair she *had* fumed. The girl must die, just like Eddie; like a cow in a cattle truck, the Lord will know His own.

My poor old Eddie; she thought of him so often now though the memories were badly lit. He seemed more alive now than he ever had when he drew breath; him and his feet and that damn ice cream van he was so proud of.

She had made love to him in that van. No, she had *fucked* him in that van with all the greed she had laid at Kate's door, fucked him mercilessly, squashing cones and spilling syrup, making him eat flakes out of her. He had been more than just willing, he had been fanatical. They had fucked everywhere with abandon apart from the one time it really mattered, apart from the Moss.

She had to talk him into it then, tease him, bribe him. He kept protesting someone would see; this from a man who'd taken her against the church gates. She practically raped him, and even then he wilted before she had milked him dry. No matter, the seed was sown in the place Samuel had shown her, the exact spot where Paul had taken the corpse of that other babe of the Moss, Eileen, and the place where Dobson would bring forth his own.

It had been summer.

It was always summer of course, even then just coming out of her teens the sun never ceased to shine, still illuminating her memories with a warm safe glow. Eddie Heather was a couple of years older—and hadn't that been attractive after years of immature boys pulling on her tits—with a wisp of a moustache that looked both ridiculous and debonair, and those bloody clogs. Eddie had *awful* feet. Athlete's foot he claimed but it was more like leprosy, the skin between his toes falling away in huge dead flakes as he powdered them on the bed; and the smell, like sour grave roses.

All that summer he had worn those huge, shapeless, wooden clogs. You could hear him clomping down the street as soon as he turned the corner. "Here comes Frankenstein for you," her dad used to say, a good ten minutes before the tentative knock on the door. The kids in the estate had a field day with them. Lining up at his van for 99's and wafers, there was always some cheeky little sod asking for a "Clog Ice."

Eddie never had a sense of humour; he was too thin skinned, even a bad pun from a scruffy eight year old could hurt him.

It was the dog end of July, a million Clog Ice queries in, when he snapped, ramming a Cornetto so hard into some urchin's face he left his lips in rags. He ended up losing the only job he ever loved.

After that winter came early, moody days spent at his parents' house with the big clock ticking like a Hitchcock plot, and the television turned off until seven because "it could go afire." The only relief coming when the neighbour's girl, Eileen, dropped in and Joyce had someone to chat to.

And because she was older the girl listened to her—all eyes and pent up breath—how good it was to be respected! Oh, how she loved that girl, her beauty, her innocence. And when Eileen told her, a little blush on her angelic face, that she had been born in the Moss— "My mum went for a walk with my dad and pop! Out I came! Guess that's why I've always been outdoorsy"—Joyce knew she wasn't just perfect, she was a godsend.

She never regretted telling Paul. One day she would meet Eileen again, and Eileen would be able to thank her properly; Eddie too.

Samuel assured her that in the times to come his role would not be a footnote. Such a hassle to get him to the Moss! Satan had been whispering in his ear but she lulled him down and, after prolonged and tedious foreplay, he had managed to fuck her on that holy ground.

When the brothers came calling she knew her husband's time was up; Paul had been dead eight years by then, and Samuel was barred from the house. Eddie rarely put his foot or his fists down but when he did he meant business. He wanted no mention of the name Cunningham in his house.

"He'll kill the boy," Paul said. "When he finds out what he is, when the Devil's voice finally convinces him. We can't risk that, Joyce. Samuel will help. Be strong and pray."

She began to go to Group, taking Dobson with her despite Eddie's protests. The end times were approaching, her child heading toward manhood fast; a black eye or a cracked rib was a small price to pay, especially when you remembered what the blessed martyrs had suffered for faith alone.

Poor Eddie; she could feel him smiling on her even now. When they met in the great beyond she wouldn't even say, "I told you so."

So many bad memories today, and all because of that presumptuous little whore. And here was the bitterest one of all, her biggest trial, and though she had passed it still hurt to think of Eddie and that thing—

No, she must be strong and not listen to the lies of doubting Satan.

She had sent Dobson off to school with a kiss, then she had rang Samuel and waited. Eddie was lying on the couch as usual, but instead of waking him and nagging him to find work she brought the quilt down from the spare room and tucked him up snug, stroking his hair until unconsciousness reclaimed him.

Soon after she had opened the door and let in Samuel and the thing—no, not a *thing*, a child, it was blasphemy to call such a miracle a *thing*, a child born of death, a beautiful child, or at least Paul said it would be—and she could not bear to look upon it.

Samuel ushered it in, putting his hand on Joyce's shoulder as the child went snuffling along the hall. "Fortitude woman! We all knew this day would come."

She brought them into the living room. Eddie lay, drool seeping from his gaping mouth (no flies in her house when Eddie was around), as the child dropped down on all fours, stalking his prone form; arching its back as it edged ever closer.

"Sustenance, child, here is true sustenance," whispered Samuel, drawing out the sibilants like he was deflating. "Better than any old cat."

The child leapt on Eddie, his eyes springing open as it clamped its mouth over his and began *sucking*, a horrible squelching, as he writhed helplessly beneath.

Joyce turned her back, looking out on Romannon Street.

On the other side of the window she could hear a motorbike grumble and fart, the hammering and yammering of workmen and, high above, she could see a plane of optimistic people going out, or perhaps disappointed people coming home. The sun was turned up full. Even though the window was open, a bluebottle banged against it when it would have been easier to fly away. She heard a squeal, then the sigh of a bus.

She concentrated on her neighbours, trying to blank out her mind, the people she had known and despised all her life. Was this what her husband was dying for? To save the likes of Sheila Weir, who spread rumours about her in the butcher's, or Moonface Bob Turk, who thieved her knickers from the line?

"It was for the whole of mankind," said Paul, and she supposed that would include a lot of people she didn't like, but that just made her sacrifice more noble, didn't it?

The slurping and the sucking grew louder, wetter. She heard Samuel issue an embarrassed cough. Was it eating poor Eddie alive? How could she ever explain that?

She didn't turn around; she just moved her eyes to the wall where, under her wedding picture (Eddie so handsome, and smiling!), she saw the shadow of the child, hunched and undulating, barely human. She bowed her head, trying to drown out the awful tearing sounds and think of how she could break the news to Dobson when he got home, full of talk of China or chipmunks or whatever else he had learned that day.

She would buy him a pet to ease his grief; she would fill the house with life.

"It is done," said Samuel.

She nodded, keeping her eyes closed until they left, holding her breath as she heard the panting child pass by. Only when the front door clicked and she heard the bad-tempered racket as Samuel wrestled with the van's engine did she turn to look at her husband.

She expected a riven mess, but he lay serene under the quilt, not a mark on him save for a few extra lines on his pale face. Here was a miracle that gladdened her heart.

His hair though, his hair was white, falling from his forehead in great pristine waves like the ice cream he once sold. Later the doctor would speak vaguely of weak hearts and she would cry and they would be real tears, but for now her tears were for her lack of faith, for the worry that when the time came she would not be able to give her son over to that *thing*, yes, *thing*.

She put down her novel and dragged the heavy Bible toward her, rucking up the tablecloth. She opened it at the dedication, relishing the spicy smell of its thin pages; it had smelt ancient from the day Samuel had given it to her, the day Dobson was born.

To Joyce, more loyal than any Ruth—he had written in his flowing, feminine hand. He alone had always valued her.

How much of this doom-laden tome she had already committed to tape she could not say. When the darkness engulfed her, as engulf her it must, she would not be short on the Word.

She skipped to Ezekiel, passing over prophets and kings with an eager wet thumb. Samuel had gotten her to read his bible favorites, his Job and Jeremiah, his Leviticus and Revelation, so often she could quote them by heart, but it was Ezekiel that she loved. Clearing her throat she lifted the mike, keeping place with a Day-Glo nail.

"'I will punish you more severely than I have punished anyone before or ever will again,'" she intoned over the quietly clicking spools.

"'Parents will eat their own children, and children will eat their parents.'" Her tears fell unchecked now.

Why, she wondered for the umpteenth time, *did God the All-Powerful, the Almighty, not just do things the easy way?*

Outside an ice cream van trundled down the street and her fat tears fell on the spidery script, and the thin pages offered up a scent of cinnamon guilt.

Chapter 23

Even Gus Hamill's dogs, whelped on raw meat and bred to bite, were scared of Sherman. Pruner had told Dobson not to bring him along, mainly because he was terrified of the thing, but Dobson had insisted, pointing out the dog would be good protection and claiming it could help track Skinner in the sprawling Moss.

"I'll carry the tent and everything," he said, but Pruner had taken that burden, unwilling to be left holding Sherman's chain. That fang-ridden beast had a look in its eye that suggested it was not above sampling a human bollock, and, besides, Dobson was the only one the damn thing ever obeyed.

Now, as they made their way through the rusting maze of cars that littered the yard, Gus's two sleek pinschers mewled through the wreckage with their knobby tales crawling up their butts. If only Sherman has the same effect on the famous Hamill shotgun—he had felt the sting of buckshot on many an occasion as a kid, fogging the Hamill orchard.

The run up to the house resembled the nest of some enormous mechanical bird and the smell of burning tyres hung thick in the air. A Morris Minor estate, its wooden paneling chewed off, sat with its back doors open, a makeshift kennel. Sherman gave its contents a cursory sniff, then pissed on its bedding.

Gus appeared from behind it, oiled to the elbows, his vast torso wobbling on spindly legs, a child's drawing of a man—a face not so much lived in as squatted in, hairs sprouting from his ears and his nose in thick grey clumps as if his skull were little more than a busted mattress. He clutched some engine part in his hand like he had been busy eviscerating a robot, but he had no gun.

"I hope you're not of a mind to be taking a shortcut through here," said Gus, scratching at his sandpaper jaws as he clocked their rucksacks. "You can just go on round Horseshoe Lane. This is no bloody public thoroughfare."

"We came to see you actually, Mr. Hamill," said Dobson.

"It's the Heather boy, isn't it? And Billy Rose. After some parts, are you?"

Pruner watched the line of crows on the barn roof and a chill ran through him; a memory of crows and blood, and of a crawling, howling—

"Young Rose," said Gus, "this buckcat Heather rubbing off on you? I said are you planning to camp on my land 'til you find a gearbox?"

"No, we came to see Skinner Morris. We need to talk to him."

Gus's face knuckled up instantly. "And what gave you the idea Skinner's here?"

Told you this was a bad idea, Dobs, thought Pruner. *Now the shotgun will spring forth and our arses will soon resemble Swiss cheese.*

Behind the house crouched the Moss, fecund and wild, smelling of gin and nettles and rich peaty earth. The clearing where the house stood looked to be the last outpost of civilization, fighting a losing battle against its inevitable, intractable green spread.

All the rotted hulks of cars pointed away from its dank marshes and hoary trees, as if humanity had fled in exodus from its grasp only to die on its borders. *If Skinner was hiding in there he was welcome to it,* thought Pruner, *let him rot there like everything else.* He would stay until the sun set, then persuade Dobson to give up the ghost and go home.

The Moss would be only too eager to give up its ghosts, and they would be many, of that he had no doubt.

"We don't," Dobson was saying, "but we think he might be in the Moss. We're going camping down there. We thought maybe you could narrow the search down for us a bit."

"Like I told the law and anyone else who'd listen, I've not seen him, and if I did I'd knock seven bells of shite outta him. Murdering little bastard that he is."

"I don't believe that," said Dobson.

Gus stuck his face down into Dobson's; up close his nose resembled a ballerina's toe. "You calling me a liar, wee man?" Sherman issued a wet throaty growl but Gus ignored him.

"I don't believe he's a murderer, and I don't think you do either."

"And why's that, lad? You know who chopped up his wee wifey then?"

"C'mon, Dobs," said Pruner. "I told you this was a waste of time. If he's down in the Moss we'll find him ourselves."

"Be careful," said Gus. "There's them down there that have more than one skin."

"What?"

"Look, Mr. Hamill," said Dobson, "we're not accusing you of anything, we just want to help a mate out is all. If you do happen to see him tell him we'll be camping by the Umbrella tree. I know you two were close; we just thought if he was in trouble he'd turn to you first."

Sherman was slavering now as he fought against his chain, garrotting his thick neck. Strangled, almost human sounds coming from his throat as his black eyes locked onto the barn, focusing on it with such intensity it seemed he would decapitate himself in his singular intent to get there. His paws were embedded in the dry earth, digging for a hold.

Damn thing's rabid, thought Gus, *it's a wonder the boy can hold him, he's no more than a pipe cleaner; it's like an elephant tethered by a straw.* Yet no sweat broke on Dobson's face. He stood with a casual nonchalance, oblivious of the wolf straining at his side. *That's exactly what that mutt is*, thought Gus, *a bloody Timber wolf with a grizzly bear for a father.*

"I know you mean well, lad, but I ain't seen him, nor expect to. You three were always thick as stew growing up. Reckon if he'd stuck with you two instead of marrying that harpy, God rest her soul, he wouldn't be in such a mess right now." He nodded, chewing on his lip. "That old Umbrella tree's no spot to pitch, all gnarly roots and night birds. If I were you I'd strike up camp on the other side. You know the Babby Swing?"

"Still got the bruises to prove it," smiled Dobson.

"Aye, course you do. Well, that's where I'd pitch up. Now, on your way before that hound of yours makes my dogs shit kittens. I've no time for jawing. In fact, I wasn't talking to you at all, was I?"

"No, Mr. Hamill. Thanks, Mr. Hamill."

"Gus is fine, now skedaddle, I'm a busy man."

As if responding to a cue, Sherman plunged forward, yanking the chain from Dobson's hand, bounding toward the barn.

"Sherman!"

"Christ boy, get him quick, I've chickens in there!"

Despite the heavy doors being firmly closed, Gus had a sudden image of the dog ripping through them with a single bite. The sound of Sherman's nails digging frantically on the slats was like a savage hail storm. The beast was growling with such hateful intensity Gus felt his testicles seek refuge in his belly.

"Don't let him in there!"

If it broke through the doors, what then?

Would his secrets be brought out squinting into the sunlight? When exposed would they lose their hold over him, cease to whisper to him in the dark, prove once and for all he wasn't crazy like his brother? But his secrets, he was certain, did not care to be illuminated. He had a feeling they would exact a terrible price were they forced out into the workaday world before their time.

He watched, paralysed and sweat chilled, as Dobson grabbed the chain and hauled the dog away, its claws scratching on air as it reared up like some mighty hell horse. Dobson cuffed the dog across the snout, causing it to sniff and sneeze, then look shamefaced at its master. *Boy has stones*, thought Gus, relaxing a little, *you had to give him that. Perhaps he'll be able to help Skinner. Someone needed to.* Gus positioned himself between the boys and the barn.

"Sorry," said Dobson, mistaking the protruding vein on Gus's forehead for anger instead of fear. "It must be the country air getting to him. We'll be off now, thanks for everything."

Gus didn't answer, afraid his voice might betray him. He watched them go, the dog still staring over its shoulder, right through him and into the barn, as it was dragged away across the dusty yard.

"Get orf moy land," he heard the Rose boy snigger when he thought he was out of earshot. Gus didn't mind, he was used to that kind of thing. When you were a kid farm types were the coolest things in the world, then when you shot up a bit they were nothing but a joke. He felt it himself. He watched their retreating silhouettes until his eyes began to water with the heat shimmer. Already he could smell the tar bubbling on Horseshoe Lane. It was going to be a brutal summer.

He heard a sound from the barn.

His joy, a lovingly restored Triumph Stag, was in there. He had dreamed of owning one since he was a nipper and saw one zoom past, a yellow spear, on the Madden road. His cars were a hobby that had become an obsession. Now they were his children's inheritance. He would pay off the guilt he felt for neglecting them by giving them what he laboured on for so long, yet he could not bear the thought of his son's flogging them for some quick cash.

The Stag was tainted now; it still bore the smell. He rarely drove it now; he should never have let—

The sound again, like something trying to hide unsuccessfully. He steeled himself, opening the barn doors with a sepulchral creak, a shaft of light bursting by him and slicing through the sucking heat.

Dust motes swarmed in that bright blade like golden snow. His nostrils filled with the familiar smells of oil and grease and hay— smells he associated with love and precision and care—and something else, something rotten, like the sinister smell that hid beneath the antiseptic waft of hospital wards.

He squinted past his beloved cars, shrouded in dust covers, and the skeleton frame of his latest project. The sunlight that pierced through the slats was not sufficient, but he hesitated to turn on the harsh fluorescents.

A furtive sound, over by the love of his life, a vintage Riley RM Drophead and his Ducatti 900ss replica that he had rescued from an auction in Rosshaven.

What else have I rescued, he wondered, his scalp prickling. *What else have I restored?* He hit the lights.

"Is that you, Augustus?"

He flinched at the inherent sarcasm. Augustus. How he loathed that name. Three syllables that had been hammered into him all his life to remind him he was a hick. Because of that name, because his brother was called Wendell and said "cababbage" instead of "cabbage", because they had been bigger than their teachers and smelt of pig dung.

Because the scent of the Moss was on them no matter how hard they scrubbed.

They mocked them for their plaid shirts and country manners but mainly, in hindsight, because Wendell was a strange fish. He had always been odd—"Takes after his granny Gee," mum used to say— and spent all his time down the Moss despite dad's warnings. "The burrs down there'll snag his brain. He'll sink in one of those bogs and there'll be no bringing him back."

And sink he did. Gradually at first.

Wendell was always mitching off school down there and sleeping out. Gus loved it as well, but in the same way he loved the roar of the chainsaw; he sensed the threat of it too. At first it showed as just nonsense; Wendell talking of flying flowers, of watering daffodils with milk to make them grow thorns, and making strange guttural noises whenever a girl was near.

Guess what I saw today, Gus, a seagull in a bubble, floating right over the Babby swing!

And he would laugh, and Gus would too, thinking his brother had been buying some of that funny blotting paper they sold outside The Cove on a Saturday night. Then Wendell's tales grew darker, and the scratching came at the windows in the early hours. Now Wendell was in the Crunchy house on the other side of Ellsford, drooling in his soup between tablets.

Dad had been right. The husk of his body lay medicated in Evanston Home but his brain had sank like a stone, never to be retrieved, in the Moss's dark mires.

"Have they gone?"

Gus moved between the shrouded cars. "They're gone. The mutt too."

Dooley was hunched by the Riley's front wheel, half covered by the tarp, fatter than the last time Gus had seen him but still light enough to cough into a corner. *My God*, thought Gus, *he's actually scared*. The realization cheered him. The little raggedy wraith was actually frightened of something. Gus, as his yard attested, could never bear to throw anything away; he tucked that little piece of information up neatly and filed it away.

"You sure?"

Still, it was wise to make certain. "Yeah, course I ... Ahoy hoy! Here it comes again, it's more like a lion than a dog!"

"Bar the doors! Quickly, bar the—"

"Too late, Dooley. Run!"

Gus burst into laughter watching Dooley trying to leap over the bonnet, sliding off onto his bony ass. *Yes*, he thought, *you are terrified you little ghoul, and now I know it.*

Dooley's face was awash with sweat, it ran in an oily slick across his sepia skin. The thin man heaved, vomiting a long string of gruel. "Very clever, Augustus," he panted. "You're quite the monkey. I'd watch that sense of humour of yours, I surely would."

Gus stopped laughing, the sound killed instantly in the heavy air, but not because of Dooley's implied threat for in truth he had not heard him. He was staring at the small puddle of puke on the barn's grainy floor.

"I shall need some transport again," Dooley was saying. "I think I'll borrow the Stag again."

Gus nodded dumbly, his attention firmly on the cat's paw and the two human fingers marooned in the bile of Dooley's guts.

Chapter 24

Lately the Reverend Brian Craig had begun to think that God was insane. By the time his early morning pilgrimage brought him to his daughter's grave he would be convinced that his Lord and Saviour was stone-cold dead.

His faith had been withering rapidly; once so vital, but now so dry and desiccated that its charred remains in his soul (Soul? A body, a machine, nothing more) appalled him. He had greeted the haggard stranger in the hallway mirror with a heartfelt, "Fuck you, God" this morning, and the stranger had grinned back in agreement.

"Fuck you, God," he whispered, so that the shell who called herself his wife would not hear and resume her sole function of crying (so many tears, the woman was filled with brine, not blood), and he would be forced to trot out more empty platitudes.

She believed, more now than ever, her faith feeding on the very void that consumed his, a parasite growing fat on misery, and he pretended to share that greed. Now all he could do was marvel that no-one had ever punched him, spat in his face, as he sat in the centre of their despair spewing out nonsense about a benevolent deity and a peaceful hereafter. They must have felt as he did now. They must have wanted to tear Christ limb from limb.

His façade was crumbling, his mask slipping; he was aware of that. He could not keep this up much longer. There was a crack in the dam and at any moment all the poison and anger within him would burst forth and wash away this lie he was living. He had felt the mask slip at the Spence boy's funeral last week; the snake thoughts rushing up, almost spilling from his mouth.

That had been a hard day.

So many memories reunited from the moment the hearse arrived and four stern men delivered a corpse from its paneled womb. It had rained, first day in weeks. Someone must have booked it after all; a cheap act, but it plucked on all the right heartstrings.

"We are gathered here today—"

We are gathered here today because Alan Spence couldn't drive, he thought, *because, to be brutally frank, he was an idiot.* But the truth was never invited to funerals. Young Alan, oiled up more than the engine, hit a tree by the community centre at fifty miles an hour. He had been driving his mum's Metro, which explained why he hadn't been going faster; in fact, it probably explained why he'd been liquored up—imagine dying in a second-hand shoebox like that. He should have crawled out and pretended he'd fell. The Reverend had to stifle a laugh with a well-timed cough.

"—to celebrate the life of—"

What was there to celebrate? He was only seventeen. Most spots in the dole queue? Feeling up some tart in a car park? I bet the father says, "I warned him about that bloody car, but would he listen," and if he does I'll scream at the banality of it all, thought Brian.

Spence was just a boy, a boy who hadn't the time to do anything. He was older than Nadine though, he had longer than her. Celebrate?

"—Alan Leighton Dawson Spence—"

Leighton Dawson! Christ, in the midst of death we are in embarrassment.

"—and pray for his safe passage—"

Brian watched as the coffin was carefully lowered, as if its contents were valuable and not pie filling, into its final resting place. Final. Nothing else. No harps, no horns, no gossamer wings. If there were a Heaven it was bound to be full by now, so what was the point in mumbling words and spilling tears over a hole in the ground?

Not for dumb Alan, indifferent now to their salt tribute. It was because one day they would be lowered down too, in a ridiculously overpriced coffee table, and that would be that, and that touched something base, that jammed the needle right in the iris.

You cry for yourselves!

Brian paused momentarily, unable to carry out the bog standard death rap, so meaningless now; he wanted to shout in their stupid wet faces. *Look what they bring for your safe passage, Alan; teddy bears, flowers in the shape of Brother, Son. Can you not see how tacky this is?*

Why not send a tree-shaped wreath, or various mangled-limb assortments. Why not go the whole hog and dump the coffin down the hole at fifty miles an hour whilst everyone makes skidding noises.

You cry for yourselves!

It seemed the whole town had been there though the boy couldn't have been that popular. If he could see this lot he'd think he was in debt big time. Funeral groupies the lot of them. Ellsford had gorged itself on death of late, become addicted.

Somehow he got through it, even when Mrs. Spence flung herself in after the coffin, bleating and wailing, he got through it, his mask intact.

He knew that pain intimately, yet all he could think as she lay prostrate in the grave beneath was: *Start shoveling now boys, bury the silly bitch with her moronic son*; and all the while his understanding smile never wavered, and all the while he carried on preaching divine forgiveness.

Was he too now expected to forgive?

If only he could get his hands on that Skinner boy he would spend hours, months, years exacting the slowest of revenges. Hell was a small price to pay when you were already there. Inbred hick—he would shit on his puddle of a corpse when he was through!

As if to underline the thought he threw the Bible he habitually carried; it bounced off a headstone, lying on the marble chips like a broken bird. He did not know why he still carried it; he supposed it was much the same way an alcoholic clung to an empty wine bottle.

He bent to retrieve it. It had his name inside it and it wouldn't do for someone to find it and start gossiping. Leaning over the grave he caught the inscription—*Cissy Cunningham, Asleep With Jesus*—and felt a chill run through him although the morning was already hot.

It recalled the dream to him, the one he'd been having on and off these last few weeks, the one where Paul Cunningham was standing in his garden, his pale face half shaded by the pines, and in his arms Nadine, naked and smiling as Cunningham *licked* at her.

It was his own scream that woke him, yelling for help to an empty room. He had the sweats from the nightmare just like when he was a boy, except then he had thought of them as NightStallions, his heart galloping down the final furlong to consciousness, the terror racing through his veins.

Whenever his courage returned his arm darted out from the duvet, seeking the balm of the light bulb. He flicked the switch and sent the shadows back into hiding. As his breath was reined in he heard the bulb crack and tick as if something inside it were about to hatch, something dark that would shatter the light.

He shivered the memory away.

Not so long ago he would have taken this for a sign. Now he knew it for what it really was, one of life's nasty little coincidences. An image of Cissy came to him, like a vision in the perfect morning, the way she was the last time he had seen her, just before her passing almost ten years before.

A stunted little thing cowled in black, hard to believe she was the mother of such massive sons. Perhaps that was what weighed her down, or perhaps she was buckled under her family's reputation; a murderous son and a fanatical husband.

Free of them both, though still saddled with Samuel, she had come to him when the cancer had moved up a gear and her ravings at the iniquities of the world were almost spent.

"Oh Mr. Craig," she said. It was always *Mr.* Craig, as if by denying him his title she repudiated the "soft" teachings of his church. "Oh Mr. Craig, the flesh of my breast is rotten and I haven't long. I wish to God the cancer had taken my womb years ago for I have raised a devil, Mr. Craig, a devil."

"Cissy, you cannot blame yourself for Paul's deeds. Don't listen to the poison that narrow minds spread."

"Paul? I'm not talking about my dear, sweet Paul, Mr. Craig. He was easily led is all. No, I raised a devil in Samuel, and when I'm gone he will go unchecked. You must keep an eye on him, or others will suffer as Paul did."

Brian dusted down his bible and sighed. He had no time this day, or the bleak days left him, for the rantings of the Good Book's many victims; was he not one himself?

I have raised a devil …

No, Cissy, just another frightened fool gulled into believing in a Heaven because earth could be such a Hell.

He moved on, his heart as grey as his hair. He felt like an ice cube held in a warm hand, sweating away his existence and growing ever smaller. He had no time now for gods and devils, sins and penance.

He did not believe his daughter's soul was an object of debate in some celestial court. Only weather and worms bothered her now.

He felt a sudden foreboding coil deep in his belly, perhaps merely the remnant of last night's dream, or the recollection of Cissy and the cancer that ate her with a gusto that time could never hope to match. It was enough to make him pause, to breathe deeply, and try to still his inner writhings.

At the far end of the cemetery the green hedge that loomed over its eastern border rose in an unassailable wall, and for the first time it seemed to him threatening. He was aware now of the unmistakable feeling of being watched, yet he was sure he had the marble orchard all to himself, with only the jackdaws that congregated on the crumbling ruins of the Agnew plot for company. A solitary cat hunted for meagre prey among the dead flowers over by the bins.

The cemetery was preternaturally quiet; perhaps that's what irked him.

Usually the sound of traffic seeped through the hedge, and birds sang in the rowan trees. He shook himself and began walking the twisting length of the path until he reached his daughter's grave, stopping short when he saw the mound of earth on either side, parted like soily labia.

Turn back, he thought, *this is God's final joke, the final turn of the knife for you who mocked Him. Turn back now.*

But he couldn't, was already moving forward on unsteady legs, his smile slipping, his mask falling, as he reached the graveside and stared down into the pit, struggling to comprehend.

He unleashed a bellow as something deep inside him shook loose. He felt unfettered, that he might just drift off and float away into the blessed ignorant abyss beyond, howling all the while.

Beneath him his daughter stared back at him through the ruins of her coffin, her eyelids peeled off, her mouth a hateful rictus sneer, her pastel dress ripped from her, her body mauled, eaten in places, half her dainty hand gone, missing.

As Brian Craig's voice finally cracked and broke, his throat only emitting jagged rasps of incoherent rage, the jackdaws soared up; their ragged chorus the laughter of an indifferent deity, or an echo of his daughter's.

Chapter 25

Despite the voice squirming in his head, despite the fugue states that found him sleepwalking toward the Moss, Malcolm fought it, turning back each time, aware that sooner or later he would inevitably succumb. The voice was getting louder, the fugues longer.

He had been sleeping rough behind the Fire Station. He felt he could fall no further, but also, at times, he felt a strange euphoria at his plight. It was as if a new colour had been revealed to him. Not just an original mix, a startling hue, but a brand *new* colour, one that no eyes had ever seen before. This new colour burned in him, glowed, but he lacked the words to explain it for how could you explain colour, let alone a new one, to the willfully blind?

And all the while the Moss was calling.

His subconscious was intent on making up his mind for him, burning bridges, forcing the play. He had sprayed obscenities all over his uncle's house before leaving, been caught stealing a newspaper he didn't even want from the Stop N Shop, and last night managed to get himself barred from The Cove; he had punched a girl, or at least had a vague memory of doing so.

He stood by the bar blowing the dust, blowing away a universe, wishing he was smart enough to work out the trajectories of those floating motes, the mathematics of their flight. It was a form of music, a dance of numbers, the oldest magic.

He turned to the girl beside him seeking only to enlighten her.

"Did you know that trust contains rust? It's doomed to failure, rotten from within."

She smiled as if he had offered her a profound truth and, despite the numbing caul of alcohol, he felt a warm stirring in his groin. *Here is your redemption*, the Brainworm urged, *she wants you, take her now!* Malcolm moaned as the beckoning beauty wet her full lips with her pointed tongue. *Take her now, Malcolm, are you not owed?* Malcolm snatched at her, grasping her dress by the cleavage and pulling her toward him, planting his mouth on her exposed and glistening breasts. The Brainworm laughed, but the laughter was replaced by a jangling chaos as something struck his jaw with enough force to send him crashing to the floor. He looked up to see Cyril being restrained, and his mother, her huge swaying dugs wobbling in time to her sobbing, being led away. The barman hauled him out through the cheers and the heckles; "Your own mum? You're one sick fuck, Weir. Don't let me see you in here again."

The only victory that night had been Drew's helmet.

He could hardly stop laughing as he squatted over it, his contortions affecting his aim, biting down on his lip as he focused on evacuating his bowels. When he had finished he hung the helmet back on the handlebars, making sure his mystery parcel was tucked away safely inside. Then he took Drew's gloves and flossed lustily between his cheeks. He allowed himself a manic laugh, the terror of what he had done sending his adrenalin soaring, before staggering home to his new life amid the lepers.

He could see Drew vividly, steaming excrement plastered over his dome, head striped like a backstreet Colonel Kurtz, and he could barely breathe with joy. Maybe he wanted to be caught, maybe if Drew hospitalized him it would keep him from the Moss.

He stank. He was down to his last tenner and he had nowhere else to go but the Moss. Last night he had heard the dead girls' chorus and he had held his ears and shouted "Alrightalrightalright!" until they had stopped, and the colour within him shone brighter than the fire beacon above him. He would buy himself something to eat (when was the last time he'd had a bite?) and walk the long cut out to Troughton's.

Above the Frying Saucer was a billboard warning of the penalties of letting your dog foul the footpath; you couldn't buy that kind of advertising. Malcolm stepped inside to find a combover audience; a few rows in front, nothing at the back.

He was impatient to be gone already. People were talking in hushed tones, muttering about the Reverend's daughter, but the details buzzed, were lost in the static. He felt no curiosity, only contempt.

"Life jackets on your chips?"

"What?"

"Lots of vinegar?" sighed the pasty girl behind the counter. Why couldn't she just ask properly? He reddened. Now he didn't even want the fucking things. He felt his blood turn to salt, silting up his heart. The bitch was sweating lard; her tired eyes looked as if they might slip out and roll down her shiny face.

"Sure. Vinegar. Why not."

They were all so dirty. He could kill them all, wipe their filth off the earth with a godlike stroke. He would go to their funerals just to see the ripples he had caused, but that joy would be more fleeting than the kill. He could tear off their smocks and fuck their cooling corpses over the hotplate. The very idea of doing it with one of these sluts after he had squeezed the life out of them made him uncomfortably hard. To caress their cold skin, to come on their pliant bodies, would be a final victory over their kind.

Clutching the grease-stained paper bag he turned to go and walked right into his mother; or rather, the familiar woman whose role in his life had become as indefinable as her title.

"Mum." She looked as if she had been slapped. "Sheila."

She had nowhere to go, trapped between the missing cat posters and the drink coolers. He was squeezing the bag too tightly; he could hear the Styrofoam and the fish bones crack. He tried to look her in the eye, to keep his gaze away from her chest at all costs.

"They may all think it's Skinner but I know you were in on it with him." Her eyes flicked constantly over his shoulder, drawing strength from the crowd. "Did you dig that wee lassie up now he's gone?"

"Mum, please … Can I—" He couldn't ask her—couldn't say those two words: *Come home.*

"I would've turned you in if I wasn't such a coward, if it wouldn't sully our good name. Not that you're a Weir, never were. To think of the hard time I gave Mrs. Cunningham, never knowing what was going to end up on my plate. Let Skinner take the blame. Leave town and let it be over, let it be done."

Hunger left him along with hope.

He pushed out past her, dropping his chips, out into the street where he could cry and she would not see him. He had only walked a few paces when a car pulled up alongside; a ridiculous looking thing, a rich man's toy. Malcolm climbed in. In truth, he had been expecting it.

The stickman sat behind the wheel, though in truth not so twig like now; he had filled out, his lips fattest of all, hiding his tombstone teeth. He winked at Malcolm before pulling out into traffic.

A blur of music, of full bore dissonance, assaulted Malcolm in a physical blast and he felt the voices return in a screaming crescendo as his empty gut tried vainly to heave itself up his throat on a wave of fetid air. The noise was emanating from the stickman himself, he realised, oozing from his pores. Malcolm closed his eyes and tried hard to hold onto consciousness. Then the stickman was leaning over him, his stench cutting through the cacophony, opening the door and pushing him out. The stupid little car fled the scene, its passenger door flapping like a broken wing.

He didn't need to look around to know where he was. He got up gingerly and headed into the Moss, the bracken and the black water, the scorched earth and the creeping things. The voices were a hook in his mind, pulling him on and on. He let them reel him in until the paths got tangled, darker, and he was hopelessly lost.

He hid only once, behind a dense knot of alders when a figure appeared, scaring up a few prissy teal until it passed; Catman with a hammer and a saw and a spring in his step. He felt no surprise, just the need for silence.

And, as the sun was reduced to a thin lattice above him, he got his wish. The voices stopped abruptly, the hook withdrawn, and he was stranded in a maze of pools and listening trees, his skin a mosaic of angular leafy shadow.

I am an archetype, he thought, *a little boy lost in the woods, shunned by those who should love me, by a wicked stepmother. A fairytale boy sent out to be eaten by the monster. I am insane. I am a hunter of ghosts, no, worse, a seeker of ghosts.* He stopped, finding faces everywhere in the brambles, hearing applause in the wafting ferns.

I seek death. I come to die and I come willingly.

He began to cry. The voices, the visions—all self-destruct buttons he had pressed knowingly.

I come to die and I am unafraid. I am a pariah dog. I am the monster chased from town by indifference rather than burning staves and pitchforks. When

I am dead they will cry, they will hurt. I will have my revenge though it costs me my life. My death will be so horrible their black hearts will stop to hear of it.

But I want to live! Go back, apologize, beg—

No, said a voice on the fern's soft breath, *you are already home. Walk further, just a little bit further, into the darkling trees. What could possibly harm you here?*

He brushed on through the cotton grass, swatting at the clouds of insects, going forward, forward, forward for there was no going back. The path ended abruptly in a high clump of crumbling peat swarming with sluggish beetles. Falling against it, raising his head, eyes protruding like a dragonfly's, Malcolm peered over the mound and laughed.

Standing in a dense thicket of willows was a large wooden shed, roughly built but sturdy, incongruous in the overgrown waste. A rudely hewn cross tilted before its door catching the sparse light that filtered through the thick canopy. Brendan had been a busy man it seemed.

"You've built me a new home," he said to the heavy air. He could imagine living the hermitic life, growing a beard and feasting on chewy pike and plump water hens whilst the outside world slipped by unnoticed, uncaring.

Perhaps the girls had left it supplied. Perhaps they would live here with him, a harem of the beautiful and willing dead.

Hoisting himself up, he ran to the ill-fitting door expecting a bulbous creak as it opened, but it swung inward on a smoothly oiled sigh. He stepped in, closing it behind him. Several wonky chairs and the battered backseat of a car were facing a rudimentary altar where several thick candles gave off a reluctant glow. Painted behind the altar was the most disturbing depiction of Christ Malcolm had ever seen; Jesus held a baby in one hand, the baby's heart in the other.

He moved closer to see what was strewn between the candles, wrinkling his nose at the odour mingling with the plywood and paint. On top of the altar lay several dead rats and a headless rabbit, and something else, something pale and gnarled. He lifted it, holding it close to a candle flame to examine it properly. A finger?

"That's mine," said a voice behind him. "Or at least it used to be."

Malcolm spun round, dropping the finger, sending it skittering across the uneven floor. At first he thought the man by the door was Silver; the same large nose, piercing eyes, and outmoded quiff. But this man looked more vital, a thin moustache smeared over his lip lending him an air of cruelty that Silver did not possess.

"Don't worry," said the man, regarding the spinning digit. "It's only a symbol of my completion, a test for my brother Samuel."

The voices began to chirp in Malcolm's head once more and he struggled to find the name he sought through the menagerie. "Paul?"

The man smiled. "Samuel will be here soon; then we can begin. You are to be a coming of age present, a final gift. My child has hankered after you for so long. Do you remember lashing out in the sewers? Now, I'm not one to hold a grudge, but my offspring ..."

"I don't understand."

"You and the rest of this wicked world. I have—" He broke off as the door flew open and Silver came in, boiling in a heavy coat. "Ah, brother," said Paul, "we were just talking about you. Look at what fate has brought us."

"What is he doing here! He can't—"

"Nonsense! Things have moved on apace. The whole Moss is offering up its dead. Everything is coming back, the time is almost at hand."

"Coming back. Like Dooley?"

"Like Jackie Paper! Remember how you used to tell me that story, Sam, Puff the magic dragon? It always made me cry. I used to tell it to the baby, but there not much to cry about here. All fear evaporates in the dark. I have raised a dragon here, a dragon all by myself."

"You should've told me about him, Paul."

"Don't be so churlish, Sam; I didn't see that one coming either. A stray dog dug him up but he would've emerged sooner or later. Everything is coming back, everything that was buried here. So strong is the child's will, as it grows it radiates its power outwards. Nothing lies quiet in the Moss anymore."

"'Why should it be thought a thing incredible with you that God should raise the dead?' Acts, twenty-six, eight."

"Just so, brother, amen. The child couldn't live on fat little dogs, and Dooley has special needs of his own. Thankfully the child heeded my lessons well and made provisions years ago, with Dooley's help. The Lord provides, hallelujah forever and amen. So ask me now, brother, ask me the question you've burned to since I returned. Ask me if I have seen the face of God. Yes, I have, Samuel, and what a dark and monstrous beast he truly is! Soon His face will darken the very skies!"

"Praise His name!" Samuel shook in his rapture. "And this boy? Is he to work with us for the end time?"

Paul laughed, his form shimmering slightly. "No, he is a treat, a morsel for an unavenged appetite. Better than a chunky pup, eh?"

Samuel stared at the floor, shamefaced. "Paul, I tried … maybe if you had explained … the animals were enough in the beginning."

"And the hamsters the old biddy brought? I fed them to Dooley. Luckily my darling thought ahead and found another to provide what you turned from in disgust like an old maid."

"I'm sorry, Paul. 'Cursed be he that keepeth his sword from blood.'"

"Make up for it now and mayhap Christ will forgive you. Hold the offering, the child draws near."

Malcolm, hoping to inch his way out the door unseen, could contain his contempt no longer; the girls had not mentioned spending eternity with two bible bashers. "You two are fucking nuts, you know that! Fucking—" His words were snipped off cleanly as Samuel gripped him by the throat and thrust him on the floor. He struggled but was no match for the big man's penitent strength.

"I knew you would not fail me," Paul was saying. "Through your belief these long years the Holy Trinity will live again—Me, my child, Dobson—the three-personed God, and their seed will usher in the New World!"

The boards vibrated with a guttural grunting. The candles flickered as something scratched and padded through the door. Malcolm tried to look but his face was pushed deeper into the knotted wooden floor. Above him Samuel closed his eyes.

"Look, brother, look! Don't be squeamish at this late hour. It's time you two were reacquainted. Look, Samuel, look into the eyes of salvation!"

Malcolm felt something jagged pierce the back of his neck. He stopped struggling as an icy numbness flowed through his veins, his heartbeat drifting away in ebbs and tides. His last conscious thought was that he might never stop falling.

He heard Silver gasp above him, "But … but you are *beautiful*," then he faded, dropping down, down, down, weighted by the brothers' laughter.

Chapter 26

"Would it make a difference if I told you the truth? The whole truth mind. I fucking hate camping."

And I always have, thought Pruner, *hate it all, the damp boots, the crinkled clothes filled with the lingering smell of wood smoke, everything.* The noises in the night as if the darkness heralded the onset of some crackling demonic party. The morning dew on the inside of the tent. The trapped insects. Awaking half-man, half-slug in a sleeping bag with a zip indentation running across your head like Frankenstein's monster. It always rained when you pitched a tent, as if what you were really doing was erecting a shrine to the god of depressive gloom. To camp is to embrace decay.

"You used to go camping all the time!" argued Dobson.

"But that was with women." Camping with women was great— the outdoors tended to strip them of their inhibitions, and their clothes. You could point out the stars to them, make up constellations, make yourself seem all sensitive. And they'd cook for you.

"Well, if you get frisky in the middle of the night you can always snuggle up to me. What happens in the tent stays in the tent."

"Kate not enough for you, eh? Need some real lovin'?" Pruner felt good, the best he had in months. Just being with Dobson did the trick. He had forgotten life could be so simple.

"So, what do you think of her?" Dobson asked with as much casualness as he could muster, but his face was pale as water.

"Kate? She's nice. Can she sing? Maybe I'll get her to sing on my album."

"Nice? C'mon, Pruner, if you don't like her then fine. Don't fob me off with nice."

Pruner laughed at his friend's sudden anger; fool *was* in love, got it *bad*. "You need me to like her?"

"No, I want you to is all."

"I like her, Dobs, I really do. You're punching way above your weight and you know it." He was too. Pruner had been surprised at just how tasty Kate had turned out to be when he had finally got to meet her last week in The Cove. He spent most of the night sipping her with his eyes. He would have hit on her if she had been with anyone else but Dobson. Or would he?

He was finding women ever more annoying. The girl he'd brought along (no way *he* was playing gooseberry for little Heather), bored him so much he had to remind himself to breathe. She was of the type usually labeled "bubbly," but he just wished she'd put a cork in it; she got right up his nose. She laughed like a sea lion.

At least Kate was polite, quiet.

"Demure."

"What?"

"Your Kate, she's demure. You're a lucky boy, Heather." Dobson beamed like a man who had won the lottery, and in a way he had; the relationship lottery, where the odds were the longest of all.

"So, it's a done deal then, the whole marriage shebang?"

"Yeah, why not?" said Dobson. "After the baby though. Kate wants to do things her way, have the kid at home and all that. We've a place lined up and everything, move in next month."

"I know. You've already roped me in to help remember?"

"Yeah. Just excited mate. My own place! Gonna have a hell of a party, Bill!"

Yeah, thought Pruner, *if Madame Ovary lets you*.

It was hard to believe Dobson was engaged. Like a toilet, someone had shut the door and began crapping on his life. And here was another weasel thought—what if Kate went away? Sure, Dobs would be unhappy for a spell, but wasn't that better than leaving your best mate all on his lonesome? Skinner was long gone (this was a fool's errand and no mistake), Drew was too bitter to stomach, and Malcolm ... well, he didn't count, wherever he was. Malcolm had descended to the bottom of the barrel, last seen heading deep south. Without Dobson, Pruner would be totally isolated, and the thought scared him more than he cared to admit.

He would have loads of time to work on his music then, find that perfect but elusive coda, but who else would understand it save Dobson? Lately he'd got to thinking he had been fooling himself, a bad case of the Emperor's new clothes; it was all just noise, the sound and the fury signifying fuck all squared. It seemed an age since he had worked on it.

The baby, this damn rat, was the spoiler. A girl as cute as Kate would soon tire of a plug like Dobson and head for loins anew, but the baby was a knot that would bind them together regardless. Now they were getting their own place, and how welcome would he be there, drinking and talking Krautrock with a pregnant brood mare tutting in the background.

She could always have a miscarriage, or maybe it would be born strangled by its own cord, or so messed up they'd be forced to put it up for adoption before the doctor stamped on it. The grief would tear them apart; you read about things like that all the time.

"I'm really happy for you, Dobs."

Hitching up their rucksacks they delved deeper into the Moss, every step reminding Pruner he'd rather be anywhere else. The air was awash with dandruff seeds and a jam of flies. In the scar-lashed and twisted trees the electric flex of squirrel tails sent up a cloak of starlings, their call a perpetual argument; the dog roses, like organic speakers, seemed to him to amplify their racket. The berries on the bushes were browning already. The entire Moss was a boiling pot of birdsong and furtive rustling.

It was all a veneer, a plaster over a wound, a pretty poster over damp and exposed wiring. Am I the only one who can see this? No, they all sensed it sooner or later, it was tangible in the undersmell; they felt it in their bones and gave the place a wide berth.

Something was wrong here, always had been.

They said Cyril Troughton, who had built half the town and gave his name to this wilderness, had blown his brains out down here back when High Street was just wide enough for a horse and cart. It was wrong, and getting worse by the feel of it. All the old stories added to the dark mystery of the place—hadn't they once spent an entire summer searching for the exact spot that Silver's brother had dragged his victim's exhumed corpse to?—but now all the rumours and whispered legends just made him uncomfortable.

He had never, not once, been here after dark, and he had no intention of losing that cherry tonight. He had a feeling that after nightfall the poster would be unceremoniously ripped down and the wiring gleefully revealed.

If Skinner had come here, then he was already mad or dead. As he tramped behind Dobson on the hollow-sounding path he began to wonder if there was any difference between the two.

"Is it much further?"

"Can't you remember?" asked Dobson. "We used to come down this way all the time."

"Yeah, years ago. You come down much since?"

"Just for a shag. I can hardly do it with mum hanging round the house all day."

"Yeah," said Pruner. "She'd probably join in."

"Fuck off, Billy!"

"Okay, okay, mate. Just messin'. Don't have a fit!"

Dobson's face scrutinized him, dropped as if he found something in that inscrutable set of stone that he didn't like, something that hurt him.

"I didn't mean—"

"I don't fit, Billy. That time at Silver's, that was a one off, down to tiredness the doctor said."

"Don't get pissy about it, I just meant—"

"Everybody just means. I'm sick to the teeth of it."

"Look who's grew a pair! But if you do start break dancing I have no medical training, and I reserve the right to laugh."

Dobson shot him a black look before breaking into a smile, and for the millionth time in his life Pruner wished he could be more like his friend—unable, unwilling to hold a grudge. He couldn't lose him. If he did, he would be lost himself.

"Let's have a rest, Dobs. I'm sweating my taws off here."

"Just round the corner, old man, then we can pitch up."

And sure enough, as the path grew thicker and they had to beat their way through an old drainage channel choked with bogbean and water horsetail, they came out into a vast open spot and the swing dangled in front of them, twirling memories in Pruner's mind.

"It hasn't changed a bit," he marveled. "How the fuck is that old tree still standing!"

The original swing had reached right across the river, a gushing tributary of the Cloy that ran across the southern border of Ellsford. You could still see the half branch that once held it jutting out over the water, snapped off in some long ago storm.

It had been replaced by a lower, smaller swing—the Babby swing—tied to a knobbly protrusion on the alder's trunk. Its arc didn't cover the river's span no matter how hard or fast you pushed off from the bank. You merely hurtled back at twice the velocity in a dizzying circle, ripping your knuckles, your face, your knees against the trunk; either that or plunge into the viscous water. It was a macho test of endurance, not pleasure, a game that only people like Drew truly enjoyed.

"Fancy a go?" asked Dobson.

"Sure, then we can pick blackberries and play Ring-a-Ring-a-Rosie. Grow up and give me a hand, this thing won't put itself up." He threw the tent down hard enough to send up a plume of dust, causing a couple of teal to squabble away from their hidey holes in the bank.

They erected the tent in silence as Sherman sat and watched. The hound looked at home here, a throwback, an urban legend in its proper context. His lower shanks were plastered in a dripping black tar where he had been wading through the bog. He was chewing on something in a contemplative manner, something he had found wriggling in the mire, the snap of small bones punctuating the unnatural quiet.

"I think Gus was shitting us," he said, feeling free to speak once more. "Why would Skinner be here? It's too open for a start."

"Maybe that's the point. Maybe he's nearby, and he'll see us, know we're here for him."

"So, we just sit here fiddling with our dicks and wait for him to drop by? If that were the case, don't you think he'd just phone?"

"We'll go look for him," said Dobson patiently. "But if he can see us, get used to the idea we're here, then he might be easier to find."

Dobson put his fingers in his mouth and let out a strident whistle. Sherman came bounding out past them, tail flicking like a metronome, as they headed down an overgrown path half hidden by clutching trees.

"If Skinner isn't the killer—"

"Don't start that again, Pruner. You know he's not."

"You ever think the *real* killer might be hiding out here then? We could be walking right into his lair. If we had blonde hair and big tit's the audience would be yelling "Turn back, you stupid fucks" right about now."

"I don't think so."

"Why not? It's the perfect place to hide out. You said so yourself."

"I just … I don't know … You ever see anything strange, Pruner?"

"I saw Jenny Bell's inverted nipples once."

"Seriously. You ever see a ghost or something?"

"What!"

"It's just I've seen … What if the killer isn't exactly, y'know, alive."

"You think Casper's got an axe? Fuck me pink with a whitewash brush, Heather, you are one freaky little fucker!"

"Listen, Bill, straight up—"

"Dead's dead, Dobson. Things are bad enough without going all Sixth Sense on me. You dream of hell so I don't have to, just keep it to yourself."

Up ahead Sherman unleashed a howl that stopped them in their tracks.

"What the—" began Pruner, but Dobson was already running by him, hurdling a large mound of peat that blocked off the end of the path. By the time he caught up with him he felt compelled to finish the question.

"What the fuck?"

Sherman was sitting beneath a large wooden cross behind which, tilting at a slight angle, stood a large rudimentary cabin.

"Looks like Skinner's just opened the first branch of the Troughton Travel Lodge," said Dobson. "After you."

Pruner tried the handle and the door fell open on a well-oiled hinge. "Holy hell," he said, stepping inside, "what have we here?"

"It's a church," said Dobson standing too close behind him.

"It's a tip is what it is. Is that meant to be Manson?" said Pruner, indicating the mural on the far wall. "Did Manson eat babies, or was that Dahmer?"

Dobson wasn't listening. He was rifling through some things on top of a makeshift podium by the light of a burning candle. "Christ, Pruner, I think this is a finger! A fucking finger and a pile of dead rats. Let's get outta here. I think you were right, I think we found the killer's den. Is that blood on the floor?"

"Probably varnish. I'll tell you what we found. Silver's wanking hut."

"What?"

"Who else? Big scary Jesus guy painting, rodent sacrifices. Who else but Voodoo Sam is crazy enough to build a shack like this in the arsehole of beyond? Well, let's give the Surfer a taste of his own brimstone, shall we?" Pruner took out a small can of lighter fluid he had brought for the camp fire. "Let's torch the fucker."

"Wise up, Pruner."

"Think about it. It might smoke Skinner out too. He's bound to come for a look-see."

"You can't."

"Why the fuck not?"

"It's ... It's unlucky."

"Talk sense, dickhead! It's not a *real* church, it's a fucking shed. Look at it," Pruner made an expansive gesture with his hand, spraying lighter fluid as he did so. "I mean, really look at it. You ever see a church like this, huh? You ever see a church with vermin for relics?"

"But ..."

"But cock!"

"But someone took the time to make this."

"Yeah, some sick cunt."

"Exactly! Some seriously twisted individual took the time to get all Handy Andy out here, doing fuck knows what kind of juju in the process, and he could be watching us right now. I don't think we should go pissing off someone like that."

"It's just some kids who've been watching too much HBO and reading the local rag."

"Nah, Pruner, kids would've done the whole Satanic bit, pentagrams and shit. Look at the quotes on the walls—no matter how fucked up kids get, they never read the Bible."

"So, it's Sam then. If he's watching, I say we give him a show."

Pruner began squirting the fuel out of the can, pumping it so hard it sounded like an android's heartbeat. With his back to Dobson he looked like a small boy taking a whiz; *and that's exactly what he is*, thought Dobson, *a little boy acting out a childish rebellion against something he doesn't understand, something that might just bite both of us in the ass.*

"It's all dry wood," he was saying. "It'll catch no problem."

"Maybe we should go to the law, Billy. If this is the killer's den, we'd be heroes. There might be a reward."

Pruner stared at him incredulously. "You really want him caught? The best, hell, the *only* thing that has ever happened to this town, and you want him caught so as you can get your dial on the front page of *The Chronicle* again? Really?"

Dobson was about to answer when he caught sight of Sherman through the open door. The dog was cowering, hackles raised in short spikes, his whole body quivering as he let out a series of pathetic little yelps.

"What's wrong, Shermy? What's the matter b—"

The building started to shake as if in the grip of an earthquake, the wooden frame rattling wildly, sending candles and chairs shooting across the bowing floorboards. The floor began to buckle upwards as if something beneath were trying to force its way through. Something huge. Then the pounding started.

Dobson bolted for the door on seasick legs. "Run, Pruner!" he yelled, but Pruner was trying to spark up his Zippo, his face a mask of retarded concentration, oblivious to the fact that the candles had already ignited the fluid, that flames were already licking the trembling wood.

Pruner stood silent as the shed settled around him, the banging ceased and the floor sank back down. He walked back outside, flames dappling his skin, into the glaring sun.

"Dobson!" he called, shielding his eyes. He could hear Sherman barking, but of his owner there was no trace. Smoke blurred his vision and he turned to find the quasi-church engulfed in a crackling inferno. *Did I do that? I think I—*

A figure appeared on the path above him, standing on the peat mound, blocking his exit. It began to slowly descend.

"Little boys shouldn't play with matches," it said.

Pruner recognised that voice. He stepped backward, squinting through the smoke and the blaze of the sun.

"No," he said in a small strangled voice. "Nononono." He fell on his ass on the hard turf, trying to scramble crablike from the apparition looming over him.

Carrie Anne smiled. "Time you got burnt, Sweet William."

He found his feet and ran headlong down a path that looked more like a tunnel through the trees, the heat too thick to breathe, ran until sparkles danced before him in the green-black shadows. He chanced one quick look over his shoulder but no-one was there, then burst into a clearing that felt like a bruise upon the earth.

He had a momentary recollection of Dutch Holland screaming, of Drew running by him. The clearing had not changed in all the years since he had last been here save that no dead birds hung from the tree. This time, Skinner was tied to it.

His stomach was hanging out, still steaming; sparrows pecking at his entrails, tugging on the bloody offal. Skinner's eyes were open wide, gazing on some eternal distance; they seemed so dry, so terribly dry. From every corner of the clearing, from every thicket and bush, from every pond and sucking bog hole, crawling, limping, dragging themselves, came cats.

Cats with only one eye in their owlish heads, cats with their bellies clawed out, with their legs stripped to the bone, cats jerking in a horrible parody of their natural grace as fat maggots fell from their clotted fur and writhed helplessly on the sun-bleached grass. A few crippled birds, some beakless, their wings torn into rags, lolloped among them.

Pruner was overcome by such a miasma of decay that for a moment he was blinded, the world around him reduced to a hazy watercolour, a surrealist blur. He could feel them curl around him, their half-chewed tails encircling his paralysed legs. They set up a broken purring; the hum of a death wasp. One cat rubbed its head against his shin and left half its face glued there; it looked up at him with a sly skeletal grin before making way for another of its kin.

He tried to scream, but his chest was so cold nothing could escape. The cats began such a frantic racket he thought his teeth would crumble loose along with his mind, and a naked girl stepped out from behind the tree.

She stroked provocatively at Skinner's corpse, smearing his blood over her breasts, between her legs, her face twisted in a mockery of lust. She seemed to shimmer; each pulse, each flicker of her being, revealing stab wounds and bite marks, blinking on and off like the ghost of murder beneath. Her eyes held him. Her eyes were mirrors.

If you look into a mirror at midnight you will see the devil, or so he had been told, but now Pruner only saw his own reflection and believed it was the dark one's true face. His skin was full of boils in those pools, diseased slug-like growths. He thought he would drown in those eyes, descend all the way to Hell and meet the source of his reflection, cackling wildly for staring too long into his own mad eyes; what was hidden in those depths longed to devour him.

"My name is Eileen, the Holy Mother," she said, breaking the spell as she pawed at her groin. "Will you worship me?"

She picked a greying flyblown lump from Skinner's intestines and placed it delicately on her tongue, moaning as if she dined on ambrosia, not putrid flesh.

"Worship me and what I have begot, and I will tell you such secrets. I will take the coldness from your heart, release you from your burden. All you have to do is kiss me. Kiss me and remember."

She was close now, close enough to see the gorge in her skull flicker on and off. The ground beneath his feet glowed an unearthly red as it split and turned as if the very fires of Hell were oozing up through the crust of the Moss. The cats fell silent. He felt her lips on his and the ice in his chest spread over his entire body, and he knew then that no mere fire could ever consume him.

And he remembered.

He remembered everything.

Chapter 27

That had been too close for comfort, mused Bob Turk as he loitered with little intent by the Pigeon Club, checking his watch with increasing and pointless regularity as he waited for Cully to shut up shop. If the wife had come into the boys' bedroom one minute earlier, just sixty seconds earlier, he would have been … He nipped the thought in the bud.

It would have been a blessing to have been caught … He smothered that one too, and quickly; there were no blessings here, only curses. He had to be more careful is all, he had to—

He had to stop is what he had to do, stop now before it all got out of hand, but he couldn't, his urges were leading him on and he was helpless in their maddening pull. He was the *real* victim in all of this.

He'd had so many affairs—no, liaisons was a better word—over the years, and he was sure Elsie, who was no fool, knew about them all. She turned a blind eye though, never dropped a hint, and he had always taken that for tacit acceptance. If she ever so much as caught a sniff of his latest indiscretions, however …

He checked his watch again as his heart thudded in his temples. Barely a minute had passed since his last peek. A minute. That was what had stood between him and utter ruin. And for what? I mean, it was all so *harmless* really.

He had sailed close to the wind before—that time with Joyce Heather had been a nail biter, but nothing had shaved so damn near the eyeball as this morning.

It was a sign, a warning. Of that he was certain.

Turk was unsure if he believed in God (though when Cyril invoked the Big Man he was always first to back him up) but he did believe in Fate, and Fate had been tapping him on the shoulder since Christmas. This morning it had bellowed in his ear.

The women had been a bit of fun, something to brag about over the click of pool balls in the Legion. It was a man's duty to dupe his wife. Joyce had been a mistake, and a frequent one at that, but even old pious Cyril had made that one too, so what was there to regret?

He had watched Joyce a long time before he pounced. He could see her now, holding court in The Cove, trapped in gin, not amber. A white blouse like the skin of an egg covering her glorious yolks; magical in their scandal, alive with sexuality. "I'm a lady," she declares. "Everybody knows that. Everybody!"

It was all he could do not to laugh in her face.

Sitting at the bar drinking Bacardi at eleven a.m., surrounded by men ready to fight over her like dogs over a bitch in heat. Could she really believe she was fooling anyone, even herself?

After that, whenever Eddie had been out flogging 99's, he had begun calling on her so often he started to wonder if that rubberhead son might not also be his. Watching that little moron running up and down the street, toilet roll hanging out his back pocket, pretending to be a Red Indian scared the bejesus out of him for a time, for idiocy ran through the Turk line. It was only when the boy shot up a bit that he could rest easy; he was the spit of Ed Heather, and every bit as gormless. He had been so grateful he had even taken him on as an apprentice at the park.

Then the bitch got funny, the way they always did, talking about how the boy needed a father figure, and he had told her where to get the fuck off in no uncertain manner.

The next day a large list appeared in the window, stuck up for all Romannon Street to see; *All The Men I Have Fucked*, it proudly proclaimed. It was an exhaustive census of the male population of the street and its immediate environs. There, right at the top of the heap, was the legend Bob Turk. Only Cyril Weir, who had scraped into the top five, managed to talk her into taking it down or Christ knows what would've happened.

Still, half the bloody town must have heard about it; how his bitter half hadn't was a mystery. She knew, of course she did. How many times had she answered the phone to silence, smelt cheap perfume on him, scrubbed the stains from his pants? She knew alright, but she kept her own counsel.

This morning was different. There would be no ignoring *that*.

He had ditched Joyce easily, not out of anger, merely at the realization of how many knobs had ploughed that same furrow. The urges he had now—the urges to delve where no knob had or should have ever been—could not be stilted by shame; revulsion only made them stronger.

He needed to talk to someone, to pretend to be a man again—it had worked before, it would work again—and Cully, the dirty sod, was the perfect foil.

He didn't dare try it on with Cyril. Cyril would read it in his face; he was good at that type of thing, a real badger. If Cyril even so much as suspected what he was, he would kill him. Cully would never suspect all his fanny chasing over the years had been a cover-up, an attempt to hide the truth of what he really was.

He needed to feel like a man again, and this was the easiest way. He could take the wife out, wine and dine her, but nowadays the babysitters were far too young. It would be asking for trouble. Then, after the meal, she would be expecting … The thought of sex with a woman, let alone Elsie, turned his gut; all that saggy old flesh put him off his stroke. The problem with ageing women is that one night, fumbling in the dark, instead of finding a little sliver of seaweed between the legs you find a baby octopus. No, better a good brag, then in time he could return to normal relations.

Baby steps, Bob, he told himself, *baby steps*.

Whilst he was fretting, staring at the graffiti that tattooed the Pigeon Club walls and imagining his own name there in the long shame roll of local perverts, he glimpsed Cully in the corner of his eye. The butcher ignored his calls and was already at his back door by the time Turk caught up with him.

Cully looked at him nonplussed, his key hovering over the lock. "You okay, Cully? Someone short change you?" The butcher muttered something as Turk followed him into the working kitchen. "You're looking well anyway," he said to the back of the butcher's head.

Cully sighed, dropping a bag of choice cuts he had brought from the shop onto the floor with a meaty thud. "I feel like death warmed up."

"Ah, come off it, you old reprobate, you're fighting fit. All that old army training, eh?"

"Aye, fighting for breath and fit for fuck all."

"Stop your griping and put the kettle on, you fat cunt. The sex mechanic is in town with a tale to tell. There's a wee lassie working down the library I'm planning to dip the wick in and I thought I might share the sordid details with you."

"Think I'll have something stronger than tea if you don't mind, Bob. Care for a tot yourself?"

"Go on then, but the good stuff mind. None of that paint stripper you bring out on poker nights."

Cully rummaged in the cupboard under the sink, producing a couple of glasses and a half-full bottle of Glenfiddich. He poured two hefty measures, downing his own before Turk had even smelt his.

"Steady on, Cully, what's the occasion?"

The butcher grimaced, pointing to the living room door. "Bony's come back."

"What! Ah, Cully, I'm chuffed for you, mate. Sincere. And after all this time, who would've thought?" Turk tipped his glass, letting the whiskey burn away some of his anxiety. "Set 'em up again, we should celebrate."

"Really?" Cully's smile resembled a rictus sneer. "Come and see, Bob, then tell me what you think."

Turk followed him into the poky living room, saw the fat little dog sniffing round the hearth, unsteady on its feet. It smelt *bad*, like damp rubbish, but it exuded a vulgar life.

"That's one old dog," he said. "What age is he now? Eleven, twelve?"

"He was twelve when he died," said Cully.

Turk thought he had misheard, was silent awhile as they watched the dog spin around slowly, curving its spine, before flopping down with a grunt.

"Twelve when he what?"

"When he died," repeated Cully tearfully. Turk was staring at him as if he were senile, but the butcher held his gaze. "I know what you think, Bob; I think so myself sometimes. But there he is. I'd kill him but I don't know if he'd die. He's not Bones, not really. I couldn't bear for him to come back again ..."

"Cully, mate—"

"It's the truth! Jesus, can't you smell him? Can't you see the fucking dent in his head?" The dog growled deep in its throat and Cully closed his swollen eyes. "You see, Bob? I'm not mad. Do you see?"

Turk did see. The dog's head was totally stoved in, and the smell he had dismissed as garbage was unmistakably the scent of death.

"I don't know what to do," Cully was saying. "Honest to fuck, I'm lost. Feel like I'm losing my mind. Maybe I should go to that bin-lid Cunningham's meeting tonight, see if he can heal *me*." He laughed sourly. "You never know. Old Wooden Tit Stone's walking round larger than life, and he's got half the wine team off the soup, cleaned up and preaching. That's a miracle in itself. These are strange days, Bob, and who knows, maybe he has a gift after all." He nodded at the dog. "I believe anything's possible now."

Turk made his excuses and left, unable to bear the smell or the terrified look in the butcher's eyes a moment longer, nor the half-heard laughter from a higher source.

Could Sammy heal *his* sickness? Did he even want to be healed?

Of course he did (and the laughter grew louder) but how could he explain, how could he vocalise this most shameful of ailments?

No-one would believe Cunningham if he decided to trumpet it all over town; he might even empathise, his brother had suffered something similar. Fate, God, or blind luck was pushing him toward Cunningham regardless; he felt like a straw in the face of a hurricane. He would let it blow him where it would.

He wandered in a daze through the narrow streets of Ellsford, baking in the evening sun, avoiding eye contact with all who passed, afraid that his predilections were stamped across his sweaty forehead, trying hard to walk like a man, to look like a man, cowering from any passing children, his eyes sticking to their hairless flesh nonetheless.

He found himself paralysed by the pelican crossing, staring at a little boy no older than five on the other side, holding onto his mother's hand. As the green man began to flash and the child glided toward him, the urges fired up again.

All these kids were alike, all clones, there must be machines somewhere churning them out. He smiled to himself, of course there were; machines they called whores.

I am sick, he thought. *Worse, I am evil.* Even as these thoughts clawed at him he was assailed by the image of himself flinging the child down into the road, ripping at his clothes, bathing in his tears.

If Silver could not help him he was doomed.

Only this morning life had been so simple. So simple until Elsie had come back early from the shop (a picture of Dustin Hoffman in her purse, oh yes, he knew all about that, the tart), padding softly up to the boys' room to ask him for the car keys, "So I can nip over to the Mall instead."

"Ah, there you are," she had said, and if she'd been a minute earlier…

A poster flapped lazily on a substation, catching his eye: *You Are Welcome to An Awakening—A Night Of Healing And Wonders! Seek Out The Lord Before He Seeks Out You!*

Fate was tugging him ever closer. He picked up his pace and set off toward the community centre, his head full of dead dogs and unspeakable pleasures. A vicious doubt nagged at him as he walked— had he left his laptop out? The boys wouldn't dare touch it, not after last time, but what if the wife decided to go on eBay or something and buy one of those gaudy baubles she was so fond of hoarding.

True, she could barely spark the damn thing up without his help, and learning her how to use the mouse had been akin to learning a chimp how to use a knife and fork, but what if Fate scrolled down for her and she found his downloads? They were only pictures, but she wouldn't see them like that. She would see them as evidence of evil, and so would others.

Things had been escalating rapidly, like some dark light had been flicked on inside him, ever since Christmas, ever since they had found the Reverend's daughter.

He remembered how her eyes had been wide open, and so dry, so terribly dry. He remembered how, when the others had been squabbling and retching and calling the police, he had reached out and cupped her breast, ran his tongue over her desiccated orb and how, suddenly conscious of his erection, he had feigned illness so that he could flee into the bushes and deal with it.

His excitement was not fuelled by her nakedness, but by the fact she was dead. Pictures were no longer enough.

He found himself opposite the community centre, standing by the tree where the Spence boy bit the bullet a few weeks ago; skid marks still stained the road, and small shards of headlight glass sparkled amid the flowers strewn round its paint-flecked trunk. When he died there would be no wreaths, only nettles on an unmarked grave. The injustice of this appalled him.

He hawked up a hefty wad of snot and propelled it onto a smiling photo of Alan Spence tied to a fading bouquet of roses. *Am I evil? Am I good? Show me which side of the coin I will land on, show me once and for all and be done with this torment.*

Ignoring the blast of horns he stepped straight out into traffic, flipping the finger to motorists in a gesture almost serene, then pulled on the centre's heavy glass doors and made his way into the main hall. At the far end by the stage he was surprised to see Wheezel and Sniper Hanlon busy arranging chairs. What surprised him most was not their sobriety, or the fact both were dressed in suits, but how *clean* they looked. Cunningham really had turned wine into water. Could Sammy Boy perform the same trick twice, could he purge his filth?

"What's the score, lads? you gotta court appearance coming up?"

Both men stopped and eyed him suspiciously. "Group doesn't start for three hours," said Sniper. "What do you want?"

"Wind your neck in, Hanlon, I want a word with the Messiah. He about?"

Wheezel and Sniper exchanged a look, then Wheezel shrugged and Sniper nodded toward a door backstage. "He's not to be disturbed. He's preparing himself."

"Don't worry, boys, I'll be gentle." Turk stopped mid-stage, turning back to Sammy's little helpers. "Hey guys, I hear Asda's doing a three for two on selected wines and spirits. Thought you might be interested." Then he entered into a small dressing room, slamming the door behind him.

Cunningham, dozing in a chair before a large dusty mirror (he'll say he was meditating or some shit), almost jumped out of his skin. "Moonface!" he said, then blushed, realising his faux pas. "I mean Bob. What brings you here?"

He was fidgeting nervously. He was scared. Turk grinned; he felt like a man again, a powerful one. He noticed the silver streak in Cunningham's hair was more pronounced than ever.

"I've come to be healed," he said.

Samuel looked momentarily perplexed. "Group's not until eight."

"I know. Your little alcoholic elves already filled me in but I can't wait, and I certainly don't need an audience. I need a quick fix. In private. Now."

"I have to reserve my strength, I need to keep it for—"

"Someone more deserving? Listen closely, you old skunk, this is life and death, and not just mine. So fire up your mojo and fire it up fast. Capiche?"

"It doesn't work like that, Bob. I can only pray and turn my mind away—"

"Uh-oh, doubt's about! Not good enough, Sammy, not good enough at all."

Samuel's eyes scanned him quickly, narrowing at the threat he posed. "But what's wrong with you, Bob? You look fine." He chewed nervously on his lip. "Cancer?"

"Could be. Cancer of the heart, of the mind. Cancer of the thought. Cancer of the fucking balls. I get these urges, Sam, terrible urges, and you're gonna make them go away."

"I've been meaning to talk to you actually," said Samuel rising from his chair. "Have you seen Mrs. Heather lately? I've been trying to contact her but I can't find her anywhere."

Turk flinched at Joyce's name; was Silver reading his mind? "That whore is of no consequence. Stop changing the fucking subject. Work your holy wonders, and work them now."

"I've told you, Bob, I can't just switch it on and off. I need to prepare."

"Sammy, Sammy, Sammy. You're a big man, but you're a coward. Not like your Paul, he was game as fuck. Remember when I beat the crap out of him in Miss Wilson's class? Knocked seven bells of shite out of him I did. Remember why? He stole two Jawas from my Star Wars box. Two Jawas, Sam. I nearly killed your hardass brother over two shitty little bits of plastic, so imagine what I'll do to you over something as important as this. Lay your hands on me, Cunningham, or I swear I'll lay mine on you."

Samuel looked toward the door as if he expected Sniper or Wheezel to come to his rescue. That made Turk smile, and that smile, in all its malicious glory, sealed the deal.

"I'll try." He gestured toward the chair he had just vacated. "You had better sit. Sadness is a weed that grows unchecked and chokes. This might not work. It chooses its own candidates. I'm only the conduit, I cannot direct it."

"Save the spiel for the pensioners, I'm in a hurry. I need to get home and … tidy up."

At first Turk noticed nothing save the sweat from the big man's paws dripping down onto his forehead, mingling unsavorily with his Strepsil breath. Then an old familiar smell came to him, a smell of vinegar and pine, of wood smoke and rich loamy earth, the smell of the Moss he had played in as a boy. He began to quiver uncontrollably, voices babbling on the edge of hearing, and when the tingling subsided he felt an immense surge of peace inform his every nerve and sinew. He drew in a rattling breath, pushing away Cunningham's hands as he stood up.

"Bob?" There was excitement in Samuel's voice. "Did you feel it, too, Bob?"

But Turk was already out the door, ignoring the stares of the two derelicts, ignoring Samuel's vehement cry, "Behold, another convert, men!" pushing his way outside into the too-bright sun. Already the memory of this morning's indiscretion was fading; fading with all the speed he had used to pull up his zipper when he heard his wife on the stairs.

Over the road, by the bus stop, a small boy was engrossed with a plastic dinosaur. A vision struck Turk with all the intensity of a double decker bus.

In his vision he was at home, squeezing the boy's neck, watching the gelatinous balls of his eyes pop outward, and he couldn't help himself, they looked so wet and sticky, he had to have a lick. They tasted salty, horrible, so he squeezed harder out of spite and there were clickings and gurglings and the boy went limp and his eyes didn't look so tasty anymore.

The vision burst as Turk ran back into the hall, scattering the bespoke drunks who bent Palm like in his wake as he leapt onstage and back into the tiny dressing room. Samuel was wearing the same expression Turk had worn that morning for his wife's untimely arrival. He gripped Cunningham by his broad shoulders and planted a kiss on his forehead.

"Thank you," he said. "You've taken away my fear. I'm a better man than I give me credit for. At last I can embrace the beast. The coin has landed, Sam, Fate has chosen!"

Samuel smiled nervously.

"Don't look so puzzled, Sambo. Talking of puzzles, riddle me this—What's white and flies across the sky? The coming of the Lord!" He ran one hand gently through Samuel's hair, tracing the silver streak. "Looks like you got splashed, my friend."

Turk brought his forehead forward with such power he felt Cunningham's nose smash like an egg across his cheeks. As the big man fell to the floor he put the boot in, kicking him until what lay at his feet no longer resembled a man, more something out of Cully's window display. A silent scream pulled back the bloody chevrons of Cunningham's lips, letting out little squeaks like a thirsty wheel.

"There is a God, Silver, I know that now." He leaned closer to the ragged pepper of his victim's ear. "His address is South of Heaven." For the first time in his life he felt completely free, felt he was under the protection of a power much greater than himself.

When he died and God played back the movie of his life on Judgement Day, this would be the bit he would keep rewinding, the scene he would watch over and over again. He aimed one final, thoughtful kick at Cunningham's temple.

"And don't *ever* call me Moonface," he said.

He ambled out into the glaring streets of Ellsford to begin his own ministry. Above him pale smoke rose from factory chimneys like a plea for help to faraway towns.

Chapter 28

Pruner hadn't left the flat in weeks, months; it was hard to tell. The air he breathed was stale, had grown a thin membrane like old coffee. He turned on no lights, watched no television, listening only to the rasp of his lungs as he lay shipwrecked in his own body.

He tried not to sleep, to avoid the dreams that plagued him. Dreams of mammoth wasps that regarded him with knowing eyes as they nonchalantly flicked their wings, laying egg after villainous egg, each one spawning a foetal and grotesque Dobson. He would awake with his red duvet now purple, smelling yellow.

He bathed constantly but was still convinced his skin crawled with parasites, with the bloated denizens of the Moss. He began to tidy the flat with the concentration of one whose mind is irretrievably lost. Wallowing in a porn-hot bath his chest remained icy cold; *I'm Baked Alaska*, he thought, *served up and ready to eat.* He contemplated slipping under the steaming water, staying there until his thoughts drowned, immersed in vile humours of black bile, but he was too frightened of what lay behind the veil, too aware of the terrors that awaited him to find any solace in the notion.

The silence of the flat eased his frayed nerves. No more music, he had abandoned his Great Work. He had only been fooling himself. He was ... What was the phrase Dobson used about such people? He was a pig with a view of Heaven.

He didn't know whether to laugh or cry at the thought, though trapped here in what felt increasingly like the submerged hull of a prison ship, he had cried with alarming regularity. He could never remember crying before, not since he had been plucked unwillingly from his mother's bleeding belly.

The things he had seen, had remembered, and the things yet to come!

He was sparring with sadness and wrestling with joy.

Am I bad, or a victim robbed of choice? Am I even sane?

The blessed healing silence was shattered by a pounding on the front door that caused his heart to scramble up his throat, splashing water and suds onto bare tiles of the bathroom floor. It was after midnight, who the hell could that be? What if it were a clown with a balloon, or worse, a little giggling girl dressed all in wh—

The pounding again, insistent as a migraine.

He pulled on a dressing gown and made his way up the hall, wincing inwardly at the wet footprints he left on the laminate floor— would they stain? He opened the door, holding his breath.

She was drunk, that much was obvious. She hurried by him leaving contrails of Pernod and flammable perfume, a Superking dangling precariously from her slack lips.

"I can't be seen," said Joyce in an attempted whisper as he closed the door. "I thought you were never going to answer. What were you doing? Milking yourself I suppose."

Pruner began to answer, faltered as his mind slipped gear, frowned, tried to change track mid-sentence, but succeeded only in standing with his mouth ajar as Joyce stumbled around his home on a self-guided tour, picking up everything and anything that caught her bleary eye before setting it down askew. He would have to rearrange every single item when she left, dust them too, or he would not be able to settle. He followed in her lurching wake, adjusting things as best he could for the time being.

"Is something wrong?" He was floundering. "Has something happened to Dobson?"

She glared at him. "Dobson has done an awful thing." She spoke so softly he could barely hear. "But you are going to help me fix it."

"What's he done now?"

She turned her back on him, running her fingers (too hard, too hard) along the spines of his CDs in their wall-mounted racks. "Nice place. So many lovely, lovely things. So many lovely, *expensive* things.

Tell me again, what is it that you do?"

"I'm on the dole, got a dicky heart, Joyce, but you know that already. I'm not fit to be on the wage wheel but I get by. I listen to a lot of great albums to pass the time."

"Too good to work, aren't you. Too superior. A little fragile angel, all gossamer and air. Or are you a rebel! Yes, that's more like it. A wild bohemian living on a higher plane than the rest of us." She produced a bottle of vodka from her handbag and took a prodigious glug.

"I remember you running around, barely out of nappies, your hair all punked up and your biker jacket on. Oh, so dangerous! Bet all the little girlies soaked their panties at the sight of you. Your Joy Division albums and your Bowie. Big smug grin on your face like you'd invented them. I was listening to them when you were still in your dad's balls! How is your dad by the way? Oh, that's right, he done a bunk when you were still sucking rusks. You ever catch his name?"

"Get the fuck out of my house, you drunken old slut."

"Slut? That rings a bell. I've been staying at a Bed and Breakfast in Blackmore this last while. Can't let Samuel know I've been such a fool … A B and B in Blackmore, that ringing any bells for you?"

Pruner chewed on his lip, eyeing her warily. In his mind he heard the lies race to be born.

"That's right, silly me, your mum owns a place out that way! Maybe the very one I'm holed up in. Tell me, what's she like? About my age, brown hair, cock mad? Don't you get on your high horse with me, you've margarine in your fridge harder to spread than your dear old mum!"

"You've been talking to her?" Pruner felt a rush of panic for no discernable reason; the thought of his family always gave him the sweats.

"Oh yes, we had a good old natter. Bit of a catch-up, y'know. Says she never sees her sweetheart of a son, though she still sends him cheques. Well, blood is thicker than diarrhoea and all that." She lifted his iPod from its docking station and ran a garish nail down its screen. "Is this a phone? Mummy *is* good to you, isn't she! Works hard, sends you money so you can act all James Dean. You're no rebel, you're just a spoilt brat. If my Dobson were in your shoes, he wouldn't play at it; he'd be the real deal. He's already rebelling against the highest authority there is."

Pruner snatched the iPod back and returned it to its rightful place, sighing at the greasy thumbprint she had left on the dial. The lions were roaring louder; it was all this talk of his mother, stirring up memories of his childhood. Memories of simple things spiked with fear. Simple shopping trips that haunted him yet.

I couldn't wait when mum told me we'd use the zebra crossing, he remembered. He had visions of himself astride that magnificent beast, fingers knotted in its mane. He even gave consideration as to what to wear; he didn't want to be too bright and blow its cover. Miss Wilson had said their stripes were a way to confuse predators. He didn't want to mess with nature. But when he got there it was just boring paint on a road and his disappointment was a vast inner tundra. His mother yanked him across the road when he started to whine, the ogling motorists making him whine all the harder.

"But where is the zebra, mummy?"

"The lions got him," she said. "The same way they'll get you if you don't come along."

Possessions made the roaring go away. It was only right she should pay for them.

"What do you want, Joyce? I've no time for this crap."

"I've come to offer you the chance to be a real outlaw for once. How would you like to fuck your best friend's mum?"

Pruner laughed despite himself. Was this what the drunken bitch was after all along? Did she really think he'd buckle to a shark? How fucking *boring* this world was at heart, how ripe for destruction.

"Sorry," he said. "Sheila Weir's not my type."

Joyce was unfazed. "Malcolm was never your friend. Even Dobson doesn't really like him."

"Well, I think Skinner's mum's dead."

"What a witty little snake you are! I'm not talking 'bout Skinner, or that other one, whatsisname, spare parts for Frankenstein … Proctor. No, Dobson's the only real friend you've ever had. We're both going to lose him if we don't do something quick."

This was something that had been gnawing at him during his exile. Dobson was tangled up in all that he had been shown. He watched Joyce flop down on the settee, her skirt riding high, her legs wide open.

"Aren't we being a drama queen?" he said. "What has Dobson done now that the fear of dead daddy can't put right?"

"He's *done* Kate Callaghan," she said, her breasts jutting against the thin confines of her blouse, propped up by a roll of belly fat. "That little tart has to vacate the scene pronto."

"Dobson mentioned you weren't a fan."

"You've seen him? How is he? Are they still—"

"Not for a while," he said; she wasn't the only one in hiding.

"He's turned on you too then. That's always the way of it. She'll make him burn all his bridges then there's no going back. He'll be as dependent on her as crack cocaine. I know; I was that soldier."

"She's not so bad. You should be happy, grandkid and all. He's punching way above his weight."

"Exactly!" hissed Joyce, leaning forward excitedly, her cleavage almost squirming free. "Don't you think that odd? That a girl like that would sink her claws in him and ignore you? Doesn't that grate on you, Jimmy Dean?"

"It takes all sorts," shrugged Pruner taking a seat opposite her. It did grate, that was the hell of it, hurt his pride no end. If he'd had her first, then Dobson would be more than welcome. He would have given him his slops graciously, but this rankled, this went against the grain.

"See, all this is meaningless," said Joyce, waving an arm round the room. "When you get older the knickknacks gather, anything to soften your coffin. You're way too young to have so much stuff. And everything so neat, so tidy. It's not natural in a boy your age, unless of course you're a little bit lavender. Is that it? Are you a closet homo?"

Pruner took the bottle from her and took a swig, curling his lip and burping in answer.

"I remember when you first came round ours, back when my Eddie was alive. I used to hate you, you know that? I thought you were bad news. He's loud, selfish, and apt to kick dogs, I says to myself. Dobson hadn't an arse in his trousers, and you with your brand new trainers and football tops, all the latest gadgets and doodads. Eddie died and left me nothing but my asshole to whistle through. I was the one who had to tell him no after you left—you can't have this, you can't have that. It was all he heard growing up. You gave him ideas above his station."

"A pig with a view of Heaven," said Pruner quietly.

"I hated you for that, but you were the only one who stood by him even when it would've been easier to leave him behind. That's why I'm hoping you'll stick by him now and help me get rid of this Kate.

Trust me, we don't have a choice."

Pruner lit a cigarette and took another drink, tasting her lipstick mingled with the acrid spirit, then handed the bottle back to her.

"I'll do it. I'll split them up. Easy as pie. But not because you asked me. See, I don't care about you, or Dobson for that matter. I've realised lately I've only ever cared for myself. Truth is," and the damn tears came, though he tried to pass it off as smoke in his eyes, "I'm gonna do it because seeing your son happy when I'm so miserable makes me fucking mad. It's all back to front, and I intend to redress the balance. Isn't that sad, I mean, isn't that the most tragic thing you ever heard?"

Joyce clapped her hands, jangling the bracelets manically on her wrists. "Kick her in the belly, ball her in front of him, break his heart!" she said, and she actually had the gall to wipe the top of the bottle before she took a drink, like *he* was the one with the pox. "As long as it gets done. I knew you were the one to come to. It's God's will."

"I saw your God," said Pruner. He regarded the end of his cigarette, glowing like the peat mounds in Troughton's wasteland. "I swallowed something jagged down the Moss. I saw Him, was privy to His works."

Joyce moaned and leaned closer. There was a sloshing noise, from the bottle or her it was impossible to tell. Her hand reached out to him. "You know," she whispered. "Then you know."

Pruner nodded, stubbing out his smoke.

"He's awful, isn't He?" she said, sounding like a little girl. "Evil."

"He's a complete bastard. We had a lot in common."

She drained the last of the vodka, her eyes wearing party hats; they rotated as she belched. "You're a classy lady," said Pruner.

"No," she smiled, "I'm a dirty MILF who needs comforting. Fuck me. I'll let you put it in the brown bin." She rose unsteadily. There was no finesse. She stripped off her clothes as if she were entering a concentration camp. Her body was firm, taut, and the light flattering, but it was just meat to him, rancid meat; a birthplace for bluebottles, something for a rat's tail to wind round.

He could smell her odour, her juices, could imagine the blood flowing down her thighs, and it repulsed him. Roadkill was more enticing than the human body. Her eyes were twinkling as if she thought him turned on and he realised he *should* be, for she had the kind of body that usually came with staples across the navel, yet he felt nothing but nausea.

What is wrong with me, he thought, as she sprawled out across his sofa, her buttocks squeaking on the PVC; *now I'll have to rub that all down in the morning.* He turned away as she parted her legs.

"I'll be back in five minutes, and by then I want you dressed and ready to leave. You're embarrassing the both of us."

He strode quickly into the kitchen, hearing her scream her frustration at him through the door. He poured himself the last of the gin from the back of the cupboard. As he downed it he strained to hear her making her exit. It was very quiet in there, maybe she had passed out. Maybe she was still there, fingering her manky steak, waiting. Jesus, it would be like ramming your dick into a blocked-up sink.

He steadied himself before returning, flinging open the door, unable to fight off the impression of a saloon entrance, a showdown with a midlife Mata Hari.

She was perched on the arm of the sofa clutching her knickers in her hand, her tufted gateway exposed like a pig with its throat cut. She was grunting, a look on her face half delirium, half bliss, reddening as she exerted, her rusty sheriff's badge widening, her doughy ass cheeks wobbling (*Those aren't piles*, he thought, *they're speed bumps*) as she defecated, giving birth to a monstrosity that slithered off the smooth settee; he could hear the liquid slap of her clench, see her hole undulate like a puckering fish mouth.

The stench assaulted him with a hammer blow, his very skin seemed to be absorbing her filth. She kept on gurning, trying her best to turn herself inside out, farting as if there were no end to her sewer. Then it was all over, with a squirt of urine as a convincing full stop. Silence.

She lifted up her chin proudly, defiantly. For the first time in so long he felt him himself stiffen; *depth answers unto depth*, he thought.

"Now," said Pruner, undoing his dressing gown. "*That's* more like it."

Chapter 29

Dobson didn't want to annoy Kate, especially now her time was so near, but despite all his efforts to don a happy face he still looked like a wet Sunday. Too many worries chewed on his guts to allow him to force a smile.

He hadn't seen Pruner since that day in the Moss, had caught sight of him only briefly through the letterbox as he begged him to open the door but Pruner had retreated into the shadows, refused his pleas. He hadn't even helped him move, something he had promised to do, and Pruner never broke a promise.

On top of that his mum had disappeared. His first thought was that the killer had struck once more; he had been frantic with worry until he had found a letter in the hall, (no stamp, no postmark) and his fears had given way to a nagging sense of desertion.

He had done his best to hide his vague despair from Kate, who was so vulnerable right now, but after a few pints down The Cove and a chat with Mosey Campbell it was impossible to keep up the pretence. He was feeling systematically rejected.

Mosey was a sentinel, a guardian, a statue that spoke only wisdom, a Sibyl who would prophesy for a double Bush. He told him he had seen his mum go into Pruner's only the night before.

"Plenty drunk, little fella, looked like she was there to party." The sentinel lacked tact, but his heart was in the right place.

Now as Kate lumbered downstairs, her belly entering the room a good few seconds before the rest of her, he plastered on a smile and got ready to serve up some of what he was already beginning to think of as Dobson dilute. She flopped down beside him, so big, so beautiful. Her eyes ripped off his mask in a single glance, saw right into his heart the way she always could.

"You okay?"

"I'm fine. Just don't know if I'm in a good mood or a bad one."

"Ah Dobs, don't fret, pet, I'm all you need." She patted the smooth round mound of her stomach. "And Junior of course."

"Is he kicking?" He pressed a hand over hers.

"No. Think *she* might be biting though."

"I can't wait, Kate, I really can't. I'll do all I can do to be a good dad, I swear I will."

"You'll be a *great* dad!" She looked deep into his eyes and he felt weak; gloriously, joyously weak. "I know these things, don't I?"

"I can't really remember my own dad anymore, he's fading every week. I see his face less and less clearly. I don't want my son growing up not knowing his dad's face, even if it is as gormless as mine."

"Your son, is it? You got a scanner in that hand of yours?"

"Your meant to say, 'Your face isn't gormless'."

"I know," she giggled, tickling him, "but I don't want to lie in front of the baby."

"I think we should go see your old man."

"I told you Dobs, no way."

"He should know, Kate."

"He will. When it's a done deal. We don't need anybody, love. Not your so-called friends, our parents, nobody. Just we two. And baby." He turned away, wiping at his face. "You crying, soft boy?"

He looked at the single red rose on the mantle that he had bought her on the way back from the pub, could almost hear it slurping greedily on the sugar water it floated in, then back at her, his eyes distant.

"No, nothing like that," he said, his voice serious, keen to open up. "My dad would've seen that as a sign of weakness, or womanly I suppose. He wasn't very romantic, not that I can mind anyway. Him and mum just sat in most weekends with a few bottles and a takeaway. More often than not they'd be at each other's throats when the drink kicked in."

He looked away for a moment, back to the rose.

"But every now and then he'd take her to the pictures. That's what they always called the cinema. Mum would dress up real nice, her eyes all sparkly, and I'd lie awake all night waiting for them to come home. I'd hear them, their voices so happy, every sentence sounding like a song. Then mum would sneak up into my room, her eyes still on fire, and kiss me while I pretended to sleep."

He was crying now, no longer trying to hide it.

"I'd no idea what the pictures were. I thought it must be like an art gallery, and underneath each picture would be a single rose in a vase. I didn't always like my dad, but those nights my mum kissed me goodnight I loved him. Now I've lost her too, and my best mate. Mosey told me she sneaked into his flat last night. I doubt Pruner will ever make her eyes glow. He'll just use her the way he uses everyone, and she'll let him cos that's all she's ever known."

The sobs racked him. Kate hugged him as best she could with the baby bump between them, shushing him as she stroked his tangled hair. "It mightn't have been your mum. After what you've told me about Pruner and women, it could've been any old slapper."

He freed himself from her embrace, got up, and went to the window.

"Aw Jesus, Dobs, I'm sorry. That came out all wrong." She lumbered up after him, placing a tentative hand on his shoulder. "Blame it on the hormones, babes, they're all over the place."

"I know you don't like her, Kate, and with good reason, but she *is* my mother. After you, she's all I've got."

"I don't hate her. It's just hard to feel close to someone who keeps pushing you away. She'll come round when the baby's born, you'll see. She won't be able to resist."

His mother pushed everyone away eventually, there was no use denying it. Even when it had been just the two of them he had played second fiddle to the animals. He looked around his new home, his fortress of independence, and found it haunted by her.

It reminded him of the house on Romannon Street when his dad was still alive. He could sense her in the echoes of its Spartan-ness; save for the fridge magnets. Mum would never approve of such frivolity. His dad had brought some home once and he could still see his mother running her fingers down their small fruit shapes as they clung like surreal barnacles to the fridge door, disdain etched on her face.

"What a waste, Edward."

"No big deal," said dad cheerfully. "Brightens the whole place up."

"Oh, but it is. People who have money to burn decorating their fridge have money to fill it. We, however, are not *those* people."

As if the whole class system boiled down to Mr. Banana, or a turtle driving a cherry car. Cue another row on the Heather jukebox.

He would be given a Mars bar and put out into the hall. Drowning out the shouts and recriminations, he would pretend that the patterns on the carpet were layouts for a city that he bestrode all powerful. If you zoomed up wouldn't Ellsford resemble nothing more than a pattern on a rug, a stain on faded lino? And what if God above, looking down, was just another lonely boy with chocolate round his mouth and tears in his eyes, and above him ... And on and on; like in the barber's with the mirrors before and aft, his image repeated endlessly, an eternity of wonky fringes.

He wished the thoughts away, trying not to let the emptiness of the house bother him. They had a lifetime left to accumulate junk.

"I think I'll pay Pruner a visit. Find out where she's at. I'm out a fortune feeding her bloody cats as it is."

"I don't think that's a good idea, hun."

"Why not?"

"Because ... Pruner has ignored you for ages now. Snubbed you. And if he and your mum are ... How you gonna handle that? It'll end badly and I want you happy. *Need* you happy for the little one."

"But I can't just—"

"Yes, you can. You can do whatever, whenever. You're not accountable to anyone anymore. Especially to people who've shown they couldn't care less. Sorry pet, but it's true." Dobson felt the sting of it, but he couldn't argue. How could they all turn on him like this?

"Why don't you go and see Silver. At least he never deserted you."

"Why the hell would I want to do that?"

"You went to see him when he was in hospital, didn't you? You must care a little bit about him."

"Felt sorry for him, that's all."

"He's lonely. I bet he's missing your mum too. It's pretty obvious he's in love with her."

"Fuck off!"

"Shh! No Anglo Saxon in front of Junior."

"Well, don't be at it, Kate. Jesus! The thought of it."

"I think it's sweet."

"He's ... strange."

"And what are you always telling me people say about you? Am I going to be settling down with a hypocrite, Mr. Heather, hmm?"

"You don't understand, love. Silver's odd with a capital weird. He's always been ... His brother was a murderer, killed a wee girl, then dug her up and brought her out to the Moss. I think it might run in the family."

"The way being a drama queen runs in yours?"

"I'm telling you, Kate, he's not the full deck. When I went round his house to visit him he was ... beating himself."

"What?" She let out a loud porcine snort, something his mother did that always set his teeth on edge, yet he found it endearing in Kate. "You found him masturbating?"

"Christ, no. He was whipping himself with a kettle flex. You wanna see his back, all cut up to fuck, big red welts. He's not compos mentis."

Kate stopped giggling with an effort. "Maybe that kicking he got did more damage than you thought."

"Dunno. A lot of those scars on his back were *old*, like he'd just reopened them."

"He should have reported that Turk to the police. I can't understand why he let him off with it like that."

"Probably scared Moonface would come back and finish off the job if he did."

"I hate it that you have to work with that thug. Seriously, it gives me the shivers to think he might do the same to you."

"Don't be silly, pet. Bob's a psycho, but he's selective in his grudges. He doesn't even acknowledge me now. I may as well not exist. I don't think he's said two words to me since. He just buggers off and lets me do all the work. We've the whole park between us, which suits me fine."

"You be careful, okay?" From the kitchen window the mighty roar of Sherman shattered the moment. "We've got to get rid of that monster, Dobson. When the baby comes, he goes."

"Sherman's a pussycat. He loves kids." He kissed her frowning mouth.

"You can't get round me like that," she said, his kiss now lingering on her neck. "We'll talk," she whispered into his mouth, "about it another time." His hands began to wander but she slapped them away.

"I want to go out," she announced, smiling at his obvious frustration.

"You fancy something to eat? We could go to Benson's."

She wrinkled her nose. He had brought her there before, a special treat, the dearest in town, and they had taken a painful fit of the giggles over the menu— "*a conversation between warm raspberries and vanilla panna cotta in a caramelised pastry case*"— and ended up in The Frying Saucer instead.

"No, thank you," she said. "Let's go for a stroll, then the cinema. A walkie then a watchie."

Since she'd got pregnant she craved movies the way some women craved coal. He had a natural aversion to cinemas though, he could never fully relax there and much preferred a DVD. Eating crisps at the flicks, crunching loudly over the tuts and sighs, he felt adrift in a dark and lonely sea wondering if he dared produce the hard brittle toffee, praying for a car chase or a shootout to cover his tracks. Never bring food to an arty movie—that was one of the lessons he would teach his son. Snacks were for the aural apocalypse of the blockbuster, not the Weepie. They should have signs up—No crunching during break-up scenes, or when the child is ill; yet he found dramas were not that dramatic when you *hoped* the cutesy kid died.

The first time he had brought her to the movies he had behaved himself, fasted for the duration. Kate munched the whole way through, draining her Coke through a straw hideously, needlessly loud, then belched like Vesuvius. It was impossible not to love her.

In the end they settled for a walk around the backstreets before Kate began to complain of backache and sore ankles.

Later that night, his true love lying beside him, a vast hillock of slumber snoring cartoonishly (and even her snores were endearing), Dobson struggled to fall over; he could not stop thinking about his mother. She had always warned him to keep his distance from others. That was the key to not getting hurt she told him, but he felt so *connected* to others, especially those he loved.

He saw that connection as a glimmering golden rope that bound him to them. No matter where he was or what he was doing, he only had to think of his mum and he could see her, *see* her absolutely, tell how she was feeling at any given moment.

All he had to do was tug on that sparkly rope, give it a mental yank, and he was right there with her.

Now the rope had gone slack and he could not see her anymore.

He caught a glimpse of her though, as he fell into a yawning pit of sleep; she was stranded in a red clearing, all alone, a red clearing stained by blood that fell from a vermilion sky. The scarlet vista scorched his mind, blistered his dreams, reduced the golden rope to ash. There were others there too, crying, somewhere out of sight.

He awoke sweating and confused, spending time measured in thick syrupy minutes trying to find his bearings. The new house had yet to feel like home.

Rising gently from the bed he made his way to the dresser—a woman's domain, filled with powders and unguents untold—in which he possessed, after much wheedling debate, a single drawer. A drawer filled with equally pointless things; long dead batteries, elastic bands, an empty bottle of Gaviscon, and a small wooden box.

He took out the box, sighing softly as he flicked it open, unaware that he had begun to rock as he fingered its contents. Kate watched him in the sparse glow from the streetlights that flowed through the unadorned window, closing her eyes as he closed the drawer and tiptoed back to bed.

She did not respond, save in a mock sleepy whistle, to his kiss. Soon he was sleeping again, untroubled now, occasionally fidgeting through more pleasant pastures. She waited until she was sure he was over, then slid gracelessly out of bed and went to his drawer, removing the box that had so captivated him.

Opening it in the sodium pool by the window she saw two necklaces curled snake-like inside; Carrie Anne engraved on one, Eileen on the other. She stifled a gasp, turned to look back at him moaning in his sleep, then back at the shining muted silver in her hand.

She sobbed quietly, soundlessly, so as not to wake him.

Chapter 30

Think of it as a heart, this pulsing glow deep in the Moss.

It has beaten slowly for an age, fed sheep by peasants who would appease it and who name it God, name it Devil; either was fine, for both names were redolent of power and fear, both incited awe and worship.

Once a turf cutter stove in a colleague's skull with a peat iron and a hunger came upon the heart and made it race, until it was no longer satisfied with rainwater, vermin, and buried pets. Soon it will see with human eyes, feel with human nerves, and taste with human greed.

Autumn arrives bleaching the green, but it is winter it waits for. Winter when its voice is loudest, winter when what passes for blood is warmest and the heart beats strongest. It reaches out its tendrils now, vapours and fogs and thin plague airs; misty fingers stroking Ellsford.

Think of it as a voice, worming into susceptible brains. Yes, a Brainworm; that's how one thought of it once, one who believed and gave it the strength to burrow ever further.

The town is quiet, subdued. Its day in the sun has passed. The journalists have gone west (there are other cancerous spots on the earth), a shooting spree in a mall; the press feed on blood too. This is good, for in the reflective pause of winter people listen more, listen to the Brainworm even behind locked doors.

It snakes its way into Molly Stone as she makes her way down her garden on borrowed legs. Womb thirty-six years due south, what good is she? It is too late to whisper to her. As it exhales its fetid vapours (think of it as a breath) she is already tumbling down by her ornamental well, the slippers her nephew bought her sliding on black ice, hurtling down the bank of her spacious lawn, her fall broken by a massive oak.

As she lies bent into an ungainly V, her brittle chalk bones crumbled inside her saggy skin like oats in a nosebag, she spots a gnome (another present from her nephew, such a *thoughtful* boy) peering down on her. Its vacant expression, its ruddy complexion, is so reminiscent of her father she cannot help but laugh. She carries on laughing when her bladder releases, steaming between her contorted legs, laughing even when the pain kicks in and her brays are indistinguishable from screams.

No-one comes to aid her. Pepper's Trees is too affluent to countenance despair so raw, and even the Brainworm refuses to console her with its madness. She has served her purpose; she made the Preacherman believe. It is of no matter now. Her purpose is spent.

There are others to play with.

Others like Bob Turk, sequestered in the bushes of the park overlooking the playground that, despite the cold snap, is still doing brisk trade. The Brainworm fogs up his mind, itches at it, until he undoes his flies with trembling fingers, tugging at himself with painful velocity.

The grunts, are they pain or pleasure? It is hard to say.

The Brainworm goads him on. He has been seen at this before. He needs little cajoling. An undercover policeman interrupts him before his taboo crescendo, and he is cuffed with his pants still around his knees; this is enough to cool his amorous blood. Later his laptop will be seized and his excuses of relieving himself in a more innocent manner will appear risible.

As he is led away, emitting strange gurgling noises, a breeze rattles the treetops, a soft numeration that drowns out his protests. Think of it as laughter.

The Moss's vapours move further into town, unseen fingers brushing past strangers, nipping them with fleeting images of misery and hopelessness that flash through their unguarded minds, seeking out the weary and the vulnerable amongst people it does not know. Not yet.

Soon it will have such fun, soon it will *walk* among these flesh bags and devour them oh so slowly, savouring every dark emotion they hide.

A tentative wisp, soft as a sigh, enters the home of the butcher, finds him in his bathroom running cold water into the tub, adding to its depths with warm tears.

Cully calls the little dog who sits watching him through grey and rotted fur. He is struck once more by how *old* the dog is. You never see old dogs on a lead, he thinks, never see them being walked by teenage girls (who love a furry accessory) or even by lonely men oblivious of fashion. Perhaps dogs grew old so quickly to throw off that yoke; perhaps they still walk the world in paw-kicking dreams.

Bones smells bad now, surrounded by a halo of flies, and something that Cully would rather not look at is writhing in the chasm in its head.

"Here, Bony boy."

Cully's heart is breaking. He loves the dog, has told it so many times, shared with it all his petty triumphs; yes, he loves its very ... bones. He can't bear to see its broken gait, or smell the putrescence that belies its shambling animation. He would rather it was his wife he were about to drown (*And why not her!* urges the Brainworm), but he can't go on living alongside this grotesque mockery of his beloved pet.

Bones does not struggle, not even when he is fully submerged and the water numbs the butcher's wrists, bubbles bursting the surface in a miasma of filth. The dog goes to its second death, not wagging but drowning, with a stoic calm. In a way this hurts Cully even more, frightens him in a way he cannot comprehend.

The fear oozes from him, greasing his flesh, and the air around him shimmers in anticipation. Think of it as hunger.

The vapours float on aimlessly awhile, drifting toward Evanston Home, finding the husk of Wendell Hamill seated by the expansive bay window overlooking the looping driveway between the pines.

Oh this is a bonus. It has forgotten dear old Wendell, has missed this old playmate!

It burrows into his mind, easily dispersing the pale chemicals that try to shackle it; it squirms along and around Wendell's feelings.

It was nothing o'clock and he had no map to Reason, no light to guide him to that mythical place. Reason wasn't illuminated; it hid in the dark, guarded jealously so that inveterate tasters of guilt could never find it. It was protected against curdlers and their monomaniac self-hatred. The pills were chimeras, phantoms that dissolved under any hint of scrutiny. Sad had no co-ordinates. Sad was everywhere. Sad *was* you as much as you were Sad. Sad was the very fabric you were made of, but if the stitches were loose, then the light could sneak in. All this Wendell knew.

Almost too warm to breathe here, a dry sapping heat that sucked out what little health remained. Uncomfortable chairs faced an unwatched television. Pretty nurses, plain nurses. Pretty, plain nurses. Badly spelt names on the whiteboard; your own existence could be wiped away just as quickly. Old men with their mouths open so wide, like snakes who swallow cows; no flies on this ward. Clean your hands! Clean them now! You are a walking cesspit, clean yourself! That's what the signs meant, Wendell could read their secrets. He knew too, that disease lingers on unwashed signs, and that hand wash smelt of Christmas aftershave.

Sickness waits like a tiger cat, crouching amid the wrinkly pyjamas and the jugs of tepid water, biding its time in this way station of the netherworld.

The Brainworm pulses. Wendell's eyes focus for the first time in weeks, lit from behind, as a swarm of memories assail him. Memories of violence and secrets, of squeezing his Art Teacher's balls in the canteen until he passes out; still not letting go, squeezing harder, as the other teachers punch and claw at him and the dinner ladies start to cry. "He made fun of my free dinner ticket," murmurs Wendell, still affronted after all these years.

Memories of bubbles filled with animals (Balloonamils he'd called them, trying to explain them to Gus), that lure him deeper into the Moss, and the voices there, and the man who could not be, the man who was dead, the man who came to his window, talking to him through the long summer nights.

Wendell shakes himself to dislodge the visions. He turns his massive head on a neck that cracks through lack of use to regard his neighbours. Beside him, skin like rhubarb and custard, is an old mollusc of a woman propped in a chair. She is frightened and vulnerable. This makes him smile. The air is punctuated by bleeps and blips, by the glint of needles and the smell of rubbing alcohol. The rustle of half-read magazines riffles through this flowerless limbo.

Then Mary, the young cheery nurse, is there, her face hanging above him like a bizarre mobile. He likes Mary; she is the only one here who ever really speaks to him. He never answers back. He hasn't spoken in years—no, not a single word, not so much as a "cababbage."

He tries to croak something, but it comes out as a wad of phlegm. Mary is ecstatic, however, her eyes widening like a lottery winner. He likes Mary.

"Did you just say something, Wendy?" she asks, leaning ever closer even though he smells like a trawler. "Did you try to tell your wee Mary something?"

He grips her shoulders with shovel hands that have barely moved in months, pulling her toward his bucket mouth, chewing on her pretty face, swallowing her smile, almost choking on the gush of blood and cartilage, but nothing can satiate this sudden rapacious desire. Yes, he really likes Mary. She is delicious.

Her howls disappear down his gullet with her tongue. He manoeuvres himself further off his chair on wasted legs, his full nappy sloshing, as the old woman burbles happily beside him.

The Brainworm is loathe to leave (think of it as a homecoming), there is so much to eat here, but there are other things to see, other games to set in motion, new friends to meet. When it has bones of its own it will return to show Wendell undreamed of pastimes.

Sliding out now, through cracks and vents, floating on the chill air like blood on water, gaining in size, going where the cold wind blows, seeking out the hot spots it has long pondered on, making sure all is in place, all is ready.

It stops awhile over the Proctor house, caressing itself around a motorcycle parked by the front gate (how Dooley would love such a thing!) before stretching out beneath the door, slinking upstairs, mingling with the odours of good home cooking, finding Drew packing in his room. It no more than grazes the boy's thoughts; like scraping at a blister; they are ugly and tangled. The Proctor boy is a waste of skin.

The Brainworm is glad that he is leaving town; it cannot understand the emptiness within him. It seeks nerves, emotion, a panoply of pain and joy, but there is nothing here but a dull throb, with anger as its only bitter condiment. It will have to learn why there are such people, perhaps it will find value there, but it must wait until it is stronger, when it can walk unaided. Until then, let the boy go unmolested. He is too sad to be a playmate, akin to a worm himself.

Sailing high over Ellsford, coiling itself around the spire of the Presbyterian church, it feels free, more, it feels itself a mighty serpent like the one Paul is obsessed with from that story of the Man God and his strange adversary—both with so much power yet they refuse to use it, refuse to play! The graveyard below is filled with tilting stones and grassy mounds; the Man God is *so* hungry.

Seeping down into the church it finds the Reverend Craig on all fours between the dusty pews bellowing at the stained glass, bellowing for his Nadine (who has been such good company—what fears she possesses for one so young). It is Dooley who has driven him to this, Dooley and his appetite for rotting flesh. In many ways Dooley has been the best company of all.

There is no need to whisper here for the voices in the Reverend's head are babbling so loudly it is a wonder he can stand it. It is better to float, to watch. Watch the silly little creature rage at his pointless little God as he tears at his face, at his clothes. Such a ridiculous spectacle, why is their faith so weak?

Naked now, the Reverend stumbles to the font and urinates in it, splashing himself, splashing the floor, breathing in deep of the metallic twang of paint that lends a heady top to his anger. He has sprayed the walls with every swear word he knows from fart to cunt, a childish surge of liberation enveloping him. He has daubed an inverted cross on his flabby chest, its running streams resembling a botched attempt at self-surgery. Is this pathetic creature truly the image of the God it so fears?

The Reverend picks up a hymn book and hurls it through the stained glass just as Nellie Brown comes in to rearrange the flowers. Her yelp of surprise is drowned out by a satisfying thud as the book strikes the Son of God in his brightly lit chest.

It leaves a ragged hole where His heart should be. Think of it as a revelation.

Enough, the game has grown pitiful.

Outside, back into the air, hovering over the sodden High Street, it watches the dispirited denizens below. The Brew Crew are out in force, causing more havoc now they are sober than they ever did drunk. They point out Christmas shoppers, haranguing them with cries of "Sinner!" and "Harlot!" jostling them, beating their heads with Bibles, righteous murder on their minds.

It could enter these minds so easily now, travel along their blasted synapses, as a wind enters a derelict house or blows across a barren burnt out field, but it would be wasteful. Samuel has set about his work well, his voice resounding in those empty domes. There is no need to add confusion to their sudden clarity.

Besides, a baby is gasping its first lungful of air and birth fascinates the Brainworm, transfixes it more than death though it remembers neither. It rushes toward the sound, shaking lampposts and power-lines in its haste.

It passes over Dobson—oh, beloved conduit, blessed nuncio—and the Rose boy as they pass each other unseen, unaware they are intent on paying a visit to each other's home, not knowing the Brainworm has spared them both out of newfound feelings of ... Think of it as love.

This unseen thunderbolt crashes down, a supersonic crack that can be heard in Blackmore where Christa Finchley stops pinching her crying baby for a moment, looking out the window with sunken eyes, oblivious to the baby flesh and blood under her tattered nails, before returning to her task with renewed vigour. The baby's skin is a palimpsest of pain as his mother creates a new orthography, writing over old bruises with new cuts and welts.

It finds Kate in the bathroom, blood between her legs, a squirming thing of grey and red in her arms, and the windowpanes rattle at such a sight. Think of it as awe.

Soon it will live through the offspring of these two children of the Moss, soon it will be done with whispering and watching; it will tear and rend with its own hands, it will taste blood and lick the last salty beats from dying hearts.

It has no time to enjoy this miracle, this mixture of obscenity and wonder. Someone is calling its name, an event rare enough to draw it back, back, back whence it came. It goes willingly. It has time.

The Preacherman is seeking it out. The Preacherman seeks answers but will find only instruction.

Stagnant streams run on both sides of Samuel, their inky water almost solid enough to walk on; what grabbing hands beneath there, what pale sucking faces? The wind strikes up, mimicking the lonely calls of the few hardy birds that remain; bereft cries that remind him of the pterodactyls that flew across the TV screens of his youth. They terrified him, and Paul would laugh. He was always so much more grown up. He could never fill his brother's boots—even the moustache he tried to grow after his death was an immature insult.

The earth pulses, glows, *beats* beneath Samuel's heavy tread just like ... Well, think of it as a heart.

Chapter 31

He could have brought Sherman with him, but that show of strength would only have made him look vulnerable. Did he really believe he was going to pick a fight with his best mate in the first place? Was he hoping to find him weaker, lessened in some significant way? Most likely they would smooth things over and end up down The Cove, laughing at their misunderstandings over a pint.

The closer he got to Pruner's flat the more he believed this scenario to be wishful thinking, a Disney version of events concocted to make him feel less nervous about the inevitable conclusion, the pointless sundering.

Pruner had let him down, turned his back on him, for no reason he could think of. He had scuttled their friendship without a second thought, and though he was going to ostensibly ask after his mother that was the real answer he sought: Why have you abandoned me?

Christ, that sounded needy—but he *was* needy.

He felt guilty for even being here, for lying to Kate and leaving her on her own when she was ready to pop (how she hated that phrase), but he needed a clean slate before the child was born, needed everything to be just so, to be right, the way it used to be.

Another lie. Things had never been right, not really. He just wanted things back closer to the approximation in his head, but he had always been the odd one out, even at school.

They ignored him back then too, engaged in grown up talk that didn't concern him at the heady age of twelve. He laughed it off, grew an armadillo shell; safe but ugly. He should've told them at the time instead of bottling it all up.

Now he was at the front door he still didn't know what to say. Just like the day before, and the day before that. He had been here every day for a week and still hadn't mustered up the courage to knock. Once he had peered through the window and saw only vague shadows. It ended here today, one way or the other.

He would kick the fucking window in if he had to, he would see Pruner face to face and ask him what the fuck was going on. He would be denied no longer. He pounded his fist against the door, grabbing the handle in his fury. The door opened.

* * *

Pruner strode the alley that led to Dobson and Kate's Xanadu with a swagger and a smile. Originally his plan had been to come like a thief in the night but what was life without a show, a dramatic cocky gesture. He would go in all guns blazing and his victorious smile would never leave his kissable lips.

The sight of Sherman, prowling the other side of the fence, caused that smile to waver momentarily; the dog flashed between the slats like a caged bear as it turned relentlessly in the small concrete pen. He leapt the fence in a single artful bound, pleased to see the mutt flinch at this unexpected intrusion; even more pleased he hadn't landed in one of the termite mounds of shit that littered the backyard.

"Hello, Shermy," he said jovially. "Are mummy and daddy home?"

The dog looked at him warily, a half growl of confusion snared in its throat. Pruner gave him a friendly pat and strolled right in through the back door, the dog following in his buoyant wake.

* * *

It was like walking into a showroom, a dollhouse. Pruner's flat was tidier than he remembered it. Dobson felt completely out of place, completely other, in the calm of this overwhelming sterility. His breath felt dirty here, he could almost see it cling to the shiny surfaces and stain the dust free air.

It felt wrong here, unnatural.

"Bill?" His voice was small, unwelcome. This was not a home, this was a stage set. The air was stale with accumulated sighs; whatever drama was to be played out here was long overdue. "Pruner? Where are you?"

This was a place of ghosts, quiet as an unmarked grave. The longer he stayed here the more he felt like a shade himself.

He moved into the kitchen, stepping from one catalogue picture into another, his heart sliding over the blinding Formica and splattering on the gleaming floor tiles. His mother's knickers—how many times had he seen them on the line, fluttering like some brazen flag—lay by the sink. A leopard skin print, a feline fanged mouth across the crotch. She had been here then, and unless she had met with a sudden inexplicable accident whilst making coffee, she had fucked his best mate right there on the worktop.

Tears stung him. He wasn't angry with her, he wasn't disappointed. He had long known his mum filled her emptiness with sex the way some women filled it with biscuits, but he could not forgive Pruner this trespass. This was over the line, a crutch too much.

* * *

Looks like your bitter half is quite the homemaker, Dobs, thought Pruner as he surveyed the wreckage of the kitchen. *You've shacked up with a younger version of your mum.* His bin was cleaner than this place. The sink was buried under a precarious pyramid of grimy dishes, the floor strewn with all manner of scraps and leftovers; Sherman set to it with gusto, chewing on the upturned lino as it removed a puddle of congealed gravy.

Pruner wrinkled his nose and moved out of the kitchen to see what other hygienic enchantments awaited him. He was offended to the core at this mess, not daring to touch anything, wary of the stink-filled air that seemed to stick to him. He was glad to be offended, delighted by the rage that swept through him at this squalor; it made things so much easier.

He stopped in the hallway, a Hoover blocking his way, its nozzle still attached to a vacuum storage bag; several others full of brightly squashed clothes were stacked like Lego bricks against the wall.

There was movement at the top of the stairs. He turned to see Kate glowering down at him. She was pale, almost translucent, a visible sheen of sweat on her arms and face. She wore no makeup, her oily hair scraped back in a harsh ponytail, an angry red scar snaking across her temple. There was blood on her bare legs, dripping from the oversized t-shirt that swamped her small figure.

"Hello, gorgeous," he laughed. "I've come for a chat with you and Brainiac."

"Dobson's not here," she said. "You'll have to come back. And next time, ring the fucking bell."

Did a God need to announce his presence? He began climbing the stairs. "Oh, you'll do fine for now, my love." His smile illuminated the dim hallway, making each sticky riser glow. "You'll do just fine."

* * *

He started by smashing plates—he realised it was childish, but he needed the release—throwing a mug through the spotless pane above the taps, hurling the doll-size microwave to the floor. If he could have summoned up a good piss he would have drenched the place gleefully but he was dry inside, withered; he couldn't even summon up a wad of saliva.

He returned to the living room, spending the next ten minutes systematically destroying it, using his pocket knife to tear apart the settee. Breaking mirrors, busting shelves, crippling the enormous plasma screen (who knew mutiny could be so sweet!) but none of it sated his rage. Only one thing could do that, but Pruner wasn't here. The flat would have to bear the brunt.

He surveyed the carnage he had wrought, trying to calm himself, to plan his next move, telling himself he would wait here for Bastard Billy Rose to return, just sit and study the look of horror on his womanly face before plunging a knife in his treacherous heart, sending his blood spraying all over his prissy flat.

In the midst of the wreckage his eyes lit on one item that had escaped the destruction, flew under the radar of his wrath. Pruner's laptop—the ultimate prize! He had it in his hands, about to sail it to techno hell in the innards of the telly, when it struck him how he could *really* hurt his erstwhile comrade.

He flicked it open and fired it up, searching through the music files until he found what he was looking for. The pompous fuck had saved it under *My Masterpiece*.

* * *

"Dobson will be home soon."

"And what will *he* do? Runaway and leave me like he did down the Moss?"

For a moment anger got the better of him, and his smile evaporated. He swallowed it, reined it in; it was important to be calm here, to remember he held all the high cards. He changed the subject back to safer ground than Troughton's bog land.

"You know, I thought you'd be all bloated, a real pudding by now," he said, stopping on the stair below her. "But you're still a dainty little thing. I bet I could put my hands right around you."

He reached out, delighted that she recoiled. "You've every reason to be scared, love."

"Is *that* what you're trying to do? Am I supposed to be scared, Billy Big Time? *Please.*"

The scorn in her voice hurt him, but she *was* scared of something; her eyes kept darting back upstairs, then down to the snuffling sounds of Sherman foraging noisily in the kitchen. "I came to chat, s'all," he said nonchalantly, wondering if the little bitch called him Billy Big Time to Dobson, or if it were Dobson who had come up with that spiteful moniker all by himself.

"What have you got to say that I could possibly want to hear?"

"Just some gossip I picked up from a girl. Eileen. You know her?"

"She's dead."

"That's the funniest thing, Katy, see, she told me you were too."

* * *

He wasn't sure what he had been expecting, some amateur version of Pruner's beloved Krautrock perhaps, but not this; never this.

For all of Pruner's talk of his "talent" (and he would never need to hire a PR) he had never actually shown any sign that he could walk the walk. Whenever he pontificated on his "great work", his "opus for the new age," Dobson would go along—not out of duty, but because he *wanted* to believe—even though a single note had never been forthcoming.

Dobson was a dreamer, and as such was open to anything that so much as hinted at grandeur, self-promoted or not. However, this was beyond the scope of his dreams; even his nightmares had not skulked these dark backstreets. His hands hovered over the keys, unable to turn off the sounds that now tattooed his brain, and the images that accompanied them.

There was a rhythm to it, a subtle one, almost indiscernible at first, but after the initial shock its hidden structure became more apparent; a mangled melody became more insidious, the beat more pronounced and awful.

Screams and cries assailed him, cut into loops repeating over and over, layered in pleadings that wove serpentine through it all, grinding out a song of death almost majestic in its elaborate torture.

On the screen, segueing from one pain to another, bleeding into each other, returning again and again with each signature wail, were images as shocking as the dying voices they belonged to.

These pictures weren't downloaded from the net or hacked from some police file. Pictures of Nadine, Carrie Anne, Beth—flashing on and off in time to their last plaintive howls—images of the girls in their final moments, their begging eyes pooled with the terrible knowledge of their own death. Like the soundtrack, these were images only their killer could have captured.

* * *

"And what are you?" asked Kate.

"Detached. Cold. Forgetful, or at least I used to be. Now it's all so clear. It courses through me, this ... power. I've never been so alive. Can you say the same, Kate? Or is that even your name?" He flicked at her necklace, the one that read *Eileen*. "What did your mother name you?"

"Power!" she scoffed. "You're a funny boy, I'll give you that. I'm very far from dead, are you blind as well as stupid? I guess at this stage of the game you can call me whatever you like, and Kate's as good as any. I liked Kate, one of my favourites, a wild little thing who runaway and hid in the Moss when you were just a babe. They never found her after I did. Sharp little mind, squirmy as a hawk's. I learned so much from her. Pretty too, don't you think?"

"Once perhaps, not now. You look like you're decaying. The only remotely attractive thing about you is that scar."

"You've acquired strange tastes," she said, unconsciously tracing the welt on her temple. "A present from your friend Malcolm when I was vulnerable, hiding in the sewers. Now the time for hiding is almost over."

"I remember now, all those songs the Moss put in my head," said Pruner, "such wicked songs, and I learned them all by heart. The darkness that put them there would be proud of the symphony I've created, for it taught me to play note by note, but I'm the conductor now, Sweetie, I'm the one calling the tune." He stretched his arms out toward her. "Your time's over, full stop. Kiss me, Kate, let's part as friends. I've come to show you my power. You'll be the final note in my masterpiece. Don't scream, I want it to end ambiguously."

"You really don't get it, do you," she said, her face so close now he felt a sickly heat emanate from her in cloying waves. "It was I who made you what you are. I who licked your tiny heart when I could have devoured it whole. I who gave reason to your worthless life by teaching you the power of the kill. The body is just a plug, the soul electric. It was I who charged your soul. The Preacher would have me dine on rats—you were my fast track to something more nourishing. The power you crow of is lent, borrowed. You're a wet nurse pretending to be mummy, nothing more."

Her eyes had grown bog black, hypnotic. Pruner was paralysed by their dark grip while all the while her mouth opened wider and wider until it filled his whole world.

"You don't fool me with your disguise," he mumbled. "Show me your true face, if you dare."

"I am how you see me, boy. Some think me beautiful and name me virtue. People's idea of evil is other people, so that is what I manifest as. It's all just a game of dressing up."

Up and beyond a baby cried, breaking the spell, Kate spinning her head toward the sound as her eyes drained to a lacklustre grey.

"And baby makes three," said Pruner, grabbing her shoulders and heaving her downstairs. He could still hear her heavy descent as he entered the bedroom.

* * *

He was ready to fling the laptop against the wall but stayed his hand just in time. This was evidence. Evidence for the police and the powers that be, evidence for himself to confront Billy Rose with. The name felt strange in his mind, jagged, unwieldy—it conjured up no memories now, just a shocked, blank space. The man he'd known all his life had been a lie, a construct, laughing at his gullibility, sniggering at his trust.

There was no real anger, not yet, more a fear so strong it felt like elation at this knowledge, this mystery revealed.

Was his mum dead? Dobson clung to the slim hope that Pruner's victims had all been young girls in their first bloom. Girls like Nadine, Beth, and … and a memory came rushing back through the blinding nothingness that tried to suppress it; Pruner's face, dappled by the sun through the crabby little trees in the Moss, his voice so clear, echoing even now, ringing out in Dobson's head the answer to what he thought of his girlfriend, his lover, his all.

Can she sing?

He fled the flat, railing against the sickly despair, praying that he made it home before Kate passed her audition.

* * *

He walked slowly toward the cot, in awe of what might lie there. What twisted, malformed creature would be tucked up there, swaddled in blankets, twitching its tail as it waited for its limbs to grow strong enough to crush the world. Would he worship it, or usurp its place?

He peered over the cot's edge, his shaky hand causing it to rock slightly, as its inhabitant looked back at him with disconcertingly lucid eyes. He sucked in a deep breath. The baby was bland, Churchillian ugly, a half-sucked sweet spat out onto a pillow, its skin raw, stained where the tears had festered. A normal, healthy, horrible baby.

The child's eyes lit up, vocalising what its throat could not, focusing beyond Pruner's shoulder. The little gurgly bastard even managed a grin.

He spun around to face Kate, or what he presumed was Kate; the slavering thing coming toward him still wore the baggy t-shirt, the necklace still dangled from the gnarly neck. He dropped to his knees as his bladder let go—to think he had thought himself a God! Here before him was the real deal, a Queen, a creature of such *beauty* he was almost breathless. And this creature was merely a vassal to usher forth the real power, the one that lay sucking on its fingers behind him.

Christ? Antichrist? Satan? No, he didn't think so. None of those tired names. It was Nature, or Nature's dark bastard.

"I didn't know." He was transfixed by the insectile eyes trained on him. "How could I know? I done everything you put in my heart, and I can do so much more. I'll serve you, I'll—"

The thing roared, its grassy mane shaking, its mouth of thorns gleaming as its larval tongue flicked over its cracked earth gums. Its very breath seemed to burn.

"Please ..." He ran a supplicating hand over the rough bark of its legs. "I'll be your little boy."

It plunged a root-like claw into his chest causing fire to blaze where only ice had burnt before and Pruner howled, or was that Sherman? He could see the indistinct shadow of the lunging hound, hear the snap of wood, and a scream so high it momentarily deafened him.

As the rain began to pelt against the window, and the child began to cry, he sank into darkness and dreams of the Moss.

* * *

Dobson was soaked by the time he had made it as far as Hollywell, and as he turned the corner onto High Street the wind almost blew him back down to the church. He battled against its sudden fury, fighting for breath like a dog with its head lolling from the window of an express train.

People were falling like tenpins, blowing like refuse down the street, hurtling into stalled cars, whilst others sought refuge in the flickering shops. The storm blew on, uprooting the bedraggled Christmas tree and plunging it through the windscreen of the No. 38 to Blackmore, shedding garish polystyrene presents in its wake.

As Dobson clung to a shuddering phone booth door, a pram sailed by at breakneck speed, a small girl strapped inside, her wail lost in the fury of the wind. Across the road Catman was wrapped around a lamppost, his eyes and hair as wild as any wilderness prophet. The tempest swallowed his words whole, spewing back only the occasional phrase—"The End is here!", and "Prepare to burn!"—along with gobbets of lunatic laughter.

The storm abated as suddenly as it had sparked, leaving only an icy breeze as a dying breath and a heart drench of rain as an epitaph. Dobson ran through the ruin of High Street, oblivious to the cries for help, the pleas accosting him from all quarters.

"Too late!" Catman was yelling into the stillness. "You have all been judged and found wanting!"

He ran faster, heading for his house of straw, praying the big bad wolf had not got there first.

* * *

Pruner ignored the wind that threatened to spiral the house to Oz. He was watching Sherman sniff disdainfully at Kate's dismembered corpse; a mix of limbs and leaves, of guts and ground. He had prevailed, and for that there must be a reason.

His work, always important, was now vital—why else would he have been spared? There was a higher force in operation than that Pretender that had crawled from the bogs. His chest felt like it housed an arctic blast but he ignored it, waiting until Sherman padded downstairs with something unspeakable in its jaws before getting up and going to the cot.

He regarded the baby awhile, nauseated by the thick drool that seeped from its scrunched-up face. How could they inspire such affection? Hard to believe he had been one once; his childhood was gone, lost to him now, and for that he was thankful.

He had a distaste for what he had to do. It would be better if he had someone to do it for him—he was, if not a God, then something close—but he could not come this far and leave his work unfinished. It didn't have to be mundane, he could still make a game of it.

His thin lips arched into a smile as he remembered the Hoover at the bottom of the stairs. "Back in a mo, Babykins," he said, tickling the child under its sticky chin. He returned, almost tripping in his haste, with the Hoover and a large vacuum pack storage bag.

"Tada!" he said, flattening the bag out on the small patch of floor the child's mother had not fouled. He took out his phone and set it on Voice Record then picked up the squirming baby, stuffing it awkwardly into the storage bag, pinching him to make him cry louder. Then he attached the Hoover's nozzle to the bag's connection, sighing with relief as he flicked the vacuum on and its teeth rattling drone drowned out the squealing child.

He couldn't help but clap his hands as the air was sucked out and the storage pack shrank with the rapidity of a crisp bag on an electric fire. He let out a small yelp of glee when he was left with a small, tidy, perfectly wrapped and perfectly silent package.

"Marvellous," he said, and began to take some photos.

* * *

He found what was left of her in the bedroom, lying on what appeared to be kindling. Her head had been almost severed. He had to roll it around to face him to make sure it was really her; her mouth was full of mud and grass, her hair … What had that bastard done to her!

Katekatekatekatekatekate—the word became his heartbeat, the only thing that kept him going.

He tried to lift her, but there were too many pieces. Somewhere in the soup of her guts was their baby, but he could not find it, could not differentiate between infant and offal. It had been cut out, trampled. He began a strange keening, rocking gently back and forth as something inside him gave way.

The air was filled with music, a simple, childish refrain that tried in vain to soothe him; the burping, colourful notes of an ice cream van. He sang along as he rocked, kissing the mess of organs and sinews, muck and briar that he clutched in his hands, hoping at least some part of it was his son.

* * *

There was no escape from the rain.

The wind hounded him, freezing his blood, but it felt good to him, it felt just. He should go home now, finish his opus, leave it for the world to find. It would be years before it was understood, but that was of little consequence. His only regret was that perhaps Dobson would not fully appreciate it now.

Although the storm had died, the streets were empty. There was nothing as mistrustful as a small town. The deluge had only served to make things unclean, to drag all the secrets back indoors.

Yes, he should go home now, but something was pulling him toward the Moss and he was too weary to fight it. The ice in his chest was speeding unchecked through his body. He felt so cold and brittle that one awkward jolt off a kerb almost rendered him to dust.

He headed toward the outskirts on automaton legs, his breath sharper with every step, his skin tighter, shrink-wrapping his bones as it wrinkled and drained itself grey. The roof of his mouth was dripping blood. He pondered the world from behind the wheel of a damaged machine. His back began to stoop, borne down by some weight akin to time, but he barely noticed.

In his head all he could hear was music. Music was all.

I kill because I love music, he realised, *and the music I love is not audible until death is close. It is the sound of cat paws on wet streets, of dogs' retching, of unnatural silences in waiting rooms, of inner screams backed by unheard orchestras.*

Listen to the symphony I have written on your heartstrings!

The caw of a crow, the cry of an orphan, the industrial hum of a factory (death on a grand scale), the revving of an engine, the blip of a flatline, the chink of scant coins in a pensioner's purse.

All are my instruments. Only I hear the melody, only I play by ear. You tut, not realising I conduct you, that your tuts and sneers are percussive chimes to my black rhythms. Soon you will beat me like the thunderous kettle drum and the piece will end.

Perhaps he should call it, "My Death By The Roadside," for he realised now his death would be a fitting coda.

I'm running out of moments. Soon they will plunder my flat, their opinions hardening when they find the diaries I wrote and could never read again. I am a living diary now, my blood ink, my eyes full stops. And when they have finished with the penbane of my journals they will consider my music collection—punk, reggae, a soupcon of the blackest metal—taking note of the cartoon Satanic imagery of their covers and reach the same old tired conclusions. They will fashion an entirely new me, one they can label Evil, one fit to adorn a tabloid's bragging headline. I will be their taboo piñata, to beat in front of society until all their demons fall out.

They will never know how those songs protected me from the darkness until I wrote my own and ushered in that glorious void. Will they listen to my work before they orgasm in righteous ecstasy? No matter, it will be left for the ages and others will surely follow.

His feet ticked on. His journey was witnessed only by a hardy few, revealing to each what they long suspected.

Mrs. Proctor saw him through her twitch-free curtains and tutted wetly; *drunk,* she thought, as she watched him stumble, and at this hour! He was a bad egg, she always said so, led her boy astray. When Drew returned (and he had been an *awfully* long time at the shop) she would tell him again, you needn't fret over that.

Mrs. Cully saw him next. She was returning from visiting that poor Mrs. Turk (oh, her poor, poor boys), offering comfort whilst fishing for gossip. She had been bitterly disappointed there had been no outward signs of scandal, and that Mrs. Turk was adamant there had been no clue to her husband's predilections (the Lord loathes a liar!), but she had *sensed* an evil air about the house and was ruminating on how best to convey that sense to maximum effect down the hairdressers, when she hit pay dirt spotting the Rose boy; at least, she thought it was him. This was far more substantial than evil air.

AIDS! He was so bedraggled, thin and sickly, and he had hidden himself away by all accounts. It *must* be AIDS!

The tales of his rampant philandering were legion—and they said he'd got that young Finchley girl in the family way—and at last he had been smitten. Long runs the fox. She picked up her pace considerably, the negative vibes of Casa Turk now forgotten.

Jenny Bell, driving the dinky pink car she believed spoke volumes about her fun personality, passed Pruner near Horseshoe Lane thinking at first that the storm had blown a scarecrow out from the fields and onto the roadside. *Oh Billy boy*, she thought, a fat tear welling for her own lucky escape, *I knew the drugs would get you in the end*. She drove on, never slowing, finding a way to blame it all on that Love Me Do bitch Finchley between third and fourth gear.

What Gus Hamill saw lurching painfully past his house was an old man. He never contemplated helping him; the Ellsford way was to ignore and move on. He merely watched awhile, thinking how a good solid fart would break that old fuck in two and send him drifting off like a dandelion clock, before returning to his daydream of an old Triumph he had heard was up for sale.

Pruner made it to the Moss unaided, ageing with every jarring step, his body burning with ice, yet still a smile on his sunken face. He stumbled on the scars of mucky tyre tracks; it looked as if the road had taken a beating too.

There was music here—a music wilder, more discordant, more death affirming than any he could ever conjure from pallid flesh, for it took its beat from the pulsing drone of the abyss.

He dropped to the ground, his spindly legs snapping, the melody of venom singing through his veins. His bones powdered as his flesh dissolved, returning gladly to the earth, wide awake and dreaming, to dance to that tune forever.

"Can I see my boy?" she asks as Samuel holds the door for her. It is the first time she has set foot in this house, and without Dobson here it feels like she is breaking and entering.

"Later, Joyce," he says. "He's at the hospital. I think they'll send him to Evanston Home, to be with the rest of the unfortunates."

"No, no, no, I'll not have that. I'll take him home with me. He belongs with his mother."

"We'll see. First things first, we have much to do."

Sighing, she walks into a synthetic meadow. The house is spotless; she has misjudged Kate in so many ways but, really, how could she have known? If only the girl had not been so fond of playing silly games, so willful like her father. Samuel says it is all a test and—

"I cleaned the place up," he says. "Such squalor. How could anyone live in such a … Expletive deleted. Pardon my inference."

"Where is she?" It seems wrong to call her Kate now, like calling Jesus by a nickname.

Samuel sucks on his teeth. He has huge horse teeth—funny, she never noticed how big they were before, how white. He doesn't smoke or take coffee or hard liquor. His body is a temple, he walks the walk, practices what he preaches.

"I buried her in the Moss, returned her to the source, dust to dust, anon and on. It made me so close to Paul. I felt like I was communicating directly with him by sharing that chore. I realise now the torture he must have went through with the sainted Eileen. Father God never makes it easy."

"And the baby?"

Samuel rubs a nonexistent stain from his tie. It is one she has bought him *and, until now, she has never seen him wear it, not once. It makes her feel a little giddy.*

"I hope you're hungry," he says, opening the door to the kitchen, unleashing the rich aroma of casserole into the hallway. "I don't normally cook, but it is a special occasion and I could hardly impose on you."

He ushers her in. The table is set for two; candles, napkins, all shining silver and twinkling glass.

"Samuel, you sly old romantic you!"

He reddens instantly, his berry head apoplectic against his immaculate white shirt.

"Have a seat, it's nearly ready," he mumbles, holding the chair for her; no man has ever done this for her. God is in such details. Is this love? At last? She thinks so, and finally she has a chance at what has always been denied her. All praise to God and second chances.

"Should I have left out some bread?" Samuel is ladling two hefty plates of steaming stew. He looks good, but pale. He lost three pints of blood during the beating he took, and that was a hell of a round in anyone's book. She laughs though; he is so comical in his desire to please her, to make everything just so.

"Come and sit down," she says, patting the chair beside her. And he pads over like an obedient dog.

"I was going to play some music, but you like that rock-n-roll and I like hymns. I thought silence would be the less controversial option."

"No matter. My heart is singing. Can't you hear it, Sammy?"

He mutters something to cover his embarrassment. The foolish old thing has even forgotten to say Grace in his discomfiture. Yes, it is easy to love this dear, befuddled man.

"The onions are nice," she says.

"Not too much? I thought I went a little overboard."

"No, just right."

"The stock? I followed the box on that one."

"Perfect, Samuel, really."

"The meat? Too tough? There's no real recipe—"

"Stop fussing. It's lovely, pet, honestly, very tender. A lovely séance picnic."

Samuel visibly relaxes. "Good, good. I was worried, I admit. I mainly used the belly meat and the, ah ... testicles et cetera. All the cuts that Paul suggested. I buried his little head and the leftovers with his mother. I thought you might approve of such a gesture."

"You've done a wonderful job, Samuel, but ... will this work?"

"Ah, sweet Joyce, look where lack of faith got us last time. No more shows now,

vanity got the better of me I'm afraid. Now I would crawl under a moving bus to hide my God from them. We must not doubt Paul again. He has shown me the way, and we must follow."

He holds her hand and a shock runs through her; has he ever touched her before?

"You'll make a truly excellent mother."

She feels like bawling in his big strong arms. "And you the best of fathers."

"Eat up," he beams. "We must be full to the throat and bursting to the teeth, consume all we can before—"

"Before we make love."

"Yes, before we ... do our duty."

"You are so adorable," she says, and she means it. "You are a big man, Samuel, and what is Kong without a helpless beauty in his grasp."

They are silent awhile, but it is a companionable silence. She thinks of her grandchild as she chews, placating it—You are safe here, inside my mouth.

Occasionally, frequently, they share glances that linger longer than usual, and she stifles some wind in order not to ruin this beautiful unlooked-for moment.

"I'm still hungry," she says.

Samuel starts to rise. "There may be a little left in the pot."

"No, love. Hungry for you." She kisses him, sucks the blush right out of his mouth, leaves him speechless. "I always knew I'd get you." She feels a saccharine love that burns and blisters. She takes him by the hand and leads him to the stairs, complacent now; Samuel will never judge her.

"No, Joyce."

"Don't be frightened, my love."

"No, I mean, not here, we—" The doorbell interrupts his protests. He hurries to let in an eager Dooley. "Ah, our chauffeur, right on cue," he says. "Is all ready?"

"The foundations of the church have been cleared. I'm sure you'll find it very comfortable." Dooley can't help but smile for he has been told he can watch.

"Come, my dear," says Samuel.

"Where?"

"Hallowed ground for the seed to take root. There must be no mistakes if we are to be blessed this time around. And after all is done I will give you a fresh year in a box, softened by the hay of days."

Taking his hand she makes her way down the path. She is thinking of that Psalm, the one that goes, "This is the Lord's doing, it is marvellous in our eyes." The sun comes out from behind a dishcloth cloud to brighten the day, but she feels that somehow it is she who is gleaming, that all who look on her will be blinded by her

divinity as they catch a glimpse of Heaven in her eyes.
  They climb in the sharp little car as Dooley fires the engine.
  "To the Moss," says Samuel.
  To Joyce it sounds like Home.

ABOUT THE AUTHOR

Stephen McQuiggan spent the first twenty years of his life in a chicken coop before being rescued by a friendly Quaker family who shaved his hands and taught him how to speak. He lives in N. Ireland and still has an aversion to eggs.

Press
Presents

The Caribbean Sea, 1708 AD. In Port Royal many have heard the legend of the Black Brig, a ship of the damned bringing a fate worse than death to the isolated colonies of the Caribbean Sea. But few know the true story behind the tavern tales. As the war between the Northern Alliance and the League of the Antilles looms on the horizon, an old captain is ready to embark on a venture to cease the blight of the Black Brig once for all and have his revenge. Set in an alternate historical setting, where a supernatural plague caused the fall of the European powers and where what was left of humanity struggles to survive in the New World, *Dead Men Tell No Tales* narrates the ghastly voyage pirate captain Daniel Drake Davies underwent in 1676, and the events that will force him to confront those same horrors thirty years later. For the dead do not rest peacefully in the Devil's Sea. Pirates, voodoo, and seagoing undead await you in this fantastic journey in a land that never was.

Welcome to Deathlehem

A chilling collection of holiday horrors benefiting the Elizabeth Glaser
Pediatric AIDS Foundation

Twas the fright before Christmas And all through the town Not a soul stirred
No one dared make a sound... Welcome to Deathlehem, where...
...Krampus, not Santa, brings the holiday cheer... ...the lights on the tree, so
festive and bright, skitter and crawl and possess a lethal bite... ...malicious little
elves, not a jolly fat one, know if you've been naughty--or nice... and ...family
gatherings and office parties often turn deadly. So enter...if you dare.

CRANIAL LEAKAGE

An eclectic collection of tales that will have you turning on the lights and looking over your shoulder.

An otherworldly artist finds beauty in man's depravity… One woman's therapy session frees more than just memories… A fertility ritual delivers more than just an abundant harvest… An artist's creations prove fatal to his subjects… An obsession with dreams pushes one woman over the edge… … and many more!

ATTACK! of the B-Movie Monsters
Night of the Gigantis

We survived The Beast from 20,000 Fathoms. Then came THEM!,
It Came from Beneath the Sea, and The Deadly Mantis.
They were merely practice runs.
Now prepare for...

Rampaging Rodents!
Terrifying Tentacles!
Bone-Crushing Claws!
Scientific experiments gone dreadfully wrong!

For some, death is not the end. There are those who are doomed to walk the earth for all eternity, those who are trapped between one plain of existence and the next, those who, for whatever reason, cannot or will not let go of the lives they left behind. These are the vengeful spirits, the tortured souls, the ghosts that haunt our realm. Welcome to FROM BEYOND THE GRAVE, a collection of 19 original ghost stories.